AIR FORCE EAGLES

Books By Walter J. Boyne

Nonfiction

Weapons of Desert Storm

Gulf War

The Smithsonian Book of Flight

The Smithsonian Book of Flight for Young People

Phantom in Combat

The Leading Edge

The Power Behind the Wheel

De Havilland DH-4: From Flaming Coffin to Living Legend

Boeing B-52: A Documentary History

The Aircraft Treasures of Silver Hill

Messerschmitt ME 262: Arrow to the Future

Flying

Fiction

Trophy for Eagles

Eagles at War

By Walter J. Boyne and Steven L. Thompson

The Wild Blue

AIR FORCE EAGLES

WALTER J. BOYNE

CROWN PUBLISHERS, INC.   NEW YORK

Copyright © 1992 by Walter J. Boyne

Published by Crown Publishers, Inc., 201 East 50th Street, New York, New York 10022. Member of the Crown Publishing Group.

CROWN is a trademark of Crown Publishers, Inc.

Manufactured in the United States of America

Library of Congress Cataloging-in-Publication Data

Boyne, Walter J., 1929–
    Air Force Eagles / Walter J. Boyne. — 1st ed.
    1. United States. Air Force—History—Fiction.
    2. United States—History, Military—20th century—
Fiction. I. Title
  PS3552.0937A74   1992
813'.54—dc20   91-41143
                                                        CIP

ISBN 0-517-57609-0

10 9 8 7 6 5 4 3 2 1

First Edition

*This book is dedicated
with love
to the two greatest grandchildren in the world,
J. D. and Grace Teague.*

AIR
FORCE
EAGLES

PROLOGUE

Ramitelli, Italy/July 18, 1944

Heat crusted the land, wilting the scrub pines clinging with twisted roots to the flint outcroppings and making the memory of Alabama's red clay and green trees seem like paradise. He sprawled rag-doll lazy across the wing, greedily soaking up the warmth, knowing that in just a few minutes he'd be freezing.

John Marshall was thinking of his shy wife, wanting to possess her at that moment, to engulf her ripe-peach sweetness in his mouth. Suddenly laughing, he vaulted from the wing and began shadow boxing furiously, sparring off his sexual tension.

"Whooee, you a real Henry Armstrong today, Lieutenant. Whatchou laughing about, sir?" As he talked, the crew chief kept on polishing the gleaming aluminum to gain a little more speed for his pilot.

"Nothing I can talk about, Sarge." Marshall smiled again at the impossible thought of his shy wife making love in the daylight, in the open, on the warm wing of his Mustang.

He shook his arms to loosen up, then sat down and took a lined yellow tablet from his kit. With short, bold pencil strokes he

1

sketched the Group Headquarters on the pad held in his lap. It was a classic peasant farm building of arches and angles, the rumpled red-tile roof slanting over the tarnished yellow stucco exterior. In front, an olive-drab Army ambulance stood next to an abandoned oxcart worn colorless by time. At the corner of the building he drew a little flop-eared dog with a big spot on its side. It was Banjo, Saundra's beloved beagle, and it figured in every sketch he sent her.

"This wouldn't be a bad place, Sarge, if we could bring our wives along."

"Not too many of us has wives, sir. You the lucky one."

"That I am, that I am." Yet tough as it was to be away from her, it was fine to be there in the sun, waiting for the takeoff signal.

A short, round pilot plopped down beside him; there was a ruby tone to his deep black skin, shiny with sweat and smoothed by the weight he so carefully fostered.

"Pretty good drawing, man." Lieutenant Walker was the biggest eater and the best pilot in the outfit—and one of Marshall's few friends. It always made him feel good just to see Walker's lazy, ever-present grin.

"Thanks, Jellybutt." Most everybody else had nicknames, some funny, some cruel, all accurate. Marshall envied them; he hadn't earned his own yet.

Biting savagely into a Hershey bar gone soft in the sun, scooping the runny brown into his mouth, he leaned back against the Mustang's tire. "When you were back in Tuskegee did you ever think you'd make it all the way to combat?"

Marshall stood up to stretch, pressing his hands against his sweat-soaked back.

"No. I figured we'd all be washed out to some infantry outfit, or wind up digging ditches."

"Me, too, especially with all the trouble you got me into."

Marshall had twice run afoul of the South's rigid segregation—once going into a drugstore to ask for a Coke, once drinking out of the wrong fountain. Walker had been there both times to smooth things over with his deferential good humor, a forelock-tugging, toe-shuffling routine that soothed white feelings. It was just an act, but a good one.

Jellybutt sat up, licking chocolate off his fingers. "Well, at least there's none of that segregation shit here."

Marshall glanced at his wristwatch and carefully packed away his tablet. "That's cause there's no white troops here. Wait till they put us on the base with a regular outfit—you'll see all the 'Whites' and 'Coloreds' signs you want, then."

Walker laughed. "Maybe. But by then you'll be a big ace and won't give a damn."

Marshall flushed, wishing he never said anything to Walker about his ambition to be the first Negro ace. He'd never let him forget it.

The siren suddenly wailed as red flares arched in the sky. Walker sprinted toward his plane as Marshall jumped up on the wing of his own.

Fifteen minutes later, the entire 332nd Fighter Group was climbing in great sweeping arcs to rendezvous with the majestic combat boxes of Fifteenth Air Force Flying Fortresses en route to bomb southern Germany. As they climbed, engines straining, their lazy turns converted speed into distance to keep them even with the bombers they were covering. It was a dream mission—they were not assigned to any specific group—free to hit hit any target they chose.

Marshall shifted in his seat, not yet chilled, the warmth of the sun through the canopy countering the forty-below-zero temperature outside. He wove a continual cross-check of the instruments with quick glances at the lethal beauty of the formations spread out across the blue Italian sky. To the left, a blur of midges blossomed into a flight of Mustangs that suddenly banked ninety degrees, flashing their silhouettes to the trigger-happy gunners in the stately bomber formations. Head-on, a Mustang looked like a German 109.

To the east, the Gulf of Venice glittered, the coastline slashed with the reflected light of lagoons and canals. They had just passed through twenty-nine thousand feet, flying in loose formation, about two hundred feet apart, zigzagging to stay with the bombers, when Marshall heard his flight leader call, "Hard right turn. Strip tanks."

Marshall booted rudder and aileron as he sent his external fuel tanks spinning end-over-end toward the checkerboard mix of barren hills and yellow-green vineyards below. As the flight leader went wings level, Marshall saw the Messerschmitts straight ahead, one thousand feet below them.

The Germans, bobbing along in their untidy finger-four formation, were getting ready to attack the bombers. Marshall's target, a dirty mottled gray, grew in his sights. At two hundred yards, he could see every detail plainly, the strange, goiter-like bulge just forward of the cockpit, stalks of radio antennae, black crosses outlined in white, a wide white stripe around the aft fuselage. Breathing hard, the cold oxygen drying his throat, Marshall reveled in the roar of his guns as his long burst exploded the Messerschmitt like a bursting balloon. As he pushed his Mustang into a steep dive to dodge the debris he thought, One down, four to go!

Wild with excitement, but still aware that it was dangerous to be alone, Marshall pulled his Mustang level, scanning the sky for his flight. Then, below and to the right, his peripheral vision caught another Messerschmitt, diving away. Instinctively, he jammed the throttle forward and dove after the quarry; he was merged with the airplane, the impulses from his brain transmitting directly into the Mustang's soul.

The 109 was moving fast, jetting full-power trails from the exhaust stacks. Gaining rapidly, Marshall began firing from three hundred yards out, watching his bullets tearing chunks from the frogskin-green camouflage mottling the enemy plane. As he closed he saw that it bore the new Italian insignia, vertical slashes of green, white, and red that proclaimed that some still followed Mussolini.

The smoking Messerschmitt slowed rapidly, skidding drunkenly to the right as its awkward landing gear slanted down. He passed just over it as the pilot plunged out of the burning aircraft to tumble over and over, white face and brown helmet alternating like a flipped coin.

Marshall banked hard left, trying to find his flight, glad the pilot had been able to bail out and hoping to see his enemy's parachute open. Alone in the Italian sky, he exulted, "Two in one day, not bad for a colored boy from Cleveland!"

The two victories replayed themselves in his head until he found himself roaring inches above the Ramitelli runway. Drunk with pride, he pulled up to do two perfect victory rolls, the sky and ground swapping places, knowing and not caring that his commander would be furious with his flagrant violation of the rules.

Marshall's landing was smooth. As he taxied in he could see his ground crew dancing like kids, waving a big captured German flag to share his triumphs.

Marshall stood on the brakes, jerking the Mustang to a nose-bobbing halt.

Oh, Mother of God, forgive me. The two Messerschmitts flashed in his mind again and the same sense of guilty dismay he'd felt when he'd accidentally run over his neighbor's pet dog swept over him. He had just killed a man—maybe two, if the Italian's chute hadn't opened.

He shoved his oxygen mask over his face and breathed deep. Then, shaking off the regret, he told himself, "Forget it! There's going to be more!"

Jellybutt was on the wing before the prop stopped ticking, yelling, "Two kills in one day! John, we're going to have to paint a skull and cross bones on your plane to warn the Germans off."

As Marshall pulled his helmet off, Walker smiled as he conferred the nickname. "That's it. From now on, John, you're Mr. Bones."

Mr. Bones, Marshall thought. Not bad. It sure beats "Jellybutt."

The Pentagon/August 6, 1947

"Hiroshima, Bandy—the big bang, just two years ago today! And since then the Air Force has gone from a world-beater to a country club."

The general limped around the table to jab his finger at a wall map. "If Russia starts something, they'll shove us out of Europe in six weeks."

Frank Bandfield stood up, stretched his six-foot frame, and rubbed his back muscles, still tight from the morning's flight in the new Republic YP-84. "Come on, Sam, we could stop them with atom bombs in a minute."

"Sure we could, if we had enough of them. But we don't. You wouldn't believe how few we have, even if I could tell you. Two years after the war, and. . . ." The big man pursed his lips, aware that he was disclosing too much even to his old friend.

Bandfield dropped back into the red leather chair, uncomfortable in his just-a-shade-too-tight pink and green uniform, absorbed in the memories of the many sessions he'd had with Henry Caldwell in the same room during the war. It seemed like ancient history and it seemed like yesterday.

Varney painfully eased himself to a sitting position on the edge of his desk, rapping a ruler against the palm of his hand. They'd served together in combat in the South Pacific, and again in the war against the bureaucrats at Wright Field after V-J Day. It was there that Varney had flamed out in one of the new jets, a P-80, in a repeat of the accident that had claimed America's ace of aces, Dick Bong. Trying to save the new fighter, Varney had bellied it in a farmer's field, breaking his back and getting severely burned in the process. With his flying career over, Varney had channeled all his energy into staff work, handling the postwar demobilization with a ruthless skill that earned him the nickname "Meat-axe."

"But here's the good news. We're still cutting back in size, but we'll be picking up in quality. The Air Force has some tremendous planes coming off the drawing board, new fighters and bombers. Even your old buddy Troy McNaughton has a couple."

Bandfield walked over to the window overlooking the courtyard, running his hand through his shock of salt and pepper hair. "Don't mention that guy to me, Sam, he's no buddy of mine. How come the Army is still contracting with him, after all the dirty tricks he's pulled?"

Varney's huge shoulders heaved in a shrug. His height, pushing the maximum for a pilot, was only part of his truly commanding presence. His steel-gray brush-cut was set off by burning blue eyes, and he had a boxer's nose, broken in two places, over a tight-lipped mouth that rarely smiled.

Bandfield, in contrast, glowed with health and an inner contentment that he was back doing the only thing he liked doing—flying. His broad shoulders and barrel chest gave him a wrestler's build, and the long hikes in the Sierras with his wife Patty had toughened his legs. At forty-two he weighed only ten pounds more than when he had been preparing to fly the Atlantic, and today the unfamiliar pinch of his uniform made him resolve to get rid of the extra weight.

The general had once sung in his church choir; now his voice was as gravelly as Andy Devine's, the effects of a shard of Plexiglas driven through his throat in his crash. "It beats the hell out of me. If I had my way, I'd have shut down his plant years ago. But you know, he's got a lot of political influence, and when he merged with Vanguard Aircraft, he acquired some good engineers and managers. It's not so much a one-man show anymore."

"I'll never believe that."

"Maybe not, but he's got two good prototypes in the works. One's a rocket-powered research plane, real Buck Rogers stuff, and the other's a flying-wing bomber. Both of them were Vanguard projects originally. They're the real reason I had you recalled. Since they won't let me fly, I need someone to ride shotgun for me like you did for Caldwell, sort of a roving ambassador."

Bandfield snorted derisively. "You mean your own personal inspector general. Or spy—I've been called that in the past."

"Who cares what they call it? I want somebody who's not bucking for general to get out there and find out what's going on in the factories. Somebody who can fly anything in the inventory, and still go down to ride herd on McNaughton two or three times a month, to make sure he's staying honest."

Bandfield ran his finger over a silver manufacturer's model of a P-51 that sat on one side of Varney's desk. He'd never been happier than when he was working for Caldwell—in the field, facing new problems every day. His plant back in Downey was building prefab houses now, and he gladly let his wife run the operation. Hadley Roget had talked him into two more projects in Salinas, and they were batting .500 as usual. One idea was sensible, converting Stearman trainers into crop dusters, and they made a little money doing it. But all they made they had lost in Hadley's real passion, a flying car.

The truth was that Varney's recall notice had been a lifesaver—the only flying he was able to do was in puddle jumpers, with no real challenge. Still, Bandfield was careful not to appear too eager—he might need to win a few concessions.

"Don't you have military factory representatives anymore?"

Varney snorted so hard he had to grab his handkerchief. "As soon as they're on the job for two months, they become advocates.

Especially with these neat new jets. Hell, I'm giving you the chance of a lifetime, fly all this new iron, get the VIP treatment wherever you go. I'd do it myself if I could."

Varney pulled up his pants to show the braces over long medical stockings that hid his injured legs. "You know how it is, Bandy, the guys all fall in love with the airplane they're working on. Hell, it's their career, why wouldn't they? And McNaughton isn't the only slick customer in the business."

Laughing, Bandfield tapped Sam lightly on the arm. "Hell, he's got to be the slickest. I've never been able to figure him out." Then, suddenly serious, he said, "But this is only part of the package. I can tell you've got something else on your mind."

Varney stuttered "Yah, yah, in a—in a couple of minutes, Milo Ruddick will be coming in. Do you know him?"

"Never met him. Some sort of under-secretary or something?"

"Assistant Secretary for Defense—not much of a title for the guy who really runs the place. He was a Congressman for eight terms, ran the House Armed Services Committee from behind the scenes. Old Milo is a political powerhouse, with Roosevelt's charm, Harry Hopkins's brains, and John L. Lewis's clout."

"You seem mighty impressed by him."

"You're damn right I am. He still likes to be called 'Congressman,' and he calls the shots on defense. If he says yea, it's yea, and if he says nay, it's nay. I've never met anybody who had the military buffaloed like this guy."

"Then why is he coming here rather than us going to his office? Looks like you'd be at his beck and call."

"I am, I am. But he wanted a little privacy."

"What does he want with me?"

"Well . . ." The door popped open and a tall, slender man, impeccably dressed, flowed into the room as silently as a Wodehouse butler. He set down a bulging leather briefcase on the polished wood floor, folded his arms across his chest, and stood looking at them as if he were impressing their image on his mind forever.

Bandfield understood why Varney was impressed. Ruddick's entrance had not been theater but presence; there was an electric aura of power about the man. He was handsome in the manner of an aging Hollywood star, with thinning curly gray hair, perfectly cut, a contrast to his bushy eyebrows, which seemed to range forever across his broad brow. As he gazed at them his aquiline nose quivered slightly, as if he were sniffing out their personalities, while behind his wire-rim glasses his eyes were thin blue shields, as cold as liquid oxygen.

Suddenly he stuck out his hand in Bandfield's direction and with that simple movement seemed to change his whole persona from master inquisitor to lifetime friend. "Nice to see you, General Varney. And this must be Colonel Bandfield. I've heard a lot about you from your old friend, General Caldwell."

They sat down and Ruddick drawled, "I greatly admired Henry. Look there." He pointed to a photograph on the wall of President Roosevelt pinning on Caldwell's third star. "There I am, in the background."

His voice seemed very familiar; Bandfield tried to place it as Ruddick fixed him with a benevolent grin.

"And that's where I want you to work for me, in the background."

"Yes, sir, just tell me what you want me to do."

Ruddick confided, "First of all, let me tell you why I'm so supportive of the services, particularly the air forces. I always wanted to fly myself, but didn't have the time or money. Both my son Bob and my son-in-law are pilots. Bob flew McNaughton Sidewinders during most of the war."

Bandfield shook his head. "And he lived through it? He must be damn good to survive a tour on McNaughtons. Troy McNaughton should have been prosecuted for sabotage at the least, and maybe for murder."

Varney turned ashen and Bandfield knew that he'd said the wrong thing. Yet Ruddick's manner did not change, his tone still johnnycake and honey.

"Now, I'm right sorry to hear that, Colonel Bandfield. Troy McNaughton's always been a good friend of my colleague, Congressman Dade, and I admire them both. And my dear son, Bob, swears by McNaughton aircraft—he wants to fly one in the Cleveland races someday. I hope your feelings won't affect your objectivity."

Ruddick lowered his head so that his eyes popped up owlishly over the top of his glasses to stare at Bandfield as he smiled. In the background Varney was white-faced and shaken.

"Sorry, Mr. Congressman, I meant no offense. If your son liked McNaughtons, they are probably better airplanes than I thought they were."

Ruddick purred, "Let's change the subject. How much do you know about the Gillem Report?"

"I've read a little about it—it's a recommendation on how best to utilize Negro servicemen, isn't it?"

"It's more than that—it's an attempt to bring about integration in a practical way. But most people don't like it. The services say it goes too far, and the coloreds, especially the NAACP, say it doesn't go far enough."

A skeptical look crept across Bandfield's face. "How do you feel about it?"

Ruddick glanced at Varney. "Well, you warned me that he was very straightforward." Then, "Colonel Bandfield, what do you think a man who represented the people of Little Rock in Congress for sixteen years feels about integration?"

"You're against it."

"To be honest, I am not, personally. I think it's inevitable, but not in my lifetime. My former constituents are against it one hundred percent, but I have to determine what's best for the service."

He spoke without bombast; it was a statement of political fact, but Bandfield was always suspicious of people who used the phrase "to be honest"—more often than not it meant they were lying.

"How do you see my role? I don't know how I can help you."

"General Varney's told me about your assignment for him—test-flying the new prototypes, visiting the factories, being his leg man, if Meat-axe will pardon the expression."

Varney nodded eagerly—it was obvious that he'd pardon Ruddick of anything.

"Colonel, all I want is that you just keep your eyes and ears open as you go around the country. Ask questions on the flight line, in the officers' clubs. Try to find out how service people feel about integrating the military. Form a picture of the real situation, and give me the pros and cons. If integration isn't going to hurt the services, I won't oppose it and I'll try to educate my former constituents to accept it. But if—as I fear—early integration will be harmful, then I'll fight it tooth and nail."

As he spoke, Bandfield placed his voice—it was Edward R. Murrow's, with a Southern drawl, richer in tone, warmer, and laced with indulgent good humor. The man could have made a fortune in broadcasting.

"I can do that, but what good will it be? I'm just one man; I can't gather a genuine statistical sample."

"Colonel, you have a reputation for being hot-headed, hardworking, and totally honest. I don't want a six-inch-thick report that shows the third standard deviation of a multiple choice questionnaire. I want someone with some common sense, somebody who can get a gut feel for a situation. Varney says you fill the bill."

Bandfield felt the same uneasy ambivalence about Ruddick that he might have felt about a likeable car salesman. The man had a marvelous personality, and he was direct and to the point. Yet in his eyes there was a thinly veiled hint of mockery, a cozy awareness that he was playing his game, and playing it well.

"Sir, I don't even know what my own feelings are. A good friend of mine, John Marshall, was one of the Tuskegee pilots. He fought in Italy and scored a couple of victories. John worked for me for a while in California, after the war. There were no problems with anyone. But the racial climate's different there. There's no way for me to guess what a guy from Alabama or Georgia might be thinking."

"You don't have to guess about Southerners—I already know what they're thinking. But integration's coming. Truman wants it because he needs the black vote. It's just a matter of when and where, and if it should be delayed. And for me, the major question is whether it should come first in the armed services. What do you think?"

Varney, tense as a torsion bar, watched Bandfield tussle with the question. "I don't know. The Constitution applies to everybody, black, white, or in-between. Everybody has a duty to serve. But I'd have to see what it does to military efficiency. I know from my friend that the guys from Tuskegee, the 332nd, did well enough during the war."

"Did you know that General Eaker didn't think so?"

"No, I didn't. What did he say?" Eaker was one of the most respected men in the Air Force, a war hero and a gentleman.

"General Eaker argues that the Negro units required too much support relative to the results they produced. He says that the service shouldn't be a testing ground for race relationships, or for advancing the prestige of the Negro race."

As Bandfield chewed this over, Ruddick went on. "Remember that the 332nd was an elite, segregated unit. Segregated Negro units have done well in every war since the War Between the States. But today the issue isn't proficiency, or bravery, or even patriotism. The issue is integration—when, how much, and where."

Varney's face was now even paler; he was openly apprehensive, like a child caught smoking behind the barn. Bandfield feared that he might be on the verge of a heart attack.

"Are you okay, Sam?"

Varney nodded, and Frank said, "Mr. Ruddick, I'll be glad to work with you, to find out all I can and give you an opinion. But I can't tell you how much confidence to place in it."

"Don't worry, you won't be my only source."

Bandfield stood up and turned to Varney, who seemed to be recovering. "Where do I start?"

"I'm sending you to North American first, to check out in our first jet bomber, the B-45. Then it'll be Convair, Martin, and McNaughton. Somewhere along the line, I want you to spend time at Lockbourne Air Force Base—that's where the majority of the segregated Negro units are located now."

"Great. My buddy Marshall is at Muroc—working for McNaughton of all people. I'll try to get some background from him. What else have you got for me?"

Ruddick handed him the bulging briefcase. "Here's the Gillem Report, with the back-up documentation. When you digest that, I'll have more."

En route to Lockbourne Air Force Base, Ohio/ September 6, 1947

In splendid solitude, far above everyone in the sky, their four jet engines churned out long white trails of vapor glistening in the sun, an endless cone of icy crystals tracking the silver bomber's path. Below, brilliant alpine cloud tops belied the black turbulence they concealed within. John Marshall lolled in the back seat of the bomber, glad to have this unexpected respite from the demanding research flying he was doing at Muroc.

"Well, Bandy, you must have a lot of pull to get a plane like this for cross-country work. I'm glad you decided to take a poor old reserve lieutenant along for the ride."

"Just part of my job. How does this bucket compare to your rocket plan?"

"Like the Queen Mary to a Chris Craft."

Silent as a sailplane, the XB-45 flew at eight miles a minute, six miles above the ground. From behind them, rays from the setting sun gave a feathering of orange and purple to the line of thunderstorms percolating on the horizon.

Marshall's voice suddenly lifted an octave. "Holy-moly, check the fuel gauges!"

Bandfield glanced down; the main tanks, one-quarter full only moments ago, were registering empty. He glanced at the "how-goes-it chart" on his clipboard where he had carefully plotted the fuel consumption for their four-hour flight out from Muroc. Everything was on the button—either they had had a sudden massive fuel leak, or the gauges were out.

Marshall echoed his thoughts. "Might be the gauges."

"Famous last words."

Bandfield had taken a cram course on the aircraft systems at the North American plant, followed by a three-hour check-out flight in the local area. But the XB-45 was a complex airplane, and he still had a lot to learn.

"What do you want to do, Bandy? We're only a few minutes out of Lockbourne."

"Nothing right now. Can you see if we're streaming fuel?"

Marshall, seated behind Bandfield in the narrow cockpit, turned and searched behind them, craning his neck to see out of the long slender canopy. "Nothing out there. I just wish I was home with Mama."

Bandfield's direction-finder needle began to move as they crossed over the Lockbourne ADF facility. He called his position into Lockbourne as he cranked the bomber into a holding pattern.

He was furious with himself as he visualized the blueprint for the accident unfolding, a series of small mistakes. First, he should never have taken an experimental aircraft on a cross-country flight when he only had a few hours in the plane. Second, while Marshall was an experienced test pilot, he'd never flown in the XB-45 before. And stupidest of all, they'd overflown Scott Field, confident that there was plenty of fuel. That's how accidents happened—not one thing, but a series of minor quirks that added up to a catastrophe.

The airplane was wonderful, fast, smooth, powerful, and easy to fly, a tremendous advance over any bomber he'd ever flown—when all was going well. But he was far from proficient in it, and things were beginning to unravel fast. His flight plan called for an hour's fuel remaining when he arrived, and now the tanks were bumping empty and the field was socked in with a stack of traffic waiting to land.

"John, I'm sorry about this—I'm too old for this kind of shit. I should never asked you to come along."

Marshall ran his finger around his new hard hat trying to ease the pressure points, yearning for his old leather helmet, and ill at ease only because he couldn't help.

"Listen, this is a great experience for me. I'll see how an old pro handles a problem."

A few weeks before, Bandfield had rung Marshall up at McNaughton's Muroc flight test facility as soon as he'd left Varney's office. Marshall was glad to work with him on the integration issue, and he suggested that they visit Lockbourne together, to show him exactly what segregation meant in the service. Varney sent orders authorizing them to use the XB-45 for some cross-country work. It sounded like a good idea, killing two birds with one stone, but now Bandfield realized that he should have known better. The airplane had completed its company test program, but it was too new, too trouble-prone, to take this sort of liberty with it.

"You going to declare an emergency, Bandy?"

"Not yet. If we've got fuel that's not showing up on the gauges, I'd just as soon hold here until we're cleared. We might . . . oh, shit."

They both watched the engines' RPM counters begin to spool down as the tanks ran dry, first number three, then one, then two and four together.

"Lockbourne Approach Control, this is Air Force Niner Four Eight One over the beacon at thirty thousand. We've just lost all four engines."

"Roger, Eight One, are you declaring an emergency?"

Over the intercom Bandfield called, "No, you stupid fucker, I'm diverting to Honolulu." But on the air he said, "Ah, Roger, Lockbourne, we're declaring an emergency, two souls on board, zero fuel remaining, descending now through twenty-eight thousand."

"Maintain a minimum rate of descent until I can clear the traffic out below you, Eight One; I'm going to have to divert half a dozen planes in the holding pattern."

Marshall's voice was cheerful on the intercom. "Well, Bandy, at least I can get into the Lockbourne club with no problem; we'll have to buy a few drinks for all the guys we're delaying."

Bandfield was too busy for the comment about segregated clubs to register, and he mumbled, "How does it feel to be in the biggest, fastest glider in history?"

Lockbourne Approach came back on frequency with the weather.

"Eight One, Lockbourne reporting one thousand scattered, two thousand broken, light rain, wind variable, gusting fifteen to twenty. Cloud tops reported at angels twenty-two, with turbulence and lightning in all quarters."

"Roger." Not good, but not too bad, and it didn't make any difference, they were going to have to make it on the first approach. He wasn't about to bail out of a prototype, especially since the handbook had warned that the airplane was not easy to leave.

Silent as a shadow, they slipped into the cloud layer at twenty-four thousand feet, plotting an exacting orbit around the station, two minutes out, 180-degree turn, track back in, 180-degree turn, then two minutes out again, descending all the while at a constant one thousand feet per minute.

"Lockbourne, Eight One. How you doing on the traffic, I'm passing sixteen thousand now."

"Roger, Eight One, you're cleared for approach and landing, runway twenty-three, emergency equipment standing by, runway wet with standing water at approach end, braking action reported poor."

The cockpit lights dimmed as Bandfield cranked the big jet around to its final approach.

"We're losing the battery, John. I don't know what that'll do to the gear and flaps. Strap yourself in tight, babe, I may have to belly in."

Even as the needle of his automatic direction finder turned as they passed over the beacon at 1,700 feet, Bandfield reproached himself again for not knowing the airplane well enough, trying frantically to recall the emergency procedure to lower the landing gear—there wasn't time to look it up, and the hydraulic system was complex. A little back pressure brought the nose up, slowing them to 130 miles per hour, just as they lost all of their electrical power, lights going out, gauges sticking or flopping like dead ducks. Then, as if on cue, the clouds parted and he saw the welcome convergent white streaks of the runway lights ahead.

"Field in sight."

Marshall spoke for the first time in minutes. "I'll bet old Daddy Johnson will be there to meet us."

"Gear going down."

The silence was agonizing as the landscape slid toward them, seeming to roll up, the trees at the edge of the runway rising, the lights getting brighter, aircraft and trucks now visible on the ramp. Bandfield's hand automatically went through what he remembered of the emergency gear–down drill.

"Brace yourself, John, I can't verify if the gear is down or not."

Hands sweating, Bandfield mouthed a silent prayer that the fuel had really burned off and wasn't pooled in the belly, a bomb waiting to go off when they touched down. He leveled off just short of the runway, slightly nose high, and when the big jet's main gear kissed the runway the two pilots bellowed in relief.

As the nose gear touched down, Bandfield eased on the brakes to roll out on the taxi-way leading to the ramp where the fire trucks and ambulances were now converging.

"Good job, Bandy, but now you're really in trouble."

"Hey, babe, after that, nothing's going to seem like trouble."

"Oh, yeah? Look who's waiting for us."

At the side of the runway, West Point training showing in his ramrod-stiff stance, was the base commander. Colonel Joseph J. Johnson—"J-Cubed" to the troops—had led the all-Negro 332nd Fighter Wing into combat. Utterly demanding of himself, uncompromising with others, he got results.

Johnson took their salute, ignoring their outstretched hands. Then, in a clipped voice that brooked no nonsense, said, "Into my car, gentlemen. Mr. Marshall, running out of fuel is the one unforgivable mistake. I hope you flight-plan better for McNaughton than you did for this trip."

. . .

Johnson was only slightly more relaxed when they met again the following morning in the freshly painted Headquarters building. His adjutant came in with some urgent papers to be signed, and Bandfield had time to study him. He was very tall, six three at least, with closely cropped hair and coffee-colored skin. Eyes dark as black olives were wide-set in his oval face, and he had the barest trace of a mustache beneath his patrician nose. Johnson tore through the papers, occasionally looking up at the adjutant to ask a question in a quiet, commanding voice. He was obviously in top physical condition, without an ounce of surplus flesh.

When he handed the papers back to the adjutant, Bandfield sought to break the ice with a compliment.

"That's a beautiful bed of red flowers outside, Colonel."

"They're called flaming salvia, and I planted them myself, part of the base beautification program. This is the only Army Air Force base in the country run by Negro officers, and I want it to look good."

He paused momentarily and went on. "We can have anything we want here—as long as we provide it ourselves."

After talking with Marshall about his test-flying, Johnson was listening to Bandfield's explanation of his assignment from Ruddick when a secretary came in to serve coffee. She was heavyset, close to sixty—and white. She slowly set the tray down on Johnson's desk while Bandfield's face betrayed his surprise.

"Mrs. Blodgett, could we have some cream and sugar for the coffee?" With a sigh the woman turned for the door as if this irrational request was the last straw in her sad life.

"Colonel Bandfield, I can see your surprise that we actually have white employees working for us! You'll note that I was careful to choose a"—he groped for the right word as he watched the door for Mrs. Blodgett's return—"mature woman for my secretary."

Johnson was silent as the cream and sugar was brought in, then went on. "The truth is, the good people of Columbus, Ohio, would rather not have a Negro unit here—but they'd rather have a Negro unit than no unit. Now we're getting to be just like Patterson Field, with Negroes working alongside whites with no problems." He sipped his coffee and added, "At least not on the job. Your friend Mr. Ruddick would be quite upset, I'm sure."

Bandfield plunged in. "Are you for integration or for the segregation of Negroes, Colonel Johnson?"

"Not a very astute question, Colonel. I've accepted segregated units because I've had to, and because they at least give my people a chance to show how they perform. But no American citizen, white or Negro, should accept anything less than complete integration. Any man should be able to take any job, any place in the country, on the sole basis of his performance in that job." Even though it was obvious that these were words he'd used often, his correct military manner didn't conceal his suppressed anger.

"Marshall, did you ever tell Colonel Bandfield why you left the Army?"

"No, not exactly."

"Then I will. John Marshall here is as fine a pilot as there is in the world. But there was no place for him to go at Lockbourne. We were short then—and we're short now—on planes, on mechanics, and on pilots. But the real problem is that we are short on a mission. We're just quota-fillers, without a real role in the war plan. It's a political ploy, giving Negroes enough to say 'we've had a chance,' but not enough to do a job."

Marshall was fidgeting. Johnson's personality was so powerful that he hesitated to interrupt. Finally he said, "That's not the real reason I left, Colonel. I had a good deal here, checked out in both P-47s and B-25s. I'd have stayed as long as they'd let me, enjoying myself. I got out because my wife couldn't take it. There wasn't any base housing then, and we were living in an old run-down boarding house, cooking on a hotplate, fighting off the cockroaches. That wasn't the worst of it. She's a teacher, and they needed teachers badly in Columbus. The school board wouldn't hire her, even though there were other black teachers. A friend told her why she wasn't hired. The school board didn't want any 'uppity Negro woman from the base.' The fact that I was an officer kept her from getting a job."

"Why did you stay in the Reserves?"

"Colonel, I shot down two planes in Italy. If there's ever another war, I'm going to get three more and be the first Negro ace. So, I had to keep my hand in."

Bandfield pressed the issue with Johnson. "If you can't get fair treatment collectively as a segregated unit, how do you expect to get fair treatment individually in an integrated service?"

"I don't. The service has never been fair to me, not at West Point, not at Tuskegee, not in Italy, not here. But I don't care, not as long as I get to show what I can do." There was a slight shift in his tone as he reverted to his formula presentation. "And that's all that any Negro should demand. No preference because he's a Negro, but no handicap either."

Johnson suddenly leaned over to Marshall, striking like a cobra. "Damn it, John, you should never have left us. I need people like you, and you walked out on me. You should have told your wife to learn to take it. We're not going to change things by running. I've taken everything they've thrown at me ever since I entered West Point, and I'll keep on taking it."

Obviously taken aback, Marshall hesitated. ". . . Colonel, I didn't think you even knew who I was when I got out."

Johnson, obviously controlling his emotions, replied in a raspy near whisper. "I know *everyone* in my command, officer and enlisted. I keep people at a distance because a commander has to. But I had plans for you."

"I'm sorry, Colonel . . ."

Suddenly Johnson stood up, close to losing his iron composure. "Enough of this. You go back to your big job with McNaughton, flying rocket planes—there are plenty of other good pilots here."

There was a stunned silence and then Johnson said in a broad, commanding tone, "Now get out of here, both of you. Colonel Bandfield, you can tell your Mr. Assistant Secretary Ruddick that Lockbourne is doing just fine. And you can tell him that no matter how he fights it, integration's coming!"

Palmdale, California/September 27, 1947

Ginny collected appreciative looks like hookers collect sailors. Now she was enjoying some from herself, leaning forward into the tri-fold mirror in their bedroom, cherry-red lips almost kissing their image. She was an ardent movie magazine fan and had devoted a lot of thought to her switch from a summer Lana Turner look to her own version of Rita Hayworth. Mouth slightly open, she was practicing a head-tossing laugh to check the bounce of the hair she'd brushed to curve over her right eye.

With a parting sigh, she rose to go in to give her husband another little dose of encouragement. Quick-marching out, she winked into the full-length mirror in the hallway, liking the way she moved, shoulders straight and sweater tight. Without knocking, she entered the spare bedroom that her husband used as a combination gym and den.

Ginny watched him exercise for a few moments, knowing he liked to show off for her, all the while contrasting the apartment-house beige of the ten-by-ten room with the luxury of her family home in Little Rock. Their drab apartment was exactly like the other twenty in the building, the building exactly like four others on the street. In a city it would have been subsidized housing; here it was where the engineers and pilots from Muroc lived. Finally, she drawled, "Like I was saying, this Marshall must think he's some kind of airborne Jackie Robinson."

Stan groaned as he finished his push-ups. She was off again! He loved her madly, but she drove him crazy.

"Listen to me, Stan, please! I'm tired of being a poor captain's wife, living in this desert-rat shanty. What's the point in my having a big-wheel daddy if you won't let him help you?"

Coleman stood up, not for his rights, but to do jumping jacks, pounding the shaky linoleum floor and bouncing the pictures on the wall in the next room. Six-feet tall, his blond hair was sweat-knit into a cap of curls.

Her tongue flickered over her lips, wondering if she'd ever be able to make him realize his potential. He was a big, good-looking man, a curly-haired Van Johnson type, and that counted in the Air Force as it did everywhere. With his looks, her brains, and her daddy's influence, he could go all the way to the top. If only he had her daddy's gumption, his get-up-and-go!

Stan got up and went, fleeing into the tiny bathroom to brush his teeth. Following, she nudged the door open with her foot, watching him with a tingling mixture of desire and frustration. Ginny loved his wide-set, heavy-lidded eyes; when he listened, they closed slightly, as if there were nothing more important in the world than what the speaker was saying. He had the leanly muscled physique of a tennis player; after they made love she liked to lie with her legs wrapped around him, squeezing him dry.

She stood there arms crossed, her foot tapping impatiently. Coleman had a battered metal tube of Ipana toothpaste on the edge of the sink and was forcing out a last spurt of the yellowish paste with the edge of his toothbrush.

"Staving off death again, Stan?"

Coleman shook his head sheepishly. His fear of death was quirky, bound up in a rueful conviction that only so many things remained to him—so many meals, so many Cokes, so many tubes of toothpaste. He was always stringing things out, getting the last squeeze from the tube so he wouldn't take another—perhaps the last!— from his fate-fixed supply. He fought this battle even with sex, rationing their encounters, firmly convinced that he had only so many orgasms allotted to him, intent on spreading them out. She could never convince him of her own use-it-or-lose-it philosophy.

He turned and, mouth foaming, shot her a wink, relying on his infectious good humor to soften her mood. Rinsing, his automatic broad smile snapped open as swiftly as a camera shutter to reveal even white teeth.

Immune to the grin, she asked, "When are you going to stand up for your rights?"

"Look, pussycat, your dad's already helped me, just getting me assigned at Muroc. I can't just go in and demand to fly a secret test aircraft."

"Some secret! Everybody knows about it. The real secret is that the test pilot is a jigaboo. And a civilian at that!"

"Don't talk like that, honey. Marshall got two kills in Italy, and he's one hell of a pilot." He put his hand out to her shoulder and she shrugged it away.

"If the Air Force can let a West Virginia hillbilly like Yeager fly Bell's airplane, I don't know why they can't let you fly the McNaughton. You know what they're saying out at Pancho's—the first man to break the sound barrier will be able to write his own ticket."

The reference to Pancho Barnes's ramshackle watering hole, which served as an informal club for the top test pilots, made him uncomfortable. A light drinker—there were only so many coming to him—he felt completely out of place at the boozing contests that went on there every night. Ginny loved it, drinking hard and then often going off to ride horseback with the other pilots at night. At least he hoped she was riding horseback.

"Yeah, sure, if he doesn't bust his ass! Nobody knows what will happen. The airplane could break up or go out of control."

"Yeager wouldn't be so hot to trot if he thought he was going to kill himself. I can't believe it's any more dangerous than what you're doing."

He hated it when she tried to sound knowledgeable. She couldn't tell a brick from a biplane, but that didn't keep her from speaking with authority. It came with the rich-father territory.

"Honey, I don't want you to do anything dangerous, I just want you to get ahead. If I don't push you, you'll just hang around flying airplanes for the rest of your life. There's no money in that, and no rank, either."

She was right. He liked to fly airplanes—and that wasn't enough to get ahead, not in peacetime, not with the Air Force melting like a lump of ice cream on a hot sidewalk. Promotions had been assured during the war, as the military expanded and the leaders were killed off. As soon as Japan surrendered, the services had collapsed in a frenzy of demobilization.

Ginny bored in. "Tell me this. How could a die-hard Southerner like Troy McNaughton ever let a colored pilot fly his airplanes anyway?"

He tossed a towel on the molding heap in the corner of the bathroom. "Hell, he probably never met the guy. From what I hear, McNaughton's all wrapped up in their secret programs in San Diego. I've never seen him at Muroc."

They were quiet for a while, then she said in the low, slow voice she used when her mind was made up, "You know, maybe I'll just talk this over with Daddy. He'll know how to handle McNaughton."

Muroc Army Air Base, California/October 7, 1947

Trucks jammed with racks of communications and telemetry gear were parked around the hangar doors like jackals feeding on a carcass. As signals from the twin SCR-584 radars filled the green screens, the men inside moved like a surgical team, keeping conversation at a minimum, eyes constantly flicking from the instruments to the aerial ballet unfolding above them.

A technician in a white jacket reached across the console to adjust a knob and the operator slapped his hand away.

"Hands off, Jack, I got this baby tuned the way I want it."

The team members' edginess was honed by the pervasive film of white grit intruding into instruments and lungs, as abrasive as the long-running competition between Bell Aircraft and McNaughton to build the first supersonic plane. Bell had gotten off to a faster start, but it had followed a more methodical test program; so far its bullet-shaped XS-1 had reached only .92 Mach. The McNaughton had been delayed in production, but its test program had rushed it ahead of the Bell entry. Last week, the swept-wing MS-447 had touched .95 Mach. Today it was going to try to go supersonic, to shatter what *Popular Science* called the sound barrier and what they hoped was a myth.

In the clear blue desert sky twenty thousand feet above them, tucked like a baby kangaroo in the B-29's bomb-bay pouch, the sleek research plane's white skin was frost-crusted from the chilled liquid oxygen in its fuel tanks. The bomber, its undersurfaces still painted in wartime black, droned in a holding pattern, waiting for permission to drop. One P-80 chase plane was escorting the bomber, another was positioned five miles ahead to pick up the rocket plane after it had expended its fuel and was gliding back.

A gray Cadillac pulled up and Troy McNaughton catapulted out of the back, shouting "Don't let them drop." Grabbing Bandfield by the arm, he pulled him into the hangar. "Goddamn it, why didn't you tell me Marshall was a Negro?"

The two squared off like fighting cocks, not for the first time in their lives. McNaughton was an inch taller and forty pounds heavier than Bandfield, but the younger man was in far better condition. As they stood there glaring, fists clenched, Bandfield remembered another day at Muroc when he'd almost hammered McNaughton. Four years had passed since then, and time, sun, and whiskey had not been kind to Troy. His once-silver hair hung yellowish-white over a florid face dotted by suspicious-looking brown spots, large and hard-edged.

Controlling himself, Bandfield moved back and said, "Look, General Varney called you and told you why I'm here—to ride herd on you! You saw my orders—and I'm going to protect the Air Force's interest. I don't care if the pilot is black, blue, or purple as long as he can fly the airplane."

"He's a friend of yours! They showed me your letter of recommendation."

"Sure, I recommended him. And he's been doing a great job. He'll make McNaughton famous when he goes supersonic today."

McNaughton motioned Bandfield to follow him into one of the tiny glassed-in engineering offices that lined the hangar. The dusty cubicle was in normal GI disarray, filled with wall charts showing which airplanes were in commission and which parts were in short supply. A stack of seven squared-off baseball betting pool sheets recorded the Yankees' recent World Series win over the Dodgers.

The older man slammed the door, then lowered his voice.

"Frank, you're supposed to be here to help me. Now, goddamn it, do it! I've been spending all my time on the ballistic missile program. I didn't even know that Marshall was colored, but now someone's tipped off Milo Ruddick! He asked me if I knew my test pilot was a nigger! I felt like a damn fool."

Bandfield suddenly understood his uneasiness about Ruddick; the man was playing a double game, pretending to be open-minded about integration when he was really a segregationist at heart.

Sputtering, his red face a patriotic flush against his white hair and blue suit, McNaughton went on. "Ruddick tells me that if I make a hero out of this nigger, I'll never get another contract."

"Milo Ruddick's too smart to say something like that, even if he believed it. And even if he did, you can't let some bastard bigot tell you what to do."

"Hell, I let everybody tell me what to do. Look how I let Varney shove you down my throat."

The older man picked up a dusty tech order and slammed it down on the battered desk. "Ruddick is calling the tune for Defense, and when he plays, I dance."

Bandfield modulated his voice carefully, masking his anger with sweet reason. "Wait a minute, *think* about this! You've got the entire range alerted, the telemetry is up, and we've got two P-80 chase planes just about ready to run out of fuel! You can't afford not to drop. The next time Yeager flies, he'll break the sound barrier, you can be damn sure of that! There'll only be one first time, Troy. If Yeager's first, Bell will pick up all the marbles."

McNaughton, as decisive as an executioner, stormed out to the communication truck. "Get me Marshall on company frequency."

The speaker crackled and the B-29's pilot said, "What the hell is the holdup down there?"

"Major Carrera, this is Troy McNaughton. Is our pilot on this frequency?"

Marshall's voice came on. "Roger, that. I'm reading you five by five."

"I'm going to give you some instructions, Mr. Marshall, and I want you to obey them. Do not, I repeat, do not take the aircraft beyond Mach .95. Do you understand?"

"Roger, I read you. But why? Everything is—"

"Marshall, my instructions are that you don't go beyond Mach .95. I'll explain everything at the debriefing. Now that's final! You can drop whenever you're ready."

High above them, the test pilot scowled in anger. The whole process was so risky that it wasn't worthwhile to make the flight just to go to Mach .95 again. He was sitting on a bomb—1,400 gallons of liquid oxygen and 1,300 gallons of diluted ethyl alcohol. If the two were mixed properly in the huge RLX-15 engine, he'd light a fire generating eight thousand pounds of thrust that could take him supersonic. If they didn't mix properly, if there was some leakage, some pooling of fuel or vapor, he, the MS-447, and the B-29 would disappear in a single gigantic fireball.

His teeth chattered uncontrollably as the freezing-cold metal seat sucked away his body heat through his thin flying suit—there was no room for leather coveralls. Marshall rubbed his gloved hand across the inside of the canopy, slick with Drene shampoo to keep it from frosting up. For the last forty minutes he'd been cramped into the tiny cockpit like an olive in a pimento, preoccupied with the long checklist, and alternating between savoring the prospect of being the first man to break the sound barrier and worrying about what might happen when he did. All of his own analysis indicated that things would go smoothly—but there were still those who predicted a catastrophic breakup of the aircraft.

Suddenly it hit him. It was Tuskegee all over again. McNaughton must have selected a white pilot for the honor, probably one of the guys who had done some of the early glide tests.

It was worse than unfair—it was stupid. He was the only one who was fully qualified, the only one who had made powered flights.

His anger built as he went on with the checklist litany, his gloved finger pointing to the propellant pressures, flicking the telemetry switches on, checking the trim. The airplane had only a few flights on it, but the instrument panel was already nicked and worn, the green priming showing through the matte-black finish.

The hell with McNaughton. There was nothing to keep him from following the original flight profile—just let the little rockets run and they'd push him right through the speed of sound. It wouldn't matter if they fired him. Even a colored pilot could get a job anywhere if he was the first man to break the sound barrier. Then he smiled through his anger, knowing that his father would disapprove, would tell him simply, "Do what's right, son!"

He tucked the checklist inside its metal jacket as the pre-drop countdown began. Carrera nosed the B-29 over into a slight dive, full power on all four engines, airframe quivering as it slanted through the crisp air toward the whitish-green desert below. When the countdown reached zero, the bomber would be passing twenty thousand feet at precisely 250 miles per hour, only two knots over the MS-447's fully loaded stall speed. It wasn't nearly as fast as Marshall would have liked, but it would be all Carrera could get.

"Three . . . two . . . one . . . zero!"

The bomb-bay's scissor clamps released and the rocket plane jolted down the retaining rails to burst like a bomb into the slipstream's blast. The explosion of sunlight slashing into the cockpit momentarily blinded him as he fell away, yawing slightly in the silent glide beneath the bomber's belly. He eased the control wheel forward to accelerate. Now gliding faster than the B-29 could fly, Marshall felt speed cloak his gleaming white plane with stability, the crust of frost flicking off in a brief sparkling funnel of light. With two movements of his finger, Marshall fired the first engine. Igniting the rocket slung the rocket plane forward like an arrow out of a bow, leaving the B-29 and the chase plane behind instantly.

At Mach .86, Marshall applied a touch of back pressure to rocket the MS-447 into its climb. It was a delightful airplane to fly, unstable at low speeds, but rock-solid now as he leveled out at thirty-six thousand feet and fired the second engine. Once again there was a jolt and the Mach built rapidly to .90, .92. He was blasting toward the sound barrier, toward certain fame—or certain destruction, if the doomsayers were right, if speed built the air into a brick wall to shatter the aircraft and sent it tumbling out of control.

"Do what's right, son."

He'd heard the words a thousand times in his youth, and they came to him now. McNaughton was the boss, he was paying him—his dad would have said he was "laboring in McNaughton's vineyard." With a sigh, Marshall reached up and flipped off both engines as the Mach meter touched .94. He was still accelerating, only seconds away from being the first man to break the sound barrier—seconds away from the record books—as the deceleration thrust him forward in his harness.

A wild surge of regret flooded Marshall. The war had ended before he could be an ace; this had been his one last opportunity and he'd tossed it away. His daddy would be proud of him, but that wasn't enough. He'd blown his chance!

The chase plane came up beside him; Marshall could see the pilot shrug and put his hands up as if to ask, "What the hell is going on?"

Descending at four hundred miles an hour, Marshall rolled the elegant MS-447 around the P-80. As he turned, keeping the Lockheed riveted firmly in the center of his canopy, he told himself, "Never again." Never again would he lose an opportunity like this, no matter what his daddy would have said, no matter what Saundra said. He'd had the world in his hands, and he'd thrown it away.

On the salt flats below, a technician looked up and said, "He hit just about Mach .95 on engine cutoff, sir."

McNaughton whirled on his heels and walked toward the waiting car. Bandfield raced ahead of him and asked, "What the hell am I going to tell Marshall? What am I going to tell the Air Force?"

McNaughton stared at him. "That's easy. You tell Marshall he's fired, and you tell the Air Force that we'll make another attempt in two weeks. Tell them to send us a pilot as good as Yeager—tell them to send us Stan Coleman."

Bandfield watched the door slam behind McNaughton, thinking how consistent the man was, always a bastard, no matter what the circumstances. He dreaded the coming session with Marshall.

Little Rock, Arkansas/November 8, 1947

The view from his offices on the top floor of the Arkansas Commercial Bank, the tallest building in the city, was remarkable. The Arkansas River crooked lazily toward the southeast, and beyond the line of hills was still faintly green. His wife's father, Judge McCallum, had once owned almost all the land spread out before him. When Alma had died the year before, title for the estate had passed to him. He drew immense pleasure from the knowledge, for he knew how important land was. His parents had been sharecroppers, poor white trash farming a section for the McCallums. From where he stood, he could see the old farm now above the bend in the river, a bluish haze from burning grass hanging over it. Milo Ruddick had worked many hours on that ground and knew that land was sacred, just like the blood of the people who owned it.

Most of the land was in jeopardy now, of course, but he'd make that right. There had been some necessarily extravagant spending. The organization he was developing was expensive, and some of his investments had gone bad. Against his will, he'd had to mortgage much of the property. And he'd had to do the same with the land in Texas, the real source of the McCallum wealth—now his wealth. The rich bonanza reaped during the war had disappeared in a glut of overproduction. He didn't like mortgages—they were a sacrifice of control—and Ruddick lived to control everything, land, oil, money, and people. With a sigh, he pressed the lever on his office intercom. He hated the gadget; once he'd have simply yelled for his secretary, but she was older now and hard of hearing.

"Cathy, I want to do some thinking in here, but I'm expecting some calls. The most important will be from Dr. Burton here in town—you know what that's about. The other will be from Secretary Woodson in Washington. And I'm expecting a call on my private line. I'd really prefer not to talk to anyone else."

It was unusual for him not to take calls—even when he was in Congress he liked to answer the phone himself, surprising his constituents with his accessibility. But events were closing in on him. Ruddick stepped into his private bathroom and splashed water on his face, then glanced in the mirror, surprised at the un-accustomed stubble on his chin. Wherever he was—Washington, Little Rock, on travel—his morning started with a trip to the barbershop for a shave and facial massage. Today he'd simply forgotten—a sign of how pressure was building. He frowned, patting down his tousled hair.

The intercom buzzed and he ran to the phone. "It's Dr. Burton, sir."

"Hello, Dick, how is Marny?"

Burton's voice was thin and reedy; he was almost eighty and had doctored the McCallum family for the last five decades.

"Milo, I don't think she's going to make it. She needs a complete workup, and if my guess is right, some intensive abdominal surgery. It will be expensive, and I'm not sure it will do any good. Marny has been moping ever since Alma died."

"I know, Dick, I tried to get her to retire, but she wouldn't listen to me. I would have kept her salary going, covered all her needs. But she insisted on coming in every day, puttering around, storing Alma's things. But it doesn't matter what it costs—please see that she gets whatever she needs—I'll take care of all of it. And tell her I'll be down to see her tonight."

They talked a while longer and he hung up, a lump in his throat. Marny had been "given" to his wife as a companion when they were only three, a practice inherited from the days when the McCallum farms had been the McCallum plantation, worked by slaves. Marny and Alma had grown up together, inseparable, servant and mistress but the best of friends. They'd rented her a little cottage down in darktown, and even when she'd grown older and wasn't really efficient, he kept paying her an unconscionable amount, twelve hundred a year, plus all the little perks—lunch, leftovers, clothing from the family.

Marny was a good woman, and she'd sent two children to college on her salary. It showed what a good Negro could do, if they were treated properly. She'd fallen ill after Alma's death, and the situation became awkward. Ruddick had moved her into the little apartment in the basement that hadn't been used for years. Her daughter had refused him outright when he'd asked her to come there to help, acting strained and resentful, quite a different person than her mother. In the end it was Marny's son, Nathan, who'd come to live with her in Ruddick's house. He was a fine strapping lad, a football player in college, and well mannered; he took beautiful care of Marny, and he even helped around the house.

The phone rang—it was the Secretary of Defense's assistant.

"This is Milo Ruddick; yes, I'll wait."

There was irritation in his voice. Woodson was calling to ask a favor, and he had to hold the line and wait for him; he was obviously losing his grip, as if he were under some terrible stress. It had sometimes been the same during the war, when they were working so closely on the delicate oil transactions.

"Milo? Sorry to keep you waiting—I was just picking up the phone to talk to you when the President rang."

The Secretary's voice was tightly contained; Ruddick could close his eyes and see him, his faced lined, intense, waving his pipe as he leaned forward over a desk piled with files.

"How is Harry doing?" Ruddick asked.

"He's enjoying himself hugely. I wish I was."

"I understand that he's serious about integration, that he's going to make an executive order directing it."

"No question about it. He knows he needs it for the election. The timing will be critical—probably do it next summer."

Ruddick grunted and Woodson went on, "You know why I'm calling. I'm going to need your help."

"You know you'll have it." When he had been Secretary of the Navy, Woodson had opposed the idea of reorganizing the services into the Department of Defense, fearing that the Navy would be in a permanent minority in votes with the Army and the new in-dependent Air Force. Partly to offset those fears, Truman had named him as Secretary of Defense. Ruddick wasn't sure he could handle the job; once during the war, when the deal with Germany over oil and tankers was about to be exposed, Woodson had come perilously close to self-destruction.

"I'm having a palace revolution over in the Navy Department.

They say I'm bending over backward to favor the Air Force, to appear neutral."

"Nothing wrong with that."

"No, but I have to throw them a bone. I'm going to come to you to carve fifty million from somewhere for that classified project we talked about the last time you were here."

Ruddick grunted. Woodson meant a new aircraft carrier, one large enough to carry bombers with a nuclear capability. It would be tough to sell, with dozens of World War II carriers either in storage or being broken up.

"Pretty risky, Mr. Secretary. You're rocking the rolls-and-missions boat. If we have to pare the Air Force down to forty-eight wings to stay within budget, new carriers won't sit well with anyone."

"I know that, but if I give them this one they'll be satisfied for a while."

"They should be; they should name the ship after you. Of course, I'll find the money, but I'm going to have to twist a few arms."

"There's nobody better than you at that."

Ruddick expected a little additional small talk, but Woodson went on for twenty minutes complaining about his office staff and, of all things, his desk—it was an antique, he couldn't get rid of it, the drawers stuck, the veneer was peeling, a childish catalogue of annoyances. The conversation was worse than trivial, it was bizarre, and the Secretary's quivering voice rose with the intensity of his complaints. Ruddick was glad to say good-bye finally. If the man was this troubled, it might mean big trouble for Milo Ruddick.

He walked to the window to gaze over his property again. When the phone rang this time, it was with the high-pitched bell of his private line.

"Ruddick here."

"This is Dixon Price. We need to talk." Price's voice varied with the situation, suiting his tough, chameleon-like personality exactly. He'd have been at home on a carnival midway, on the docks in San Francisco, a stage in New York, or pleading a case before the Supreme Court. Whatever it took, Price had it, in spades.

"What's the problem?"

"The same as always, money. I've recruited half a dozen new organizers to send to Georgia and Mississippi, but I'm having a little problem with my bank."

Ruddick was silent for a while. During the war, Dixon Price had run McAmer, the McCallum family's oil company. He had managed the complex series of deals with Woodson, involving Brazil and Switzerland supplying oil to Germany via Spain. After the war, Dixon had created the largest law firm in Little Rock and had become a part of the governor's kitchen cabinet. Many people— Ruddick included—thought that Dixon really ran the state. The *Gazette* had once run a cartoon showing the horse-faced governor sitting on the birdlike Price's knee, a ventriloquist's dummy. It wasn't exactly fair, but it was a political fact of life that Price and the governor were more than close.

For the past five years, Dixon had been deeply involved in Ruddick's special project and had used his own funds for the recruitment of potential Klan leaders. Dixon was indispensable to the future of the Klan.

"Let me see what I can do. I know you've really extended yourself."

"I'm glad to do it, Milo, but I'm just caught short this year. You know what's happened to prices. Do you want me to contact our overseas friend for some new merchandise?"

Ruddick pursed his lips and whistled. "I don't know, Dixon. We pretty well have the best of the crop in hand now, and—"

Dixon's rough laughter interrupted him. "And you don't want to part with any of them. I know. But there's still a market out there for the second-rate material, things we can still have shipped in."

He was right, of course; the basement of Ruddick's home was filled with racks of paintings, the heart of the "lost" Hermann Goering collection. Only he could enjoy them—and that was the way he preferred it.

"You're right, as usual, Dixon, much as I hate to admit it. See what you can do and get back to me."

Ruddick leaned back in his chair to examine again the hazardous course he was charting. He knew in his heart that the emotional basis of the Klan ran too deep in Southern culture for it to ever die. But the Klan was an object of national ridicule, and rightly so. A primitive Rotary club, its members were largely ignorant rednecks hating blindly without a cause. But loosely organized as it was, it had potential. After all, Hitler had started his political career with a party with seven members. There were still thousands of Klansmen, and millions more would join if the Klan could be revitalized. It was a question of organizing it properly, giving it the right goals. And the name had to be changed to something ambiguously popular.

There was no doubt that Dixon could get some more paintings— the man had his hand in everything—but if he got them, would it be possible to give them up?

Salinas, California/December 24, 1947

The party got more comfortable as the adults got more to drink—the men Old Forester bourbon, the women a rough Italian table wine from a local farmer—and the children came to the point where they knew each other well enough to play and not yet well enough to fight.

The U-shaped frame and stone house progressed from the original clapboard Roget farmhouse, which was one wing, to the new stucco addition where the Bandfields lived. Nestled between the two wings was a courtyard with a swing set and a swimming pool for the kids. Clarice Roget had chosen the site carefully. Both front porches overlooked a dry river valley winding its diminishing channel out through parched rocks and scrub pines to the town. Hadley Roget was standing with his arms on the railing, staring out at the flickering lights that each year reached out closer to them from Salinas.

Bandfield came out and slipped his arm around his old friend's shoulder.

"Bet you're thinking how happy Clarice would be to see this shindig."

Hadley nodded. "This place is a monument to her, you know. She built it because she was tired of you and me running around playing with airplanes. She wanted it to be just big enough for two families—with lots of babies."

"Well, even Clarice would have enough babies to go around tonight."

"How's little Ulrich getting along with your kids?"

"He's a nice boy, shy, after all he's been through. Lyra watches over him like a tigress—I think she's a little too protective."

"Patty still crazy about Lyra?"

"If she liked a man as much, I'd shoot the bastard. I think they get along so well because they both know how miserable it is to be married to a pilot."

Roget turned and eyed him quizzically. "I hear what you're saying, but I can tell you're not too happy. What's the matter?"

"I'll be honest with you, Hadley. I don't like having people living in our side of the house. You and Clarice were always over in your own wing, but Lyra and Ulrich are just down the hall. I can't walk around in my underwear, and Lyra is so nervous that I'm afraid I'm scaring her."

"Did you tell Patty this?"

"She just laughed at me, told me I was gone most of the time, and that it wouldn't be forever."

"Be patient, son. After all Lyra went through—the Nazis, the bombing, losing her husband, everything—she'll need a little time. And Patty's right. The Air Force keeps you on the go most of the time; you're more like a boarder with bedding privileges than a husband."

"Well, that's not all. I think Patty's drinking too much. She's got a glass of wine in her hand all the time. And she's putting on a little weight."

"Aw, Bandy, you're full of it. What the hell is that in your glass, milk? She's just relaxing from her worries." They stood together quietly for a while, then Roget said, "I guess Patty told you that we're starting to lose our ass in the housing business."

Bandfield put his fingers to his lips and pointed—two deer were walking quietly in the shadows at the edge of the old flying field. Then he whispered, "Yeah, cut-throat competition from jerry-built houses. She says we're trying to build quality houses like we built quality airplanes, and we've priced ourselves out of the market. The question is, are you willing for us to fold our tents and get out of the business?"

Roget stood and stretched. Two inches taller than Bandfield, he had the ropy, hard-knit muscles of a man who'd labored all his life. He was letting his white hair grow long again, a sign that he was at last beginning to overcome the melancholy that had engulfed him when he lost Clarice. Once it had been his trademark, one of his few vanities, a great mound of silver that made him look like an old-time prophet. Clarice had always taken care of it for him, shampooing it, only trimming it when absolutely necessary. When she died, he'd had it cut off and buried with her.

It bothered him that for all the years they'd been married, he'd been preoccupied with work; now that she was gone he thought of her constantly, missing her, and grieving that he had not paid more attention to her. The sorrow had changed his nature, too; once he'd been a punster, always ready with a joke, usually a bad one. Now his long rugged face was etched with lines and tinged with sadness.

"Hell, Bandy, I've folded more tents than a tribe of Indians. I never liked building houses, anyway—the damn things don't fly. How long a tour of duty are you going to have to pull with the Air Force this time?"

Bandfield laughed. "Depends. Patty says we've got plenty of money, but I figure I ought to stay in for twenty, anyway, and nail down a pension in case we go bust again."

"Pension, you don't give a goddamn about no pension, you just want to fly the new airplanes. Don't try to bullshit old Hadley."

Bandfield nodded and grinned. It was true—but he couldn't admit it to Patty.

Roget's voice went up an octave. "Your marriage is as weird as mine was—I hope you take better care of Patty than I did of Clarice." They drained their glasses and Roget went on. "Anyway,

I've got some ideas about going back into the airplane modification business, and I'm not so sure I can handle it without you."

Bandfield groaned. The only time they'd ever made money on airplanes was during the war, when Patty was running the plant, subcontracting parts for the bigger contractors. Every time they'd try to build airplanes themselves, they'd been squeezed out of the market.

"Don't you groan at me. I've got some good ideas, can't miss."

"Like the Aircar?" Roget had dumped a small fortune into a combination car-plane that was a bad car and a worse airplane.

"That was a fluke, Bandy, and you know it. No, I think—damn it, I know!—that there's going to be a market out there for big airplanes that can drop water and chemicals on forest fires. God knows we've got enough forest fires every year to make a market. That's one thing. The other is converting surplus airplanes to executive planes—you know, taking a Lodestar, stripping out the military gear, cleaning it up, putting in a luxury interior, and selling it for a company plane."

"Sounds good to me, because you and Patty can handle it here in Salinas. We know who all the good workers are—start small, and work up. If it gets to be too much for you, I'll ask to be released."

They shook hands and Bandfield continued. "I think converting airplanes to fight forest fires is the best bet to start with—the whole west needs help with that."

They heard Patty laughing and then she called, "Bandy, get in here and watch Lyra set the house on fire." Bandfield rolled his eyes and tilted an imaginary shot glass back.

Roget scowled, "She ain't drunk, Bandy, don't kid yourself. And even if she was, she'd still be able to handle you."

Inside the group was gathered around a table that had been cleared and covered with a rough canvas tarpaulin. In the center was a hot plate, with a pot bubbling on it, the smell of hot metal searing the air. On the floor was a washtub filled with water.

Roget handed Bandfield a fresh tumbler of whiskey and whispered, "Looks like your visitor friend is loosening up."

"A little dago red will do that. She's sure looking better. I wish she'd do a little walking around in *her* underwear."

During the war, Lyra Josten had been in the German resistance movement, doing espionage work for General Henry Caldwell. She'd arrived from Sweden six months before, pale and painfully thin, her eyes dull with fatigue and anxiety, a sharp contrast to plump, rosy-cheeked Ulrich. It was clear that she had been denying herself to make sure that her baby was well fed. Now both were looking beautiful, thanks to Patty's tender care and lavish diet. As Lyra busied herself with a ladle and gloves, Roget said, "I'd never thought two young women would get along in one house like they do."

Bandfield nodded. Patty was a wonder. When she'd heard that Lyra needed help to get into the United States with her baby, Patty had roared into action. Within a few weeks she'd secured all the paperwork and arranged for their transportation over.

Lyra was bubbling with pleasure. "Ladies and gentlemen! We're going to play an old-fashioned Russian Christmas game. First, you stand up and tell where you were last Christmas and where you want to be next Christmas. Then you pour a splash of molten lead into the water. When it cools, you fish it out, and the shape of the metal will tell your fortune."

Waving the ladle she said, "Patty, you go first while I make sure the children stay back."

Patty took the ladle, saying, "I was here in this house last year; I hope we're all here next year." She poured a stream of lead into the washtub; there was a hissing stream of steam as the lead settled toward the bottom.

Lyra scooped it out. "See, it looks like a star! That's a good omen, it means your wish will come true."

"Who's next? Bandy?"

"No, let young Lyra go next."

Lyra took the ladle and began to speak in a quavering voice.

"This really works, you know. Last year in Stockholm, I wished we would be in the United States—and look at us here, with you good people."

She stepped over and took Bandy by the hand. "Come here, because the wish I make is going to please you."

"I wish you all a Merry Christmas—and for next year, I wish Ulrich and I will be in our own home."

Bandy blushed as Lyra poured the lead into the water—she had him figured out, no question. Patty was smiling as Lyra pulled a long silver strand from the tub and flourished it.

"What is it? I can't tell what it is."

Bandfield took the still warm lead and slowly rotated it. "Well, if you hold it this way, it looks a little like a map of Argentina. But if you turn it this way, it looks like a bear."

Lyra took the metal. "I'm going to put this away so we can look at it next year and see what it was trying to tell us."

2

Nashville, Tennessee/January 8, 1948

Relaxed as a stroked kitten, Ginny luxuriated in the unaccustomed comfort of the fieldstone rambler that served as the McNaughton Aircraft Company's guesthouse, taking advantage of Stan's absence to play her private hair game. Placing her right hand at the top of her head, her fingers worked incessantly until they had grasped an individual hair. When she had it secured in solitary splendor, she pulled it, stretched it out in front of her mouth and bit it in half. It was a reflexive habit she'd had since adolescence and it drove Stan crazy.

Walking in suddenly, he caught her.

"Honey, you're doing it again. That's worse than biting your nails and I don't think it's healthy. Shouldn't we talk to a doctor about it?"

"I'll talk to a doctor about this, if you'll talk to him about the way you save things."

They stared angrily at each other, in the rough eye-contact of marital silence. He broke the impasse by throwing a magazine against the peeled-pine log wall.

"This crummy place looks like a Sonja Henie movie set."

"That shows what you know. It must have cost Troy a fortune—it's better than a ski lodge. Even has a heated swimming pool." She glanced around, mentally ticking off the prices of the expensive Ethan Allen furnishings.

Then, trying to make up, she said, "Sorry, baby. We're just nervous after all that's gone wrong. Maybe things will work out after all."

Coleman shook his head, his voice bitter. "Fat chance. We were better off before you got your dad involved."

"Better off! At least you got a chance to fly McNaughton's rocket plane."

"Big deal. Yeager goes through the sound barrier, and they cancel our program."

She lit a cigarette and drew deeply on it. "Why the hell couldn't he have crashed? Or even just bailed out?"

"Because he was good."

Sounding genuinely contrite for a change, she said, "I'm sorry, honey, I was trying to help."

"Yeah, just like today. The only reason Troy McNaughton is going to talk to me is because of your stepfather. I know that, he knows that, and it makes me feel like a jerk."

Ginny reached out and stroked his arm. "That's not true. You're here because you're a great pilot, and McNaughton needs you."

She managed him by switching subjects like a conman shifts the pea under the shells. Plopping herself down on his lap, she asked, "What's his wife like?"

Coleman shrugged. "I haven't seen her, but I hear she's pretty good-looking—she's a lot younger than Troy—and she's supposed to run the plant single-handed."

"You be careful around her."

He hugged her and said, "Let's both be careful. When you see her tomorrow, let her do the talking, find out all you can. This might be our big chance. And maybe our last one."

. . .

The next day had gone quite well for Stan Coleman; Ginny thought it had gone well for her, too.

Coleman was early for his nine o'clock appointment, and McNaughton gave him a quick tour of the huge plant. Only three years before, it had teemed with workers as Sidewinder and Mamba fighters poured off the production line for Russia, three shifts a day, seven days a week. Now most of the bays were empty, chained off, lights darkened and populated solely by the birds that inevitably found their way into the gloom of empty hangar space. Some modification activity was going on, but no new production. The empty plant made Coleman uneasy—McNaughton Aircraft looked as if it needed a funeral director more than a test pilot.

"Sad, isn't it? We took this place from a cornfield to one of the most modern aircraft plants in the world in just a few years. Now we'd be better off turning it back into a cornfield; we could get a few niggers in to run it. Might as well—the whole South's being taken over by them anyway."

"Somehow you don't look like a corn farmer to me, Mr. McNaughton." Stan traded on repackaging what people had just said, giving it a humorous conspiratorial twist. He'd already caught McNaughton's prejudiced view of Negroes and played to it. "We've got a few hundred thousand colored down in Arkansas we could send you, though—it'd be good riddance." Coleman hadn't been exposed to Negroes before he married Ginny; since then he'd adopted her family's attitude toward them.

They were sitting in Troy's trophy-bedecked office—photos of famous pilots, film stars, politicians, models of McNaughton aircraft, and Troy's sporting trophies. Coleman made a practice of knowing the name of the best of everything, and he quickly complimented McNaughton on the brace of Purdey shotguns and the Greenhart fly rod.

Troy went to the window to adjust the blinds. He moved around the office constantly in short little runs, from his desk to the sideboard, from the sideboard to the window, as if he could burn away his problems with his energy.

"The long and short of it is this. We desperately need to get a new product in production or just shut down. We were doing fine in our San Diego plant until the idiots in Washington cut the funding for missile research and development."

He tapped a Camel out from a pack and Coleman's lighter appeared like lightning. Troy took the light, his eyes narrowed to avoid the smoke.

"Stan, I understand you're in line to do the test work on Boeing's new bomber. Have you flown it?"

"Just once, up at Moses Lake. Pardon my French, but it's fucking sensational. Handles more like a fighter than a bomber."

"But it's too short-ranged. It needs aerial refueling and that won't work in wartime."

Catching the scent, Coleman jumped in. "Yes, you sure couldn't send tankers over enemy territory."

Nodding in agreement, Troy went on, "And the B-36 has enough range, but it's too slow. Let me show you something."

McNaughton moved a long, narrow box over to the center of his desk and lifted its lid. Inside was a model of a flying-wing bomber, not unlike the one Northrop had built, but much sleeker, with longer, narrower wings and six jets clustered in the center on the trailing edge.

"Ever hear of the Horten brothers?"

Coleman shook his head.

"They designed dozens of flying wings in Germany and flew a lot of them. They had a first-class jet fighter ready to go at the end of the war, faster than anything on either side. After the war they moved to Argentina, like a lot of the Germans, and they kept up their research, working in secret for Vanguard Aircraft. When we bought Vanguard, we acquired the rights to manufacture it."

Coleman ran his finger over the model's smooth black skin. "It looks like a boomerang someone tried to straighten out. Where's the cockpit?"

"Well, that's my little secret. We'll talk about that later. I call it the 'Manta'—it looks like one. It'll be faster than the B-47 and have a longer range than the B-36. And it's so slim, they tell me you won't even be able to pick it up on radar."

Coleman was impressed but felt the need to assert himself. "Why not a new fighter? That's what you've got your experience in."

"I'd like to, but North American and Republic have too much clout—they've got the market sewn up tighter than a politician's wallet. Our last fighter, the Copperhead, got frozen out, even though it was a better plane than the F-84 or F-86."

His eyes bored into Coleman like an IRS auditor checking deductions.

"I want to build a flying wing. That's why I want to hire you."

Coleman nodded as if he fully understood as McNaughton went on. "I've got to take the long view on something like this, Stan, it's a four- or five-year process. We'll have to make some smaller airplanes at first, just like Northrop did, to get the hang of it."

Coleman stood up, wanting to say something strong, insightful. "Well, what about Northrop's wing? It's already flying."

"Yes, but it's an old design—all they've done is stick jet engines in a piston-engine airframe. I'm not worried about them. Boeing's the outfit to beat, and I don't know if anyone can beat them, even us. But the budget's tight and getting tighter, and I've *got* to get the development money. That's where you come in."

Coleman nodded judiciously, understanding that it was the Ruddick connection. He should have minded, but he did not; McNaughton had a soothing, almost hypnotic effect upon him.

Troy hurried to a sideboard cluttered with decanters and soda siphons. He poured himself a Dr Pepper, offering one to Stan. Coleman was thirsty, but he shook his head no—who knew how many Dr Peppers he had left?

"Stan, I've got some political connections, but you've got the best I've ever seen. I'm an old friend of your father-in-law's, but I want you to tell me all about him, how you see him."

Coleman nodded. This was comfortable ground; he far preferred talking about his father-in-law than the engineering merits of a flying wing. "I suppose you know most of what I know. His wife's family was Old South aristocratic and Texas-oil rich. She's left half of Arkansas and a good chunk of Texas to him."

"How did she die?"

"She'd been sick a long time and finally committed suicide. It was tough on the kids, particularly Ginny."

McNaughton was quiet. It seemed terribly convenient for a politician to have a rich wife die.

"Ginny's just his stepdaughter, from the wife's first marriage, but she loves him more than most people love their real father. They're thick as thieves. And you have to give the man credit. Ruddick made a ton of money on his own, too, during the war and after. He was a Congressman for eight terms, and he's one of the few politicians rich enough to contribute to other politicians' war chests. He's smart and knows the defense business backwards and forwards, so he has a job no matter which administration it is. And mainly, he knows where the bodies are buried."

Coleman twisted in his seat, then went on. "Milo likes to run things. If he's got a fault, it's that he doesn't like to delegate anything to anybody. I understand he drives the people in his company crazy, checking into everything."

"Got any weaknesses, any vices?"

Coleman thought it was a hell of a question to ask about his father-in-law but went on. "Not that I know of. He's a churchman, attends every Sunday when he's in Little Rock, runs the vestry with an iron hand."

"How does he like you?"

"Oddly enough, he thinks I'm tops, because I'm a pilot. That's his one frustration in life—he always wanted to be a fighter pilot. But his eyes are bad, never had a chance to fly himself."

"Did you get any kills during the war?"

Coleman hung his head modestly and said, "Three." He hesitated and added, "Only one of them was confirmed."

He didn't talk about his victories too much—he'd been stooging around in Bavaria, late in 1944, and had come across a flight of three German training planes, little Focke-Wulf biplanes. He had shot one down, and the other two had dispersed like rabbits in the woods. When he came back, he claimed three victories, but they gave credit only for the one on the gun camera film.

McNaughton went back to business. "What about Ruddick's son?"

"Oh, Bob flew during the war. He's a closed-mouth, private sort of guy, but we get along pretty well. I understand he's a good pilot. But his dad intimidates him like he does most people. Like he does me."

"What's Bob doing now?"

"He's running a small airport outside of Little Rock. He's talking about getting into air racing, but his Dad's not willing to foot the bill."

"How would Milo Ruddick feel about it if someone else gave Bob a little help?"

"He'd love it. He always talks about Bob being another Roscoe Turner, racing at Cleveland. But he won't put up the money it takes. I don't know where all his money goes, he must be socking it away. The Ruddicks live well, but not lavishly. Sometimes I wonder if he doesn't have a little tootsie on the side who he spends his money on."

McNaughton shook his head. "I doubt it. It always seemed to me that he preferred power to pussy."

Coleman smiled and Troy went on. "You know, it might be good publicity for McNaughton Aircraft if we converted one of the Sidewinders into a racer."

Coleman leaned forward at the word *we*.

"It looks to me like the kid's the way to his father's heart. We'll work on Bob, convince him about our capabilities. Then maybe the three of us can convince his father that we need twenty million in start-up money for the wing."

"Twenty million! That's a lot of money; Boeing only spent about half that on the XB-47."

"It's a lot, but it's only a down payment. Let me level with you. The Manta bomber is just a stalking horse. I don't care if we ever build one! I want to build guided missiles, flying wings with a long range and an atomic bomb load."

"Is that why there's no cockpit on the model?"

"Exactly! I want the money for applied research, mainly for a robot navigation system we acquired from Vanguard. It'll be far more accurate than anything humans can do."

Self-interest flashed in Coleman's eyes like a neon sign.

"Missiles are the key to the future, Stan. Nobody will need bombers in twenty years, believe me. But those idiots in Washington won't see that. Theodore von Karman, one of the greatest scientists in the world, says they are possible, but Vannevar Bush says they are not. So they believe Bush and cancel development."

Coleman nodded; he'd met von Karman, heard of Bush.

"Where does the competition stand with missiles?"

"Good question. Convair's had a lot of money funneled to them, but they're off on the wrong track, trying to build ballistic missiles— like big V-2s. They won't be ready for eight or ten years. With the present technology, you just can't build a rocket big enough to throw a ten-thousand-pound atomic warhead from here to Russia. That's why I want to build flying-wing guided missiles. Manned bombers are obsolete—with the atom bomb, you don't need them anymore." He waited for this to sink in.

"So, you see, I've got to take the money where I can get it, and put it where I know it will do the most good. The Air Force will go for developing the wing, I know—if Ruddick backs us."

"How can I help?"

"I've watched you for the past few months. You know how to handle people. You're a natural-born salesman, and I want you to sell the two Ruddicks. They already know you and trust you. You're an insider, part of the family. Your wife can help, too."

Coleman's feigned reluctance didn't fool McNaughton. "I don't know, Troy. I've got a great flying job, and I'll probably be promoted in the fall."

"I'll double your salary, and put Ginny on the payroll at whatever you are making now in the Air Force."

"Gee, I'll have to discuss it with her, Troy."

Sticking out his hand, Troy smiled. "No, you won't. I'm sure she and Elsie have already come to an agreement. Now don't say a word to anyone about the wing, and especially not about the missiles."

The two wives had in fact already come to several agreements, the first of which was that they disliked each other intensely. The second, almost equally important, was that they nevertheless would have to work together.

Elsie McNaughton had been waiting in the grand old Maxwell House Hotel dining room for half an hour, passing the time with bourbon poured from a silver flask into a thick tumbler of ice water. She much preferred the sweeter taste of a Manhattan, but you still couldn't buy drinks in a Nashville restaurant. She glanced at her wristwatch, then poured more whiskey over the ice.

As she sipped, Elsie impatiently tapped a crystal vase with a spoon; she had carved out a career in the almost exclusively male aviation industry by never waiting for anyone or anything. Knowing her temper, the Negro waiter watched her as nervously as a mouse watches a cat.

She had started as a secretary for Bruno Hafner in the old Hafner Aircraft Company, unable to take shorthand, barely able to type, but young, virginal, and eager to learn about everything. The first thing Bruno taught her was sex, but after the first rough edges of his lust had been knocked off, he found she had brains as well and began to treat her as his girl Friday. When Hafner Aircraft went belly up in 1936, Troy McNaughton had bought up its assets—among them Elsie Raynor.

With the experience she'd had with Hafner, she quickly assumed a major role at McNaughton, developing an easygoing, bantering managerial style that did not quite mask her voracious appetite for power. Troy valued her knack for going to the heart of business problems. Sometimes she used sex as a weapon, exploiting the weaknesses of the men she worked with, but most of the time she simply worked harder and gathered more information than anyone else she was competing with. She had used both approaches with her old friend and lover, the late General Henry Caldwell, and it had paid off handsomely over the years. Elsie was a wealthy woman, with a large interest in McNaughton Aircraft held in her own name.

When Ginny finally appeared, clicking in on four-inch high heels, the two women experienced the polar opposite of love at first sight. Elsie thought, A frigging flamenco dancer—where are the castanets? even as she realized the truth—Ginny was too young, too pretty, and too much in love with herself for Elsie to endure. As Ginny walked over, Elsie's eyes swept up and down. Ginny was taller and she had a gorgeous figure—much like her own had been only a few years before.

Elsie sat up straight and stole a quick glance into the mirrored column next to her. She sighed. Twenty extra pounds had mugged her body, making the flat round and the firm sag. Her once silky, copper-gold hair had been turned to dime store henna by too many weekly treatments. In her youth, she used just a touch of makeup, but now she was layered in a rose-pink Elizabeth Arden haze.

Ginny, piling up impressions at equal speed, let her best beauty-contest smile blossom as she thought, She looks like a whorehouse madam.

Elsie half-rose from her seat to greet her. They shook hands formally, each momentarily lost in appraising the other.

If Ginny's first mistake was to be attractive, her second was to dominate the conversation. Elsie tried to interject at first, but soon gave up, confining her remarks to "aha"s and a few "I see"s.

"I just love your guesthouse; you must have had a professional decorator in."

Elsie liked the old guesthouse better, where she had roistered with Caldwell and many others. The new place was too luxurious for her, and it didn't even have a mirror by the bed! She started to say that she had done the decorating herself when Ginny went on, "'Course, I'd never hire anyone to do my home. I've got a natural talent for decoration, everyone says so."

Elsie smiled, thinking: You probably love blue-tinted mirrors and movie-dish tableware, you cracker bitch.

In the next hour, Elsie learned far more than she wanted to know about Ginny's aristocratic family, her powerful father, Stan's cleverness, and how much the two of them could do for McNaughton Aircraft. She also saw that as mendaciously cunning as Ginny was, she could be a useful tool—and would never be a threat.

Finally, Ginny ran down, saying, "But goodness me, I've been doing all the talking. Tell me why you all want Stan to come work for you."

Smoothing the silver-threaded tablecloth with her hand, Elsie decided to tell Ginny the simple truth.

"Because of your contacts—your stepfather, of course, and all the others. And because your husband will make a good salesman for us. He's much smoother than Troy. Troy's ways were fine for the old days, but the government's more sophisticated now. I understand that Stan has a very winning manner, and that he looks the part."

Ginny was excited, visions of managerial perks dancing in her head. "You don't want him to be just a test pilot?"

The white-jacketed waiter, silver-haired and sleekly deferential, served dessert, orange sherbet for Ginny and bourbon black bottom pecan pie for Elsie.

"Oh, sure, he'll fly as much as he wants to. But Troy wants to use him in Washington to sweeten up the brass—you know, buy them dinner, take them fishing and hunting. Troy always says you sell a hundred times more airplanes on the golf course than you do on the flight line."

"Stan will be perfect for you!"

Elsie just smiled. Maybe he would, at that. She pushed the pecan pie away untasted—perhaps it was time to find out if there was life in the old girl yet.

Cleveland, Ohio/March 17, 1948

God bless his father. Usually his calm presence, so benign and filled with good will, made everyone feel better. Now he was mad as hell, veins purpling out in his forehead, arms waving, and everyone was uneasy.

"Start at the beginning, son. I'm tired of wondering what's going on. You and Saundra have been sharp with each other all morning."

The Reverend John Stuart Marshall, Sr., three inches taller and fifty pounds heavier than his son, was built more like Joe Louis than Father Divine. Curly white hair ran around the monklike tonsure of broad black scalp, and his eyes normally sparkled with humor. Now they flashed an urgent warning that he wanted straight talk. Despite his anger, Reverend Marshall instinctively pulled Saundra close with his beefy arm; she gladly folded herself into him, grateful for his love and warmth, sorry that their bickering had bothered him. She had never really known her own father. For some reason still unrevealed, her sternly religious mother had forbidden even the mention of his name. Their life had been work and church, yet until she'd met John's father she couldn't believe that ministers could laugh, that religion could be comforting.

"Dad, the problem is work! I can't get a flying job. I've been all over the country. If I didn't have Mr. Bandfield's word on it, I'd think I'd been blacklisted by McNaughton."

"Oh, you're 'black' listed, son, we all are. I thought you found that out at Tuskegee." His mother shook with mirth, eyes lit up and crackling white teeth smiling through skin as shiny as a polished pan. Her face was long and narrow, her nose slightly hooked, her smile wide. The family had always had fun, no matter how hard times had been. When everyone was home it sometimes seemed as if laughter would jump the little frame house on Connick Street right off its concrete block foundations. Mary was a tall woman, thin and strong as the lengths of hickory she used to apply to John Jr.'s backside. His copper color and hooked nose came from her side of the family. The senior John Marshall always joked about there being an Indian somewhere in his mother's family woodpile—but never when Mary was around.

She busied herself around the battered oak kitchen table, the center of their life, passing out plates of fragrant stollen, heavy white frosting dotted with raisins, oven-warm and their standard Saturday morning treat. Working for a German family in Shaker Heights for almost twenty years, Mary's cooking style had changed over time to mix its purely Southern origins with German-American dishes. John's favorite meal was still neckbones, sauerkraut, and liver dumplings, a Dixie-Bavarian mixture he'd daydreamed about when eating K-rations in Italy.

"Don't laugh, Mom; at least Tuskegee taught me to fly—I'll always be grateful for that."

Tuskegee Army Air Field had been the experience of a lifetime—and an utter nightmare. Tuskegee was an experiment, to see if Negroes could learn to fly, and the Army handled it in a curious dual fashion. On the one hand, the training was just as arduous and fast-paced as at a white flying school. On the other, segregation was preserved almost as strictly as it was in the nearby town of Tuskegee, where the drinking fountains were marked WHITE and COLORED and hostility lurked behind every glance. Like most of the other aviation cadets, John had endured the humiliation because he loved to fly and because he felt that a chance to be a commissioned pilot offered the best way for Negroes to advance.

"Dad, the only people hiring pilots are the airlines, and of course they're not taking on any Negroes. I thought about seeing if I could get back into the Air Force, but after our problems at Lockbourne, I decided against it."

Saundra's smile was tight. "No, no more Lockbournes, please."

The old man's manner softened. "I have to tell you, son, I was worried when you left the Air Corps." He would never call it anything else but *Air Corps.* "I knew that when that McTaggart outfit offered you a job, they didn't know you were colored."

"McNaughton, Dad. And they must have known; there was a box to check for race on the application, and I told them that I'd learned to fly at Tuskegee and fought overseas with the 332nd. No white boys did that!"

"No matter. When somebody realized who—and what—you were, they took care of things. Just like I said they would."

His mother broke in. "Amen. He said that the very day we got your letter saying you were going to work for them."

John Sr. looked at her and smiled. They'd been together thirty-five years now, survived two wars, a depression, and two race riots, one in Detroit, and the other in East St. Louis. They'd had five children, and three had lived to maturity. She was still a good-looking woman.

"What's this business you're in now?"

"I don't know a whole lot, and most of what I know I can't tell. All I can tell you is that I've got a job, flying for a foreign government, and the pay is good—six hundred dollars a month, as long as I'm there."

"Six hundred dollars a month! Whooee! Sure beats a dollar a day at the foundry. But where are you going, John?"

"That's what I can't tell you. As soon as I can, I will, and I won't be gone any longer than I have to. If Saundra can stay here with you, I can save a lot of money, and maybe come back and start a business of my own."

"You know that Saundra's welcome here. You just be sure you come back." He paused. "It's not this 'ace' thing, is it, son? You don't have to prove yourself to anyone, you've already done that."

John Marshall flushed; as usual his dad was on target.

"No, no, Dad, it's nothing like that."

His father smiled and said, "Son, you forget a daddy can tell when his son is fibbing, and you're fibbing now. I just hope it's a good cause."

"It is; you'd join yourself if you knew what it was." Then he laughed and added, "'Course, you're not exactly in the line of work they'd want to use," and made his father angry because he wouldn't tell him any more.

That night Saundra lay next to him, cradled in his arms, crying softly because he was leaving, again. His parents, knowing they would want to be alone, had said good-bye that afternoon, driving to St. Louis in their two-tone gray 1940 Nash Ambassador to see the Reverend's sister. The elder Marshall loved the Nash because the front seat folded back to make a bed, and they never had to worry about finding a place to stay that would accept Negroes. They packed a big hamper of food, slept in the car by the side of the road, and used the woods for a restroom.

"Don't cry, honey, not on our last night for a while."

"I should be better at this. We've had almost as many 'last nights' as we've had nights together."

It was true. They'd been married less than a year when he went off to flying school—just in time, it turned out; a few months later married men weren't being admitted to the program. Since then only his job with McNaughton had given them any kind of home life, even though the little house they'd rented in the desert had been lonely and primitive. There'd been no place for her—no place livable—when he came back to Tuskegee, and their experience at Lockbourne was too painful to recall.

"Do you mind staying here? Would you rather go back and live with your mother?"

"Never! I love her, but I hate being with her. Mother is always scrubbing life on the washboard of religion. Your parents are so different—you're so different."

"That's why you love me so." They kissed for a long while, and she pulled away to ask, "What's this 'ace' thing your daddy asked about?"

He'd never discussed it with her, and knew he couldn't now. She'd never understand. "Ah, when I went to flying school I told my daddy that I wanted to be an ace, shoot everybody down—just foolish young man's talk. Don't think about it."

"Your father's not the only one who can tell when you're fibbing."

He licked her tears, little salt kisses, savoring them. Her big brown eyes had been the first thing that attracted him to her when they'd met at school. Widely spaced, her eyes shimmered with a serene intelligence that had captivated him at once. Just over five feet tall and weighing only a hundred pounds, her energy and imagination belied her doll-like size. She could be formidable when really angry—he'd learned long ago when to back off. And, he confessed to himself, he loved her figure best of all—small, well-formed breasts, a flat stomach that V'd into a wild mound of curly hair that she was ashamed of and a darling rounded bottom that he could never keep his hands from.

She was tense in his arms, her anxiety causing her to exude a musky scent that excited him. He let his fingers drum on her deliciously soft inner thigh, tapping a little song of love.

"Stop that." Saundra sat up and turned on the lamp. The light made a halo around her loosened jet-black hair. She tucked the sheet modestly around her.

"Are we ever going to settle down and live any kind of a normal life? What if I'm pregnant, what happens then? What if I'm pregnant and you get killed?"

He tugged the sheet down, letting her breasts spill out. "Well, you've still got Banjo to take care of you."

She tucked the sheet up angrily and snarled, "Damn it, be serious with me."

He kissed her brow. "I hope you are pregnant. I'll be back before the baby would be born. And I'm not going to get killed, I'm an old pro at this. When I come back, I'll start a little business, a flying school maybe, out in California. There must be lots of guys like me who want to fly."

She nestled back in his arms. "I'd like that. But how many colored boys would have the money to pay for flying lessons? How many white boys would take lessons from a Negro pilot? If you are going to start a business, do something I can help with. Start a little store, hardware, or maybe even groceries. Something that I can be with you every day." Her voice was earnestly beseeching, sending out an emotional SOS.

Reaching out, his finger traced the outline of her breasts, circling her nipples as they blossomed beneath the sheet.

"That's what we'll do. A little store, just you and me," she said.

He rubbed her nose with his own and said, "Honey, you have to understand. I can't give up flying, not ever. I've been in combat, I've flown rocket planes! Not many men, white or colored, have done that. I'm not going to wind up selling apples from a cart or pushing a broom in a factory!"

She melted against him, and their mouths met. How funny, he thought. She's so shy in so many ways, but her tongue is so aggressive, as if it has a mind of its own, as if there were fires burning in her that hadn't warmed him yet. He toyed with the idea of telling her about her tongue, then decided not to—it might make her stop. And he didn't want her ever to stop.

She broke free and whispered, "Put Banjo out of the room and close the door."

Nashville, Tennessee/April 15, 1948

The big man sat like an unwashed Buddha, stewing in his own rank heat, brown splotches staining the sweat band of his fedora, sleeves rolled up, folders piled around him. Baker's round face was pockmarked and shady with a day's growth of beard; his small, mean brown eyes had the expectant look of a bird dog with a quail in its mouth, eager to be rewarded but reluctant to give up its trophy.

McNaughton had hired him as chief of security in 1945, and he hadn't done an honest day's work since. But he'd done many dishonest ones and that was why McNaughton paid him $15,000 a year, more than his best test pilot made. Porterhouse steaks and bourbon whiskey had padded Baker's big frame just as blackmail and bribes had padded his bank account.

They watched each other as carefully as two sumo wrestlers about to grapple. McNaughton eyed Baker's horse blanket–plaid sport coat, his white plastic belt, and brown and white shoes.

"Rushing the season a bit, aren't you?"

"Nah, this is my Little Rock outfit, looked right at home there." He sipped his drink watching McNaughton carefully, trying to see how much Troy already knew, how little he could tell and get away with, selling his information as a dishonest bartender dispenses drinks, short-measured and watered.

"It's all there, Chief, enough to send this cockie to the chair."

"Proof?"

"Chief, if I'm lying, I'm dying! It ain't like this guy was no Sherlock Holmes or nothing. He never could've gotten away with this if he didn't have the coroner and the chief of police in his pocket. He's got to be a little bit nutso."

Baker had worked with Naval Intelligence during the war, an inquisitor running "special" security checks on people in sensitive positions. It was better than a college education; he learned how to pick locks, break into homes, bribe police officials and in general acquire the criminal talents necessary to be a skilled private investigator. Baker assumed all his subjects were guilty; if they weren't, he was content to frame them. He cultivated evidence like a crop, and if the yield was poor, he planted more.

"The dumb broad never had a chance! He'd had her so isolated for years that people thought she was crackers."

"Sum it up for me. I'll go through this stuff myself later."

"Sure. First he gets her isolated, like I say. Then he begins to spread rumors about her threatening suicide."

McNaughton interrupted. "Dick, how do you *know* that?"

Baker lolled back in the chair, picking his nose with practiced enjoyment. "I talked to her beauty operator, a good-looking doll named Leah Fanning. Mrs. Ruddnick stops coming in, and when Leah calls, old man Ruddick tells her, 'Mrs. Ruddick is not well. She tried to kill herself.' Other people said the same thing."

"When was all this?"

"Hell, that's the amazing thing—he started this whole caper in 1942, worked on it for years. I checked with their druggist, nice old guy named Kallme. 'Kallme for Drugs' was the sign for his shop. She was getting more and more prescriptions filled for all kinds of stuff—bromides, morphine, everything."

"He told you this?"

"No, Chief. I talked to him first—then I had to break in and look through his records. Everything neat and tidy on three-by-five cards. All the prescriptions were from the coroner. I checked him out; he's a rummy on old Milo's payroll."

"Go on."

Baker paused to finish his drink, handing the glass to McNaughton to refill. "Anyway, Ruddick spreads the rumor a couple a' times about her killing herself, once even has an ambulance come out and haul her to the hospital to pump her stomach. Then one day she's found in the garage, the old La Salle's engine running, vacuum cleaner hose attached to the tailpipe."

"Any autopsy?"

"Not so you could notice. Papers full of her 'long brave battles with illness,' lots of stuff like that. So he inherits everything."

"Pretty well fixed?"

"Yeah, on paper. But he's land poor, and he has lots of expenses. I don't know who all he's paying off, or bribing or what, but I think he's hurting for cash."

McNaughton's eyes went up. "I guess you busted in the bank, too?"

Baker smirked. "No, but I did go through his desk drawers; found his checkbooks, all of them, back for years. He's got neat handwriting and keeps good records. He's spending a *bundle* on art, all to a New York importer, and he's funneling dough to a lot of local politicians, plus he's funding the state Ku Klux Klan organization all by himself."

McNaughton paused to savor the information. Even if the murder was impossible to prove, the stuff on the Ku Klux Klan was dynamite. If he was still running for Congress, it wouldn't keep him from being reelected—hell, it might help—but it might prevent him from getting confirmation for a presidential appointment.

"What a fruitcake! How'd you find out about all this stuff, the art, the Klan, all of it?"

Baker belched, then tossed a handful of peanuts in his mouth. "I was busier than a one-legged guy in an ass-kicking contest. Mostly I found out from the checkbooks, but Little Rock's a one-horse town. The Railway Express guy likes White Owl cigars and beer as much as he likes to talk. Said it was amazing how much artwork gets shipped in to Ruddick, all out of New York. The name of the company he gave tallied with his checks. I'll get more dope on it if you want me to."

"Yeah, go ahead. What kind of art is it?"

"He didn't know, never saw it unpacked. Says it goes out to Ruddick's house and that's it."

McNaughton was uneasy. "You believe this Railway Express guy?"

"Yeah, he's proud of Ruddick, like he's bringing culture to Little Rock. He's a Klansman himself, and he sort of sounded me out, real clever like, asking me what I thought about niggers, before telling me all about it. I had to walk finally; he was telling me more than I needed."

They were quiet for a while, the silence broken by Baker's munching and slurping. He got up and fixed himself another drink, long on bourbon, short on water. McNaughton sighed, saying, "Help yourself, Dick. What about the children?"

"You know the daughter is from his wife's first marriage. The boy flew your airplanes during the war; he's running a little airport now. Seemed like a nice guy, kind of quiet. Everybody I talked to had a good word for them both, although they hinted the girl was a hot number. One guy sniggered something about 'backseat Ginny.' "

McNaughton rifled through the folders, as a silence fragile as gratitude hung in the room. Finally he looked up and said, "Baker, your expense account is pretty high for just giving out White Owls and beer. Don't you have any conscience at all?"

It occurred to Baker that having a conscience would be inconvenient at this point, inasmuch as he was fucking McNaughton's wife regularly, and he replied, "Christ no, boss, look who I work for. How about my raise?"

McNaughton shook his head. The information might be worth millions in the long run, but Baker mustn't know that. With a reluctant grunt of resignation, he muttered, "Two grand a year. Don't spend it all in one place."

Ekron, Israel/May 29, 1948

"I feel like a popsicle." Sitting with two other pilots, blankets draped around their shoulders, Marshall prayed for the dawn even as the chill stiffened his weary muscles.

"Chocolate-flavored," came a voice from the background. Marshall took no offense at the joking tone. In the ten-day crash course in Prague to check out in their aircraft, he and the other pilots had quickly grown close because each of them was a pro they could trust in combat.

Like the others—an American, an Englishman, and four Israelis—Marshall had entered training with a false name and false identity papers. The Czechs were so glad to get hard American currency for the planes and the training that they only glanced at his passport, even though a Negro pilot was an obvious oddity. Marshall regretted not being able to wander around war-damaged Prague, poverty-stricken yet beautiful in its melancholy, but the pace at the school was too swift. Instead, they'd gone directly from the long sessions at the airfield to their shabby rooms at the once-magnificent Flora Hotel, where barely edible food was served in absurdly tiny portions.

The Czech instructors had been a saving grace. Most were ex-RAF pilots who spoke English well enough, and who were following the new Communist line only because they had to. Many of them had flown Spitfires, and they bitterly derided the brutish Avia S-199 fighters they were teaching them to fly. Lacking the standard Daimler-Benz DB 605 engines, the Czechs had shoehorned in surplus bomber engines, great Junkers Jumo 211F power plants that made the already fractious Messerschmitt design even trickier to handle. The Czech pilots had rightly nicknamed it the "Mezec"—mule.

Yet as tough as it had been in Prague, the last seven days in Israel had been real killers. As soon as the course was over, they'd flown to Israel nonstop in a war-weary Douglas C-54 crammed with the parts of a disassembled fighter plane. It transpired that he hadn't been hired as much for his flying skills as for his maintenance officer experience. Three more C-54s had shuttled in to spill out their cargos, a bewildering assortment of wings, engines, and parts. Marshall and a small team of mechanics had worked night and day to assemble four of the hybrid Avia/Messerschmitts, painting them in Israeli colors with the Star of David insignia.

Now, completely outfitted in captured Luftwaffe flying gear, Marshall waited for a signal to fly in the defense of the new nation of Israel. It would be the first takeoff on the first combat mission of the first Israeli fighter squadron. The "Messers," as they'd come to call them, were in camouflaged revetments along a runway that was no more than a strip of roughly flattened sand. The Egyptians had complete control of the air, and the primitive birthing of the Israeli fighter force was being conducted in absolute secrecy.

Marshall felt the tension more than anyone. Before his trip to Prague, he'd never seen a Messerschmitt except through his P-51's gunsight. A translator had helped him decipher the few German technical manuals that the Czechs had sent along, but assembling the airplanes had been mostly a cut-and-try operation, facilitated by good mechanics willing to die from overwork. Now they were waiting to go out on a combat mission, and not one of the Avias had been test-flown, nor had any of their guns been test-fired! He wasn't sure that the bombs would come off—or that the wings would stay on.

The squadron commander, "Moddy" Myers, limped over to brief them, still favoring a leg injury an Arab car bomb had inflicted on him. Short and bald, he spoke with a lion-like ferocity.

"We'll take off just after dawn. Egyptian troop columns are moving on Tel Aviv. Less than two hundred fifty Israeli soldiers are available to block them. If we don't stop the column from the air, the war is over."

He paused and roared at them, "Over, do you understand? Israel will be gone, a two-thousand-year dream destroyed. We've got to delay their attack until reserves are scraped up from somewhere."

"We're supposed to stop them with these firecrackers? What are they, two-hundred pounders?" The speaker, an American who'd joined them only yesterday, ran his hands over the small bombs under the Messer's wing.

Myers shrugged and turned his hands palms up. "Seventy kilos. It's all we've got. If you're on target, they'll take out a tank. Follow me and do what I do."

They were veterans, and they understood.

The new pilot spoke to Marshall. "I think we met at Ramitelli. You were with the 332nd, weren't you?"

The man stepped forward, hand outstretched. He was well over six feet tall and moved with a rangy ease.

"I'm Bayard Riley—they call me "Bear,' mostly, but around here my name's supposed to be 'Moshe Niv.' "

Marshall recalled him at once. Riley had been a fifteen-victory ace with Quesada's Ninth Tactical Air Force—he'd been sent to Ramitelli to give a dive-bombing demonstration and a pep talk. When he left, he'd put on a dazzling twenty-minute display of low-level acrobatics.

"Sure, I remember. You really beat up the runway in your Mustang." Then, with a diffident grin, "They call me Seffy Mizrahi here, but I can't get used to it."

Riley commented, "The Red Tails were a good outfit. You never lost a bomber you were escorting, did you?"

Marshall liked him immediately. Few people—even Air Force pilots—had ever heard of the pilots from Tuskegee, much less of their combat successes.

Riley explained that he'd arrived the night before, direct from his training in Prague. "Only had five days of training, half a dozen hops in one of these crates." He gestured to the fighter's fuselage with his elbow. "Pretty sorry after a 51, huh?"

In just the few moments of their conversation, the sun had crept up enough for the soft morning light to light up the chiseled angularity of Riley's face. He'd pulled his poncho off, smoothing down a shock of straight black hair. His skin was almost as dark as Marshall's, whose normal copper tone had burned jet black after only one week under the desert sun.

They had no friends in common, so they talked of Italy and Prague, and Riley asked why Marshall was flying for Israel.

"I couldn't get a flying job back home. No one will hire Negroes—and I'm too stubborn to give up flying. Besides, I sort of like the idea of fighting for a minority—it's in my blood, so to speak. What about you? You could be flying with the airlines if you wanted to."

Riley hesitated for a moment. "Sorry I brought the matter up. I can't tell you. Please don't ask."

Marshall was considering that when Myers came over and told them that Riley would be Marshall's wingman. The field telephone rang loud in the crisp desert air and the adjutant emerged from the tent, yelling, "Cockpits, please."

The pilots turned to their aircraft, busying themselves with the pre-takeoff chores, plugging in the radios, adjusting the harnesses.

Erich Weissman climbed up on the wing with a rag, polishing the thick armored glass for the fifth time that morning. Marshall liked him; he was conscientious to a fault and full of the skills he'd picked up working as a slave laborer building jet engines for the Nazis.

In Prague, Erich had told him about his years at Dachau, where the Germans had beaten and starved him so that his body was as twisted and gnarled as a Monterey pine. In a flat voice, he poured out unbelievable stories of mass death and grisly cremations, portraying the scenes of horror with a powerful immediacy. Talking as he worked, his emotions tearing him to bits, Weissman wielded his wrench as if the bolts were the heads of Nazi prison guards. Weissman had strengthened Marshall's belief in his current mission and made him think about home. Racism in the United States might not be as ghastly as racism had been in Germany—but it was still racism, and he was increasingly aware that he was going to have to fight it.

"Tell me Erich, what are you going to do when this is over?"

Weissman breathed on the windscreen, rubbed it, and said, "I'm going to get even with a few people."

"Nazis?"

"Of course. The ones who got away. It wasn't just the concentration camps like Dachau and Auschwitz, you know. They used slave labor in factories. I was a worker at Nordhausen, building jet engines in a factory tunneled into the mountains. Thousands died there, building it and working in it."

He paused, eyes gleaming, mouth working. "It took a lot of people to kill six million Jews, not just a few SS guards, but businessmen and officers, people trying to win the war no matter what the Nazis did. And at the end, most of them just stopped their murdering, took off their uniforms and walked away."

Marshall shook his head in disbelief as Weissman went on. "I'm going to go after the ones I know personally and the ones I'll find out about. And then I'll kill them." He turned back to polishing the canopy, his intensity leaving Marshall shaken.

A green flare shot up and they started engines, the prop blast swirling diamond-sharp facets of desert sand into a glittering rainbow of colors. Behind the short line of fighters, the sun's rays reached out to reflect off the dark line of distant green hills, hinting at the heat that would crisp them by the time they returned. If they returned.

There were no taxi-ways and they went quickly through their warm-up drill in the revetments before wheeling out to takeoff, the angular Avias dipping and bobbing on their narrow-tread landing gears past clusters of cheering ground crew.

In two minutes they were airborne, Myers and the quiet man from New York, David Lipschitz, in the first section, Marshall leading the second with Riley tucked in on his wing. The Messers climbed at a steep angle that still surprised Marshall, slanted back in his seat, his feet nestled in the straps of the unfamiliar German-style rudder bar. Everything about the plane was different—its German smell and hostile German angularity were so different from the P-51. Still, it climbed well, clawing upward at three thousand feet per minute before they leveled off at eight thousand feet. He noted gratefully that all four planes had survived the toughest test, the takeoff, and that none were streaming oil or coolant. So far, so good.

They headed for the sea in a loose finger-four formation, ignoring the wildly inaccurate fire as they passed over the Egyptian anti-aircraft batteries at Ashdod.

Sweating in the cramped cockpit, Marshall felt a surge of sympathy for the poor German pilots who'd had to fly this dog in combat. He could hardly see out of the fortresslike visor, and the lack of control harmony warned of a malicious plane ready to turn and bite if the pilot was careless for a moment.

He glanced to the left and his heart jumped. Riley had the wing of his fighter tucked so close he could have touched it. Marshall waved him away, frightened. A midair was the worst flying hazard, worse than combat, worse than fire—the tremendous speed and mass meant that the slightest kiss of one airplane against another could tear them apart.

Riley shook his head, edging in closer, holding up his hand to show three fingers. Marshall looked away, not wanting to encourage the madman, knowing what was coming. Riley sidled in and tapped his wingtip three times—*skitch, skitch, skitch*—against Marshall's fuselage, in a touch so sure, a tap so light, that Marshall barely felt it. Riley then pulled out to a normal combat formation.

It was extraordinarily delicate flying—a stronger tap could have thrown the airplanes together, sent them tumbling to the sands below. Strange guy, Marshall thought. Quiet on the ground, almost as if he had something to hide. Then he shows off like this.

The front line was never far away in embattled Israel. Ahead, Myers waggled his wings. The target was a long column of Egyptian trucks, dust roiling behind them, each one crammed with troops. A spearhead of tanks and half-tracks was spread out in loose marching order across the road to Tel Aviv.

Myers's wing lifted and they dove at the head of the column, each pilot picking a target for the two little bombs his Avia carried, hoping for a lucky hit that would stop a tank. They flashed through the erratic flak barrage, most of it from multiple barrel 40-mm

Oerlikons, then arced back up for the strafing runs. Free of its bombs, the fighter felt much better in the climb.

Marshall armed his cannon and plunged toward the brown sand again, firing at the trucks, noting the black smoke pouring from two burning tanks, one at each end of the column. The ailerons of the Avia stiffened alarmingly as he gained speed, until, at the pullout, it felt as though he was steering a runaway concrete mixer.

Now there were half a dozen trucks burning. Completely panicked by this first attack from the air, the Egyptian infantry was abandoning the trucks, scattering on foot into the desert. As Marshall tucked into a vertical bank to set himself up for another run-in, he saw an Israeli airplane crashing at the side of the road. It was like a film—he'd looked just in time to see it whole, a slight stream of smoke behind it, nose down at an impossible angle, and then it merged with the ground in an instantaneous change from machine to a fire-gutted cloud of black smoke. He knew that it was either Myers or Lipschitz, for Riley was tight on his wing.

Remembering his role as a maintenance officer, Marshall felt a stab of apprehension. He mumbled a prayer as he turned for a final pass. "Dear God," he prayed, "if it had to happen, please let it be from gunfire, don't let it be from my mistakes."

They flew back to Ekron to refuel and rearm and found that it was Lipschitz who had crashed. Myers's airplane sat forlornly in its revetment, streaked with sheets of sand-crusted oil from hits in his oil cooler. Their first battle, and 25 percent of Israel's fighter force was destroyed, and another 25 percent was out of commission.

"Well, Moshe, shall we go again?"

"Call me Bear. I'll never get used to Moshe. Now that the Gyppos know we're here, why don't we take a crack at air-to-air? I hear they've really been working Tel Aviv over."

The Egyptian bases were only fifteen minutes flying time from Tel Aviv. They had been bombing twice daily, using modified Douglas C-47s as bombers and ex-RAF Spitfires as escort.

The ground crew worked hard, and soon the planes were climbing again, back toward Ashdod, Riley in the lead.

Marshall saw them just as Riley waggled his wings at the enemy formation, two C-47s acting as makeshift bombers, escorted by four Spitfires. They were loafing along at about five thousand feet, confident that the Israelis had neither flak nor fighters. The F.22 Spitfires were lovely things, with squared-off wingtips, tall rudders, and cowlings bulging like a bosomy woman's blouse from the big Griffon engines. Moving like sidewinders in great S-turns above the two Dakotas, the Spitfire pilots were eager for the bomb drop to be made so they could strafe the city streets with their cannons.

Riley's flat voice crackled through the radio. "Bombers first."

They flashed through the surprised Spitfires, pulling behind the C-47s to fire. It was a slaughter. Marshall saw his cannon shells explode a Douglas's fuel tank, tearing off the wing to send his victim spinning erratically to the ground, incontinently spewing out bombs like beans from a bag. Riley's smoking target was slanting toward the sea south of Tel Aviv when the Spitfire escort hit them.

Still unfamiliar with his plane, Marshall heaved the stick over and booted rudder to turn left ninety degrees in a vertical bank, applying full power as he pulled the nose up in the ridiculously high angle of climb of which the Avia was capable. Two of the Spitfires, their speed bled down by his turn, foundered after him, falling behind. He stood his plane on its wing and saw Riley diving away toward Ekron, the other two Spitfires on his tail, almost close enough to fire.

Stall-turning, Marshall dove through his own pursuers, flinging himself headlong after the planes on Riley's tail. They grew quickly in size from little crosses into lovely Spitfires shining in the morning sun. His altitude gave him speed and he gained rapidly, firing a long burst at the first one, just hoping to scare him. Instead the long intermittent lines of 20-mm shells magically converged into the glistening Plexiglas, blowing the pilot's head off and sending the airplane vertically into the ground. The other Spitfire turned and ran. Marshall cranked his neck around to see if he was being followed; then, fuel and ammunition low, he eased back the throttle and dove down to catch up with Riley.

It was a near-fatal error. A Spitfire came from out of nowhere and Marshall's instrument panel disappeared in a blinding explosion as cannon shells hammered into him. One minute he was flying a fighter, the next he was trapped like Houdini in a safe. He jettisoned the canopy, loosened his seat straps, and kicked the stick forward, sling-shotting himself out of the fighter; not waiting to slow down, he pulled the ripcord while he was still tumbling, jerking to a halt as the canopy blossomed.

He had less than a minute to survey the carnage of four crashed aircraft—his own and the three Egyptian planes. As the Spitfires disappeared to the west, Riley's airplane, the last fighter in the Israeli Air Force, headed toward Ekron trailing smoke.

Marshall hit the ground, rolling as he punched the quick release button on his parachute harness. He'd somersaulted to a stop, and lay still for a moment, eyes closed, catching his breath, gingerly trying to determine if he'd been wounded or injured. He opened his eyes to a Roman circus scene. A scowling gladiator-muscled farmer was poised with a pitchfork over his throat, about to pin him to the ground forever. Behind the farmer an angry group had gathered, muttering ominously. He thought he understood the Hebrew word for Egyptian.

Marshall closed his eyes, wishing that his Luftwaffe flying gear had some Israeli insignia.

When he opened his eyes again, the pitchfork was still there and the muttering was growing louder. He took a breath and shouted the only Jewish words he could remember: "Gefilte fish, gefilte fish," and then, in English, "I'm an American."

Putting down the pitchfork, the farmer said in a cultivated accent, "Why didn't you say so? You're the damnedest, blackest American I've ever seen. Thought you were one of the Gyppo bomber pilots. I was within a toucher of pronging you."

Marshall told the story to Riley that night at the pilot's hang-out, the Atom Bar in Tel Aviv. Bear laughed and said, "I tan so easily, I'd better watch it. In a week, you'll look like a Swede next to me."

They were quiet for a while and Marshall said, "You know, that makes four for me. One more and I'll be an ace."

"Don't bust your ass getting there, John. Being an ace isn't everything."

"That's easy for you to say. You're already one. But there's never been a Negro ace. I'm going to be the first one."

"I hope you run out of wars first, John. Besides, the Air Force won't give you official credit for these Gyppos."

Then, more seriously, "John, I owe you a lot. If you hadn't blown that Spit off my tail, I'd have had it. My engine was already cooking; I'd never have been able to fight them off."

"Glad to do it."

"I know that. But I want you to know you've got a friend for life. I'll never forget it."

Marshall was sure he would not.

Nashville, Tennessee/June 5, 1948

Milo Ruddick glanced at the sign and smiled approvingly.

" 'RaceCo,' eh? Good name. Who's chairman of the board?"

"I am, sir. Bob is the president and Troy is the treasurer."

"Well, it's his money, I don't blame him for wanting to be treasurer. How much has he spent so far?"

Coleman nodded his head sagely and whispered, "About a quarter of a million."

Ruddick whistled. "Whooee! Well, I know a good old boy like Troy has figured out some way to charge it off to the government. But I thought surplus airplanes were dirt cheap."

Letting the sarcasm pass, Coleman said, "The planes were cheap enough; we got four Sidewinders for six hundred bucks apiece from the storage yard at Kingman. But it takes dough to modify them."

"How they coming along?" Milo always dropped into his Little Rock drawl whenever he was enjoying himself.

"Great. We've kept two stock, for trainers, and Abe Corrson, one of the all-time great speed merchants from the prewar Cleveland air races, is converting two into racers. Troy's named them Viper I and Viper II."

"Can I meet him?"

They walked into the brightly lit shop where Corrson was bending over a workbench, and Ruddick whispered, "Looks like Tony Galento."

The mechanic had the ominous aura of an all-night filling station operator, with a sloping brow, beer belly, and a once-powerful physique covered by hair that tufted into surrealistic topiary art around his tattoos. He barked a few orders and walked away from the team of mechanics busy transforming two obsolete fighters into racing machines, Sidewinders into Vipers.

After the introductions, Coleman asked, "What are you working on now, Abe?"

Fat as he was, Corrson was a ruthless specialist in airplane weight reduction. "We're knocking off pounds. I got them stripping every surplus ounce. We're pulling all the war gear—gun mounts, firing controls, armor plate, radio equipment, even the emergency systems."

Ruddick gulped. "Is that safe?"

"I don't believe in safety; I believe in winning races. Look at this."

Abe took them over where his men were reaming out existing holes in formers and boring new ones.

"You save a fraction of an ounce here, a fraction of an ounce there, pretty soon you save a pound. That means you need less fuel, so you save some more."

Milo kicked a soft amorphous bundle of rubber. "What's this?"

"It's the self-sealing fuel tanks. We don't need 'em, nobody will be shooting at us. We'll be putting in lightweight neoprene fuel cells from U.S. Rubber."

Waddling toward the wall, he said, "You wanna see a hunnert-pound saving—take a look at dis."

The Sidewinder's regular canopy was sitting on the floor; next to it was a lightweight Plexiglas bubble just larger than the pilot's head. Ruddick looked dubious.

"How will Bob be able to see out of this?"

"He's going to be out front—all he'll have to do is look straight ahead." Pride registered in the fat man's voice. "And if you think this is something, take a look at dis."

He led them to the wing, sitting forlornly on a dolly, the tips a jagged mass of metal.

"We've chopped six and a half feet off each side, gives it a wingspan of twenty-five feet, just about the same as the old Gee-Bees—but with three times the horsepower."

Coleman was no engineer, but he knew that clipping the wings cut down on both lift and drag.

"What's this going to do to stall speeds during the turns?"

"They're going up, Stan." Corrson's voice was contemptuous. "You don't get sumpin' for nuttin'. The guy that flies this is really going to have to be a pilot, not just a limp-wristed pylon pusher."

Ruddick gulped and asked again, "Is it going to be safe?"

Corrson quietly put down his tools, spat, and said, "Shit no, I tole you it ain't gonna be safe, it's gonna be fast. You want to win the fucking race, or you want to be safe?"

Seeing Ruddick's appalled expression, Corrson relented. "Look, it ain't all bad. I'm moving the radiators from the fuselage to these streamlined wingtip fairings. They'll act like endplates and make it easier to fly." He hesitated and said, "Easier than it looks now, anyway. And I'm changing to a thirty-six-volt electrical system; it'll pull the gear up right fast, and get your boy off to a quick lead."

Corrson's face split into a gap-toothed grin, as if he'd solved everybody's problems.

Coleman smiled back weakly. "Tell us about the engines, Abe."

"Hey, they're completely rebuilt. The Allison in a Sidewinder put out about thirteen-hundred horsepower with a three-bladed prop. This's got a four-bladed prop and a two-stage supercharger."

He patted the engine fondly, as if it were a favorite puppy. "This little devil will deliver twenty-eight hundred horsepower at sea level. We'll be pulling a hundred fifteen inches of manifold pressure at thirty-three fifty rpm, running on a special Shell triptane fuel."

Ruddick poked around the piles of parts for a while, then walked out shaking his head, Coleman trailing behind. Turning, Ruddick asked, "Tell me the truth, Stan—is it safe for Bob to fly this thing? I don't want him killed."

"Don't worry, Milo, I'm not going to let Bob get into trouble. He's been practicing in the stock Sidewinders, and doing real good. Today's he's flying practice laps on the race course Troy had laid out—fifteen miles long, four pylons. He's due back about now—let's go down to the operations office and wait for him."

"Well, no offense, Stan, but I'm going to get a second opinion."

Coleman felt relief—he didn't like being on the hook. "Good idea; get somebody to look the racers over, maybe have them fly with Bob. That's the way to go."

"Don't say anything to Bob about this. I don't want to spook him. I'll work it in sometime after the racers are ready to go. Understand?"

"Gotcha."

Washington, D.C./July 16, 1948

"Honest to God, Bandy, I don't know what you're thinking about. I understand Milo Ruddick asked you to see him two weeks ago."

"He asked; he didn't tell me. I had stuff to do."

They were sitting on a horsehair-stuffed leather couch in Ruddick's outer office, sweat-stained from the D.C. heat outside. Bandfield moved his foot and a spittoon clanged.

"This place gives me the creeps—you'd think Daniel Webster was going to walk in."

"I wish to hell we *were* visiting Daniel Webster instead of Milo Ruddick. He's pissed off that you didn't report as soon as he asked you to."

"I didn't report to him because I don't want to tell him what I'm going to have to tell him."

"Which is?"

"That he's a bigoted horse's ass."

"Don't kid around, Bandy, this guy's too important to the Air Force."

"I won't be rude, Meat-axe, but I'm going to give it to him straight about integration."

The pleasant-looking secretary nodded, and they went inside. Ruddick moved around from behind his desk, smiling, clasping Varney's hand in his, then putting his arm around Bandfield's shoulder.

Ruddick was dressed in an expensive pinstripe suit. Bandfield had never seen a shirt like the one he was wearing; it had a white collar and long French cuffs, but the rest of the shirt was a deep blue. He didn't like it, but he knew it had to be expensive. Everything about Ruddick seemed expensive—especially his goodwill.

"So here's our elusive Colonel Bandfield. You know, Colonel"—it sounded like *Cunnel*—"when I call a military officer in, even a four-star general, they're usually pretty prompt."

"Sorry, sir. I was tied up with some business on the Berlin Airlift."

"A good answer, Colonel. Not true, but a good answer. But I've got some questions I want to ask you."

"About integration?"

"Yes, but later. Right now I want to ask you for a favor. You flew in the Cleveland air races, I believe?"

"A long time ago." He didn't even like to think that it was sixteen years before.

"Well, a firm is modifying two McNaughton Sidewinders into racing planes. My son is supposed to fly one of them in the Thompson Trophy race at Cleveland."

"This year?"

"No, they won't be ready by September, they're shooting for 1949. Sometime between now and then, I'd like you to go out to Nashville and look at the racer. Then fly with my son and see if he has the skill to handle it."

"I'm sure General Varney will give me time to do that. But your son is probably qualified—you told me he flew McNaughtons during the war, didn't you?"

"Yes, but these are going to be highly modified. Frankly, they scare me. I'd like you to take a look. Now, tell me what you learned about integration."

Bandfield looked down and scuffed his foot on the thin carpet. "Mr. Ruddick, you're not going to like what I have to say. I talked to a lot of people around the country. I talked to Colonel Johnson at Lockbourne. It looks to me like the service is making a big mistake with segregation. We're missing out on a lot of talent, and spending a lot of money doing it."

"Well, it's a moot point. In ten days, the President is going to sign an executive order that will force integration in the services. So all this doesn't sound too bad to me; I don't mind those findings at all."

Varney looked relieved as Bandfield went on. "Yes, but I also found out that you're lying through your teeth when you say you don't oppose integration personally. You had my friend, John Marshall, fired at McNaughton, just because he was a Negro!"

Varney jumped in. "Colonel Bandfield, you're out of line." He turned to Ruddick. "I'm sorry, sir, I had no idea this would happen."

Not accustomed to sharp talk from subordinates, Ruddick stepped forward in anger, fists balled, then stopped to compose himself. After a teeth-clenched moment he grunted, "I'm sure you didn't, General. This is outrageous, and it makes me wonder if Colonel Bandfield has the good judgment required to fly Air Force aircraft. I'm going to have to look into this matter."

Bandfield strode toward the office door; then on impulse he turned around, to ask, "Does this mean you don't want me to go to Nashville and fly with your son?"

Varney shot toward him bellowing, "This is no joking matter, Bandfield. You shut up before I shut you up!"

Washington, D.C./July 23, 1948

The men who'd slaved under him in the China-Burma-India theater called him "Larry the Lash." Now Lawrence Gunter sat at his

Pentagon desk, face flushed with anger, yelling, "Don't tell me he's under house arrest! Tell me you'll have him in my office in an hour. You understand, one goddamn hour!" He slammed the receiver down, cracking the black plastic.

The morning had gone well until now; his long-awaited appointment as commander of the Berlin Airlift had finally come through. Major General Gunter, with his patented combination of begging and threatening, had just finished wringing twenty of the best people in the Air Force out of personnel for Operation Vittles. But now he'd been told that the one man he wanted most was under house arrest at nearby Bolling Air Force Base, and "might not be available."

While he waited, Gunter reviewed the facts. The Russians, rattling tanks instead of swords, had clamped a blockade around Berlin on June 23rd, knowing that the United States didn't have the military power to prevent it. The United States had hung tough. On June 26th, aircraft under the command of Lieutenant General Curtis LeMay began airlifting food and coal packed in GI duffle bags into the beleaguered city of more than two million people. The "LeMay Coal and Feed Company" was doing a good job, using twin-engine Douglas C-47s to airlift as much as a thousand tons a day, and America was responding with pride.

LeMay was the combat commander who had burned Japan to the ground, but Gunter was a master of airlift, his training gained flying the Himalayan Hump. Gunter—and the men he'd just chosen— had more airlift experience than any other group in the world.

The papers on Gunter's desk were filled with the excitement of LeMay's efforts—the hustle and bustle at the terminals, aircraft lined up waiting to be loaded, tired crews staggering out for yet another flight, and maintenance doing miracles on the flight line. Twenty-four hours a day, long lines of C-47s and a few of the larger, more efficient C-54s passed through the crowded aerial corridor to Berlin, stacking up to orbit in great columns of traffic before letting down to land. And each day, the tonnage being lifted rose.

It made wonderful reading—and it was all wrong. Gunter knew that there shouldn't be any airplanes parked—they should either be in the air or in maintenance. The crews shouldn't be tired—they should be flying or resting. And there shouldn't be a stack of orbiting traffic; instead, the stream of aircraft should be regulated like a conveyor belt, moving at equal speeds, precisely spaced, and never deviating from standard procedures. If a plane had a problem, or got sent around for weather, it should simply plod back to the point of origin to rejoin the stream in a never-ending process flow. Gunter knew that you had a good airlift—and the airlift over the Hump had been the best—when it became a boring operation to watch.

The door opened and Bear Riley marched in.

"Captain Bayard Riley, reporting as ordered, sir."

"Sit down, Bear. At least they don't have you handcuffed and in solitary. What's going on?"

Riley relaxed. "I'm really glad to see you, General. This time I got in trouble just following orders. I had a job straight from General Varney to check out the various air forces in the Middle East. He got me duty with the Israelis—it was a hell of an experience."

"Why are you under arrest? I didn't make any calls yet because I wanted to hear the story from you."

"You must know Assistant Secretary of Defense Ruddick?"

"Sure, a treacherous bastard. A real cracker, but a powerhouse, he virtually runs the department. Christ, I hope you didn't get on his shit list; he's snake-mean and hard as a nightstick."

"That's it. He got me in the room alone with the Secretary of the Air Force and the Chief of Staff and chewed us all new assholes."

"What for? What did Symington and Vandenberg have to say? A cherry-assed captain like you might have to put up with that, but they don't."

"Well, they by-God did. Vandenberg was in a brace, and everytime Symington would start his smooth talking, Ruddick would yell 'Shut up, Stu!' and up he would shut!"

"Spit it out, man. What the hell did you do? Knock up some A-rab's daughter or what?"

"It seems Ruddick's got something against the Israelis—he was yelling about them controlling the press and the films, and God knows what all. He said we shouldn't be helping them, we should be helping the Arabs because the Arabs have all the oil."

"Didn't he know you were under orders?"

"Sure, but he said we just tried and killed a whole bunch of Nazis at Nuremberg who were only obeying orders. He said I was a murderer, just because I shot down some Egyptian planes."

"Jesus. Doesn't he know that we're always looking for information like this? Hell, look at the Eagle Squadron. That was as much a training exercise for us as it was help for Britain."

"We tried that argument, but it backfired. Symington told him about our buddy Bandfield, flying for the Loyalists in Spain, then going on to be an ace for us during the war. I thought Ruddick was going to go through the fucking roof! He must know Bandfield from somewhere because he started yelling about getting that 'nigger-loving SOB.' "

"He must be going nuts."

"Yeah, but it turned out that the thing on Bandfield saved my ass. Ruddick damn near had a stroke, and sort of forgot about me for a while. And I just got word from the chief that Ruddick is cooling down, and that there won't be any court-martial."

Gunter smiled for the first time.

"Good, because have I got a job for you!"

3

Berlin, Germany/May 13, 1949

"Let me remind you, Captain, that I did some extra-legal things for you."

"Helmut, you don't have to remind me. I'll never forget, no matter how much time I spend in Leavenworth."

Josten fumed as Riley told himself that it was better to be working for Gunter than being in some guardhouse back in the States. He'd arrived in Germany eager to wallow in the fleshpots of Europe and raring to do whatever buccaneering task Gunter wanted done—as long as he didn't have to cross Milo Ruddick again.

Of course, he'd not seen or spoken to the general himself since his arrival. His orders came down via a variety of adjutants, who simply handed him a sealed envelope. Inside, on a plain sheet of paper, would be a typewritten directive, undated, unsigned. At first they rained down, and Riley was in his element, bribing friend and foe alike to get the labor and materials that were unavailable through official channels. It was a basic market economy, where cigarettes, chocolate, gasoline, and coffee did well and U.S. dollars did marvels. The jokes at home were always about nylons and

Fräuleins, but little trading was done with hosiery except on a very interpersonal basis. For the bigger jobs, Riley used U.S. currency, though coffee would do. And someone in Gunter's office saw to it that he always had plenty of each to trade with.

No one in Europe had really known what would be needed for an airlift of this size. Before Gunter appeared on the scene, they were proud to be lifting 1,500 tons a day; by early September, Gunter's systematic efforts had raised it to 7,000 tons a day. Now there was no quota—it was just fly all you could, and they were dumping in close to 10,000 tons a day, 40 percent *more* than Berlin had received via road and rail before the blockade.

But the initial steep rise in tonnage had outstripped even the American resources, and it took all of Riley's piratical skills to keep the huge mechanism of the airlift lubricated. Of the many jobs Gunter had given Riley, two stood out in his mind, both had been with Josten, and one of them could never be admitted.

The first was probably the most important—against all the current rules and regulations banning fraternization, he'd found eighty badly needed German mechanics to work on the flight line. The men had been recruited by the same man now upbraiding him, a horribly disfigured ex-Luftwaffe colonel, Helmut Josten. Josten had barely survived a crash in a jet fighter at the end of the war, and he was now a free-booter on the black market. Riley hadn't asked any questions about his past, and Josten had come up with some of the best mechanics Riley had ever seen, hardened Luftwaffe veterans who were hungry for work. Later, of course, the prohibitions against use of German labor would be lifted, but at the time it was a major contravention of Occupation regulations.

Riley had been dismissive of Josten when they'd first met, thinking that he was just another one of the unlikable lot of defeated but unapologetic German officers. But early on, they had a minor disagreement about how Josten would pay the German workers he'd rounded up. Riley had been insisting on doing things his way when Josten had bristled, suddenly every inch a Luftwaffe colonel, staring at him with his lips pulled back in a death's head rictus of anger. Riley had quickly agreed to his proposal.

It was impossible, really, to like the man; coldly distant, he refused to talk about the war, except when Riley drew him out on Luftwaffe aircraft. Then he glowed with a vindictive pleasure, telling Riley how superior the German jets had been. In one argument they'd almost come to blows.

"The Messerschmitt Me 262 was the finest plane of the war. We could have had hundreds of them in 1943, if they had listened to me. And if we had had them, the war would have had a very different outcome, believe me."

"Yeah, we would have A-bombed Berlin instead of Hiroshima."

Josten did not speak to him for a few days, then, in an obvious attempt to make up, had brought in a photo taken in Sweden in 1944. It showed Josten, in civilian clothes, a beautiful black-haired woman, and their baby.

"My son, Ulrich, and my wife, the former Countess Gortchakov. Isn't she beautiful?"

"Very. Is she in Berlin with you?"

"My wounds caused us to be temporarily separated. She is waiting for me to join her."

After that, Riley had tried to like Josten, but it wasn't easy, for his manner was as scarred as his face. When he smiled, his lips pulled back over his teeth in a mirthless grin that frightened even the omnipresent begging German children, long inured to wounded soldiers. Painfully thin and stoop-shouldered, he walked slowly, with a sidling, crablike gait. Thinning white hair framed a cadaverous oval face, and the bony ridges over his dark eyes cast shadows over his skull-hollow cheeks. Even dressed in his ill-fitting old army clothes, Josten was grimly impressive.

He had also helped Riley with the second, far more dangerous task, a totally illegal mission. The continuous rise in tonnage had made it necessary to open a new airport in November, at Tegel. A runway was made in record time with the brick debris created by Allied bombers from Berlin buildings only three years before. Although it was an important addition to the airlift, cutting the transit time down appreciably, it was dangerously flawed by a two-hundred-foot radio tower sticking directly up into the approach path to the runway, a hazard at any time, but a deadly menace to navigation in bad weather. The tower was in the French zone, but the radio station itself was operated by the Russians, who naturally refused to permit the tower to be relocated. Riley made an agreement with Josten—one C-54 load of coffee and a favor to be defined in the future—and the tower was mysteriously blown up. The Russians had raised holy hell, accusing the Americans and the French of an act of war, but they couldn't prove anything. The Germans enjoyed it immensely.

No one even noticed that the ten-thousand-pound cargo of coffee was missing, for the paperwork at every level had been well-managed. But Gunter must have been spooked by the furor that followed the explosion, for Riley hadn't heard from him since.

Instead, he had been flying the Rhein-Main-to-Tempelhof run seven days a week. It would have driven him crazy if it weren't so amusing to monitor the universal hobby of the occupying forces, the exchange of German antiques, silver, art, and jewelry for American, French, and British food. Sometimes, he wondered if there could still be another cuckoo clock left in Germany, but there always was. A friend of his in Army counter-intelligence had tipped him off that his German colleague, Josten, was a principal in the process, specializing in the transfer of art works. And now he'd asked for his favor.

En route to Tempelhof/May 28, 1949

The four-engined transport groaned and wallowed in the sky, sluggish from its ten-ton load of macaroni. It was his last trip and Riley was restive, the boredom hanging in the cockpit as thick as the rank sweat from their unwashed flight suits. It had been better before, when Gunter was still using his special talents.

He called, "Air Force Six One Zero, Aschaeffenburg, six thousand," into his mike as the ADF needle swung over beacon—there was no reply, there never was if you were on course, on time, as you were supposed to be. As you'd damn well *better* be.

They were working him double on the last flight, making him give a line check. The new pilot, Major Don Wallston, had been pulled from his flourishing dental practice as reluctantly as a tooth from its socket to fly in the Berlin Airlift. A Rotary-club type who insisted on being called "Wally," Wallston was a ham-handed pilot, always following the airplane like a bad actor taking directions from a prompter. He'd just banked too steeply to the left and was now overcorrecting to the right as he brought the C-54 back near the assigned heading of 057 degrees.

Riley raised his eyebrows in disgust and whispered to Sergeant Bonadies, the crew chief, "Just so the fucker averages out."

Riley's hands were in his lap, but his right knee forced the wheel up, stopping the turn, as his left leg applied a little back pressure to the control column to ease them back up to their assigned six-thousand-foot altitude. Wallston didn't notice, just as he hadn't noticed Bear subtly compensating for his ragged flight path ever since the takeoff at Rhein-Main. A good instructor, Riley always tried to keep the student's confidence level up.

Leaning back to talk to the crew chief, Riley asked, "How long we been doing this, Al?"

"Seems like forever, Captain."

It had been almost a year since Riley had been forced into the right seat of a C-54, the last place a fighter pilot wanted to be. But within a few weeks he'd gained enough experience to become first an aircraft commander and then an instructor pilot. For almost a year they had been making two or three trips a day in the dreary twenty-mile-wide corridor through Soviet-occupied territory. Three minutes ahead of them was another of the big Douglas transports; three minutes behind was yet another, part of an endless 170-miles-per-hour chain that supplied two million Berliners day and night. What had started out as a Soviet grab of the German capital had turned into a display of Allied generosity and technical capability. In classic American tradition, the Air Force had pulled itself together for this supreme effort, draining resources from everywhere, but putting on such a show that the Russians were now desperately seeking a face-saving way out.

"You're doing fine, Major; I can see I'm going to have to give you a thumbs-up on this one."

"I'm not so sure, Bear; I've only flown this route a few times. And this weather is lousy."

Riley glanced out into the gray mess drooping like great sodden wads of cotton down to within four hundred feet of the ground. "It ain't so bad; you'll hack it just fine."

Wallston clutched the control wheel even tighter, leaning forward to fix the instruments in his gaze, as if he could wring skill and safety from them with his stare.

Riley opened a letter and pretended to read it under the shaded red cockpit light.

Perspiration beaded the other pilot's lip as his eyes stayed glued to the altimeter, trying to hold on to his altitude even as he drifted off toward the edge of the corridor. Riley surreptitiously nudged the rudder with his foot and pressed upward on the control wheel with his knee, edging the airplane back on course, thinking as he did so: The old Air "Farce" is in bad shape if it lets turkeys like this fly.

A solid sheet of rain smashed into the windscreen, laying in great flat droplets the size of his thumb.

Wallston nodded his head imperceptibly, summoning all his skill to fly the fifteen-minute straight-line course to the Fulda range, where he would have to brace himself for the turn for the long leg into Tempelhof. It was basic pilot training stuff, but he'd been behind the airplane since takeoff. Now he was desperately trying to stay on the center line, well inside the corridor, knowing that if he wandered off, he was fair game for the Russian flak. The Russian fighters weren't a problem in weather like this—they were strictly blue-sky warriors.

Riley watched the other man with scarcely veiled contempt. Why did guys ever try to learn to fly if they didn't like it? Hell, you could tell this man hated it. They wanted the glamour, the extra pay, but they didn't like the danger or the tedium, and there was always plenty of both.

He yawned and scratched, reflecting that he didn't like it much either. In the beginning, it had been a perfect assignment. There had been a rapid buildup in the Israeli Air Force, and he left in good conscience, having done his bit for the underdog, at the same time getting lots of information on the forces in the area. Yet the little dust-up with Ruddick still bothered him. There wasn't much he could do about it now, but if he could ever put the blocks to the blowhard bastard, he would.

Yesterday he had received word from Josten that tonight was the night he'd be calling in the favor owed him for blowing up the tower. Riley enjoyed flaunting authority, but he hoped this would be vaguely legal. Yet the USAF owed Josten a great deal, and he knew Riley would do almost anything short of murder, as long as it didn't hurt the United States.

The control wheel banged against his knee as violent backfires ripped apart the C-54's sleep-inducing vibrations. Riley glanced quickly at the oil pressure and cylinder head gauges, then turned to Sergeant Bonadies, asking, "What do you think, Al?"

"We must have blown a jug on number one. Let's feather it."

Bear hesitated. The Pratt & Whitney engines were tough and the airplane was overloaded. "No, we're too heavy, just pull the power back." Just then Wallston, white with fear, jabbed his hand up and feathered the prop on engine number four.

The C-54 sagged like a pricked balloon as Riley applied power to two and three, yelling to Bonadies, "Restart number four as soon as you can, then keep easing the power on number one back till it stops backfiring!"

Bonadies's hands flew across the panel—he knew that the Douglas behind them was gaining on them second by second, and they'd already dropped three hundred feet toward the stream of unsuspecting C-54s below.

"You want it, Captain?" Wallston's voice went high, pleading, not asking.

"No, no, you got it, you're doing fine. Just don't feather any more of the good engines."

Riley pulled out the let-down plates; he didn't need to study them, and they'd be picked up by the excellent Tempelhof GCA shortly, but he wanted Wallston to feel it was his airplane to fly.

Out of the corner of his eye, he watched the altitude continue to slip away as the airspread bled off three miles per hour.

"Give it some more power, Major—don't be afraid to use all you've got. Get on the trim, and keep it straight and level. Tromp down on the rudder to center the ball—crabbing like this causes more drag, and slows us down."

Wallston shot a look of pure panic at him and jabbed all four throttles forward, the number one engine belching long streams of flame back to turn the enveloping mist fiery red. Bonadies had already shoved the mixtures to full rich and the props to full high rpm, shaking his head in disgust as he pulled the number one throttle back. Wallston's spastic reaction might have blown the engine up; he was shook. Bonadies thought, Why the hell doesn't Bear take over? Or at least put the fucking magazine down.

Riley was now idly thumbing through a copy of *Flying*, apparently content to leave the situation in the other pilot's sweating hands. The airspeed was back to 170, and they were coming up on their proper altitude again. Bear nudged the control column forward with his knee and said, "Better reduce the power, Major."

He called, "Tempelhof, Air Force Six One Zero."

The bored ground controller responded "Roger Six One Zero, stand by for ground-controlled approach. Status please?"

"Ah, Six One Zero is negative."

"Negative" meant the airplane required maintenance. A damn shame, Riley thought. They'd probably have to leave the airplane there, and that meant he'd have to carry whatever Josten was bringing in somebody else's airplane to get it out of Berlin. No real problem, just a complication if Josten was sending out a big painting or a sculpture. He laughed to himself, thinking it was probably a bronze horse from the Brandenburg Gate.

Riley switched frequencies and the familiar voice of Tempelhof GCA came up. Ground-controlled approaches were relatively new, but the crew in Berlin was superb. Just the comforting sound of their lazy voices, telling you when to turn and when to descend, urging little corrections up or down, right or left, like a wife's conjugal instructions to her husband, was worth the trip.

"Air Force Six One Zero, if you read me, acknowledge and turn left to three-sixty degrees now and descend to two thousand feet."

Wallston flew straight ahead, oblivious to the call, so Riley kneed the control wheel up and applied a little left rudder. As he did, the C-54 bucked like a dying horse from a tremendous explosion that sent the cowling from the number one engine rattling back against the fuselage and tail. Riley tossed his magazine down, reached up and put his hand over the feathering buttons of the good engines, and yelled, "Al, feather number one and pop the fire bottle."

Wallston stared at the instruments, his hands frozen on the controls, eyes cod-cold with fear.

"Tempelhof GCA, Six One Zero declaring an emergency, we have a fire on number one." Riley's voice was calm. He reached over and shook Wallston's arm.

"Okay, Major, we're passing through three thousand feet. Get it trimmed up; they'll be turning you on to the downwind leg shortly."

Wallston nodded, his face as gray as the clouds hurtling by.

The radio crackled. "Six One Zero, turn left to ninety degrees, descend to fifteen hundred."

No reaction from the major. Riley shook his head and said, "I got it, you follow me through."

GCA had just turned them on final approach when the oil-starved number one propeller separated, wrenching itself from the engine and sending a blade slicing into the number two engine. Debris thundered against the fuselage again, and Riley saw the number two RPM needle surge to the stops.

"Feather two, Al. Full power on three and four. Major, you watch for the runway lights, and give me a yell as soon as you see them."

They were north of the final approach course and well below the four-hundred-foot minimum ceiling for Tempelhof. Riley concentrated on the instruments, his leg straining to keep the nose of the C-54 from wandering while he arm-wrestled to keep the wings level.

The wartime Allied bombing had not been perfect, for the

approach to Tempelhof was studded on either side with seven-story-tall apartment buildings, some still habitable. At night, in clear weather, you could look up to see the lights from people's living rooms. Riley pressed on, hoping that they would not become sudden uninvited guests.

Wallston grabbed his arm and pointed. "Approach lights!"

Mounted in a cemetery on pylons made of pierced-steel planking, high-intensity lights marked a path to the runway. Riley kept full power on as he banked sharply to line up.

"Gear down; full flaps."

Wallston clutched the control wheel in a death grip as Bonadies dropped the gear and flaps.

With a skipping crunch, the C-54 touched down on the first third of the runway. Riley was almost standing on the right rudder as he pulled the throttles back. With the asymmetric power bled off, he got off the rudder to let the airplane roll straight ahead on dark concrete glistening slick from rain. As it slowed, the glitter of the yellow runway lights merged with the flashing red signals of the fire trucks and ambulances, embracing the suddenly silent C-54 in an orange nimbus of moisture.

Riley was already going through the paperwork. "They'll have to tow us off. You've got the airplane, Major. Not a bad ride, but maybe you need one more trip before I check you out."

Wallston grinned and shook the wheel. "Hey, call me Wally. And yeah, one more ride ought to do it. That wasn't too bad a landing, was it?"

As forbidding as death itself, Josten was waiting for them as the oil-covered C-54 was towed in. As the German civilians began their quick offloading drill, muscling the cartons of macaroni as if they were manning a fast-firing 88 flak battery, he handed Riley a brown leather satchel. Riley would have no trouble taking it back out; it was standard government issue. Inside the satchel was an oblong package, wrapped in rubberized fabric and sealed with a ceramic-like glaze.

"Captain Riley, this is extremely valuable. Please don't open it. Make sure it gets to the addressee as soon as possible. He and I have already corresponded about this, and he knows what to expect—he knows its true value."

"What is it, a bootleg Rembrandt?"

They were standing alone in the bay of a hangar, but Josten lowered his voice. "I shouldn't tell you this, but perhaps it will insure that you are careful with it. It is far more important than any Rembrandt; it transcends the little matter of art. Inside this is a flag, the one that Adolf Hitler marched with in Munich, the Blood Flag of the Nazi Party. It has tremendous historical significance."

Riley was so relieved it wasn't a stolen old master that he laughed out loud. "Who the hell would want it?"

"I don't expect you to understand. I just expect you to get it to its destination."

"No problem. I'll have it to . . ." He scanned the label and exploded. "Jesus Christ, this is going to Milo Ruddick! I hate that guy. What the hell does he want with a Nazi flag?"

Josten's thin lips parted slightly—it could have been a smile. "That's none of your business. You said you'd do me a favor. This is the first part of it."

"What else do you want?"

"I want you to get me into the United States. I want to work in the aircraft industry. At McNaughton Aircraft."

Riley hesitated. The man deserved a lot—he'd have to try. "Helmut, I'll give it my best shot. I think I can get you into the United States—we've already employed lots of German scientists and engineers. And I may be able to get you a job, but I can't specify which company."

"I got a radio tower blown up for General Gunter. He can get a job for me at McNaughton."

Cleveland, Ohio/September 4, 1949

The two old friends ignored the weather as it shifted from blazing sun to glowering black clouds and scattered showers. Prowling the flight line like hunters on the trail, they submerged themselves in the rich perfume of beautiful aircraft: high-octane gas, acrid exhaust fumes, accompanied by the rumbling shriek of power as the engines were tested.

Hadley Roget's swift pace belied his six decades. Head forward, shoulders back, he took in the new technology at a glance, analyzing and comparing the fleet of modified warplanes competing in the next day's Thompson Trophy race. Normally Roget's long, rugged face was cast in a scowl, his brow, cheeks, and jaw all jutting with harsh, angular lines. Now, absorbed in every detail of the airplanes, his contentment softened his features, making him seem ten years younger.

"Take you back to 1932, Bandy?"

Frank Bandfield, his arm in a sling, just nodded, too moved to speak. Cleveland in 1932 meant many things to him. It was the year that Jimmy Doolittle, one of the greatest pilots of all time, had won the Thompson Trophy in the bulletlike Gee Bee racer. Bandy had won his own less competitive event, the Standard Mystery Derby, and with it enough money to start the Roget Aircraft Factory. Most important of all, it was at those same races that he met the woman who became his wife, Patty Dompnier.

"Look at all this iron—P-51s, P-63s, some big Corsairs. Nothing but fighter planes. Looks like the old-time builders are out of luck. You couldn't slap an airplane together out of steel tube and plywood in your backyard like we did and be competitive."

"Yeah, but the midgets are sort of like that. Let's go over and see how Marshall's doing."

As if to compensate the old-time racers who'd busted their balls in the prewar Cleveland races, the Goodyear Company had established a prize for homebuilt racers powered by modified light-plane engines. Small but fast, they depended upon the ingenuity of their builders and the skill of their pilots to win.

They found Marshall stretched out on his back underneath the wing of a neat wooden gull-wing monoplane. It was painted a light blue and carried the name *Saundra's Special* on the cowling.

Nudging Marshall with his foot, Bandfield said, "Come on out, John, I've got Hadley Roget here to give you some tips."

Marshall rolled back on the creeper grinning. "Lord knows I need them, Bandy. I'm only turning about one-thirty in the practice heats, not enough to qualify, much less win." He stood up, wiping his hands on cotton waste.

"Hey, what'd you do to your arm, Bandy?"

"It's nothing, just an operation to dig out a little shrapnel from when I got shot up at the end of the war. Just means I can't do any flying for a few days."

Roget was down on his hands and knees in front of the airplane, carefully sighting along the fuselage. He walked around it silently, then turned to Marshall.

"The only reason you're getting one-thirty out of it is because of the good workmanship. It's a mighty clean airplane, John, but you've built in too much drag with the gull wings. You've got two intersections in close to the fuselage, and the drag is eating you up."

Marshall looked appalled. Half the appeal of the airplane for him had been building a "mini-Corsair."

"Will it help if I tweak the engine for more horsepower?"

Roget loved it; he was just getting warmed up. "The drag's going to go up faster than the power. You ought to take this back home and stick a straight low wing right across the bottom. It means you've got to change the gear, but that's the only way you'll ever be competitive with this little scooter."

Bandfield shook his head. "Don't let this old gloom merchant get you down, John. Go on fiddling, you never know what might happen to the others."

Roget chimed in, "Don't blow smoke at him, Bandy. The man's competing with Fish Salmon and Tony LeVier! This is a pretty little airplane, but it don't stand a chance."

His words were drowned out in the roar of four North American F-86A Sabres streaking across the field at low level, the pounding roar of their jet engines completely overwhelming all the other activities on the field. They were scheduled to race in the next day's Thompson Trophy race.

When the silver F-86s had passed from sight, Bandfield, trim and athletic at forty-four, said, "John, excuse us. I hope Hadley didn't depress you too much. Now I'm going to take him over to see the McNaughton Viper—it'll tighten his jaws for sure."

As they left a woeful-looking Marshall, Bandy said angrily, "Damn it, you nasty old bastard, John had his heart wrapped up in the airplane. Why did you have to spoil it for him?"

"Son, I'm never nasty. I just call 'em as I see 'em."

"Well, if we get in over at the McNaughton hangar, don't call it as you see it."

As they walked, the two old friends realized that while the racers had changed, nothing had altered Cleveland's carnival pageantry, designed to provide a thrill-a-minute background for the actual races. The Navy Blue Angels had performed flawlessly that morning in their stubby Grumman Bearcats, and the Air Force Acro-Jets were scheduled for a three o'clock show in their Lockheed Shooting Stars. A pretty little wisp of a girl, Kaddy Landry, had just finished the time-honored comic acrobatic routine of a "student stealing a plane," putting a yellow Aeronca through heart-stopping low-speed, low-altitude gyrations. She was taxiing past, waving to the crowd when a roar went up. The two men looked up to see bat-winged Tommy Boyd gliding like a demented flying squirrel toward his minimum parachute-opening altitude. The wings—just cloth surfaces stretched between his arms and legs—enabled Boyd to make erratic swooping curves that brought the crowd to its feet gasping.

"Some things never change, Bandy."

"Yeah? Wait till you see how they've changed the Sidewinder."

Varney had pulled him from McNaughton after the scene in Ruddick's office, but Bandfield had made a lot of friends there, engineers who kept him posted. A guard at the door grinned and waved them by. As soon as he was in the door, Bandy said, "Oh, oh. Looks like we're in trouble."

In the back of the hangar, hunched over a table, Troy McNaughton was waving his arms in explanation to Milo Ruddick and a young man who looked just like him. Both Ruddick and son were dressed in flight suits, zipped to the collar. Bandfield wondered if they had on two-tone shirts with French cuffs underneath.

Stan Coleman came forward, hand outstretched, searchlight smile beaming at them in turn.

"Come on in, Bandy, glad to see you."

"Stan, I'm not sure we'll be welcome."

Ruddick looked up at the sound of his voice, and boomed, "Come in, Colonel Bandfield, come in. Delighted to see you. I'm glad you and your friend could drop by."

Surprised, Bandfield came forward. As Coleman started the introductions, Roget walked toward the jade-green Viper, gleaming iridescent under the overhead lights. It was well named. The grotesquely long engine stretched out behind the huge four-bladed propeller and seemed to pulse with energy even at rest, overpowering the tiny wings and tail surfaces.

"Who in hell designed this man-killer?"

Bandfield winced; Roget was telling it like it was. Both Ruddicks, father and son, scowled at the remark. Coleman rallied smoothly, "You're partly right, Mr. Roget, it's a killer to look at, but an angel in the air. Let me tell you about it."

Coleman picked up a clean red shop rag and, flourishing it like a matador's cape, walked to the streamlined radiator pod at the wing tip.

"This is the sleekest finish ever applied to an aircraft surface—ten coats of paint and fifteen coats of wax." Coleman laid the rag on the top of the pod; it slipped off to scuttle like an escaping squid down the length of the wing, up the fillet, and down to the ground. If Coleman had used a marble for the trick, it wouldn't have been remarkable, but the sliding rag, frictionless as a glob of mercury, was a stunner.

Roget nodded with appreciation, the last approving gesture he'd make as Coleman went on. "You probably recognize these pods, Bandy; they were made from surplus seventy-five-gallon drop tanks. We've installed the coolant radiators in them. Located outside the propeller slipstream like this, they have far less drag than the regular

Sidewinder belly system. And they act as tip-plates, improving the lift. Best of all, the heat exhausted out the back adds thrust like a jet engine.

Roget shook his head. "It'll heat up in a minute on the ground, though. You better have guys standing by with hoses to squirt through there."

Coleman closed his eyes, smiled, and nodded at Roget, indicating that they'd already thought of that. Then, strutting like a model on a car-show turntable—he obviously liked his new role—Coleman spread his hands and said, "You'll note that the right wing is one foot shorter than the left wing—it's a new way to offset torque."

Roget snorted. "Yeah, really new, except the Germans did it in the First World War, and the Italians did it in the Second!"

Unfazed, Coleman went on. "At max power the engine will deliver twenty-eight hundred horsepower via this four-bladed propeller. As you see, the propeller is a new design, with very wide blades and an extremely thin cross section. Costs us ten thousand dollars each, just for the blades."

Roget was relentless. "This power plant's way too big for the airframe. The goddamn torque will twist this monstrosity into the ground on takeoff like a corkscrew going into a cork. You haven't got enough vertical surface to handle that much power."

Milo Ruddick boiled over, losing his normal Southern gentleman's composure to yell, "Who is this wiseass? Bandfield, I never should have let you in the door."

Roget scowled at him and said, "Mr. Ruddick, I'm not trying to be a wiseass. I just know it's criminal to tinker with aerodynamics like this. And I know that if I were you, I'd take my boy back home, and not let him within a hundred miles of this killer."

Bob Ruddick started to speak, but his father silenced him with a peremptory wave, his accent thickening with his anger. "Bob"—it sounded like *Baob*—"already has ten hours in this airplane. Yesterday he beat ten other racing planes to win the Ohio Trophy race with it. You all don't be telling us that it's dangerous!"

Roget started to apologize and Ruddick interrupted.

"Bob here has got a damn sight more experience in fighters than Bill Odom, and he's the favorite! You go over and tell Odom not to race if you want to, but knock it off around here!"

Roget shrugged. "I'm sorry. I'm sure your son is a fine pilot. But I've got to say what I think. And I think this airplane is more than dangerous—it is deadly."

Bandfield ran his good hand nervously through his curly black hair, which was beginning to be salted with silver. He was quiet, content to let Roget express his own feelings while he observed the emotions of the others—Coleman clearly confused that his presentation was interrupted, the senior Ruddick furious, the younger Ruddick concerned and embarrassed. In the background, Abe Corrson lurked, a wrench in his hand, a sinister scowl on his face.

"If I could go on?" Coleman sounded like the host of the "$64 Question" radio quiz show when the audience got out of hand.

"Let me try to allay some of your fears, Mr. Roget. I test-flew the airplane, and I knew you couldn't use full power on takeoff. Too much torque, just as you say. But it's no problem! When Bob won the Ohio Trophy, he used half-power on takeoff, only about sixty inches of manifold pressure. We've got a quick-action gear that cleans the airplane up fast, and as speed builds, you've got more than enough control to handle the torque."

Roget threw up his hands. "Don't listen to an old fogey like me. You guys know it all. I'm not going to say anything more. I wish you the best of luck, I really do."

He turned to the younger Ruddick. "You be real careful out there, son, don't let anything happen to make you take chances."

That night in their hotel room, Hadley was still mumbling as he poured Old Crow over ice cubes in two thick glass tumblers. There was a timid knock at the door. He opened it and Bob Ruddick walked in, asking if they'd spare him a few minutes' conversation. He'd obviously been doing some serious drinking.

"I want to thank you for what you tried to do today. The truth is I'm scared shitless."

"Well then, don't race. You're not being cowardly, you're being smart. No point in pushing your luck."

"My dad won't see it that way. After the Ohio Trophy race, he's convinced I can win. And it's my fault, I've been telling him I could. The way Troy and Stan have brought me along, teaching me everything, I thought I could win it easy. But everything you said confirmed what I already knew. I've bitten off more than I can chew with this airplane."

Bandfield asked, "How was it in the race yesterday? You did okay?"

"Sure, but it was just like my qualifying heat. I was only pulling partial power, averaging about three-ninety—and I was ahead of everybody, the air was smooth. It was no different than practicing back in Nashville." He paused. "Can I have a drink?"

"Sure, if you think you ought to. You've already had a few and you're flying tomorrow."

"Maybe, maybe not. But right now I need a drink." He took a glass and poured it a quarter full.

Ruddick's voice was low, barely controlled. "You know they changed the course layout—seven pylons instead of four. And it's only going to be fifteen laps instead of twenty."

Bandfield tried to encourage him. "If you decide you've *got* to race, both of those things should help you. You can just cruise high and wide, fly a big circle, like Doolittle did in 1932 with the Gee Bee. That's how the jets will be doing it tomorrow, too. Even if you feel you have to race, that doesn't mean you have to kill yourself trying to win."

Roget swirled the whiskey in his glass. "There's lots of ways out of this, Bob. You can just say you don't think it's safe. That's the best way, 'cause it's not. But if you can't do that, abort on takeoff—say your gauges showed an overheat, or you got smoke in the cockpit. Ground-loop the bastard. Hell, say or do anything, it won't matter to anybody a week from now, not even your dad."

Ruddick's face was resigned. "No, you don't know him. As smart as he is about business, he's a fanatic about other things, just like his own daddy was. We Ruddicks are weird people, believe me."

Throwing down the rest of his whiskey, he reached for more, whispering, "There were always strong men in the Ruddick family, until they got down to me."

"Don't talk like that, Bob, there's nothing the matter with you! You flew in the war, you've already won a race in the Viper—that's enough to prove you're a man to anybody!"

"You don't know my dad—the Ohio Trophy meant nothing to him! He didn't even want to have my picture taken with the cup! I've got to win the Thompson; nothing else will do. My dad's like that. He's a brilliant man, but when he gets an idea in his head, nothing will change it. It's my fault, I know, I encouraged him. I can't explain it, but it's like his whole life is bet on this race."

"You got that wrong—it's your life that's being bet."

"Sure, but you know what I mean. He's done everything for me, given me a chance other pilots would kill for."

"You're young. Get some experience. Take the stock Sidewinder and fly it next year in the races. You don't have to win the first one you enter. Your daddy doesn't need that. He sure doesn't need to have you killed."

"No, that's the crazy part of it. He not only wants me to win, he wants me to win the first time out! He's already talking about me winning both the Thompson and the Bendix next year! This whole thing is a fantasy he's had since I was a kid, we've talked about it all my life. It's like a guy who wanted to be in the majors, training his kid to play baseball. You've seen that before."

Roget was blunt. "You don't get killed shagging flies, Bob. If your dad is this stupid, it's your duty to yourself to do what's right."

Bandfield thought about his wife, Patty, just down the hall, entertaining Lyra and the children. He considered asking her to come in—she'd know how to comfort this poor guy, tell him he was fine, encourage him to do what he wanted. She'd done it often enough for him. He asked, "Well, what are you going to do?"

"I'm going to fly. And try not to kill myself."

. . .

Bandfield spent time the next morning with Troy McNaughton, pleading with him to withdraw the Viper from the race. "Look, Troy, I know what you are doing. You want to butter up Milo Ruddick. I can understand that; he controls a lot of contracts. But if you kill his kid in your airplane, you'll make an enemy out of him for life."

McNaughton snorted. "First of all, we're not going to kill any-body. Bob Ruddick doesn't have to race if he doesn't want to. That would actually be the best thing for me—his dad would always feel an obligation for all the trouble we went to."

"Yeah, but Bob *is* going to race. I'm certain of it."

"Me, too. But that doesn't mean he'll kill himself."

"But *if* he does, Troy, think about that."

McNaughton shook his head. "How long have I known you now, Bandy, maybe ten years? In all that time, you've never gotten any smarter about business. If Bob Ruddick kills himself today, his dad will chalk it up to fate. I know the type. He can't blame me because that would mean he was blaming himself. And guys like him never blame themselves. The only way I can get in trouble with Milo Ruddick is to *not* let his son race. But you'd never be able to see that."

He paused. "In fact, if he gets mad at anybody, it will be you and Roget. He'll say you spooked the boy."

"Jesus, Troy, you must be nuts! Forget about Milo Ruddick and contracts and who's mad at who. Don't you see anything morally wrong with a young guy killing himself when he doesn't have to?"

"Look, you want me to ban the Thompson Trophy, stop car racing, crusade against boxing? Get out of here, Bandy, go do something you know how to do—like watch a race."

McNaughton watched Bandfield slam the door, thinking that the younger man had never learned how the game was really played, or what the rules really were. All Bandfield saw was that McNaughton was doing Ruddick a favor by building the racers for his son. It didn't even occur to him that there might be other, deeper ties.

McNaughton pulled out a Dutch Master cigar, bit off the end, and lit it. The airplanes he'd built for Ruddick were nothing, mere show. His hooks now were jabbed and set far into Ruddick's dark, vulnerable past. He inhaled deeply, and the cigar tip glowed cherry red. Why did people like Bandfield meddle in business when they never even saw the satisfying side of it? Any idiot could make money—the pleasure was in power and control. Hell, even Elsie knew that!

The night before at the hotel they had paired off in little groups. Bandy and Roget talked quietly, still concerned about Ruddick's chances. The Bandfield children were noisy, with George and Charlotte acting big, arguing about everything as they tried to explain the races to Ulrich. Patty and Lyra were going through the latest issue of *Vogue* magazine. They wore almost identical linen dresses; Lyra took her cue from Patty in everything from hairstyles to underwear, and Patty was flattered by it.

When the idea of going to the races had first been proposed, Lyra had demurred. Patty thought she was concerned about the expense, so she had insisted, pointing out how much Ulrich would learn about the country on a train trip, how good it would be for Charlotte and George to have someone to be responsible for. But not until last night did she understand that Lyra was really frightened to come to the races with them.

After two stiff drinks, Lyra had opened up.

"Patty, forgive me, but I hate airplanes and pilots—you and Bandy excepted. Ulrich's father was the kindest man in the world, but airplanes destroyed him."

"It was the war, Lyra. War changes men."

"It was the war, true, but it was mostly the airplane, the jet fighter—it blinded him. First he wouldn't see what the Nazis were doing—then he didn't care."

Patty patted her hand.

"Helmut changed from a decent, loving, compassionate man into an amoral killer. He became obsessed with a technology he thought would save Germany—and Nazi Germany wasn't worth saving."

"Was he really a Nazi?"

"He was worse than most Nazis because he was brilliant—he had no excuse. Most of them . . ." She fell silent, shivering with loathing at the memory of her reluctant affair with Joseph Goebbels, a brilliant monster.

"Lyra?"

"I'm sorry—I have so many bad thoughts of the war. You can't know what it means to see your lover change, day by day, into a killing machine."

Patty felt she knew something about Josten's addiction to aviation. Flying had cost her too much as well—her mother and her first husband had died in crashes. The tension and the absences had more than once almost broken up her marriage to Bandfield.

The next morning, race day, Bandfield had encouraged them to watch. Ulrich and the children wanted to go, and Lyra had to give in.

Service participation at Cleveland was a time-honored tradition; there was no better way to show the taxpayers what their money was buying than to send a few fighters to race around the pylons. Even though the eighty thousand spectators knew that it was more of a demonstration than a race, not many people had ever seen a jet. The pretty little silver F-86s, with their swept wings and raucous engines, were crowd pleasers.

Down on the starting line, Bayard Riley sat sweating, sucking on 100 percent oxygen, delighted to have a chance to compete in the Thompson Jet Trophy Race. At precisely 3:55, the four F-86s launched, streaking for the first pylon.

Riley had just finished familiarization in the airplane at George Air Force Base, and as much as he wanted to win, he was more determined not to kill himself. As they hit the first turn, the number three F-86 pulled up and out. Riley didn't see any smoke—probably some sort of a control problem.

The remaining three fighters began flying a circular course, covering almost twenty miles instead of a pylon-hugging fifteen, turning the first lap at just over six hundred miles per hour.

Riley was enjoying himself, glad that the leader was being sensible, when he noticed that the distance between him and the first two planes was widening. He shoved his throttle to the firewall, the competitive urge surging, the gap staying about the same.

It was tough flying. The air was turbulent, and they were pulling a constant 6 to 7Gs to maintain the tight circle; when they hit a gust, the Gs went up a couple of brutal notches. The primitive G-suits helped, but Riley felt as if he were in the grip of a python.

On the sixth lap, he squeezed past the second place machine, its fuselage frayed, the glossy paint trim worn away as if it had been beaten by a chain. Six-hundred-miles-per-hour bugs beating an airplane to pieces, he thought.

On the eighth lap, Riley forced his way into the lead, forgetting about his galloping fuel consumption, pushing past Mach .95, way beyond the F-86's low-level limits.

Riley was totally lost to the racing urge now, pulling the airplane even tighter, letting the G-forces build as he tried to increase his lead. A tremendous jar hammered through the stick, rolling the airplane sharply to the right, outside the race course.

A wail went up from the crowd—half-hoping for an accident, half-praying for the pilot—followed by a cheer as Riley regained control. He slowed the F-86 down and came in to land.

As he taxied by, Bandy nudged Roget.

"Look at his right wing! He must have lost an inspection panel. It's damn lucky he didn't crash."

Later, when the other two F-86s landed, Bandy took his family and friends down to meet the pilots.

"Patty and Lyra, may I present Captain Riley? Bear, this is my wife, and our friend, Lyra Josten."

A fan asked Bandfield for an autograph, and as he signed, Riley stared at Lyra. He ran his hand through his jet-black hair, wet with sweat; he wiped it on his flight suit and extended it to her. It had been months since Helmut Josten had shown him the photograph, but he recognized her instantly. Reluctantly, she pressed her fingertips against his own, as he continued to stare intently at her, wondering if he should admit that he knew Helmut, that he was working to get him into the country. In the end, he decided to say nothing.

To Patty's amused concern, Lyra had withdrawn her hand with a little shudder, wiped it with a handkerchief, and turned away.

Bandfield had not noticed the building intensity and was surprised when a discomfited Riley declined his invitation to come by the hotel for drinks and dinner.

Later Patty teased him. "By golly, Bandy, I believe you were trying to be a matchmaker for Lyra. I should have told you that she doesn't like pilots."

"Nonsense. All women like pilots. Some just like them a little more than others."

The afternoon heat hung across the field like a hot towel, soaking the tired and edgy crowd. It was almost five o'clock and eleven airplanes were being positioned for the start of the Thompson Trophy race for piston-engine aircraft. There were three of the big Goodyear F2G Corsairs, gull-winged monsters with huge R-4360 engines; six Mustangs in varying degrees of modification and preparation from stock to the superslick Beguine; a Bell King Cobra and the McNaughton Viper. The *Cleveland Plain Dealer* had picked Bill Odom, flying the Beguine, as the favorite, but the radical appearance of the Viper and Ruddick's boyish appeal had also attracted a lot of followers.

Bandfield had gone down to the McNaughton hangar to make one more attempt to talk Ruddick out of flying. When he arrived, there was an argument in process, with Milo Ruddick screaming at the top of his voice, "What the hell do you mean you're not going to fly? You won the Ohio race, you can handle this, I know you can."

"Dad, I'm scared. I've been advised not to fly this airplane by people I respect. And I've got a monster hangover. I'm not going to fly."

Ruddick grabbed his son by his shirt and shook him. "You're making a fool out of me, son. You can win this going away."

"Dad—I'm not flying."

Bandfield stepped forward. "Congressman, that's a good decision on your son's part. But I can find you another pilot, if you'll let me."

Speechless, Milo Ruddick whirled on him, glaring. "Go ahead, Colonel. We might as well try to salvage something out of this."

Bandfield turned and ran, holding his injured arm to his side, leaving a morose group to trundle the airplane out to the starting line.

As engines began to start down the line—the big growling bark of the Corsairs; the softer, melodious snarl of the Mustangs—Bandfield came trotting back, holding his bad arm, followed by a pilot in flight suit and helmet.

Suspicious, Ruddick barked, "All right, Bandfield, who's the pilot?"

The new pilot stuck out his hand. "I'm John Marshall, sir. You had me fired from McNaughton, but I'm willing to fly this plane for you."

Milo Ruddick stared at him. "Goddamn it, Bandfield, what kind of a joke is this?"

"No joke at all, sir. If my arm was right, I'd fly the airplane myself. Since I can't, I'd recommend John Marshall before anybody else."

Furious, appalled that anyone could insult his father so openly, Bob Ruddick said, "Dad, they're trying to make fools out of us. I'll fly it. I'll be okay."

By the time Marshall and Bandfield were back in the stands, the McNaughton pit crew was well into the starting process. Milo Ruddick stood on the Viper's left wing, grinning foolishly, hair blowing in the slipstream, hosing water through the Viper's wingtip radiator, sending repeated thumbs-up gestures to his son.

Inside the cockpit, head pressed against the tiny canopy, wearing a modified football helmet and an oxygen mask, Bob Ruddick sat looking straight ahead over the vibrating blur of the instrument panel, talking to himself.

"Just take it easy, fly high and wide. Don't have to win, just have to survive."

Sucking oxygen to offset his throbbing hangover, Bob Ruddick forced himself to swing his head to the left; it felt like his brain had lurched to one side and then back, like a balloon filled with mercury. His father grinned, jabbed his thumb up again.

The pilot looked back at the instrument panel, praying for a red warning light, a temperature going off the peg, anything that would give him an excuse to pull the throttle back and shut this quivering beast down. He started, sensing that his airplane was suddenly rolling backward, then, realizing it was an illusion, saw that the racers on either side of him were moving forward.

Bandfield yelled, "They're off!" as ten airplanes moved forward, the Viper hanging on the starting line. A Corsair was already airborne, gear coming up.

Roget yelled, "Ruddick's not started. Maybe he got smart and aborted."

Huddled in the cramped cockpit of the Viper, Bob Ruddick shot an agonized look at his father pounding on the wing with one fist and pointing at the fast-disappearing racers with his other. Confused, frightened, yet conditioned to obey, young Ruddick shoved the Viper's throttle full forward, leaving his father's fury behind him in a crackling blast of the Allison's exhaust.

With the other aircraft airborne and already heading for the second pylon, the roar of the Viper's engine broke across the stands, somehow louder alone than the combined noise of the ten other starters had been.

Bandfield watched the jade-green racer leap forward at full power, knowing just how frightened Ruddick was, how alone he felt.

Inside the airplane, Ruddick's leg pressed the rudder full right, as the Viper began its implacable torque-driven drift to the left, the immense gyroscopic forces generated by the engine power twisting the entire airframe in opposition to the propeller. Bob Ruddick was unaware of the complex mass of forces preying on the racer—he sat unseeing, unthinking, glazed eyes staring straight ahead, ignoring the instruments, ignoring the change in direction, the change in the horizon; his hand was locked on the throttle, his right leg rigid on the rudder pedal, seeing only his father's angry face and the fist jabbing at him.

The Viper accelerated swiftly even as it began its arcing turn, gathering lift that brought its wing up, taking the weight from the wheels, changing it from a ground-bound juggernaut into a torque-driven missile, the sucking lift inexorably driving the right wing up, up, and over. Immobile, scarcely seeing, a passenger in the last seconds of his life, Bob Ruddick huddled in the cockpit as the Viper went inverted, pausing for just a moment before its nose dipped to plow into the ground, the roar of its engine ceasing in the massive explosion that brought the expectant crowd to its feet in collective horror.

Bandfield burst from his seat toward the wreckage. Roget followed along behind at a fast walk, mumbling, "We should have stopped him somehow, driven a truck into the prop, something." As he watched Bandfield disappear ahead of him into the crowd already circling around the wreckage, the airborne racers reappeared, on the second lap. And Roget said to himself, "We should have driven a truck over his dad."

The appalled onlookers—mechanics, firemen, ordinary members of the crowd—circulated as fire trucks futilely sprayed the blazing wreckage-encrusted hole. Near the center, two circles of fire that had been the wheels sent out sparkling streamers of molten magnesium. Bandfield, breathing hard, stood recalling how many times he'd witnessed the same hopeless destruction, the same swift change from gleaming airframe and beaming life into this sickening charred amalgam of fire, flesh, and metal.

The racers passed overhead again, already on their third lap. Two Corsairs were leading. It was just registering that Odom's Beguine was not in the pack when a tremendous blow smashed into Bandy's temple, knocking him flat with a lightning blast. Pain in great pulsating currents blinded him, and he felt his stomach convulse. He was vomiting as he tried to get to his feet to run, sure that there had been a secondary explosion in the wreckage.

As his vision cleared, he saw Milo Ruddick standing over him, a two-by-four board in his hand, screaming, "You dirty nigger-loving Jew, Bandfield, I'll kill you! You and your ignorant friend scared my son to death! It's your fault, you filthy bastard, your stupid idiotic talk killed him!"

Behind Ruddick was Troy McNaughton, smiling down at Bandfield.

Roget separated them and hurried Bandfield to one of the ambulances standing by the crash site. It took them almost an hour to get off the field through the surging, crash-maddened crowd. At the hospital, the X-rays found no fracture, and a young intern asked endless questions about the race as he used twenty-two stitches to sew up the cut on the side of Bandfield's head. In the cab on the way back to the hotel, Bandfield asked, "Ruddick must be crazy. What was he saying about loving Jews and niggers?"

"I don't know, Bandy, he was out of his mind with grief. You can sue him for everything he's worth, you know that."

"Christ, I don't want to sue him. Did you ever hear who won the race?"

"Yeah, Cook Cleland in the Corsair. But the bad news is Odom—he lost control on the second lap and crashed into a house. Killed him and a woman and her little baby. I doubt if there'll be any more racing at Cleveland."

Little Rock, Arkansas/October 1, 1949

The shades were always drawn, now. Milo Ruddick sat despondently at his desk, unshaven, shoelaces untied.

A four-by-eight-foot blown-up photograph of Bob Ruddick standing in front of the Viper hung on the wall. It had been taken immediately after the Ohio Trophy race, and Bob was grinning as he held the huge cup. Ruddick was glad he had the photo now, regretting only that it was not the Thompson Trophy. But that was life.

And so was revenge.

He turned back to the file of papers on his desk. The report had been compiled by Troy McNaughton's chief of security, Dick Baker. It confirmed the material Ruddick had gathered from his military intelligence sources. His suspicions had been absolutely correct. Not only had Bandfield recommended the jungle bunny Marshall for the test pilot's job, he'd gotten him another job in Salinas. Bandfield's wife was no better; she was one of those pushy women always wanting to do a man's job. And she had brought this Communist woman, a Jewess no less, into the country with her brat.

But these were only externals. The most damning thing in Bandfield's criminal past was his flying for the Reds during the Spanish Civil War. He'd shot down eleven of Franco's planes. And the Air Corps had actually let him back in to fly!

"I wonder how much damage he's done over the years. He sabotaged the McNaughton supersonic program, hiring that nigger, that's for sure. Well, I'll get him. I'll get him."

Salinas, California/October 15, 1949

Saundra Marshall did what she'd done every morning for the past six months—rolled down the striped awning, pushed the tables out to the front, brought the boxes of fruits and vegetables out, sprinkled them down with a fine spray of water, swept the floor—and then waited.

The waiting had been horrible at first; sometimes not a single customer had come in all day. Her initial reaction was that it was because she was Negro; there weren't many colored people in the area, and the Marshalls were the only ones with a store. But bit by bit, business had improved so that she felt a little better. Today was

Saturday, and usually the weekends were better, with tourist traffic stopping for soft drinks or directions.

It had puzzled her for a long time that the majority of her customers were male Mexican laborers. Invariably, they would come in alone, poke deferentially around the store, buy one or two little items, gum or a candy bar—and then shyly buy some of the cosmetics she had prepared. Then a few Mexican women started coming in. They were far more direct, going directly to the counter, and pointing to the bottles they wanted.

She had created a simple line of homemade cosmetics—face cream, hand cream, and a general purpose lotion, all based on her sweet old Aunt Mary's recipes. No one had called her Mary—she was "Aunt Love" to everybody, and Saundra had called her line "Love's Lotions."

The ingredients were simple—regular cold cream, tinted with food coloring and perfumed with Evening in Paris, then mixed with aloe vera and glycerine. She'd designed the label herself and had them printed at the small shop on Olvera Street.

It had taken her awhile to realize that it was the new label that had caused the jump in sales. She had designed it to read

LOVE'S
LOTION

but the "s" in Love's had been looped around the "L" in Lotion, so that it looked like

LOVE'
POTION.

When she'd finally figured it out, she felt she had to change the label, but John wouldn't let her. "Honey, it's not like you were selling fake medicine that couldn't cure them. This is good stuff. And if some of your cutomers happen to think it's a love potion, it might just work for them. Besides, it's the only thing that's getting us any business. Raise the prices!"

This morning Patty Bandfield and Lyra were coming over to test her products. The three of them, from such vastly different backgrounds, had wonderful times together. In the beginning, part of it was that Lyra and Saundra were mutually exotic to each other. Saundra had never met a foreigner before, and Lyra had never talked at length to a Negro. But more important, all three of them were strong, independent women, all wanting to get more out of life than just a living.

Lyra and Patty came in laughing and spent the next twenty minutes experimenting with the cosmetics.

Lyra, ever the pragmatist, said, "John was right. These are good products; I'll use them myself. You don't have to care what people do with them—if they think they work as love potions, more power to them. Maybe I'll take an extra bottle for that myself."

Patty shot her an approving glance. "And John's right about pricing, too—you're way too low. You're not charging for all the time it takes to make them. I'll bet if you raise prices, you'll sell even more."

Enthusiastically, Patty squeezed her arm. "I think you might have something here. Why don't you think about expanding? I could help you with the finances. I'll bet you'd find a big market in Los Angeles."

The words were a reprieve. Business had picked up, but Saundra had already decided that unless things improved dramatically in the next sixty days, they were going to have to go somewhere else. She'd opened their little variety store with $4,000 in savings— blood money, John called it, from his flying for Israel. He had protested long and hard about a store, but finally, as always, had given in to her. But when she needed another $4,000 to keep going, she found that he had spent the rest of his savings on his little racer.

She'd just put out the plates for lunch when John came in, obviously depressed.

"Well, baby, they've had to let me go. I knew it was coming."

"Don't worry, John, we'll be okay. You can help me with the business. Patty's going to help me with the finances."

"No, we've taken enough from the Bandfields. Bandy got me the job as instructor; I don't want to take anything more."

She whirled on him. "Don't be foolish. You worked hard instructing, taking charter flights. You earned your keep. Patty's talking about *investing* in me, not giving me anything. She could make a great deal of money.

He put his arms around her. "Honey, I don't want to make you feel bad, but for her to make a great deal of money, you'd have to make a great deal of money. And I just don't see that happening."

She shrugged him off. "You were willing to put up with a job as an instructor, taking peanuts for pay, and you resent me having any success."

"What success? You're selling a few bottles of lotion. We'd starve to death."

"Not if we move to Los Angeles, open a factory."

"We don't have any experience, honey. Be realistic."

"You didn't have any experience building racers, either, and you were quick enough to sink our money in it."

Stung, John retaliated, "*Our* money? *Our* money? I earned that fighting in Israel. You blew half of it on this store; I blew half of it on a racer. Fair enough."

"We should have listened to your father, and stayed in Cleveland."

"Sure, I could have stayed in Cleveland, sweeping floors. That's insulting. Hell, I've been an officer and a test pilot."

"Well, maybe you'd be better off back in the Air Force."

"You mean it? Could you stand it?"

She turned away. "No. I mean without me. I'm holding you back. Somehow we've drifted apart since Tuskegee. You expect too much out of life, you demand too much of yourself. I'd be content married to you if you were just a factory hand—as long as you came home every night."

He threw his arms around her, pressing his cheek against hers. "Don't talk like that, Saundra, don't ever talk about us splitting up. I couldn't stand it. I couldn't have made it through pilot training if I hadn't had you to think about. If you left me, I wouldn't be worth anything." He tightened his embrace.

"I'm serious, John. I love you, and I know you love me. You just don't love me as much as you love flying."

"Not so, not so at all. It's different, that's all. A man has to work at what he likes."

"No, he *doesn't*. Most men don't. If you love your wife, and love your family, you work at whatever you can get. But I'm not trying to argue with you—you go ahead, try the Air Force again."

"Not if you're serious about splitting up."

"We won't split up. I'll go to Los Angeles and try to work my little business into something. We'll see what happens. If the Air Force takes you back, maybe they'll send you someplace where we can be together, where there won't be any trouble."

Marshall snuggled his face into her neck.

"Honey, I don't know if the Air Force is taking anybody back in now—but I'm going to write and find out. Maybe they'll send me someplace in California. There's lots of bases here. You've been reading how President Truman is pushing integration in the military—maybe it will be better this time."

She closed her eyes and whispered, "Maybe." But she knew it would not be.

Nashville, Tennessee/December 14, 1949

In the growing recession, the first thing to dry up were defense appropriations, and the manufacturers were reeling under the Secretary of Defense's ruthless cuts. Even Milo Ruddick hadn't been able to save McNaughton's missile development contracts, and they had had to close the San Diego plant.

But behind a huge theater curtain inside the cavernous tomb of McNaughton Aircraft's main assembly bay, a sleek new shape had emerged, a half-scale version of what was supposed to be the Manta jet bomber. There was a cockpit for flight tests, but so far only Troy McNaughton and a handful of McNaughton engineers knew that the Manta was intended to be a winged missile, unmanned, and capable of carrying a large atom bomb.

There was a quiet murmur at the arrival of Dr. Vannevar Bush and his six-man delegation from the Joint Research and Development Board, the group that was trying to manage the unruly rivalry developing among the services for the control of missile programs. The Army asserted that missiles were simply artillery; the Air Force had begun alluding to missiles as "unpiloted aircraft"; and the Navy said it needed both artillery and aircraft, and thus missiles, of its own.

Bush was dressed in a gray three-piece suit straight out of the Roaring Twenties. He moved with a birdlike quickness, his suit lapel pulled back so that the Phi Beta Kappa key in his vest pocket showed. Slicking back his silver hair with one hand, he took in the huge curtain and the battery of charts and graphs, all covered and marked TOP SECRET. Suspicion glittered in his eyes; he knew that damn Milo Ruddick was a strong supporter of McNaughton Aircraft, and that was enough to make him wary.

Bush turned to peer closely through wire-rimmed glasses at McNaughton. "Mr. McNaughton, I think I should warn you that we don't like surprises."

McNaughton, usually the consummate soft-soap salesman, knew that with academics like Bush a good offense was better than a weak defense.

"Then I'm in for a bad morning, Dr. Bush, for I do have a surprise for you. But I think you'll like it."

The lights were dimmed and McNaughton began the briefing himself, detailing the familiar facts of the appropriations allocated to the development of the McNaughton Manta jet bomber. Bush's eyes glazed, and he signaled for some coffee to keep him awake.

"We've been able to outstrip Northrop's efforts because we are using the German research on flying wings done by the Horten company that began in 1931. And, to make sure that we have a complete understanding, we've hired the top Luftwaffe test pilot to help us. Helmut Josten is our Dr. Von Braun, so to speak. Helmut, would you come forward and meet Dr. Bush, please."

Josten stepped from behind the screen, almost, but not quite, clicking his heels. The patrician Bush had difficulty controlling his shock when he saw the pilot's burned face.

McNaughton resumed, "Today we are going to show you the half-scale version of the Manta, which is scheduled to fly in six weeks. Then we are going to recommend that you cancel the program."

Bush was so amazed that he started to rise and knocked over his coffee. "What's that?"

Now in his element as a briefer, Stan Coleman stepped forward, took the pointer from McNaughton's hand, flashed his customary winning smile and said, "First, however, let me show you some improbable claims."

He flipped the first chart; it showed a sketch of the Convair MX-774, an advanced version of the old German V-2.

"As you know, after spending millions of dollars, this program was cancelled. The MX-774 was intended to lead to an intercontinental ballistic missile, to be shot out of the atmosphere to fly for five thousand miles, then descend and strike a city-size target in Russia. We think the concept is a failure—no one will be able to get that sort of performance from a ballistic missile for twenty years."

McNaughton watched Bush nodding sagely, as even wise men do when their own thoughts are played back to them. The scientist spoke: "You're right; for one thing, we don't have the guidance capability for that sort of trajectory."

"Exactly!" Beaming, Coleman went to the next chart.

"This is North American's MX-770. They call it the Navajo. It has a five-hundred-mile range—totally useless, unless we're going to war with Canada or Mexico. They are talking about a five-thousand-mile-range missile—but they say that it will need a nuclear power plant. We think this is pie in the sky."

Bush roused himself to say, "Do you always knock your competitors at your briefings, Mr. McNaughton?"

"Not always, and only if it's vitally important as it is today. And as you'll see in a minute."

Coleman, serious now, brow furrowed, went to the next chart, a picture of the Manta flying wing, devoid of any cockpit.

"We want you to cancel the Manta bomber program, and substitute for it the Manta guided missile—five-thousand-mile-range, six-hundred-mile speed, and virtually invisible to the enemy radar."

As he spoke, the curtain lifted and a battery of lights flashed on the jet-black Manta, mounted on a slowly rotating circular platform.

After a long silence, Bush muttered, "Damn impressive!"

"What's that, sir?" McNaughton had heard him, but wanted it repeated.

"You heard me. This is damned impressive, I have to admit."

"We can build a fleet of these at one-half the cost of Boeing's B-47 bomber, and one-tenth the cost of Convair's proposed ICBM program."

Bush hopped up on the turntable and walked along the length of the Manta.

"This is extraordinary, Mr. McNaughton. You were supposed to be developing a manned bomber. What happened to change your mind?"

"Don't misunderstand me. We could easily develop this into a manned bomber, if that's what the services demand. But we think a flying-wing guided missile makes more sense from both the performance and the economic standpoints."

Coleman interjected on cue. "We don't think there will ever be enough money to develop an intercontinental ballistic missile. Too many problems of guidance and weight—how are you going to carry a ten-thousand-pound nuclear warhead?"

Bush nodded in agreement—he'd been saying the same thing for years.

"The Manta's mission is one-way; it doesn't have to carry fuel for the return flight. That means we can carry a five-ton bomb load. We can build two of them for every B-47 they are going to buy, and you won't need any funding for crews."

Bush turned to him. "What about guidance? Why should this be any more accurate than a ballistic missile?"

"We're planning a redundant guidance system. The main system is brand-new—it will use the stars to navigate by, just like a human navigator, but much more accurately. The backup system will be to fly it by remote control. The Manta's radar will transmit its position back to B-29s or B-50s standing well off the Russian borders; they'll make any course corrections by radio. Not as accurate as the main system, but if you are carrying a forty-kiloton bomb it won't make any difference."

Excited, Bush unconsciously sucked his teeth, a vulgarism that would have dismayed him if he'd been aware of it. "Does Milo Ruddick know about this?"

"Yes, sir. I briefed him on it. We are personal friends, as you may know, and I generally keep him posted."

"I'll bet you do. Let me caucus with my people for a few minutes." All the McNaughton people streamed out into the hallway to wait.

Coleman slapped Troy on the back. "You handled him just right, Chief; he was all set to rip our knickers."

"Yeah, but I know how he thinks. I figure with Ruddick and Bush lined up, I can shove this down the Air Force's throat, no matter what guys like our pal Varney say."

4

South Korea/August 5, 1950

Four F-51s burst out of the overcast to dance their dolphin shadows across the sun-silvered clouds. The targets lay ahead, dispersed like a handful of seed sowed along the muddy river's bank. A yellow-ochre blur of North Korean troops, their artillery, and a column of the wicked Soviet-made T-34 tanks were paused at Ham-chang, ready to push on to Pusan and throw the Americans into the sea.

Sweat burning his razor nicks, throat dry as beef jerky from the oxygen, the rotted-rubber G-suit constricting his legs, Marshall felt short-circuited by time as he fumbled for once familiar knobs and switches in dreamlike frustration. His last attack in a Mustang had been six years ago, in Italy, against an arched stone bridge crawling with retreating German troops.

The pretty little fighter, supreme over Europe, was sadly obsolete now. Scruffily maintained, it was a poor vehicle for this re-baptism in conflict, and absolutely the wrong weapon for ground attack, for a single rifle bullet through the radiator would cook the in-line twelve-cylinder engine to a melted mass of steel within minutes.

117

They would have been better off with Thunderbolts, the big, radial-engined Republic tank of a fighter. But there were no Thunderbolts, just as there were no jet fighters that could operate out of the rough Korean fields. There were only Mustangs, and they would have to do.

So far today's mission had been a milk run, but in the next second a black cloud of flak might blow him to bits. Things happened as suddenly as the war itself; on June 24th, he'd just finished a mission in a F-80 at Clark Field in the Philippines; the next day the North Koreans had begun their massive invasion of South Korea. Two days later, President Truman authorized the use of U.S. forces to support the South Korean forces, and the next thing he knew, he was here, fighting a war no one really understood.

Sheer habit made him scan the sky—there'd been no fighter opposition since the early days of the invasion, but you could never be sure, and he didn't want to miss a chance.

The C.O.'s voice, crisp and cool, crackled through the radio: "Dallas flight, cleared to attack."

Major Seville's F-51 peeled off, the five-hundred-pound general purpose bombs under his wing marring the fighter's crisp lines. Marshall thought: Should have napalm and rockets—that's what we need. But even as he prayed for better armament, Marshall followed Seville effortlessly, his hands and feet caressing the controls, flowing to the attack like a bow on a violin string, sky tumbling upward as the ground flew toward him, concentrating on following the cross shape now pulling up below. Marshall saw a single black explosion where one of Seville's bombs had detonated, felt the gratified lift of his aircraft as his own two bombs released, then pulled the stick back hard, fighting against the dimming blackout of G-forces to lead the other F-51s back to the perch.

He was pleased with himself, and with his comrades. Like riding a bicycle, you never forget, he thought. Two weeks before, at Clark Field, they had all been hotshot jet pilots flying F-80s and kidding that jets were so fast that you had to say "Rog" instead of "Roger." Now, without any transition training at all, they were back in beat-up Mustangs, trying to halt the rampaging North Koreans and prevent an Asian Dunkirk. Jets couldn't operate from the rough Korean fields—the Mustangs could

Seville's voice, taut with exasperation, came back over the radio.

"Shit. One of my bombs hung up. We'll make a strafing run and I'll try to pickle it off."

Marshall inserted his finger in his oxygen mask's damp sump to let the sweat drip out. Bad idea—they'll be waiting. The four Mustangs dove again, twenty-four lines of bullets reaching out to scythe down the brownish-yellow-clad troops manning the anti-aircraft batteries. Marshall saw the bomb fall away just as Seville's airplane staggered from a burst of flak.

This time only three aircraft pulled up. Seville was below them, slowing down, the black smoke boiling from his engine merging gray with the phosphorescent coolant fluid streaming from the belly. There was no radio call. He simply turned and dove with all six .50-caliber guns firing, a fragile stream of ejected cartridges trailing behind to dot the path to his death. Seville crashed straight into the flak battery, disappearing in a massive explosion that shot flames and debris two hundred feet into the sky.

Sweet Jesus. He was good and now he's gone.

Marshall called, "This is Dallas Two. Form up. Nothing we can do for him now."

The sorrow-laden trip back to the field took only twenty minutes, Marshall telling himself all the way that they'd better get used to casualties. After landing, he put on his maintenance officer hat and toured the flight line, talking with the mechanics, estimating how many planes they'd have ready for the next sortie, offering advice, permitting them to cannibalize parts from other aircraft only when it was absolutely necessary, and yelling on the field phone at the supply people. He liked maintenance work—smear on enough grease and there were no color barrriers. It fitted in with his basic philosophy: You received the respect you earned, no more, no less. It was all he ever asked for, all he and Saundra had ever thought about asking for. He wondered how her application for the bank loan was coming. She'd long since closed the little retail store and was busy planning an expansion. He was glad Patty was there to guide her.

Less than an hour to the next mission briefing remained when he trotted back to exactly the same type of ten-man tent he'd used in Italy, its tired canvas sagging despite the rope lashings. He wondered how it was able to intensify the Korean summer's heat just as it used to amplify the Italian winter's cold.

Marshall glanced at the shaving mirror hanging at an angle on the tent pole above the potbelly stove. His wide-set, hazel-flecked eyes were bloodshot, and he needed a haircut—and maybe one of Saundra's dye jobs, he thought. She was always playing with her cosmetics line, experimenting on both of them, and he couldn't deny the traces of silver in his curly black hair. Rubbing the lines left by the oxygen mask, he lay down on the mildewed mattress with its sour-smelling khaki blanket. The narrow tubular-metal cot listed in the mud, threatening to dump him in the dirty stream of water running in the door of his tent and out the hole he'd dug in the rear.

The unpalatable GI rations kept Marshall lean, while the long hours kept him hard. Reaching into the chipped. olive-drab foot locker that was all he had of home, he pulled out a fifth of pinch-bottle Haig. He sipped straight from the bottle, rinsing his mouth, holding the whiskey as long as he could against its bite before spitting it out to disappear in the swelling rivulet. He didn't really like the taste, and regarded the scotch only as an antibacterial mouthwash. You needed all the help you could get to fight bacteria in Korea.

The morning's scene played before his eyes—Seville diving, his bomb-laden wing low, the stream of flak—37-mm probably—that reached out from a clump of trees to smash into the airplane, and then the sickening dive into the target.

He must have been wounded—knew he couldn't make it back. He wondered it he would have the courage to do the same.

· · ·

It had been nice in the Philippines, eating crisp lumpia in native restaurants, the hot flaky rice crepes stuffed with God knew what. At the officer's club they had played tennis on "Whites Only" courts, a term that always made him uncomfortable, even though he knew it referred only to the approved clothing. Everybody took Wednesday afternoons off for "athletics"—whatever they chose, from baseball to a romantic rendezvous, and the weekends were leisurely when the guerrillas—"Huks" they called them—weren't shooting.

He liked Clark Field even though Coleman had led a small group that evidently resented his being a Negro. He'd learned to eat early and quickly in the club, and never to visit during happy hour, when booze might get the better of some Southerner's discretion. And— most important lesson of all—he'd learned to keep his face impassive if an attractive woman, American or Filipino, walked into the room.

He found Korea a strange and bitter country where even the maps were wrong by a matter of miles and pilots flew missions out of airfields whose names they couldn't pronounce. Home base was called K-10, an old Japanese field at Chinae on Korea's southern coast, with short sod runways and derelict buildings. American bombs had twisted the hangar's I-beams into spaghetti in 1945; the caved-in roof still threatened to fall, and the long hangar doors slanted out on broken rails like a dead vulture's wings. A tent city not much different in layout from that of a Roman army stretched out behind the hangar, dust-blown or mud-sunk depending on the weather.

The irony was that they were here fighting for a people they'd never met and knew nothing about. They came in contact with no one but the acquiescent native help, whose apparent mission was to please and to steal. They had no idea why they were there, except that President Truman had decreed that they would be. No one protested—it was enough if the President said it. But it would have been nice to come to know the Koreans, to find out what they thought about the war, Communism, the United States, whatever. As it was, they fought the war in a mental vacuum, accepting that Communist aggression had to be contained wherever it appeared.

Four tents away from Marshall, Stan Coleman put down his headset and turned to the pilot next to him. Lieutenant Fitzpatrick was a prototypical Irishman, blue-eyed; his thin red hair mirrored the tint of the freckles that covered his face and arms. Only five-feet six-inches tall, and weighing 165 pounds, he was built like a "how-to-draw" artist's illustration, in stout swirling cylinders of leg. thigh, belly, and chest, conveying not so much mass as an energy-charged force. He'd earned his way through college playing the piano on Grace Line cruise ships between Honolulu and San Francisco. A natural mimic, he could dance like Astaire, bluster like Cagney, and charm like Grant, and it had been a rare cruise when he did not bed down one or more of the happy travelers, usually older women ready for a fling. His stubby fingers were agile, and he was adept at parlor tricks, with which he diverted both attention and serious conversation. His irreverent manner was deceptive. His eyes betrayed him as he calculated the angles on every event, trying to exploit everything to suit his interests to get the comparative advantage. He was patient, and often seemed to extend himself, but his quick mind ran a continuous accounting of favors given and favors received.

Fitzpatrick's personality suited the current situation perfectly. Coleman, Fitzpatrick knew, was easy to manipulate and was beginning to be resentful about the things his patron, Ruddick, did for him. Coleman wanted it both ways—to have Ruddick's help but not to have to feel obligated to him for it, and that made Coleman value Fitzpatrick as his right-hand man.

Now Fitzpatrick played his part as usual, as eager to please as a dachshund puppy, tipping his field cap with his hand and letting it bounce down his arm.

"Did you get it?"

"I got it. You're looking at the new C.O."

Fitzpatrick pumped his hand. "You deserve it. And who's going to replace you as ops officer?"

He knew it wouldn't be him. They were good friends, but Coleman needed a dependable operations officer—and that was not Dick Fitzpatrick.

"We'll do it the Army way—the next senior guy."

"For Christ's sake, that means old Bones himself! You're not serious are you? The troops won't stand for a nigger ops officer."

Coleman played the devil's advocate as usual. "Hell, I don't like it any better than you do—but you know the pressure is on all over the Air Force to treat niggers like white men."

Fitzpatrick grinned disarmingly. "If you make him ops officer, he'd be in line to get a squadron. Then what would old man Ruddick say?"

Coleman fondled his secret like a worry bead. Occasionally, it was good to keep Fitz a little uncertain.

"Don't sweat it, buddy. Let me handle it, I'll be sure it works out right."

Understanding flashed in Fitzpatrick's eyes.

"Ah, I get it. You'll set him up?"

"No. We will."

K-10, Korea/August 24, 1950

Four hours before, he had put his head down on his maintenance officer's desk to take a brief nap, still soaked in sweat from the hands-on exertions of repairing a shot-up Mustang. Now the barking sounds of engines running up dragged him from a sexy dream about swimming nude with Saundra, a torrid mixture of an Esther Williams film and their wedding night. Not that Saundra would ever have been uninhibited enough to swim nude. He worried sometimes about the strength of his erotic dreams—just the image of the pliant mound of hair between her legs was enough to awaken him, rigid with desire.

But now fatigue soaked him like oil in a wick. He had been rousing himself to a peak two or three times a day flying ground-support missions against the North Koreans, and it was difficult to sustain the high level of energy needed for his other work. He was still doing the maintenance officer's job, and trying as hard as he could to satisfy Coleman as operations officer. From a career standpoint it was great; the operations officer really ran things for the commander. If he could handle the work and get a good performance evaluation, it could get him promoted, maybe even get him a squadron someday.

But Coleman had changed so much since his promotion. He'd never been friendly before, always making snide little jokes, different than he was with his white friends. With them, he was almost too agreeable, seeming to try to get along with everyone. He had a talent for taking what they said and feeding it back to them in some crazy fashion. He'd been particularly funny kidding about regulars staying home and the reserves doing all the fighting.

Almost everyone in the squadron had arrived by different routes. Few were regular Air Force. Marshall had requested to return, and, after incredible delays—he suspected the problem was that he was Negro—had finally been called up. Coleman had been involuntarily recalled—he talked unself-consciously about the big salary he'd been making at McNaughton Aircraft, obviously not caring that Marshall had been fired from the job he'd filled. There were only a few guys like Fitzpatrick, lifers who'd stayed in only for the flying. What a pair they were—Fitz had the guts, but didn't want any glory; Coleman surely wanted glory, but Marshall wasn't sure how much he had in the way of guts.

Ever since Coleman had become commander, he'd proved impossible to work with. The other men didn't seem to be having the same problem, but then they didn't have the same responsibilities.

It had been tough enough just being maintenance officer. The airplanes had all the routine difficulties of old equipment—leaking seals, corrosion, and no spare parts—and the runways caused continual problems. They were made of PSP, pierced steel planking, sheets of mild steel perforated with round holes that allowed the viscous Korean mud to squish through. Interconnected and laid on a dry field, PSP was adequate to spread out the fighter's footprint. But when the rains came, the PSP sunk in, buckling and rolling like a living thing under the weight of the overloaded Mustangs, expressing geysers of mud through the steel like blood from a wound. The long nose of the F-51s (he still couldn't get used to the change in nomenclature; they'd been called P-51s till 1948) wiped out all forward visibility on the ground, so you S-turned as you taxied to be able to see forward. All the slipping and siding looked comical, but it ripped the tires like cheese on a grater and imposed crippling side-loads on the landing gear. Taking off was bad and landing was even worse, for brakes became useless on the slime-coated runways.

The Mustangs were worn-out hulks scabbed from wherever they could be found. Some were from Dean Hess's "Bout One" unit, which had been trying to train the Republic of Korea Air Force. The rest had been pulled grudgingly, like hibernating bears, from storage in Japan. More were supposed to be on their way from stateside National Guard sources.

The Mustangs were in use because, in staff jargon, they were the only assets available. It was hard to imagine. Only five years before, the United States had the greatest air force ever seen, with 243 groups and almost seventy thousand brand-new airplanes. Now they were flying scrapyard rejects. The few Lockheed Shooting Star jets stationed in Japan couldn't operate out of the primitive Korean fields. The F-80s had to fly out of Itazuke, Japan, to Korea to patrol over the Han River area, then return. Their lack of range was exactly the same problem the German fighters had encountered against Great Britain, only here the waters of the Korean Strait were even colder and bleaker than the English Channel.

Worse than the old airplanes was the infernal combination of bad weather and low standards of training. The Air Force was literally killing itself in Korea, throwing itself repeatedly upon the sword of unpreparedness. The week before there had been seven accidents in thirty-five minutes—eleven men killed—when fog suddenly shut down the airfields at the end of a strike mission. No one had seen anything like these Korean fogs, far worse than any English pea-souper. They would generate spontaneously, submerging the base in an impenetrable blanket of moisture redolent of the human night soil used as fertilizer by the Korean farmers.

This week they'd already lost two pilots to bad weather. The prevailing northwest winds dragged in frigid Siberian moisture to clamp the humid Korean summer down on them with heavy cloud cover and torrential rains. But weather didn't make any difference to Headquarters—air power was the *only* thing slowing the North Koreans down, and that meant the Mustangs had to launch on call, whatever the conditions.

The F-51's primitive instrumentation often malfunctioned; the artificial horizon would tumble in a sixty-degree bank, then take minutes to recover. The pilots were forced to employ the rudimentary techniques of prewar air mail flying, using needle, ball, and airspeed to penetrate weather. For navigation, they had only the defective Detrola automatic direction finder, whose needle pointed the same way whether you were going to or from the station. The Detrola was suspected as the prime cause in both of this week's accidents—it looked as if the Mustangs, lost in the clouds and low on fuel, had followed the needle *away* from the station into a barren hillside. Marshall had to go to the crash sites to see if there was anything to be learned, but there wasn't enough left of men or machines to conduct an investigation. In a few weeks, the poor pilots' families would have the closed-casket funerals back home, unaware that the military coffin would contain only scraps of flesh and 150 pounds of sandbags to simulate the weight of the body.

Marshall rolled over on his back and stared up at the droplets of moisture gathering on the tent ceiling like sweat on an elephant's belly. What was it with Coleman? Was it the race business all over again, just like it had been at McNaughton? Or was he getting to be too sensitive, too quick to plead racism as an excuse? He seemed to be popular enough with the other guys in the squadron.

Marshall wondered if it was because Coleman felt defensive about having taken his job at McNaughton. Good Lord, if anyone should be angry, it should be him! He'd lost his job and a chance at the history books.

The tent flap opened and Fitzpatrick stuck his head in. "The skipper wants to see us on the double."

Wordlessly, Marshall followed Fitzpatrick, splashing along the PSP path leading to the operations tent where Coleman greeted him with, "Sleeping in, Captain? Maybe if you didn't spend so much time eyeballing the white nurses, you wouldn't be so tired."

Marshall wanted to throw himself at Coleman, but controlled himself. "What the hell are you talking about?"

"I heard all about it—last night a couple of nurses came in the club and you damn near went crazy."

"Major, for your information I wasn't even in the club last night. And if I was, who I look at and how I look at them is my business."

"Mind your tone, Captain. I've got the book on you, and you know it. The Air Force may be integrated, but we haven't reached the interracial dating stage yet. Now shut up and listen."

Blood pounded in Marshall's head, but he kept silent. It was like a nightmare from the past, his father's old warning about *never* looking at a white woman, never talking to one first. But someone had made this up—Fitzpatrick?

"We just got a frag order in—two Mustangs to recce a valley near the west coast—here are the coordinates. They have reports of a column of friendly Korean troops ambushed and cut up."

He handed them the flimsy and pointed to the spot on the map, just north and west of Pohang. "A column of ROK troops is retreating down this valley. A forward air controller just sent us word of a possible ambush there by North Korean People's Army troops. The FAC is flying a T-6 right around the valley, reporting no flak, but suspicious movement on the hillsides." He tapped the valley with his finger. Marshall noted that Coleman's nails were clean, manicured. He was glad he was wearing gloves over the ground-in grease of his hands.

"I want you and Fitzpatrick to check it out. Even if you don't see anything, go down and plaster the side of the hills with machine-gun fire to see if you can raise any action. If you see something, call the FAC and we'll launch another flight."

Marshall said, "Right. Who will take over the scheduling and briefings for me this morning?"

"I'll find somebody who can manage it in his spare time."

Face burning, Marshall saluted, spun on his heel and walked out of the tent. Coleman was goading him, trying to get him to be insubordinate. Why didn't he just fire him? But as he walked, he thought, I can take everything that bastard can dish out.

Fitzpatrick had been silent the whole time, but sloshed out behind him in the rain, a grim smile on his face.

Even in the driving rain, the old Mustangs looked pretty, with the blue flashes painted along their sides, the jagged bolts of lightning on the tails. Marshall was flying *Zero Hero*, the name left over from World War II, just like the plane. Someone had put some tuned pipes on a shackle under his wing—in a dive it gave off a tremendous howl that was supposed to frighten the North Koreans.

Despite Coleman's emphasis on the importance of the mission, Marshall expected a cancellation call to come. The lowering black clouds spilled rain like a burst water balloon, and visibility was less than one hundred yards down the muddy runway. Fitzpatrick taxied behind him at a distance in *Eighter From Decatur*, avoiding the swirling spray of liquid mud being thrown up by the propeller of Marshall's Mustang.

"All right, Captain Marshall, let's go. What are you waiting for?"

Marshall shook his head at the insulting transmission and called "Dallas One rolling," as he applied power. The Mustang skidded to the left until speed made the rudder effective. He took scant comfort from the fact that Fitzpatrick was following in a muck cyclone.

Thirty minutes later, they contacted "Boxcar," the forward air controller. Marshall didn't envy the FAC's job, flying an unarmed T-6 trainer low and slow over enemy territory, usually with an airsick Army officer in the backseat to evaluate the opposition forces.

Boxcar vectored them to clearing over the valley north of Pohang. Marshall led Fitzpatrick in a gentle bank at ten thousand feet; below he could see a two-mile line of stopped traffic along the winding valley road. There was no shooting.

"Dallas Two, I'm going to make one low-level pass to take a better look. Watch for flak."

Marshall metered his speed carefully, letting down to arrive at the entrance to the canyon at four hundred miles per hour. He flashed over a road filled with trucks, tanks, and jeeps, a few burned out, most of them filled with troops.

The troops weren't moving. Could they *all* be dead? He pulled back sharply on the stick, letting the G-forces build in a climb back toward the entry point.

Marshall hated to go back down. If there were any antiaircraft, they'd be waiting. But he knew Coleman would want to know numbers, dispositions, estimates of casualties, the whole mess. Deliberately he let down slowly to traverse the column at two hundred miles per hour.

The carnage reminded him of the old Budweiser painting of Custer's last stand. The North Koreans had ambushed the convoy, killing the first and last tanks, then slaughtering the troops with heavy machine gun and mortars. It must have been over in seconds, for only a few bodies littered the ground; most were clumped in the center of the trucks, as if they were trying to hide under each other. Others hung over the vehicle sides, some head and arms down, held by just a leg, others bent in the middle like sacks of flour. Great splotches of blood, black in the valley's shadows, drenched the sides of the vehicles and the ground beneath them. As he flew, his whistling passage seemed to shake a black velvet cloth ahead of him as successive waves of birds rose up from their feast on the dead. Breathing hard on the oxygen to overcome his nausea, he pushed the throttle forward to climb out.

As he cleared the ridge line, glad to be away from that valley of death, a battery of 37-mm flak guns blasted his aircraft, shattering the rear of his canopy and stitching holes through his wing and fuselage. He tried calling "Dallas Two, I'm hit," but his radio was dead. Circling above, Fitzpatrick saw the flash of fire embrace the Mustang.

"Boxcar, relay to Base, heavy flak batteries at south end of valley."

Fitzpatrick's mouth suddenly went so dry he barely croaked, "Uh, Dallas, send another flight. Dallas One was hit on his second pass and is streaming fuel. Doubt if he'll make it back."

The FAC said, "Roger," and switched frequencies to call "Mosquito Mellow," the airborne controller.

Marshall's Mustang shuddered like a snapping whip as the big Merlin engine backfired. He leveled off at eleven thousand in an eerie mouse-gray translucence where vaporous columns of moisture drooped like stalactites from the lighter ceiling above to the ominous black deck of clouds below.

The barrage of shells must have missed his radiator—the engine was still running cool. If he was lucky, he might be able to nurse it back. He glanced to his left rear, vainly hoping to see Fitzpatrick on his wing. If he went down, it would be nice to have someone to know where.

Slowing the airplane down to 140, he reached forward to twist the knob that would cage the tumbling artificial horizon and lock it into position to stabilize. When he released the caging knob, the instrument's face tilted crazily again, rotating slowly like a bright coin dropped into deep, clear water. If he got back, it would be on basic instruments, the "needle, speedle, and airball" of flying school. Using the magnetic compass, he set a course of 170 degrees to take him along the coast, back close enough to the base for the Detrola automatic direction finder to guide him in. He'd just fly till he was sure he was well out to sea, then let down and creep back to the shore. He might be able to make it if the engine kept turning and the Detrola did not. He mentally computed his odds as about one in five.

Time stretched out like drooping strands of taffy as Marshall repeatedly checked his wristwatch. After an eternity, he figured he was in position and throttled back, praying that the engine would pick up power when he needed it.

The battered Mustang slipped into the enveloping black clouds like a spoon into pudding. Ordinarily so docile, the tired fighter protested its wounds, groaning and swaying beneath his hands. At the lower left of the instrument panel, diagonally below the useless artificial horizon, was the turn needle, no bigger than a paper match. His inner ear deceived him, telling him that he was turning, and it took a force of will to apply the strong stick and rudder forces necessary to keep the needle standing straight above the gunmetal ball centered in its liquid race. It was a primitive instrument, its fragile glass arc much like a hardware store level, and his life depended upon it.

He thought: The ceiling on takeoff was less than two hundred feet, but the rain was intense. Maybe it lifted.

He managed a wry laugh at himself.

Really whistling in the dark, now. If the ceiling wasn't high enough, he'd probably never know the difference and just disappear with a splash. The mean-green sea around Korea was cold, as harshly unforgiving as the country it surrounded.

A spot spread out below him, changing from hellhole black to a shiny ebony, and then, as he came closer, to a lacy green-white froth. He advanced the throttle, exulting as the faithful Merlin responded with grudging backfires. Pulling his oxygen mask aside, he gulped in the salt-tanged air, happy still to be flying. He looked hopefully at the Detrola. The needle should have been homing in on the K-10 beacon like a hound dog on point, but instead it rotated mindlessly.

He glanced around the panel. Uh-oh. Coolant temperature's finally rising. Not too much time left now.

His hands sweating beneath his gloves, mouth dry, Marshall visualized the coast again, mentally computing how far he'd flown. If he had calculated correctly, a right turn should take him toward K-10. If he'd gone too far, he'd be down in the drink; if he had not come far enough, he'd smash into one of the mountains that reached up like angry fists along the coast.

And no one would *ever* know. The lonely thought oppressed him. It was bad enough to die, but to go anonymously like this, spat out of an alien sky to be swallowed up by an alien sea was too evil. Saundra, his family, no one would ever hear of him; his body would . . .

Enough of that! I'm going to drag this dog home!

Boxcar had relayed a message back to Fitzpatrick to return immediately. No relief flight could be launched because weather had shut down the base. When he was forty miles out, he called in "Base, Dallas Two."

"Roger, Dallas Two." Fitz recognized Coleman's voice. "Any word on Dallas One?"

"No, his radio's out or else he went in. Last I saw him, he was streaming fuel bad, heading due south along the coast."

"Roger, Dallas Two. We've alerted the rescue people. You're going to have to divert. We're socked in here. Suggest you try K-2, they're reporting a three-hundred-foot ceiling and a half a mile vis. Over."

"Thanks for nothing!"

Coleman put down the microphone and stepped outside the tent to the duckboard sidewalk. An airman from the orderly room brought him a tin dixie of coffee, and he walked back and forth.

He didn't see how he could be criticized; the mission had to go, and both men were qualified. Marshall should never have made the second pass; he knew better. And if it was anyone else but Fitz up there, he'd be worried, but Fitz was an old pro.

He thought it over very carefully; Marshall was almost certainly down. Well, it was war, and better him than a white man.

As he turned, thinking that as C.O. he really ought to be a lieutenant colonel instead of just a newly promoted major, there was a flash and an explosion of fire at the end of the runway. A moment later another one erupted. Coleman saw Tommy Daniels, Marshall's crew chief, walking back from the fires.

"What's going on, Sarge?"

"I just set waste oil on fire in two fifty-five-gallon drums. Captain Marshall is coming back, and I wanted to give him something to shoot for."

Coleman's shutter-quick smile flashed. "Good man; it might be just what he needs."

It was.

As the derelict fighter groaned back over the waves Marshall saw the flames rear up like a waving flag, columns of black smoke merging with the overcast. He smiled to himself. "Old Coleman's all right, after all. He's expecting me."

The engine was bucking like an asphalt tamper, sending neck-laces of blue-yellow flame backfiring from the exhaust stacks. The coolant temperature was off the peg, and he had no idea if the gear and flaps would lower—and he didn't care. Just the sight of the burning oil had fanned his hopes, sending adrenalin charging through him like a hormonal Paul Revere. He had a sudden irrational rush of sentiment, thinking of his battered foot locker, his tent home, safety.

With sensitive hands, he coaxed the crippled Mustang around in a sweeping curve that would give him a short final approach to the runway.

Marshall debated making a belly landing; it was probably the smarter move. If he dropped the gear and it didn't come all the way down, he'd be in more trouble, and he sure couldn't go around. But he knew that Coleman would criticize him if he damaged an airplane he could have saved.

He was lined up on the approach, just bumping under the cloud ceiling when he dropped the gear. He felt it grind to a halt midway, the red warning lights shining. There were no alternatives now.

Cinching up his belt and harness, Marshall added power to keep his speed up, afraid of a stall, thinking, I'll spike it on the end of the runway and pray.

Zero Hero hit just past the two barrels of burning oil, snapping off the gear and spinning the airplane to the right, no longer a flying machine but just metal thrashing in agony. His wing snagged a strip of PSP from the runway, cartwheeling him wingtip over wingtip until the Mustang flopped forward on its nose, poised there for an agonizing moment, then crashed over on its back.

Dazed with pain, Marshall hung upside down in the cockpit, the canopy crushed in over his head, mud oozing in through the holes from the flak. At touchdown, he had automatically cut the magneto and battery switches. It was strange to reach up to push the fuel selector off. There was no fire yet, but he could hear the ominous drip of fuel sizzling on hot metal as the fire trucks pulled up.

Chest aching, he gingerly checked his limbs for broken bones. When he reached to rub his sore back, he felt moisture. Blood, he thought, then realized his fingers were tingling cool, and he knew it was gasoline. He would have preferred blood, which did not burn.

Looking up and out, he could see Daniels digging ferociously with a shovel to get room to break the canopy away. Another man was shoving a brace under the fuselage to keep it from slipping.

Brave guys. One spark and we're all three barbecue.

The fire trucks began spraying foam as other men joined them. It took endless minutes of digging in relays, short chopping strokes, to keep ahead of the sliding mud and make room to break the canopy away. Marshall kept himself balled into a knot as they slammed the sledgehammer against the Plexiglas. When the hole was big enough, he released his seat belt and fell on his head, the helmet levering his chin into his neck, stretching and bending his neck. Daniels pulled him out bodily, and they hustled him off to the medics—and the waiting Major Coleman.

It was all anticlimactic. Coleman had questioned the doctor closely about the extent of Marshall's injuries. He'd been very lucky to survive the gunfire, weather, and crash and wind up only with some cracked ribs, a strained back, and a neck injury that demanded treatment in Japan.

Coleman looked at him with contempt.

"Marshall, I'm glad you survived this. But you should never have made that second pass. It makes me question your judgment. I'm relieving you as operations officer."

He spun around and left the room without another word.

Marshall looked up at the arched ceiling of the Quonset hut. Coleman had done a job on him. But, as his daddy always said, what goes around comes around. Coleman would get his.

Las Vegas, Nevada/September 5, 1950

Both Lyra and Ulrich had blossomed physically. It would have been difficult for them to do otherwise. Patty had insisted on their living with them in the big house in Salinas, and she showered them with attention. In the early days, Lyra would surreptitiously take food from the table, wrapping it in her handkerchief to eat later. It was weeks until she could free herself of the idea of permanent hunger and imminent starvation. The boy had grown, too, the rich whole milk and fruit acting like a tonic to his system. Still very quiet for his age, wary as a wild animal, he enjoyed playing alone on the grass-covered hills around the farm, seeming to come alive only when Riley visited.

They had been dating ever since the ill-starred meeting when Bandy had introduced them in Cleveland the year before. Uncomfortable because he knew Helmut, Bear had been miffed when he felt Lyra shudder as they shook hands. Yet Lyra's air of mystery intrigued him. She did not seem strong, and he began a patient pursuit. Over the next few months, he flew or drove to Salinas to court her, always being careful to have some present for Ulrich that made it difficult for her to refuse to see him. More than patient, the hospitable Bandfields conspired with him, believing that Lyra desperately needed a man in her life. And despite her reservations about pilots, Lyra was drawn more and more to Riley's quiet, persistent pursuit.

She had been talking about European casinos one evening, and Bear had jestingly invited her to go to Las Vegas. Lyra surprised him by accepting immediately; they had not yet been intimate, and he had really expected her to be offended. Riley decided to pull out the stops, renting a nine-dollar hotel room at the Flamingo and making reservations for the biggest shows. It was a sumptuary extravagance for an ill-paid Air Force captain used to hanging out in BOQs, but he knew it was now or never. His orders had just come in for transfer to a SAC F-84 outfit in Bergstrom, Texas, and he knew he had to make his move with Lyra now.

The drive up had been pleasant, but at lunch in Reno he decided to ask about something that had always bothered him.

"Lyra, when we were introduced in Cleveland, you seemed bothered when we shook hands. Why?"

Lyra put down her knife and fork and stared at him. "Ven ve

met"—she paused, to control her accent—"when we met in Cleveland it was right after your race. Your flying suit stank of jet fuel, just as my husband's did. It was the shock of that smell, not you, that made me ill. But the truth is I don't like military men, and I don't like pilots."

"I don't know whether that makes me feel better or not. And I might as well tell you something else." Unconsciously, he looked around and lowered his voice, as if he were passing on state secrets.

"I haven't told you this before, but I know Helmut."

She stopped chewing, her face suddenly glazed over with fear. "*Lieber Gott.* How?"

"I worked with him during the Berlin Airlift. He did a good job, and the men liked him."

"Was he well?"

"He was still recovering from surgery, but he was getting stronger all the time. He showed me a picture of the three of you, when Ulrich was just a baby."

"Yes, I know the one. Ulrich was two weeks old."

Then, abruptly, "Do you know where he is now?"

"Yes. The U.S. government owed him a great deal—and so do I. We tried to repay him in part by getting him a job at McNaughton Aircraft."

Her hand covered her mouth.

"He's in America?"

"I'm afraid so."

She slumped in a chair. "Dear God, I can't believe they let him in this country. That's why I came here, to be away from him. Now he'll come for Ulrich. What am I going to do?"

"Lyra, I'll protect you. Don't worry about him."

She initially wanted to return to Salinas at once, worrying that Helmut might be on his way already. Riley finally persuaded her to rest in the room while he went down to the casinos to gamble, persuading her that the Bandfields would not let anything happen to Ulrich. After calling to warn Patty, Lyra finally agreed.

By evening she had realized that if Helmut had not come yet he was not likely to come that very night and let herself be over-

whelmed by the neon extravaganza of the Las Vegas Strip. She
didn't feel like eating yet, and they prowled the Strip, taking in the
people and the players. They stopped for drinks while she told about
the blackouts and the bombing in Berlin. He held her hands as the
words tumbled out about being trapped in the crowded bomb
shelters, about the hunger.

"You don't understand how precious this cup of coffee is! In
Berlin, an ounce of real coffee was more valuable than an ounce of
gold."

Her stories went on and on until she grew too sad and he realized
it was time to go to see Jack Benny playing at the Last Frontier. She
pretended to like it, but he could see that she didn't appreciate
Benny's understated, self-deprecatory humor. They left in the middle of his act—it was like the scene in his film *To Be or Not To
Be*—to go back to the Flamingo to listen to the Vagabonds. When
they went in to eat, Riley shamelessly plied her with California
champagne, enjoying her European style of eating. He tried working his fork and knife as he thought she did, making her laugh
openly and without reservation for the first time. Later she had
egged him on as he successfully lost money at blackjack, roulette,
and the craps table. But it wasn't until she hit a jackpot on the
quarter slots that she really glowed—and then suggested that
they go back to the room "to put the money away and to talk
things over."

Even at nine dollars, it was not a large room. She had them sit at
the small table on two straight-back chairs, as far from the bed as
they could get, saying, "Let me tell you why I've been so distant
with you. It's not that I don't feel attracted."

He nodded; he'd waited months, he could wait some more.

"My husband and I were lovers for a long time before we married.
Such things were probably more customary then in Europe than in
America even now."

He nodded again, wondering why she was telling him something
that absolutely did not matter, then taking her hand as fear filled her
eyes.

"I thought I could escape him by coming to America. I never

thought that they would let someone so involved in using slave labor come to this country."

He waited and she went on. "It's ominous that he hasn't called me. If he didn't intend us harm, he surely would have called." She looked deep into Riley's eyes. "Wouldn't he?"

"I don't know, Lyra. Perhaps he has no intention of seeing you, perhaps he's ashamed to."

She looked away, nodding as if she wanted to believe. Then, shaking herself as if she were literally shedding Helmut from her shoulders, she looked him in the eye and said, "And I have had other lovers, too. I was in the German resistance—God knows there were few enough of us—and I became one of Joseph Goebbels's many conquests. I hated it, but he gave me much useful information. And I think he might have saved my life, late in the war."

Riley was touched, knowing how much this cost her.

Lyra was close to tears. "In my own way, I'm as scarred as Helmut. Let me tell you why I have this problem of washing my hands. A group of us were on a train to Dachau. It was in the last month of the war, and the Nazis were using all sorts of people in their military. We were guarded by two members of the *Volksturm*—an old man and a young boy with a crippled leg."

She stopped, her lips working as if she wanted to say more, then she ran into the bathroom. There was the sound of running water, and then she returned, obviously embarrassed by giving in to her compulsion even as she was talking of it. She stood beside him. "I knew we would be killed when the train got to Dachau, so I made sexual advances to the older man. When he accepted, I manipulated him with my hand to excite him. As he became more excited, I was able to take his knife and . . . kill him. He bled all over my hands. I killed the young guard as well. Then, a little later, the train stopped when it was attacked by *your*"—the word sounded like a criminal charge—"fighters, and most of us were able to get away. But ever since then, I've been cursed with this foolish handwashing habit."

He rose and extended his arms slightly. "Do you think it might do well for you to see a psychiatrist?"

She reddened in anger. "You think I'm crazy? I'm not crazy; I'm washing my hands because they were soiled with the blood and semen of that filthy guard."

He reached out to her, and she slumped gratefully in his arms.

"Lyra, I don't have a lot to offer you, and I know how you feel about pilots. But I've been reassigned. I'll be going to Texas. I love you and I love Ulrich, too. I want you to marry me; I want to take care of you both, forever."

She nestled her face in his shoulder, crying softly. "Bear, I see how it is with Patty and Bandy. He's never home. I don't want to marry someone who won't be around."

He kissed her, and she stirred, pressing herself into him. Finally she whispered, "Let's forget about everything else; just make love to me now."

Itazuke Air Force Base, Japan/October 18, 1950

The two long months in the military hospital had given Marshall too much time to think about Saundra, Coleman, and his own career. He was determined to get back into combat, to win his job back as operations officer. As soon as they released him from the hospital he went to the assignment officer in personnel, a balding sympathetic major who genuinely seemed to want to help.

"Captain Marshall, you're right. The 76th is short of pilots. But I'm going to level with you." As he said it, Major Rosa shifted uneasily in his seat. "Look, Captain, I've never seen this before, but your old C.O. has specifically requested that you don't come back to his unit. It's just as well, because I've got a priority job that needs filling here at Itazuke, and you're perfect for it."

"I don't want a job in Japan—I want back in combat."

Rosa shook his head wearily. "I don't want a job in Japan either, I want to go back to the States. But I'm here and you're here, and that's how it's going to be. But I'll tell you what. You take what I give you for a few months, and I'll try to get you assigned to another fighter outfit as soon as I can."

Bowled over by Coleman's veto of his return, Marshall reluctantly took a job at Itazuke as an engineering officer, making test flights on all the planes that were in for maintenance—fighters, bombers, trainers, everything in the inventory. Working hard, he turned the maintenance unit from a job-lot concept, geared to peacetime base activity, to an industrial facility capable of doing maintenance on a mass-production basis. The system worked so well it got a name, REMCO, for Rear Echelon Maintenance Combined Operations, and Marshall got a "well-done" letter from Earle Partridge, the Fifth Air Force's commanding general.

Even working eighteen hours a day, the base was comfortable compared to Korea, and the job was satisfying, but there was no combat in Japan, no chance to kill some MiGs.

Then, in mid-November, Bear Riley showed up in the 27th Fighter-Escort Wing, transferring from Bergstrom Air Force Base in Texas. The 27th was a Strategic Air Command outfit, flying Republic F-84E Thunderjets. The airplanes had been brought over on the carrier U.S.S. *Bataan* and were badly corroded from the salt spray.

"How did you ever wind up SACumsized, Bear?"

"Old Curt LeMay wanted some fighters for himself, and what Curt wants, Curt gets."

"You'll wind up flailing a bomber around; I never thought you'd be one of those multi-motored guys."

Riley was reflective. "I tell you, pal, that might not be a bad thing. I'm trying to get Lyra to marry me, and she hates the way I've been bouncing around, says I'm just like Bandy. Maybe being a SAC bomber pilot wouldn't be too bad; they stay pretty much in place. Lyra might be able to get used to that."

"That's great, Bear, you and Lyra would be a great pair. But I don't think they'll ever get you in bombers."

Riley introduced me to the C.O. of the 27th, Colonel Blakeslee, a hard-drinking World War II ace. When Blakeslee saw the

REMCO operation Marshall had set up, and how quickly his F-84s were being put in shape, he got him transferred to his wing. Bones was already checked out in the F-84 and took over the maintenance officer job in the 522nd—the "Fireball Squadron," where Riley was the operations officer.

Wright-Patterson Air Force Base/ November 15, 1950

The base's tempo was offbeat, hesitant, not like the charging hell-bent-for-leather days of World War II, not yet like the somnolent prewar years. Instead it was slowly, inexpertly lurching toward the pace the new war in Korea required. Roget walked down the Area C flight line, drinking in the proliferation of aircraft types. There were still hangovers from 1945, plenty of C-47s, C-54s, and Mustangs, but there were all the new types, too—F-86s, two B-47s, a fleet of B-45s, stuff he'd give his right arm to fly. Yet the thing that really amazed him was the sheaf of papers clutched in his hand. After years of starving to death, losing competitions for contracts with the government, he'd been handed a $20 million order on a platter, No competing, no argument, just take the money and run!

Roget had flown into Dayton the day before, for a one-hour meeting with the commanding general of the Air Materiel Command, Lieutenant General Edwin W. Rawlings. It had been like old times—he'd known him as Captain Rawlings back in 1935 and Colonel Rawlings during the war, when Roget had worked at Wright Field.

If he hadn't been in love with flying, Rawlings could have made it in Hollywood with his square shoulders, curly hair, and deep, rich voice. "Hadley. I hear you want to get back into the airplane business."

"Yes, sir, General. Frank Bandfield and I have been futzing around with houses and stuff, when he's not off flying for you guys.

We were thinking about maybe doing some inspection and repair work."

Practically every flyable asset the Air Force, Reserves, and National Guard units had in service was already on its way to Korea. It would take months for new airplanes to start coming off the production lines—but there were literally thousands of aircraft in storage or lying surplus at airports around the country, waiting to be brought back into service.

"How about starting out modifying Douglas B-26s?"

"Sure, how many do you have and when do you want them?"

Rawlings punched a button on his desk and a harried-looking captain scurried in with a pack of papers.

"Here's the contract, Hadley, all set. I'll have them fill in the blanks when you leave. It calls for an initial lot of one hundred airplanes. We deliver them to your factory in Salinas, you refurbish them to our specs, we fly them away. Almost all the major stuff is GFE—Government Furnished Equipment. The rest of it, mostly sheet metal, control runs, stock stuff like that, you'll have to local manufacture. As soon as you can handle more, let me know, and we'll get another contract out to you."

"When do we got our first bird?"

"It's on the way as of now. You'd better get your ass back to Salinas and start hiring some first-rate mechanics. Now on your way, we've both got work to do."

He called Patty immediately, delighted with the news.

"It's risky, Hadley."

"What do you mean? I've got the contract."

"Yes, and if we were in the old plant at Downey, it wouldn't be a problem. But it means we've got to expand here at Salinas. I'm going to have to go to the bank again and get the money for it."

"Use the land for collateral?"

"That's all we've got, kiddo. It will take all our ready cash just to outfit the place we've got."

"Should I refuse the contract?"

"Yeah, sure, and have Bandy never speak to me again? No, we'll do it, but it's risky. If something goes wrong, if peace broke out, I don't think we'd come out of it okay."

"Go ahead. It'll be okay. I'm sure of it." Hadley put down the phone, wishing he felt as confident as he sounded.

Los Angeles, California/December 1, 1950

A crowd pressed around the shop window, watching the noontime television news. Late for a critical appointment, she couldn't stop to watch herself, but the shop owner had rigged a speaker, and she could hear Douglas Edwards's voice. "Two hundred thousand Chinese troops are driving United Nations forces back all along the front." She sagged with the knowledge that this meant more combat for John—as if he hadn't already had enough. He'd fought in Italy, and he'd been shot up in Korea. It just wasn't fair.

A few weeks before, he'd written from Japan, delighted to be flying F-84s, and sure that everything was almost over— MacArthur's invasion at Inchon had turned the war around, totally defeating the North Koreans. But now with the Chinese coming in and the Russians blustering, it looked as if it might be World War III.

Saundra had wanted to go to Japan to be with John in the hospital, but he had insisted that he'd be back flying before she could get there. And she was completely engaged in developing her new products—hair straighteners, skin lighteners, and special shampoos. It took weeks before she really felt they were good enough to market, months before anyone would buy them, and now they were selling even better than the "love potions."

And it was this success that made her, at one level of her emotions, glad that John was overseas. She simply could not deny the extraordinary pleasure she derived from succeeding on her own, without any help from anyone except Lyra and Patty. They'd been godsends, with funds and advice. Patty had advanced her five thousand dollars, and Lyra had given her some more face cream and shampoo recipes that her mother had used in Europe. But they didn't help in the actual business—it was she who went out and knocked on doors and sold the products. She mixed them in big stainless steel bakery vats, using a two-foot-long wooden paddle to stir, then laboriously packaged and labeled them. She even drove the truck, making sure that deliveries were on time and that no one was shorted.

When she started, Patty had advised her to go to the major drug store and grocery chains to sell her products. On the first three tries, Saundra didn't get past the receptionist, so she changed her tactics. The fourth firm on her list was Phipps Pharmaceuticals. Instead of trying to see a buyer, she called the secretary of the company president. With a little soft talk and some joking, the secretary had set her up to see the head man—Mr. Phipps himself.

She'd never forget that walk through the office, filled with hundreds of identical desks, each with a white clerk bent over it, pulling calculator handles, filling the air with the click of numbers and the whirl of paper. Apparently, they didn't see many Negro women; as she passed through she could feel their eyes following her as if she were a particularly unpleasant-looking bug crawling across each of their desks.

By the time she'd reached Phipps's office, she felt scared; when she saw Phipps himself, she was terrified. Tall and lean, he towered over his enormous mahogany desk like God at the Judgment table. Then he smiled and talked to her courteously before sending her to a buyer with a genuine knowledge of their stores' clientele. The buyer, impressed that she'd come directly from Phipps's office, placed an initial order that completely swamped her capacity. She'd been three weeks late in delivery and was terrified that Phipps—God himself—would cancel. If he had, it would have been all over, for she'd spent three thousand dollars on materials and equipment, and had another two thousand dollars on order.

But Phipps was patient, and the products had been runaway successes. Now she had a clientele of her own, four major drug and grocery chains, and she was still doing all the mixing and packaging, but at the end of the month she planned to hire some help.

John would never have let her do it. As much as he loved her, he would never have let her work so hard, take so many chances, beard so many men—white men at that—in their dens. Instead, she would have been keeping house for him, and—maybe—loving it.

Best of all, the business was lucrative. She'd be able to afford her own television set in a few months. She thought she'd get a Dumont; they were over four hundred dollars, but she liked the round screen, and they seemed to be the best. And if things kept up, she'd buy a house and a car, too.

Today's appointment was with Abe Doerker, a buyer for the Allied Markets chain. He'd been hard to reach, and it had taken a call from Phipps to get through to him.

When she got to Doerker's office it proved to be nice enough, always a sign that she had reached someone with enough authority to make a decision to buy. His secretary, Blanche, had been a little snippy, slamming the door when Doerker asked her to bring them coffee, as if she was not accustomed to waiting on a Negress.

Saundra's sales success had given her a good routine, and she felt well in control of the meeting. Doerker was tall with thinning blond hair and a paunch poised over his belt like a lip of snow over a roof, his mouth weak and jaw slack.

The meeting had started off professionally, with Doerker asking intelligent questions about discounts and delivery times. Then he'd moved around to her side of the desk and leaned over her. "Well, we're certainly going to have to have some of your products in all of our stores," dangling the word *all* as Svengali dangled the watch. "But I have other interests, too, like lingerie."

Saundra refilled her cup, thinking immediately of a friend who wholesaled a complete line of lingerie products.

"I'm sure I can help you there, too."

Doerker chuckled. "I'm sure you can." He moved closer, saying, "May I call you Saundra?"

She edged away, nodding yes.

"Saundra, you're very beautiful. And I don't mean just for a colored woman. You're really very beautiful."

Suddenly he pulled her face to his, mashing his open mouth on hers, thrusting his slimy sausage tongue between her lips, while his right hand slipped between her legs.

Revolted, wondering what on earth he could have had for lunch to make his breath so bad, Saundra raised her hand and poured hot coffee over the back of Doerker's head. He tumbled backward, screaming, tripping over the telephone table to collapse in a heap on the floor.

Blanche burst through the door to find Saundra calmly packing her samples into her case. The secretary broke into laughter as Doerker struggled to his feet, furious, eyes blazing, yelling, "You black bitch, get out of here."

Saundra smiled at Blanche. "Thanks for the coffee. It came in handy."

Later, she reflected that her average was not bad; she'd made hundreds of calls, and while it wasn't the first time that a buyer had made suggestive remarks, it was the only time she'd been assaulted. Yet it bothered her; she wished John, or someone, were there to protect her.

K-2, Taegu, Korea/January 22, 1951

Marshall had flown fourteen missions with the Fireballs and had grown to love the sleek, straight-winged F-84s. Like their World War II predecessor, the Thunderbolt, they were heavy, rugged ground lovers that needed lots of runway. The F-84s were expensive—$300,000 each—but they were reliable and nimble enough below twenty-five thousand feet.

In the past, when Marshall had taken stock of himself, he had never been satisfied, even when Saundra forced him to admit that he was doing pretty well for a preacher's son from Cleveland. The two kills in Italy, two more that didn't count in Israel, and flying the

rocket plane at McNaughton was pretty good by anybody's standards. Yet his self-esteem still suffered—he'd left the Air Force and
been fired at McNaughton and in Salinas. He had begun to build
some confidence in the Philippines and at K-2—when he had run
into Coleman's constant sneering.

It was much better now, with the REMCO achievement behind
him, and serving with the 27th, but he still had the burning hunger
to be the first Negro ace. It wasn't any of this "credit to your race"
nonsense that you saw in the newspapers. He knew that he was as
good or better than any pilot in the squadron, and that if anyone
could do it in F-84s, he could. The drive to be an ace was simply
undeniable, overcoming even his dismal loneliness, his aching
need for Saundra.

At Taegu, the only fly in the ointment was a prissy West Pointer
who'd washed out of flying school and refused other flight training,
announcing that he'd leave the service as soon as his obligated
tour was up. The Air Force didn't care for his attitude so they
sent First Lieutenant Kirby Gant to Korea to serve as adjutant in
the 27th.

Compared to the way Coleman treated him, Marshall saw Gant
as a lightweight, the comic stereotype of an adjutant, a groveling
perfectionist for superiors, a tyrannical bully to the exasperated
enlisted men who worked for him. He'd alienated everyone with his
continual complaints about everything from the noise of the engines
running up to the pilots wearing flight clothes to the mess hall.

Always defensive, Gant compensated for being a washed-out pilot
by constantly bragging about his four-letter athletic prowess at the
Point. Marshall, trying to be agreeable in one of their early con-
versations, mentioned that he'd lettered in track in high school and
college, doing the broad jump. Gant immediately nicknamed him
"Little Jesse," and had broadly patronized him ever since, obviously
annoyed that a Negro could make it through flight school when he
could not.

Gant bothered Riley as much as he did Marshall, and they'd
decided to get even, to fix Gant in some memorable way. Tonight
was a good night—a whiskey front, as they called the bad weather

from Siberia, was moving in and the weather boys had forecast a complete standout the next day.

Riley posted a KICKAPOO JOY JUICE PARTY sign on the rough board shack that served as their club, and he and Marshall went around collecting the miniature bottles of mission whiskey the pilots received after each sortie. Most of the pilots saved them for just such an occasion, and two contributed whole fifths that they'd brought back from Japan. Riley poured it all into a big mess hall soup cauldron, diluting it with gallon cans of GI fruit juices, mostly the acid orange, but with a few cans of the slightly sweeter pineapple. He dropped a big chunk of dry ice into the mixture to chill it, setting the cauldron boiling like the potion in an amateur production of *Dr. Jekyll and Mr. Hyde*. It didn't taste very good, but after the first two went down, taste no longer mattered.

Inside the hut, Riley had arranged for a few friends to egg Gant on, plying him with Joy Juice and asking him questions about his athletic ability, particularly his broad jumping. Flattered to be the center of attention for once, Gant grew pretty expansive.

While Gant was so pleasantly engaged, Marshall and Riley went to the supply shack, where enough emergency equipment to last two wars was stacked to the ceiling. They pulled two cases of dye marker, the yellow-aluminum powder that a downed airman was supposed to spread from his raft, and carted them out to the evil-smelling stream that sluggishly snaked through the center of the camp. The pilots called it the Nile; it was bone dry in the summer, but the winter rains filled it with the pestilential runoff from the surrounding Korean farms. Then they rigged a rope between two trees so that it ran across the center of the stream, loosening it so that it sagged into the water.

Working quickly, they emptied the die into the pool that had formed near the footbridge across the Nile, let it spread, and went back inside to stand next to Gant and his circle of admirers.

Gant looked up and said, "Well, well, here's Little Jesse himself. Jump any broads lately?" Everyone laughed except Marshall, and Gant drank another glass, very pleased with the good response to his sally; these guys weren't so bad, after all.

Normally Marshall just smiled and took Gant's ribbing. Tonight he said, "Well, I'll bet I can outjump you, Gant. Why don't we have a little contest, a broad jump over the Nile?"

Gant smirked. "You're on—but you go first." He grinned owlishly around the hut, reinforced by the amused approval and support from his new circle of friends.

The hut emptied at the prospect of a contest. Marhsall marked off a spot on the ground as the takeoff board, took a twenty-yard run, jumped, and cleared the Nile by four feet.

Gant was not impressed. "No sweat. I'll move the board back four feet and still beat you."

As Gant turned around to mark off his run, Riley stood by the rope he'd slung.

The pilots cheered as Gant assumed the sprinter's position, pounded down his track, and hit the takeoff board. Just as he jumped, Riley pulled up on the rope, catching Gant in midair and dropping him into the Nile like a sack of flour. Looking like a wet Crayola, Gant struggled out of the Nile to the raucous laughter of the group, going to the showers without saying a word. The next day, skin still bright yellow, he demanded a full series of shots from the flight surgeon and a transfer from the C.O.

Two days later, long before dawn, the two co-conspirators were double-timing down the PSP ramp that led from the mess hall to the operations shack. Mildly content after a wretched eggs and spam breakfast, they were still laughing about Gant's spectacular plunge. Both were a little older than the new troops coming through—this was their third war—and they knew their sophomoric high jinks had helped the younger pilots let off steam.

"What's the mission?"

Bear was puffing a little from their run. "You'll love it! They want a maximum effort, a thirty-three-airplane strike at Sinuiju Airfield. The B-29s are going to be hitting Pyongyang."

"What kind of opposition they calling for?"

"The usual heavy flak—and they've got seventy-five MiGs sitting

at Antung, across the Yalu. Intelligence says that our ground support is tearing the Commies up. We might get a reaction from the
MiGs. Maybe we'll get lucky and they'll mix it up. You know they
shot down a P-80 last week."

A hot flush of anticipation went through Marshall. Maybe he'd
get a chance for a kill at Sinuiju.

Bear read his mind. "Look—I know what being an ace means to
you. Don't press—don't get yourself killed. You've shot down four
airplanes, that's more than most of the guys who call themselves
aces have."

It was true. Lots of pilots who had one or two victories claimed to
be aces. Some of them did it so often that they began to believe it
themselves.

"Only two counted. But I won't press—and I won't let anybody
slip by me, either."

There was no more conversation. They went into the briefing
tent, then helped the ground crews pull the canvas covers off the
canopies and controls, making sure the wings weren't frosted over.
They wouldn't have had to do it, but they were pros, and they knew
that the sense of solidarity was important to the airmen on the line.

The slightly distorted Saint Andrew's cross of Sinuiju Airfield lay
350 miles to the northwest, its runways a blot on the sheet of snow
that ran from Siberia to Pusan. To the west, the Yellow Sea bulged
swelling and hostile like a sullen gray balloon inflated with some
evil gas. From its corner, a dank twisting tendril extended inland to
separate Red China and North Korea. It was the Yalu, the magic
shield of the North Korean Air Force. United Nations forces were
not allowed to cross the Yalu, and the Chinese used its sanctuary to
field their growing legions of MiG 15s that were piloted, according
to rumor, by Russians, Chinese, and even some Germans.

The river was spanned by a string of Japanese bridges that stitched
the two countries together like a zipper. The B-29s had been
hammering the steel and concrete bridges since November, but
from the Chinese People's Republic a steady stream of men, muni-

tions, and materiel poured down to the armies that had driven the United Nations forces all the way back down the peninsula. The Reds had retaken Pyongyang in December and Seoul had fallen for the second time on January 4th.

Today, the B-29s were going after Pyongyang again, trying to stop the flow of road and rail traffic. The 27th was sending out eight flights of Thunderjets, all loaded with maximum ammunition, but no ordnance. Two flights—eight aircraft—would strafe the field at Sinuiju, while the others would orbit at altitude to fly top cover.

Taking off was hairy. Each of the overloaded F-84s depended totally on their JATO bottles. These small canisters, locked on two shackles on the aft fuselage, were electronically fired rockets that provided an extra two-thousand pounds of thrust for fourteen critical seconds. As the F-84s scrambled in pairs, the moist Korean air seized upon the JATO exhaust and turned it into a manufactured fog, a grayish-white petrochemical mixture that stung the eyes and lungs. The second pair of Thunderjets had some visibility, but after that the pilots launched blindly into the fog, praying that the planes before them had cleared. Once airborne, the pilots went on instruments and jettisoned their JATO bottles later than usual. By the time the last pair of fighters had launched, the field was completely socked in with a choking haze, and the JATO bottles were sunk in fields all over Korea, waiting to be uncovered by a farmer's wooden plow.

Marshall was leading one of the strafing flights, enjoying the rock-smooth steadiness of his fighter. He loved the jets—they were swift-climbing, rock-solid in cruise, and gave the overwhelming sense of power at your fingertips. Tougher than piston-engine planes, they'd be more able to take the punishment that the airfield flak was sure to dish out. Marshall thought: Lordy, if I'd had one of these babies in Italy I'd have made Eddie Rickenbacker look sick.

The prospect of flak didn't bother him, but he was annoyed that he couldn't be flying top cover, ready to scrap with the MiGs. Moaning, he cinched the straps of his oxygen mask tight to keep it from falling off under the 8 or 9 Gs he might pull in a dogfight—if there was one.

The rapid Chinese ground advance had apparently overtaxed their early warning system, for at 0800 hours he led eight Thunderjets across a surprised Sinuiju Airfield.

Bones Marshall felt a mild disappointment. There were only a dozen aircraft on the whole field; no wonder the flak wasn't tougher.

Thundering diagonally across the field, perpendicular to the openings in the aircraft revetments, he saw his bullets ricocheting off the concrete as they walked up to Yak 9, the little Russian F-51 equivalent, blowing it apart, the fuselage half-turning as a gear collapsed beneath it, sending one wing flat up against the rear of the revetment. It was fun, but unsatisfying—the Fifth Air Force didn't count ground victories toward being an ace.

In seconds, they were across the field and climbing.

"Red Flight, let's get some altitude. Nothing left worth shooting at."

As he climbed, he looked back; all of the 84s were with him, and there were fires burning in most of the revetments. The flak was opening up now, firing just to make the gunners feel good, for the 84s were long gone. The combat glow settled over him; he felt eager, conscious only of the pertinent—arming switches, fuel state, enemy locations—and ignoring the hard seat, the parachute straps cutting into him, and the sore where his helmet rubbed.

Across the river at Antung, the flight line was a swirl of dust, and he heard the group leader calling, "Thirty-plus MiGs airborne." There was another call: "MiG formation turning north."

Marshall cinched his helmet strap and tightened his shoulder harness. The 84s were all in formation now, at twenty thousand feet, where the MiGs' speed and climbing advantages would be offset by the Thunderjet's turning ability. He felt very comfortable, aware of where all the airplanes were, friends and enemies, and glad to be "the shooter" protected not only by his wingman "Boots" Burns, but by the second element of 84s. Boots had moved into fighting position, angled back, ready to follow him no matter what he did. The old story about leaders briefing wingmen ran, "If I punch a hole in the ground, you better punch one just beside me." Boots would have punched the hole.

The fight started when the first unit of four MiGs detached themselves from their circus like hornets from a nest, thundering down from altitude, changing from flickering dots with a contrail to fire-spitting cruciforms.

Bones hesitated just long enough to sucker the first four MiGs toward his flight. Timing was critical—too soon and he tipped his hand, too late and they got a free shot. He waited until the MiGs began firing. "Red Flight, break right, now!" As he reefed his graceful, slender-winged fighter around, he knew that his second element would endure waiting another agonizing ten seconds. They were dying to break with him, to bring their guns to bear, but they had to sit as a target to avoid telling the diving MiGs what their tactics would be.

He was surprised at how pretty the Russian planes were, with their distinctive swept-back wings, high tail, and broad vertical surfaces. As they closed at better than one thousand miles per hour, Marshall observed the blinking fire from the twin 23-mm cannons, and the slower, bigger burps from the single 37-mm piece, the individual shells tiny deadly blobs reaching out to grab him. As the two flights passed head on, the MiGs were even more impressive, earth-brown camouflage coloring on the top, a lethal gray below, with a red ring around the jet intake matching the red star insignia.

A veteran now, Marshall enjoyed stalking the MiG, not firing too soon, waiting instead to stick the nose of his F-84 right up the enemy's tailpipe. A quick glance back told him that his flight was with him, and that the enemy planes were on the opposite side of the circle, trying to turn with them, a mistake on their part. At twenty thousand feet they should have been climbing and diving.

Marshall let his nose drop, gaining speed, creeping up on the inside of the flight of four. In the hot lust of battle he ignored the swift build of pressures of his G-suit, the downward smashing tug of G-forces, the raw discomfort of the mask and harness; all he saw was the flight of four North Korean fighters turning ahead of him.

Like pulling a heavy log up an incline, he tugged the nose up inch by inch until he had the lead MiG's fuselage centered in his gunsight. The MiG turned and another flight of F-84s flashed between them, spoiling Marshall's shot. He reversed and came back to find another of the MiGs settled in on an F-84's tail, matching every turn.

"This guy's a honcho," Marshall muttered, using the new slang for an experienced, determined enemy.

Ahead, the honcho saw that he was overrunning and obligingly popped his dive brakes, slowing down to get a better shot. His target F-84 was now diving toward the deck, pulling white vapor trails from its wingtips.

Marshall lined up the MiG in his Sperry sight, then took his feet off the rudder pedals to make sure the airplane was flying straight, that he wasn't making any casual control inputs that would send the bullets skittering wide. He fired a long burst of armor-piercing incendiary and saw strikes sparking from the MiG like a steel knife blade pressed against a carborundum wheel.

The MiG kept turning and Bones moved in on it, firing steadily. At first, his six .50s didn't seem to do much damage against the stoutly built aircraft, then pieces began to fly away, the tailpipe puffing a cloud of black smoke like an old train leaving the station.

It slowed perceptibly and the canopy blew off, turning wildly in the wind, the pilot following. It was like a training film; the ejection seat had a shot of flame behind it, then it tumbled away, the pilot strapped in like a mannequin.

Marshall turned to find another victim, but the sky was empty. The remaining MiGs were climbing away, heading for the safety of the Yalu.

"Red Flight, check fuel state. We're going home."

Boots Burns's voice came back, "Roger, Red Leader. I'll confirm that MiG. Congratulations, Bones!"

He had three that counted now; there were two to go. It wasn't such a bad war after all. Saundra would be proud of him—if she wasn't too busy making money.

Washington, D.C./April 1, 1951

Milo Ruddick whacked the *Washington Post* on his desk with satisfaction. Even that liberal rag had to print the story on the first page. The only thing that bothered him was that Julius Rosenberg looked just like Heinrich Himmler in the photo.

"They found the bastards guilty. Good. I hope they get the chair."

It wasn't that Ruddick was biased—he wanted *every* Communist to get the chair. But the Rosenbergs were special—they had stolen atom bomb secrets and given them to Russia.

Tom Finletter, the Secretary of the Air Force, was first up on his appointment docket. Ruddick would have much preferred to still be dealing with the Air Force's first Secretary, Stu Symington—he was a politician first and service secretary second. Despite his Foggy Bottom manners, Finletter was tough. He had become a rabid advocate of what he called "air atomic power," and he wanted the Air Force to assume the world policeman role the British Navy had played in the nineteenth century.

The Cold War and Korea proved that he was right. There was no turning back for the United States—the oceans were no longer barriers, and there would be no time to rearm in the next war. A professional military had to be continuously maintained now, no matter what the cost.

So far, Finletter had been very successful. The Korean "police action" had scrapped all of Truman's economy drives, and, in 1952, the Air Force had been given a bigger budget—more than $22 billion—than either the Army or the Navy. But Finletter was ahead of the Congress, ahead of the public; educating them would take time.

The door opened, and a death duel of courtesy began. Finletter, balding and stoop-shouldered, was a gifted lawyer and politician. Despite his senior position, Finletter was more than content to come to Ruddick's office as a gesture of obeisance to the man's informal but very real power. Finletter was soft-spoken, and his quick wry smile seemed to amplify the pain expressed by his bruised-looking, hound-dog eyes. He gracefully inquired about

Ruddick's health, asked about Ginny, and commented on the economy in Little Rock—all in the warm, caring tones of the professional diplomat. Ruddick, armed with sorghum-sweet Southern courtesy, came right back with some pleasantries about the Army's prowess in artillery in Korea, for Finletter, like Truman, was an old artillery man. Ruddick then inquired solicitously about his health, praised him for his foresight in fostering the growth of the Strategic Air Command—and got ready for the business he knew would be forthcoming.

It came: "Milo, I hate to bother you, but the Air Force needs more Research and Development money *now*, this year."

"Are you really sure, Tom? R and D funds for the Air Force have gone up five hundred percent in the last two years. The Army and the Navy will accuse DOD of arrant favoritism if you get any more."

"Very sure. You know we're hamstrung now in Korea—can't use the atom bomb, can't cross the Yalu, can't bomb Manchuria. And while we're bleeding ourselves white, Russia's going ahead with its missile progran. Worse than that, the Army's constantly trying to take over our missions."

Ruddick nodded; he'd hear the same sort of complaints from the Army secretary in about an hour.

"What do you need the money for, Tom?" *For* came out almost *Faaw*. The more Ruddick was pressed, the more Deep South he became.

"There's a breakthrough coming in the hydrogen bomb. It looks like they'll get the weight of a warhead down to about three thousand pounds, and that means we'll be able to build a true intercontinental missile—the Atlas. If we don't do it first, the Russians will have us by the throat."

They sat contemplating each other, political chess masters each thinking a dozen moves ahead. Finletter was one of the few men in government who saw past Ruddick's driving ability and Southern charm. He knew that Ruddick hated the Russians almost as much as he hated Jews and Negroes. It was crazy to have a reputed Klansman virtually running the Department of Defense—but there it was. Like Hoover with the FBI, Ruddick had proved indispensable to DOD through the years. When Truman and Louis Johnson were cutting the services to pieces, Ruddick had led the way, suggesting cuts that did the least possible harm. When the big Korean budget boom began, he had handled the expansion with equal skill. There was no doubt about his ability—or his ruthlessness. He got much by charm, more by fear. His intelligence network was formidable, and there were few people on the Hill without secrets that could harm them. And he successfully masked his bigotry from most people.

Ruddick sat quietly, contemplating the problem, which carried pluses and minuses for him. As a true patriot, an ICBM carrying a hydrogen bomb was a welcome addition to the country's strength. But he had diverted enormous R&D sums to McNaughton for the flying-wing missile. If the Atlas ICBM was successful, the Manta would be obsolete before it flew. That could mean the end for McNaughton Aircraft—and he couldn't afford to have Troy McNaughton unhappy.

"How much, Tom?"

"We need four million more this year, ten million next year, then two hundred and fifty million spread over the next three years. That will get it into production."

"Is that for the warhead only?"

"No, warhead and Atlas missile system."

"I'll see what I can do."

Finletter knew that meant he'd do it. "It's a pleasure to do business with you, Mr. Ruddick."

"Likewise, Mr. Secretary."

Ruddick watched Finletter leave, aroused by Finletter's challenge, aware that his problem now was to find substitute contracts for McNaughton's cancelled Manta missile. It would not be difficult, for the whole business of defense was a game, just like the little enterprise he had going with the esteemed senator from Wisconsin.

Little Rock, Arkansas/September 15, 1951

Stan Coleman eased the borrowed Chevy around the rise, then shut off his lights and coasted down Elmwood Avenue, where Little Rock's upper crust lived. The huge old houses sat on four-acre sites, surrounded by neatly mowed lawns and lines of magnolia trees. The place smelled of money and he loved it—marrying Ginny was the smartest thing he'd ever done, even if she was hard to get along with. When he'd gone to Korea, Ginny had gone back to live with her dad in the old family home, kidding Stan that she was going to see her high school sweetheart. She was really there to help settle her mother's estate.

He'd liked her mother, even though she hadn't been well for years. Her suicide had been a sad affair.

He let the Chevy roll to a stop at the far corner of the lot; the only light on in the rambling brick house was in Ginny's bedroom. She was probably reading. Good! He wanted to sneak up and surprise her. She knew he was coming home, but he deliberately hadn't told her when. He'd caught a MATS flight to Little Rock Air Force Base and borrowed the car there.

Coleman reached in the the backseat for the string of Mikimoto pearls he had picked up for her in Tokyo. All during the long hops across the Pacific—Guam, Wake, Midway, Hawaii—he had been building an image of her—nude, blonde hair streaming, clad only in this strand of pearls. In his fantasy he completely dominated her, fucking her brains out until she begged for mercy. He felt he had a few extra rounds to spend this time. He's been saving himself for a year, even though he'd been sorely tempted in the sexual smorgasbord lonely GIs found in Japan.

The key was under the mat, and he let himself into the darkened house with a sense of proprietary pride. He'd own this place one day, after old man Ruddick kicked the bucket.

Coleman moved noiselessly across the living room, remembering everything about it—the high-backed chairs, each with its doily, tiered tables filled with china knickknacks, the huge sofa covered with cushions, and, in the center of the room, a portrait of Alma Ruddick as a young girl. In the light, her lustrous gray eyes seemed to follow you around the room—he wondered if she watched the same way in the dark. At the foot of the huge wide stairs, he removed his shoes, and, hand on the carved railing, eased upstairs. Midway, he paused, hearing a man's hoarse cry of pain or passion, then Ginny's voice, low and urgent.

He crept down the hallway to stand by her door, listening with a sick feeling of self-contempt. Then anger swept through him like sheet lightning as he heard her say, "Fuck me, Nathan, fuck me."

Coleman kicked open the room. Just as he had fantasized, Ginny was nude. But instead of him dominating her she was covered by a huge Negro—Marny's son!—who rolled to the side of the bed, obviously terrified to be found with this white man's wife.

Unable to speak, Coleman waved his arms at them, and Ginny said, "He was raping me, Stan, get a gun!"

Coleman looked at her and mumbled, "Get out of here, Nathan. Don't ever come back."

Wide-eyed, Nathan grabbed his clothes and sprinted down the hallway, as Ginny said, "Don't just stand there, call the police!"

"Ginny, shut up. You weren't raped, I heard you talking to him, pleading with him for more. If anybody's been raped, it's me."

Coleman sagged, his shoulder against the door, the pearl necklace spilled upon the floor. All of his past prejudices against Negroes seemed petty compared to the raging hatred he felt for Nathan, this nigger who had crept into his bed and made love to his wife. How often had he done it in the past? How many other niggers had she had?

He looked after her with such loathing that she gave a little scream and ran into the bathroom. Stumbling across her discarded clothing, he sat on the edge of the bed, staring with contempt at his reflection in her vanity mirror. As bad as it was to be cuckolded by a Negro servant, it was worse to be the pawn in the games she and her stepfather played. He would have been better off never to have married, never to have taken Ruddick's favors. Now, on the tousled bed where Ginny and Nathan had romped, he felt for the first time just how truly he was trapped. He hated them all—Ginny and Nathan, Ruddick and the niggers, all of them. And, somehow, he would get even with them all.

5

Salinas, California/November 14, 1951

Hard work had burnished the wrinkles from his face as it siphoned away his paunch. Hadley looked ten years younger, fit, his skin bronzed by days on the ramp, his step as lively and enthusiastic as it used to be. He was even letting his snow-white hair grow long again, something he said he'd never do after his wife's death. Responding like an old sled dog to the snowstorm of contracts from Wright-Patterson, Roget contentedly loped the production lines from which refurbished North American F-51s, Douglas B-26s, and Curtiss C-46s were pouring, supervising everything. The big IRAN—Inspect and Repair as Necessary—facility suited his busybody talents perfectly, as he helped teach forgotten skills to a new work force. For some reason she could not explain herself, Patty had gone first class with the factory, diving deep into debt for a building that would serve for twenty years instead of trying to make do with modular metal prefabs.

Hadley was crowing, "It's better than the big war, Bandy! I never had so much fun in my life. No worries about whether it's a good design, no worries about competition—just fix the airplane and let them go."

Although his assessment was very different, Bandfield nodded agreement. Home on leave, he was contemplating a relaxing test flight behind the stick of a Mustang just as the wild-goose blare of the crash siren sounded. Responding in a way that had become chillingly familiar in the past few weeks, they leaped on the running board of the fire chief's pickup as it headed for the runway's edge.

"There he is."

In the hazy sky, a cross and a smudge of gray-brown smoke drew nearer, a schoolboy's drawing of a plane in desperate trouble. The chief's radio crackled, "Ah, Salinas tower, this is Air Force Nine Seven, four miles out, number one engine shut down and burning, losing power on number two."

"Roger, Nine Seven, you're cleared for a straight-in, emergency equipment standing by."

The B-26 grew larger, canted to the left, crabbing painfully as the pilot sought the field. Bandfield knew what the pilot was going through, sweat streaming from his face, left leg stiff on the rudder pedal, wheel cocked over, throttle jammed forward, eyes constantly switching between the airspeed indicator and the runway, praying hard all the while to keep the sick number two engine sputtering with enough power to stretch his glide to the field.

There was an involuntary cheer when the B-26 finally limped in to land on the end of the runway, the pilot immediately shutting the good engine down and standing on the brakes. Fear of fire tossed him out of the top hatch like toast from a toaster as the fire trucks began spraying foam.

"Look at him, he won't quit running until he hits the ocean!"

It was almost routine. The planes that staggered in for refurbishment were mostly derelict clunkers like this one, flying on one-time-flight ferry permits, their fabric-covered control surfaces tattered, with paint chipped and gaping holes where instruments had been. Apparently no airplane sat anywhere for more than ten minutes without scavengers savaging it.

Bandfield smiled and punched Roget on the arm. Another tired old B-26 was down safe.

Roget laughed, "We won't make any money on this one."

Bandfield agreed. It was tougher and tougher to get GFE, the Government Furnished Equipment, and spare parts prices were going up all the time. Still, the business gave him an enormous satisfaction, especially a beat-up crate like this one. The prop had hardly stopped ticking when one of their crews began breathing life back into the airplane. In three days, it would be stripped down, steam-cleaned, and fed into the two-block-long production line. Within a few weeks, the same airplane would emerge for its test flight, then be painted—ready for another war.

Patty was even more concerned with the financial risk than Bandy was, even though the first contracts had been very profitable. The Air Force was beginning to tighten up on its negotiations as more competitors entered the field, but there was still a decent margin. It was worth the risk to her to see Hadley and Bandy so happy that they were still a useful part of the aviation scene. It was important work—they were supplying airpower that wouldn't have been available otherwise, getting airplanes to Korea long before new equipment could be delivered. They were proud to do it—and would have done it for nothing if the Air Force had demanded it.

The job also pointed where they should go in the future. The Korean War wouldn't last forever—and when peace came, Roget Aircraft would be ready to go into the modification business, converting the old warbirds into executive transports, an idea Hadley had long been nourishing. Bandy, a native Californian, was more intrigued by an earlier idea—modifying some of the bigger planes to fight forest fires. The market was more assured—and he wouldn't have to be there to watch over it.

He had just walked into his second-floor office, which overlooked the line, when he saw the look on Patty's face.

"What's going on?"

"You just got a call from the Associated Press. Some senator named McCarthy has accused you of being a Communist, and is demanding that all our contracts be cancelled."

Nashville, Tennessee/February 14, 1952

Elsie was running late, and Stan was already outside on the sidewalk of the commercial terminal. She put her arms out to him saying, "Stan, you look terrible, what's wrong?"

He didn't answer, embracing her first as an old friend, then not relinquishing her. She'd sent him many signals in the past, and he had always put her off. Today he held her tight.

She sensed the change immediately and pulled him toward the car.

"What's happened, Stan—" He leaped across the seat at her like a lion on a piece of meat. Without a word, ignoring the people outside the car, her mouth met his willingly and they kissed deeply.

After a few moments Elsie pulled back. "Stan, you know I've wanted that ever since we met, and you've always been cold as a fish."

"Things have changed, Elsie. I wanted you before too, but . . ."

She guessed at once that he was having problems with Ginny, and it pleased her. She had plotted his seduction even before they'd met, purely as a way to spite Ginny. He had always been friendly but distant.

Wiping the lipstick off his face, Coleman snarled, "We've waited too long, honey, way too long. Let's go see Troy, and then we'll have a little party by ourselves somewhere."

The meeting in McNaughton's office began and ended curiously. Troy had looked at them both closely, eyes narrowed, obviously aware that there had been something going on, saying, "How was the canary you two cats have been eating?" Then, with the abstract proficiency of habit, he lit a cigarette and shifted it to the corner of his mouth.

"Damn, that's hot." He ground the cigarette out, then reached into his desk to put a little salve where the Camel usually drooped. There was a sore on his lip.

Troy went on: "I guess you know that Milo hasn't been able to prevent the Air Force from cancelling the Manta. They're putting all their chips on the Atlas ICBM program, and it's too expensive to be able to afford us as a backup."

Coleman nodded with indifference. His entire philosophy of life had changed since the ugly scene in Little Rock. He had idealized and idolized Ginny, feeling that she was so far above him that he might have understood her infidelity with someone else. Finding her with Nathan had destroyed him.

McNaughton droned on. "But he's tossed us a juicy bone. We are going to be a subcontractor for the Boeing B-47, building center fuselage sections and inner wing panels. They are expanding the hell out of that program, bringing Lockheed and Douglas in as additional sources. It's not as good as producing something of our own design, but it'll keep the plant going, and it's going to be very profitable."

Coleman stared at him. A year ago he'd been hanging on his words, trying to see what advantage was lurking. Now it didn't matter.

"I want you to ask Ruddick to get you released from the Air Force. He can do it with a phone call."

Coleman laughed bitterly. "Why would I do that?"

"So you can manage the B-47 component program."

"Hell, I'm no manager. You just want my connections."

It was a statement of the obvious.

Troy was terribly preoccupied, fingering his lip as one probes a sore tooth with a tongue, seemingly unable to marshal his usual salesman's persuasiveness. Elsie felt a sudden unease. Could that sore be a chancre?

"We need you, Stan."

"You don't need me. I just want to get back in combat."

Troy and Elsie looked at each other. They knew Coleman loved to fly, but getting back in combat was totally inconsistent.

Yet it was his story, and he stuck to it, frustrating Troy. Resigned, he told Elsie, "You see if you can persuade our friend. I'm catching a plane back to Washington in an hour."

As they left the factory grounds, Coleman slipped his hand beneath her skirt.

"Don't, honey, you'll get me so hot I'll run into something. We'll be there in a minute."

As soon as the guesthouse door closed behind them, Coleman threw himself on her, pulling her down in the hallway.

"Don't rip my blouse, honey, I'll—"

He closed her mouth with his own as he tore the white fabric away, then pulled at her skirt.

"Let me help, honey, don't be—"

Her Playtex Pink-Ice girdle, fashion's Maginot Line of chastity, slowed him momentarily, but she peeled out of it and he began flailing inside her in a demon-driven way, his eyes closed, breathing hard.

Later, he was sheepish as they finished undressing.

"I'm sorry I was so rough, Elsie. I was hot."

"Lord, honey, you're telling *me* you were hot? I hope that little romp on the rug was just for openers."

He nodded, half smiling. "I guess Ginny told you how I used to worry about saving myself. Not anymore."

Elsie reached for him, cuddling his head between her breasts. She had tasted jealousy in his mouth—his tongue, his whole body, had been probing for Ginny. Why?

He dropped off her and slept beside her for almost twenty minutes. Elsie stared at the ceiling, bemused that something she'd waited so long for could have been so disappointing. It had been a hard campaign, starting with a diet and exercise program she couldn't stick to. It took almost two years to get herself into shape to compete with Ginny—and Stan's reserve diminished her appetite for him. Yet the habit of conquest sustained her interest, and as part of the process, she saw to it that she and Ginny became "best friends." It had been easy—Ginny's vanity was as deep as her character was shallow. The better she knew Ginny, the more she wanted to screw Stan, just to show her. Elsie didn't just listen; she drew Ginny out like Stokowski drew out an orchestra, dropping just the gestures and the words to evoke an outpouring, never volunteering any of her own liberal views, content to let Ginny chatter on.

Discontented, she watched Stan snore, muttering to herself,

"What the hell does it all mean? What the hell am I doing here?" For the first time in her life she felt uneasy that she was involving herself with someone she didn't care for. She asked herself, "Ain't it enough that I've got Dick Baker to screw?"

Coleman woke up, saying sheepishly, "I guess you can tell, Ginny and I are through."

"Honey, you just tell your old Aunt Elsie all about it."

"It's such a mess—I just can't live with her anymore."

"What happened? Was she unfaithful?"

Coleman sat up. "No, nothing like that. Ginny would never do anything like that."

"Baloney, Stan. Something happened. If you don't want to tell me, that's fine. I really don't care." He must have walked in on Ginny while she was screwing somebody else. It happens.

She turned on her side, suddenly bored with the whole process. She felt a peculiar desire to be free of him, to be back in Dick Baker's trailer, not having to pretend about anything.

He put his hand on her shoulder and she turned, saying, "I'm getting too old for this."

"No, you're not, you're beautiful. I'm just a little tired and worn out."

Reflexively, she became the practiced courtesan, saying, "Honey, you just be quiet for a while. I'm going to talk a little French to Stan the Man here."

Los Angeles, California/April 10, 1952

After flying his 114th combat mission in F-84s, Marshall was sent home. Combat in Korea had been satisfying: dropping napalm, shooting up trucks and trains, and slinging bombs into tunnels. But there had been no more dogfights and no more victories. He knew he was an ace in his own mind, but the Air Force did not—could not—count the Egyptians as victories. His official score stood at three.

Despite his assignment as a flight commander with the 94th Fighter-Interceptor Squadron, Rickenbacker's old outfit, he immediately began applying for reassignment to combat in Korea.

He didn't tell Saundra that. Instead, he drove from George Air Force Base to Los Angeles each weekend, pleased at first to spend time in the flat-roofed stucco crackerbox house she'd bought in Santa Monica. It was small, studded on a block with a dozen others as identical as the white dots of sugar on a licorice strip, but she loved it. At first they used to go down to Muscle Beach to buy hot dogs from the vendors and then eat them while watching the weight lifters. Afterward they'd stroll in the sand to admire the sunset—but day by day, week by week, she had less time for him.

Lack of time was only one of the disturbing changes in her. When he'd left, his wife had been frustrated with a failing little general store, struggling to sell her line of homemade cosmetics. When he came back, she was a business executive, running a small factory and building a sales organization. Strangest of all, she was a new woman in bed.

Their first night together had been remarkable, better than any of his wartime fantasies. Saundra, always so shy in the past, was now as aggressive with her whole body as her tongue had once been, open to experimentation, eager to please. When they made love she quite literally took his breath away, kissing him so deeply that he gasped, "I need some oxygen, Babe. What's come over you?"

"Well, you just did, twice. And in a minute, I'm going to come over you."

"No, I'm serious. You're like a different woman. If I didn't know better, I'd say you had a lover while I was gone." Then, ruefully, "And a good one, too."

"You're lucky I know you're joking."

They lay quietly side by side, hands intertwined, his leg plopped over her thigh.

She yawned and stretched, then said, "But I *am* different now, in a lot of ways—I've had to be. The real world's taught me a lot."

"Maybe too much."

"Maybe. I guess the sad truth is I've gotten harder. Your sweet old

Saundra has had her sweetness ground off in the tough business world."

She didn't have to tell him; he was sick of hearing her yammer about bad accounts, about people who paid late but took the 2 percent/10-day discounts anyway, boring stuff he never wanted to be involved with.

"The Air Force is pretty tough, too."

"I know, John, being shot at—"

"Christ Almighty"—the words shattered her; he'd never taken Jesus's name in vain with her before—"the combat was nothing. Try being snubbed by blond idiots like Stan Coleman. Try looking away and not saying anything when the other guys are talking about pretty girls—pretty *white* girls; try not hearing people tell nigger jokes, try not seeing them clam up when you come in."

"Well then, get out. Do what I'm doing, make some money . . ."

The quarrel went on, but the marriage started to break down there, with the role reversal. He used to be the one who was preoccupied about making a living, who would quickly fall asleep after making love, and then wake up early, worrying. Now it was the other way around. One morning he had reached for her, to find a note saying only, *Early morning meeting—see you about six.*

It had been past ten P.M. when she returned, tired and out of sorts, passive about their lovemaking. From then on it seemed to him they were only going through the motions of being married.

His own schedule at George was full. He had to get as much flying time as possible in the F-86 to bring his experience level up, and the C.O. had saddled him—as the new guy—with all the boring, time-consuming extra duties—Form 5s, Awards and Decorations, stupid stuff. He could only get away on the weekends, when she was either bone-tired or frantically busy. For the first time in their marriage, they began to have serious, sustained quarrels that didn't end with a romp in bed. One Friday night she told them they were going to a cocktail party and dinner with some clients.

"Look, Saundra, I've only got forty-eight hours. I don't want to go to a stupid party with your clients—I want to stay home with you."

"John, these people put the beans on the table—I have to go. Why don't you find some way to get more time off?"

It was a rhetorical question—she knew that the Air Force was as demanding of his time as her business was of hers.

Marshall felt as if he'd stepped outside his body, watching the argument build toward a critical point. He wanted to beg her to stop, to give in to her, to agree with anything, and could not. Instead he said, "I'm going to get plenty of time off—from you. I'm going back to Korea."

"Oh, what a big surprise. I'd never have guessed. The truth is you'd rather have a chance at getting two more kills than be with me."

Frustrated, Marshall lunged at her, fists clenched, "I'll beat some sense into you."

She laughed and he backed away, apologizing for his idiocy. Yet a week later he had his orders—and she had decided to talk to a lawyer about a divorce.

K-13, Suwon, Korea/May 26, 1952

When he'd arrived with Dave Menard at K-13, Bones had pointed them to a rope dangling from the rear door of the transport.

"Number one Korean service."

Korea had three seasons: mud, blazing heat, and freezing cold. The battered old C-54 had settled into the black gumbo like a washerwoman into old shoes. There was no way to get out except by the rope, so they dumped their gear and shinnied down hand over hand.

Bones's perception of Korea, dimmed by the few months he'd spent in the States, came roaring back as he saw how truly desolate the country was. The monotonous landscape was sparsely studded with ruined villages, their little thatched-roof hovels hammered into the earth by the triple passage of war. And hanging over all like a rank caul, soiling the very wind, was the pervasive stink of human waste.

Young Second Lieutenant Menard, chunky and kitten-eager to please, had dropped down the rope to stand ankle-deep in the mud beside him, nose twitching, appalled.

"This is it?"

"This is it, Lieutenant, and it doesn't get any better."

They whirled to see the colonel stepping out of the classiest Jeep in the Orient. Francis Ostrowski had exercised his commander's privileges by equipping his Jeep with an aluminum top, a huge chromium-plated siren mounted on the left front fender, and a spotlight on the right. The whole Jeep had been painted fire-engine red, with a big white sign under the windshield that said THE BOSS.

Menard had stiffened into a brace as Ostrowski grabbed Marshall's hand.

"Glad to see you, Captain Marshall. I *need* some veterans! Mostly they send me green beans like young Menard here." He flashed Menard a big grin and said, "Welcome aboard, son."

Loading their kit in the Jeep, they roared toward the flight line, the exuberant Ostrowski talking to them as he drove, waving his arms, his curly head popping back in laughter. He was huge in every way—head, nose, hands, personality, the very image of a warrior enjoying himself.

"Welcome to the 61st Fighter Interceptor Wing, the best damn outfit in Korea. I ought to know, because I just came over from the 4th, and it's pretty damn good, too."

Menard was hanging on to the edge of the Jeep, trying to believe his good luck. Ozzie Ostrowski was a legend, wild, rambunctious, and an ace in two wars—not many second johns got a C.O. like him.

Ostrowski and Marshall had hit it off with the mutual approval of two people who discover they own the same breed of dog or drive the same make of car.

"Bones, come on in the ops shack; you've got a couple of old buddies waiting for you."

Marshall glanced around the base, noting that things had improved since Taegu. They weren't working out of tents. Instead, the engineers had cast concrete pads and put up two-by-four shacks framed with tar paper. The runway was concrete, there were neat revetments made of sandbag pyramids, and there was even a scattering of Quonset huts around the periphery, suggesting that maintenance was getting a little protection from the elements. If the war lasted another two years, there'd be regulation hangars, plush O-clubs, theaters, the works. Americans enjoyed fighting in a foreign country if they could bring their creature comforts with them.

When the door opened, Coleman and Fitzpatrick were waiting for him. Fitzpatrick put out his hand, and Coleman stepped back. Marshall hesitated, and then shook Fitz's hand, nodding to Coleman. Ostrowski sensed the awkwardness, and boomed, "Sit down, everybody, I want to get these new guys up to speed.

"First, the good news. We've got the best damn airplanes in the world, North American F-86Es. We can whip the MiG's ass any time he'll fight. Now the bad news. The bastards rarely want to fight. They're using this war as playschool for the Russian Air Force."

He sipped from a coffee mug. "It ain't like they're outnumbered or anything. They've got beaucoup MiGs over there across the border. Last April I saw five hundred, count 'em, five hundred, goddamn MiGs sitting at Ta-Tung-Kou airfield. If they'd let us, we could have shot fifty of them up on the ground. But no, we can't cross the Yalu."

He winked at Coleman and said, "Can we, Stan?" and Coleman shook his head. After a twenty-minute briefing Ostrowski said, "You three guys run along—I want to have a private conversation with Bones, here."

When the door closed he said, "Captain Marshall, I'm going to ask you for a favor, a confidential one. We've got a problem in this wing I hate to admit. We're *not* the best wing in Korea, far from it. We're not getting enough kills because some—*most*—of the guys aren't aggressive enough. I figure only twenty percent of them are intent on mixing it up. About seventy percent get into the combat zone, but for some reason they don't engage. I need flight leaders who will force combat to happen."

Ostrowski took a long pull at his cup—Marshall suspected there was something besides coffee in it—and lowered his voice.

"Coleman's a great pilot, none better. I've hassled with him in mock dogfights, and I know he's good. But he's been here three months, and I don't know if he's unlucky, incompetent, or scared—but he's not killing any MiGs. I want you to watch him, and tell me what you think. If he's just unlucky, I'll give him a little more time. If it's anything else, I'm going to send his ass back to the States."

"Colonel—"

"Call me Ozzie."

"Ozzie, I can't do it. I hate Coleman's guts, and he hates mine. You must have picked up on that. I couldn't be unbiased."

Ostrowski reached over and squeezed his arm. "Bones, don't give me that bullshit. I've got the book on you from the guys in the 18th and the 27th, both. You're the fairest guy in the business, that's why I'm asking you. Check that. That's why I'm telling you."

MiG Alley/June 1, 1952

Ahead, sun glinting on its wings, Coleman's F-86 was turning again; the four F-86s had about exhausted their patrol time on station—if the MiGs were going to attack, they'd do it soon, knowing the Sabres would be short on fuel.

Marshall felt guilty about feeling so at home, but the bashful MiGs made the threat seem remote. The next best thing to making love to Saundra was flying an airplane that cost nearly half a million dollars and was such a contrast to the primitive country below. To leave that abject poverty and operate this magic carpet was a joy. With more than a hundred controls to operate, two dozen instruments and warning lights to watch, and a big General Electric jet behind him putting out more horsepower than three diesel engines, Marshall felt as powerful as Superman, as comfortable as if he were in his daddy's Nash. He snuggled down in the cockpit, grateful for the heating and pressurization systems staving off the outside sixty-degrees-below temperature, letting the hottest fighter in the world fit him like skin fits a catfish. He wasn't flying it, he was wearing it, soaring eight miles above the ground at .8 Mach.

Visibility from the bathtub canopy was superb. Glancing down, he was amazed as always that the ground looked so different from the maps. On the flat surface of the briefing charts, the squiggles representing mountains were overrun with a well-defined circulatory system of neat red highways and blue rail lines. Yet the Korea spread out below him resembled an upended bowl of greenish-brown Wheaties, a topologist's dream of endlessly convoluted surface where roads and rail lines were just evanescent traces, disappearing with every turn. Occasionally, there would be a soft fragile smear of bluish vapor, wood smoke from a village that had been a self-important yellow square on the map.

Around him, the bright, impartial blue shed its death-cold light on two battle lines. One was the artificial Line Kansas, just dots marked on a map to show where the Eighth Army had been told to stop and where the Communist and the United Nations forces now stood in wary deadlock. The other was the natural battle line of the Yalu River, which formed the upper boundary of the craggy quadrangle making up MiG Alley.

Bones disliked flying number two behind Stan Coleman as much as the other man resented it. He'd been promised his own flight, and it was galling to be flying Coleman's wing like some kid just out of gunnery school, even though the C.O. had asked him to do it.

The first day Coleman had set him straight.

"Look, Marshall, I know what Ostrowski is doing, siccing you on me like a goddamn watchdog. So you just do your job in the air and keep your goddamn black ass out of my business on the ground."

His attitude didn't bother Marshall—he already knew how he felt, and Coleman's open dislike was easier to handle than hypocrisy. Yet he knew that something had happened to Coleman—his habits were totally different. He seemed driven, preoccupied, with all the old bullshit polish gone. Not much of a drinker before, now he was swilling it down. Most of the guys took an occasional drink, and lots of them would get completely snockered when they knew there was a stand-down, but Coleman drank steadily, standing at the bar until it closed, singing the inane fighter pilot songs, then puking his way back to his hut. Even the younger troops were avoiding him, and the C.O.—who did more than a little drinking himself—was worried about him.

But the most fundamental change was in his racist attitude toward Marshall. He had never concealed how he felt about Negroes in the past, but now he took pains to insult him. At first he had done it quietly, in private. Lately, he'd been bolder, especially in front of Fitzpatrick, goading Marshall like a schoolyard bully pressing for a fight. Well, if it came to that, so be it.

On the way up to MiG Alley, they flew in their close-knit "show formation," individual aircraft within three to four feet of each other, flights no more than seventy-five feet apart. Now they were in combat formation, listening to "Dentist," the radar site above K-14, tracking the various gaggles of MiGs. Traffic was heavy, as Dentist called, "Bandit Flight Number One over the Mizu," "Bandit Flight Number Two now on a heading to Race Track," and "Bandit Flight Number Three at Angels thirty-five over Antung." The calls made Marshall's mouth water—there were lots of MiGs out there to fight with. The Mizu was the big Sui-Ho reservoir on the Yalu, easy to pick out. Race Track was in the center of North Korea, where their formations tended to converge.

Coleman, hung-over and probably breathing 100 percent oxygen, chose instead to fly a routine patrol, watching across the Yalu. There, the MiGs from Antung were flying their usual parallel instructional parade, as peaceful as a Central American paseo.

Cruising across the river, Marshall counted eight flights of sixteen fighters each, 148 MiGs. Yet the MiGs were skittish, wary as streetwalkers worrying about an unmarked police car. As much as the bait tempted them, they didn't dare take on twenty-four American Sabres.

MiG Alley had become a Communist training ground, just as Spain had been in the thirties. The Russians had a regular curriculum to train their pilots at their protected Manchurian airfields. Each new class began with familiarization flights in the local area. Then came instructional patrols like this one appeared to be, just a promenade up and down the Alley. Toward the end of the course, they'd have a graduation exercise, and a few of the MiGs would take a plunging dive across the Yalu in a sixty-second hit-and-run attack. Then there'd be a few weeks of regular battles, the old class would graduate, and the new guys would come in. The Sabres flew at the very limits of their range, so patrols were often cut short or battles broken off. The MiGs took off and climbed in great sweeping circles over their own airfields. Their greater service ceiling always gave them a height advantage which easily converted into speed, and when the battle was over, they could glide home if they had to.

The MiGs could fly higher because they were lighter by almost four thousand pounds and powered by a derivative of a Rolls-Royce engine sold to them by the Brits. The Sabre had more armor, redundant systems, and better gunsights. In effect, the Russians were flying hotrod Fords while the Americans were flying Lincoln Continentals.

Bones watched Coleman begin his turn, flashing the 61st's broad bands of yellow edged in black on wing and fuselage, little wisps of vapor coming from the wingtips.

Lordy, what pretty airplanes. Too bad they couldn't cross that stupid river and wax some Communist ass.

Three hundred feet away, the flight's other element crossed over, Dave Menard flying on Fitzpatrick's wing. The remaining flights were strung out behind them, like cars on a toy train. Combat was supposed to be exciting, but not with Coleman leading.

No tiger, Coleman kept his patrol at a distance, never placing it where it might offer a tantalizing cheap shot to lure the MiGs into battle. There were fights going on elsewhere—they could hear the yips of the guys in the 4th, calling out the breaks, yelling when they got some hits.

Coleman was content to watch the enemy across the Yalu. It would have been a decent tactic if the aim was to keep them across the river—but the name of the game was to kill MiGs.

The Communists exercised an iron control over their fighters from the ground. Lately they'd taken to sending out two groups of MiGs, fifty or sixty in a pack. One would go down the west coast of Korea, another down the center. The planes would be strung out in long lines, quickly called "trains" by the U.S. radar sites observing them. The two groups would converge over Pyongyang, then let down as they headed back north, trying to pick off any U.S. fighter-bombers they could find. It was muscle, pure and simple, and the Russians knew it.

Marshall looked up to see his dream come true, two sections of MiGs diving toward them, their external fuel tanks fluttering behind them like plucked feathers.

Marshall called, "Red Leader, break right!" and Coleman responded immediately, turning into the MiGs, as the F-86s sent their own tanks tumbling away.

Marshall followed, heart pounding, fingers already trembling on the firing button, as the targets slipped away—it had only been a feint. The MiGs were already diving across the Yalu, secure in their Simon Says war, just taunting the Sabres.

Coleman's voice, suddenly high-pitched and nervous, said, "Red Flight, let's go home."

The four Sabres had just turned ninety degrees when the second flight of MiGs roared through them, their cannons burping little incandescent balls of fire that seemed to slow almost to a halt as they approached. Coleman reversed to follow them, and Marshall groaned. He should have gone up and over, they'd never catch them this way. Marshall kept on his wing, protecting his six o'clock position, feeling the G-forces build as the turn tightened.

Another flight of MiGs passed ahead of them, diving after Fitzpatrick and Menard. Breathing hard, Marshall called, "Red Three, break left," and Coleman swung in, changing places to fly as his wingman as Marshall flattened out into a turning circle behind the pretty brown MiGs.

"Take it easy, don't hyperventilate," Marshall told himself, trying to slow his breathing down as he kept the stick back. The Sabre's right wing had a tendency to stall in a turn, and he knew he'd have to flatten out a bit to keep his speed up. But with the F-86E's new slab tail, he had this pigeon cold—he could turn inside the MiG, no matter what the other guy did.

The MiG flight began to separate as they scrambled home toward the Yalu. Marshall fought off the urge to fire, even as he wished he had someone other than Coleman as his number two. He glanced back quickly, didn't see him, thought—The bastard's gone—and turned back to the MiG. He was at 410 knots at twenty thousand feet, not caring that the airspeed was above the red line. He reeled the MiG like a fish on a rod into his sights and fired, the six .50s hammering in the nose, knocking a couple of knots from his airspeed.

Fuel leaked from the MiG's wing and hot licks of white vapor streamed back out from the fuselage. Marshall's tongue stuck to the roof of his mouth as he watched his bullets sparkling on the brown surfaces, the enemy airplane making rough amateurish jinks to right and left, good for nothing more than slowing it down.

Suddenly, the MiG's rear fuselage blossomed like an opening flower as the little spade-shaped panels of the speed brakes popped out to slow it further. Marshall fired, and the MiG spouted smoke like blood from a harpooned whale. The burbling jet wash from the MiG jostled his Sabre as he fired again. The MiG seemed to smash into an invisible wall, disappearing into its own smoke and flames like a handkerchief into a magician's hand as Marshall roared past it, zooming up to the right, searching for Coleman, then reversing to come down for the kill.

Heading back, he found only a circle of white smoke and red flame marking the explosion.

Marshall was yelling, "Whooee, number four!" when his Sabre shuddered from cannon hits. Two MiGs were on his tail where Coleman should have been; they broke off as Menard came thundering after them.

Marshall tried to roll level and check the damage but could not; he was diving at Mach .95, his hydraulic pressure gone, his controls frozen. Now just a passenger in an aluminum sled, he tugged at the stick, trying to break the tight diving spiral, to escape the brown and green Wheaties earth spinning upward at him.

Throttle back, Marshall pulled with all his strength at the stick, trying to bring the wings level and get the nose up as the battered Sabre bumped at the speed of sound, the G-meter pegged. With no hydraulic pressure to help him, the violent pressure of near-sonic-speed air clamped a rock-solid lock on his controls. His oxygen mask slipped down as the sustained G-forces drained his vision away like a Hollywood fade-out.

Altitude melted as Marshall fought the airplane.

"Eject at twelve thousand feet," he told himself.

As the F-86 plunged through thirteen thousand feet, he actuated the canopy release. The pyrotechnic charge blew the canopy, but the python grip of G-forces kept it from clearing, jamming it into the fuselage structure like a chip into dip, sticking it up behind the cockpit in a great transparent air brake.

The shuddering Sabre slowed down abruptly, the speed falling through three hundred knots. Marshall evaluated the hazards of ejection over North Korea versus riding the airplane down and murmured, "Take a shot at it!"

Delaying the rest of his ejection sequence, he felt control grudgingly come back to his full-strength pull on the stick. By the time he reached 2,500 feet, he had the airplane flying again, heading back toward Suwon.

Marshall sat shivering in the cockpit, sucking on oxygen to fight off a nauseating fear of death. His fourth kill had been within seconds of being his last.

At Suwon, he made a long, careful approach, lowering the gear with the emergency system and landing without any brakes. He was towed in by a cheering ground crew, happy to see the black powder-marks of combat smeared back on the fuselage—they'd hold a drunken celebration tonight—and amazed to find the canopy sticking up aft of the cockpit like the lid of a sardine tin.

After debriefing, he'd rushed to the club, intending to celebrate.

"Hey, Bones, come join the party. Coleman got two kills."

"You're kidding me. What did he get?"

"He found two bombers down on the deck, TU-2s, and hammered them both. Come on in, he's buying."

Marshall walked away, the pleasure in his own kill gone. Instead of sticking to his wing, that goddamn Coleman—he should watch it; he was beginning to swear a lot—had gone hunting for stuff that was obsolete in World War II.

Later that afternoon, he had another private session with Colonel Ostrowski.

"What is there to say, Ozzie? He wasn't aggressive up at the Yalu, and when we swapped positions, he handed my ass on a platter to the MiGs. But then, he got his kills."

"Don't be too hard on him. He might have got slung out of position when you were turning with the MiGs, and then got carried away when he saw the bombers."

Knowing he didn't really mean it, Ostrowski shook his head. The wingman was there for one purpose, to cover the leader's ass, and nothing, not an easy shot at a target, nothing should intervene. The old "two holes in the ground" idea was the only rule—anything else and all the combat tactics became meaningless.

"Okay, you've got your own flight. Menard is coming along fast, and he has a lot of promise. Take him as your wingman. And I want you to know, I've got nothing personal against Coleman. Maybe being this close to being an ace will get him to start fighting. I'm too short-handed to send a veteran home. If he gets aggressive and starts mixing it up with the MiGs, that's all I ask for."

The Pentagon/August 15, 1952

Ruddick was not a generous man, but he gave Coleman credit for common sense. Stan could have made a lot of trouble about that insane business in Little Rock. Instead, he'd taken a gentleman's way out, simply leaving, going back to Korea.

Burying his face in hands he asked himself what was the matter with Ginny. How could she do that to him? Thank God she was only a stepdaughter.

Nathan had left town, a good thing; he'd had to have killed him. It made it impossible to continue to care for Marny—she was innocent, of course, but it had been her son. And money was tighter all the time.

It was annoying to be so dependent on the funds being funneled to him by Troy McNaughton. The Little Rock real estate market had gone from bad to worse, the oil business was stagnant, and the cost of supporting the Klan was back-breaking. Besides that, he had never been able to bring himself to part with the last shipment of paintings.

The only bright spot on the horizon was the B-47 subcontracting that McNaughton could do for Boeing. It would become a real money mill in the months to come, even if Troy McNaughton was losing his grip. He was sick, but in Ruddick's book that was no excuse. Hell, look how Harry Hopkins and Roosevelt had carried on, dead on their feet, but still running the country. The cancer was destroying McNaughton emotionally, turning him into a terrified husk of a man.

He poured himself a shot of rye whiskey and sat sipping it. He had ambivalent feelings about McNaughton's illness, taking a certain ruthless pleasure in a younger man being on the verge of checking out. Yet Troy had always been smart, and fair, being professional enough to stay just this side of unreasonable in his demands for contracts, while always being generous in return. Who knew what his successor might be like?

The thought of dealing with Elsie put him off. It was all right for her to play executive, to act as a manager, but he didn't want to deal with her personally. He knew that she was tough—but he wasn't really sure how smart she was; yet if something happened to Troy, she would be the wild card—either the solution or the problem, he wasn't sure which.

There were some options. He already had his own man in the plant. Helmut Josten had done a good job smuggling paintings out of Germany, being ingenious or ruthless, as required, and had been given the job at McNaughton as a reward. It's too bad that he was too ugly for Elsie, who didn't bother to conceal her dislike of him. With Troy gone, Josten's usefulness would diminish—it might be better to take him to Little Rock.

He overfilled his whiskey glass and drank again. Dipping his fingers in the spill, he doodled little circles on the walnut table top, trying to see the opportunities that he knew lurked in McNaughton's illness. Baker was an arrogant oaf, but bribeable. Ruddick suspected that Baker had something going on with Elsie—they were just too cozy when they thought no one was watching.

The best solution of all would be Stan. He surely didn't intend to stay in the Air Force, and he wouldn't want to stay in Little Rock, not anymore. If he could persuade Stan to take a job with McNaughton when he came back, it might work out. Stan could handle Elsie, and he could handle Stan.

Ruddick glanced up at the big schoolroom clock, black numbers on a white background. It was time to savor a little revenge. The Senate Permanent Subcommittee on Investigations was meeting today, chaired by the estimable Senator Joseph R. McCarthy. And today's principal witness would be none other than that murdering son of a bitch, Frank Bandfield, the man who'd killed his son.

Bandfield was angry, pugnacious—and a little bit scared. He'd been in combat in two wars, shot down twenty enemy planes, even been shot down a few times himself, but he'd never been as furious as this. To have his loyalty impugned by this malignant growth, this villainous, stubble-jawed senator from Wisconsin, was an infamy.

Yet it was a frightening process as well. He was intimidated by the long marble halls of the Senate Office Building, by the serried ranks of jaded reporters, by the flashes of the cameras, and by the certain knowledge that McCarthy would ask loaded questions and twist any answers. It was going to be a field day for the press. He'd been reading the papers, and while the reporters didn't seem to like

McCarthy, they made capital out of all his charges—if there had been any retractions, any apologies, he hadn't seen any.

Bandfield had three lawyers with him. Two were longtime friends from California, and they were nervous, too. They had insisted on bringing in a local lawyer, George Robinson, who had a terrific reputation and was supposed to be familiar with dealings on the Hill. A huge man, with close-cropped black hair and a sardonic manner, he didn't seem very optimistic. And Bandfield felt like a yokel when Robinson reached over and carefully cut a price tag from the sleeve of the new sharkskin suit he'd bought for the occasion.

Bandy was surprised that everything took so much time, and that there were so many interruptions. Here in the nation's capital, the whole procedure had an antic, country courthouse feeling, with people dashing in and out of the hearing room, young staffers whispering into committee members' ears, laughter rising up from remarks he didn't even understand—and absolutely nothing happening regarding his testimony.

Finally, however, the senator appeared, talking in quick asides to two young aides who seemed the personification of malevolence, one short and balding, with protruding eyes like evil soft-boiled eggs, the other with the too-soft look of a women's magazine male model. McCarthy moved quickly, holding his head down like a hound on the trail.

After a lot of flesh-pressing, the hearings finally opened, amid an interminable amount of preliminary chatter. Bandfield had focused on his anger, telling himself that he was as patriotic as any man in the room, that he had fought in a dozen battles, that—

"He's talking to you, Mr. Bandfield." The Washington lawyer nudged him.

Startled, he sat up. "I'm sorry, Senator, would you repeat that, please?"

McCarthy shot a raised eyebrow at his aide and in voice slick as drain oil, said, "Certainly, Mr. Bandfield, it was a difficult question. I asked if your name was Frank Bandfield, and if you had served in the U.S. Army Air Forces?"

"Yes, sir, to both questions."

"Did you also serve in the Loyalist Air Force—the Communist Air Force—in Spain, in 1937?"

"Yes, sir, but I was—"

"Just answer my questions for now, Mr. Bandfield. You'll be allowed ample time to make a statement later." He turned to whisper to the young aide with the evil-egg eyes.

"Now, Mr. Bandfield, were you not a friend and confidant of General Henry Caldwell?"

"Yes, sir." Bandfield was puzzled—and worried—about questions on Caldwell.

"You feel you helped General Caldwell?"

"Yes, sir, that was my job. I was his trouble-shooter; he sent me—"

"Mr. Bandfield, we have a lot of people here whose time is valuable, and it would be most helpful if you would just answer the questions"—he paused—"and leave your excuses till later. Mr. Bandfield, I'm very sure that you are aware of what I'm about to say, but others may not be. General Caldwell was one of the primary architects of the Lend-Lease plan to Russia, particularly in regard to the supply of aircraft. Do you feel that he was of great assistance to the Soviet Union?"

"Yes, sir. There were a great many other people—"

"Just answer my questions, please."

"Yes, sir."

"Thank you. I'll go on to another matter now. I believe that you and your wife sponsored the immigration to the United States of a European woman and her son. Is that correct?"

Bandfield was angry and his lawyer restrained him.

"Yes, sir."

"What nationality was this woman?"

"She came from Sweden." Robinson jabbed him hard in the ribs. "She came from Sweden, but she was originally from Russia."

McCarthy conferred with his aide again. They laughed together, more congratulatory than conspiratorial, clearly enjoying themselves.

"Mr. Bandfield, do you presently hold a Reserve commission as a colonel—a full colonel, a bird colonel, I believe it is called, I'm a Navy man myself—in the U.S. Air Force?"

"Yes, sir."

"And you are now on active duty?"

"Temporarily, yes."

The senator smiled. "Temporarily. That may be truer than you know. And, Colonel Bandfield, are you a principal in the firm called Roget Aircraft, Incorporated?"

Robinson conferred briefly with Bandfield, who said, "Yes."

"What does that firm do?"

"We rebuild aircraft for service with the United States Air Force."

"And you don't find it unusual that an officer in the Air Force, on active duty, would be the recipient of contracts from that same Air Force, contracts worth millions of dollars?"

"No, sir. I've been involuntarily recalled—in fact, every time I've ever gone into the service, it's been involuntary."

McCarthy scowled at the general laughter. "Mr. Robinson, you are more familiar with proceedings like this than Mr. Bandfield. Would you ask him to make simple, direct answers to my questions?"

"Yes, I will, Senator, but this is not a trial. I believe it would be helpful to get more of Mr. Bandfield's views on the record."

"You know that there will be ample opportunity to do so."

Bandfield started to speak, but Robinson tapped his arm, saying, "Senator, Mr. Bandfield has been a principal of this firm since 1932. His ownership is well known to the Air Force, and his having a Reserve commission has not been a factor in obtaining contracts. And, as he points out, he has been recalled involuntarily. I happen to know that his recall was at the personal request of General Varney."

"Counselor, I know you have a distinguished reputation, but I want to assure you that though I'm from a great agricultural state, which you Washingtonians think is populated by gullible farmers, I am not naive."

His voice had lowered, but now he raised it, changing the tone from soothing to savage. "Nor are the members of the press, nor is the American public. Colonel Bandfield is a blatant example of one of the great problems in our system, the mutually profitable interdependence of the military and industry. But that is the least of it."

As he stared at Bandfield, he popped two white pills in his mouth like a chicken tossing off kernels of corn, then took a long drink of water. Both pills and water had been served to him like Communion by the younger staff member. He orchestrated the little ceremony, protracting it, his eyes burning above the raised glass as if the water fueled his fire.

Then, he daintily patted his lips with a handkerchief. "That is by far the least of it, the diversion of taxpayers' funds into his pocket. I suggest, Colonel Bandfield, that although you are an officer in the U.S. Air Force, and you have acted as a contractor for that distinguished service, you are in fact a Communist fellow traveler, and there is no guarantee whatever that the products you are making millions on are not in fact sabotaged at the factory you control."

Bandfield was almost out of his chair when Robinson's huge hand pulled him back down.

The lawyer rose quietly to his feet, fussing with some papers as if he had a prepared response, obviously wanting to make sure that his voice was cool and unemotional.

"Your allegation is uncalled for, Senator. Colonel Bandfield's service in the Air Corps, in the U.S. Army Air Forces, and now in the U.S. Air Force has always been at the behest of the government. He is a distinguished combat veteran, an ace with twenty victories—"

McCarthy broke in. "Yes, eleven of them fighting for the Communists in Spain. He's an ace all right, a Russian ace!"

Robinson flushed. "It is unconscionable to suggest that he is anything but a patriot."

The young man whispered to McCarthy again, and the Senator rose. "Thank you, Counselor, for your views. I think that the subcommittee will draw a different conclusion. And I think it is criminal that a fellow traveler like Colonel Bandfield can profit so hugely from contracts from a government that he has actively tried to subvert for almost twenty years!" There was a ringing theatrical tone to his voice, a gravelly accusatory note that hung in the air above the clicking flashbulbs. He was savoring the moment, a little Mussolini behind the small balcony of his desk.

"Worse than that, this fellow traveler could be eligible for a pension, so that in his old age he would still be drawing on the blood of the country he has betrayed for so long." He paused again for effect. "Well, he will *not* have a pension, nor a commission, nor any government contracts, if this subcommittee has anything to say about it. I have to go to vote now, and so this meeting is adjourned until tomorrow at the same time."

The roar in the courtroom mercifully drowned out Bandfield's shout, "You bald son of a bitch, come down here and fight."

In the back of the room, Milo Ruddick smiled. It was enough. McCarthy's accusations had been backed by a sufficient basis in fact. The papers would do the rest. Even if nothing else happened, even if Bandfield got his story on the record, everyone would understand if the Roget Aircraft contracts were shifted elsewhere, perhaps even to McNaughton.

And McCarthy—or his staffer, more likely—was sharp, bringing up the matter of Bandfield's retirement. No doubt they would force him to resign his commission. It was a tidy bonus of revenge for poor Bob at Cleveland.

Washington, D.C./September 3, 1952

Erich Weissman liked to come into Scholl's Cafeteria on Connecticut Avenue at twelve-thirty, exactly one half-hour before he took lunch. It gave him a heady pleasure just to be near so much food, to walk down the line (outside the rail, of course—he didn't want to bother anyone) and examine the range of dishes.

Then he'd sit and imagine that he could put some of his friends from Dachau through the line, transporting them in time and space, suddenly to present them with this feast.

They were all dead, killed and burned eight years ago. But how they would have enjoyed it. He laughed to himself—they used to enjoy a potato peel, a frozen turnip, anything. The steaming line at Scholl's would have been too much for them, of course, but it was a pleasant fantasy—after all, if he could imagine those wraithlike skeletons alive, he could imagine them eating all they wished.

When he finally went through the line, he ate simply—usually some bread, bad as the American stuff was, soup, and a piece of fruit. Habit. And thrift. The stipend he received from the nameless people in Israel didn't permit high living and hardly covered the travel he had to do.

It was to have been his last day in Washington on this strange assignment. For the first time, his target was not a German expatriate but an American. He had become expert in eradicating people and making it appear like routine crimes. It was going to be tough to do that in an orderly, peace-loving town like Washington.

K-13, Suwon, Korea/September 15, 1952

Marshall knew he was earning his pay, no doubt about that, and Ostrowski was already openly referring to him as "my maintenance genius." The week after he had arrived, Ozzie had immediately assigned him the additional duty job of "Special Assistant to the Commander, for Maintenance." The job title caused immediate resentment with the group maintenance officer because it meant Ozzie considered his work unsatisfactory.

And it was. Half of the F-86s were AOCP—out of commission for parts—primarily a lack of replacement engines. Bones nosed around and found out that there were plenty of engines waiting to be shipped out to Japan for overhaul, but there were not enough engine dollies to mount them on. The dollies were relatively simple structures, designed to transport engines easily without damaging them.

He collared his young wingman Menard and told him they were going to take a personal count. They found twenty-four engines awaiting overhaul, supported on sandbags because there were no engine dollies available.

For the next four hours they walked the base, poking into hangars, looking in trucks. By six o'clock they had found fourteen dollies stuck away in odd corners, covered by tarpaulins or being used for nonessential purposes. One had been converted to an altar by stacking boards on it and draping it with cloth.

Menard kicked down the door of a locked-up Quonset at the edge of the field.

"Bingo, Bones! Look at this." There were another eight brand-new dollies, still in their crates. "Let's go to the maintenance shack!"

"No, we'll do it my way."

Bones was popular with the troops and arranged for an early morning work party of a hundred airmen from different units—headquarters, mess hall, the motor pool.

"Okay—let's put four men on a dolly and form up in a column of fours. Menard, you lead the parade in Ozzie's Jeep. I'll be in the M.O.'s office."

At nine o'clock, Marshall was talking to the M.O. about a parts problem, when the siren on Ozzie's Jeep blared. The maintenance officer groaned as Bones followed him out of the room. Menard came by, standing up in the rear of the Jeep saluting, followed by a parade of twenty dollies, each one pushed by airmen.

Marshall didn't say another word to the maintenance officer—he didn't have to.

The dollies were just a start. The Sabres were chronically short of a whole variety of parts, primarily because the paperwork and the chain of command intervened. Without any authorization, Marshall placed an order with the North American civilian technical representatives on the field for a quarter of a million dollars' worth of the items in shortest supply. North American, entirely at its own risk, chartered an air freighter and shipped the parts immediately. Within ten days of his request, the parts were on the field, being installed. As far as the paperwork went, he assumed that someone would sort it out later, or else he'd go to jail.

Dave Menard turned into a first-rate officer in the process. At first Marshall would have to pull him away from the volleyball court or the makeshift baseball diamond—sports were big at Suwon. But within days, Menard had taken the challenge, and, following Bones's lead, got his hands greasy changing brakes or pulling engines. Some of the senior NCOs tried to hard-time him at first, but by varying his good humor with tough military discipline, Menard gained their respect. Between flying days and working nights, the two men grew close, and it dawned on Marshall that Menard was the first real friend he'd made since Bayard Riley. It helped a lot.

Around midnight, another young flyer was approaching Suwon, feeling lonely and friendless. La Woon Yung was a proud man, but his shame was great as he slipped his PO-2 biplane through the pitch-black Korean night at eighty knots. Windblown and almost deafened by the irregular pop-pop-popping of the small radial engine, the young pilot peered ahead for the glimmer of lights. Under his wings were two small bombs useful primarily for disrupting sleep.

Yung had wanted to fly MiGs but hadn't been skilled enough, and they had relegated him to this laughable job of dropping firecrackers. Women pilots had flown the same wood and fabric crate during the Great Patriotic War; it was a disgrace.

The well-lit airfield lay ahead, beyond the blur of the village, surrounded by a moving ring of headlights as trucks passed around its perimeter. The arrogant Americans used more electricity on a single base than a whole Korean city used. They had not detected him yet—the lights were still on and there was no antiaircraft fire. La Woon Yung pulled the bomb release with total indifference as he passed over the parked F-86s and then turned north.

A bank of clouds ahead blossomed with the sudden reflected glare of the explosion, and he banked around to see an F-86 burning fiercely on the ramp. Keeping the little PO-2 cocked on its wing, he noted that there were other fires. Elated, he considered returning to survey the damage and decided against it. They would learn the results from the local people by tomorrow morning. He was one of the first North Korean pilots to destroy an F-86. He would surely be decorated; perhaps he could ask to be reassigned to MiG 15 training. The war had taken quite a different turn!

At eleven the next morning, Marshall began to have serious concerns about his C.O.'s sanity. Ostrowski was still raving like a lunatic nine hours after the incident, screaming that he wouldn't stand for clapped-out pissant trainers destroying his fighters. So far he'd threatened to fire everybody in the world, from Truman on down to the firemen who had managed to contain the damage to one aircraft destroyed and four damaged.

The week before, Marshall had been given Able Squadron and told to do whatever he wanted with it, as long as he got some kills. Now didn't seem to be the best time to present his new plan of operations, but he took a shot at it. "Colonel, maybe this'll help. Let me tell you how we can get another twenty minutes on station, and get some more kills."

"Kills, kills, by God I want some kills right here on base. How in hell can I run an operation if North Korean lightplanes shoot the shit out of me? I . . ."

Marshall let him rant for a while, then cut in. "We were spending too much time on the ground and in the climb-out. From now on, Able Squadron is going to eliminate the engine run-up and emergency fuel checks on the ramp, and we'll make running takeoffs. We're going to stop circling over the field to join formation; instead I'm going to head straight for MiG Alley, and the troops will form up as we climb. When we get to our combat altitude, we're going to be cruising at a minimum of .8 Mach."

Ostrowski was beginning to calm down, listening closely. "The safety officer's going to be down on you like a ton of bricks—you're talking about violating procedures."

Marshall took a chance, using Ostrowski's language instead of his own. "Fuck him." The verb stretched out as if it had four U's in it. "Who's the C.O. of this outfit, you or the safety officer?"

As Ostrowski's rage ebbed, Marshall told him the next part of his plan. Official policy, straight from the President, demanded that there be no intrusion into neutral Chinese airspace, not even in hot pursuit. But there had been signals recently that General Frank McKinley, the new commanding general of the Fifth Air Force, would look the other way on a border violation, if it was done quickly and well.

"You don't have to hear this. But if I see any MiGs I'm going to hit them, no matter which side of the Yalu they're on."

Beaming now, Ostrowski said, "I didn't hear it, but I like it! When do you start?"

"Tomorrow morning. But there's one more thing. I'm going to schedule my troops to have a practice dogfight on every mission we don't engage the MiGs."

"Go get 'em, Tiger."

As Marshall walked away, he realized he liked the sound of his own tactics, and particularly the sound of the words *my troops*.

That night, on the way back from the mess hall, he bumped into Coleman and Fitzpatrick, suited up for flying, but not carrying their hard hats.

He made an effort to be civil. Coleman was the C.O. of Baker Squadron, and they had to get along, and Bones asked, "You guys on the roster?"

As usual, Coleman didn't speak, but Fitz said, "Yeah, on Bedcheck Charlie's roster. We borrowed a T-6 from the Mosquito Squadron. Our armament guys stuffed a thirty-caliber machine gun in it. We're going out to loiter around the edge of the field around midnight and see if we can hammer him."

"Don't bust your ass."

Marshall walked away, resentful of Coleman's continuing hostility, and thinking that it wasn't very smart to risk two veteran pilots to shoot down some poor North Korean PO-2. Then it hit him. It was part of the change. Coleman had the ace bug as bad as he did—and a victory was a victory, PO-2 or MiG.

At midnight Coleman and Fitzpatrick were circling at four thousand feet. The base wasn't lit up as it was the night before, but the pressure for maintenance kept enough lights on for Bedcheck Charlie to find it.

Fitz had ferried the T-6 over from Taegu West, complete with its standard armament of twelve 2.25 aircraft rockets the FACs used for marking targets. He hadn't flown a T-6 in years, but he'd conned the C.O. of the FAC squadron into thinking that he was a high-time instructor in the airplane. The machine gun had been in storage, and it took the armament boys less than two hours to get it installed and belted up.

Airplanes spoke to Fitz the way marble speaks to a sculptor, and he was perfectly comfortable, even in the rear seat, content to be airborne, willing to let Coleman take the credit if the PO-2 showed up and they got lucky. One of a fast-disappearing breed of pilots, he had no interest in promotion or glory. He liked to fly airplanes, all kinds, fast or slow, and as long as the Air Force would let him do that, he'd be happy. He had volunteered for F-86s because they were the hottest thing around, but he had no special interest in shooting anyone down. He'd seen enough combat to know that it was mostly waiting and then blam, instant terror, as some poor schmo got killed. Guys like Coleman and Marshall amused him—they liked to fly, but they were really interested in getting ahead.

Yet Coleman was a handy guy to know, and he was probably going places—his kind always did.

In the front seat of the T-6, Coleman had turned down all the instrument lights to let his eyes acclimate. It was up to him to pick up the PO-2. Radar was no help against the little biplanes, wood and fabric ferrets slinking down the Korean valleys. But if the PO-2 crossed the field, he'd be silhouetted against the lights.

They were loafing along at 100 mph, nose high, Fitz amusing himself doing perfect pylon eights using the middle of the field as the pivot point; he'd just passed through top dead center of his turn when Coleman yelled, "I got it! There he is!"

Two thousand feet below, an elated La Woon Yung, head still turning from last night's praise, toggled off his bombs and turned his PO-2 north. Just beyond the field boundaries, he circled, hoping to see a repeat of the previous evening. There was a small fire, but nothing important. Disappointed, he straightened out as Coleman came level behind him.

"Watch your airspeed."

Fitz was nervous—Coleman was slamming the airplane around at eighty knots, nibbling at a stall, too slow for comfort in drastic turns.

"I'm just going to fire and walk the bullets in on him."

Coleman pressed the firing button. Nothing.

"Jesus, this mother's armed, but it's not firing."

La Woon Yung glanced back, saw the T-6 and half-rolled his PO-2, split-S'ing toward the ground to disappear like sugar into coffee.

"Where'd he go?"

"Coleman, drop the gear. I got the fucking airplane."

As Coleman hit the hydraulic button and slammed the gear lever down, Fitz closed the throttle and shoved the T-6's nose forward.

"Drop fifteen degrees of flaps; be ready to haul the gear up if I call for it."

Coleman was disoriented as Fitz pulled the T-6's nose up.

"Gear up—look out at about the two o'clock position, low."

Coleman's peripheral vision picked up the phantom of the PO-2 flickering over the treetops.

"You figure out the fucking guns yet?"

"Still not working."

"Okay. Arm the rockets, and fire when I tell you to."

La Woon Yung had lost sight of the T-6 and had straightened out, anxious to get back to his own lines, to enjoy again the respect given a Sabre-killer.

Fitz wallowed in at low speed behind the little biplane, making coarse control inputs to track it. Visibility was bad from the backseat, so Fitz crabbed as if he were side-slipping in to land. He knew that if the enemy pilot saw them, he would be able to evade—there was no way the T-6 could maneuver with him. As the North Korean drew closer, Fitzpatrick felt a curious mathematical detachment, interested more in analyzing the performance of an unfamiliar airplane flown in awkward circumstances than concern that he was about to kill. He realized that he was as annoyed with Coleman for not being able to make the machine gun work as he was irritated that the Korean was ruining an otherwise perfect night for flying. Still, they had business to do.

"When I say fire, salvo all twelve."

"Roger." Coleman leaned down to make sure the firing panel was set correctly.

Fitz eased the power on and slid the T-6 directly behind the PO-2, creeping up on it until he was within fifty yards.

"Fire."

The T-6 disappeared momentarily in an incandescent ball of flame and smoke as the twelve rockets left their rails. Seven of them missed the PO-2 entirely. Two hit its wings, one passed harmlessly through the fuselage, one hit its fuel tank, and one exploded when it struck La Woon Yung in the back. He had been a hero for exactly twenty-four hours.

"Great shooting, Coleman. That gives you number four."

In the front seat, ecstatic, Coleman missed the irony.

6

Panmunjom, Korea/September 22, 1952

At Kaesong, the only real agreement had been to move the conference site to Panmunjom, where the peace talks quickly grounded to a halt over a single issue—the forced repatriation of Chinese and North Korean prisoners. The United Nations insisted that it would not force anyone to return to North Korea or China against their will, while the Communists insisted that it was not a negotiable matter. While the perfectly uniformed, frigidly discourteous negotiators fumed at each other across their green baize–covered tables, neatly punctuated with water carafes and lined tablets, terrified young infantrymen on both sides died in petty attacks across the bloody ridge lines. Simultaneously, ominously, the biggest buildup of airpower in the jet age began. By September, U.S. intelligence reported that the Communist air order of battle had seven thousand planes, primarily jet fighters and jet bombers, disposed in an arc around Korea. At the sharp end of the United Nations stick were less than two hundred Sabres.

West of MiG Alley/September 22, 1952

There might be seven thousand enemy planes out there—but Marshall wasn't getting any more MiGs than he was getting sex. He wondered what Saundra was doing; the time difference made it hard to compute—he figured she'd be working at the office. It was six at night in Los Angeles—and yesterday! He could hardly wait to recross the international date line on his way back to revive their marriage.

Yet other than the pain of missing her, he was content. His new tactics saved fuel and added spectacularly to the loiter time in MiG Alley. Ostrowski had ordered the two other squadrons to follow suit and today he was flying lead with Baker Squadron, Menard on his wing, and a sour-faced Coleman in the number three position to see how things worked.

It had been an improbable week. They had flown twelve sorties and engaged only three times, but Fitzpatrick had knocked down his first MiG with a long-range deflection shot. The gun-camera films looked like an Annie Oakley trick. The MiG was just barely visible, high in the corner of the frame, when Fitz's tracers arched out like a necklace of car headlights on a hill, and blam! no more MiG.

Strangely, Fitzpatrick had seemed discomfited rather than pleased. Menard was far more elated when he got a probable. The only thing assuaging Marshall's fast-deflating ego was the fact that Coleman hadn't scored either, mostly because he persisted in spending time down on the deck looking for more sitting-duck TU-2s. Well, he wouldn't today, not with Bones Marshall leading. He laughed at the memory of Coleman's face when he announced that the flight would turn off its IFF—Identification, Friend or Foe—signal as soon as it reached altitude and maintain radio silence. Fitzpatrick had shrugged and Menard was too green to know that it meant they were going to penetrate Manchuria.

All the recent intelligence briefings had confirmed what everyone had long suspected—the Russians were flying the MiGs. One pale-faced, red-haired pilot had been observed bailing out. More important, they were operating the extensive ground radar control net. All enemy communications were now in Russian.

The Russian ground controllers exercised authority that was unbelievable to an American pilot. Ground told them when to take off, where to go, when and if to attack, what field to return to. Even more incredible, the pilot even asked for decisions about whether to eject from a damaged MiG. It was absurd—there was no way any ground controller, no matter how experienced, could tell what to do in a dogfight, or analyze what was wrong with a shot-up MiG. Yet the report was comforting—it left the airborne initiative in American hands despite the disparity in numbers.

Immediately alert as his earphones buzzed with preliminary static, he heard Dentist calling, "Hemlock Leader, I have forty-plus MiGs climbing through twenty-five thousand at Antung." The controller's Southern drawl brought back unpleasant memories of Tuskegee.

He didn't acknowledge the call. He was already clearly illegal, over the Yellow Sea, thirty miles north of the Manchurian border.

"Hemlock Leader, Bandit Flight Two, another twenty plus MiGs climbing through twenty thousand at Antung. Acknowledge." It sounded like Aaaahk-nldge.

Good. Sixty to four—the odds were just about right, for this time the F-86s would have the altitude and speed. One slashing attack through the MiG train, clobber a few MiGs, then back across the Yalu to the regular patrol point to switch on the IFF with nobody the wiser.

"Hemlock Leader, acknowledge if you read. Bandit Flight One now splitting up, about half going heading three-sixty, half one-eighty. Over."

Splitting up! Even better, now the odds were down to maybe five to one, less than the current eight-to-one kill ratio, Sabres to MiGs.

As his eyes made the customary circuit around the sky, a quick glance in the cockpit to check the instruments, then out to check the sky again, Marshall picked up the MiGs, the two flights drawing apart like frightened schools of fish. The group heading south was a more attractive target, because the line of attack would take the F-86s directly toward the Yalu. But he could see Bandit Flight Two also headed south—too many to run into after a fight.

And the group going north were probably new arrivals, out on an area familiarization flight, a bunch of Ivans just in from the farm. With a hunter's skill he closed, positioning his Sabres above three flights, eight MiGs each, level at thirty-five thousand feet, all utterly unaware that there was an American within a hundred kilometers.

Without a word, Marshall punched off his tanks, and a quick glance showed him that the other three in the flight had followed suit.

Marshall put the nose of his Sabre down. "Hemlock Leader will take the second pair, second flight, last section. Hemlock Three, you take the first pair. We'll dive right through them, then turn and head south."

There were no acknowledgments as the four Sabres, yellow stripes on silver skins, dove toward the unsuspecting MiGs.

A look back showed that Menard was right where he should be, protecting him, letting him devote all his attention to the shooting. He was turning out to be a good wingman, a good man.

Taking the classic high-side approach, Marshall closed to two hundred yards and began firing. Shedding pieces from its tail like a molting pigeon, the MiG rolled sharply as the pilot ejected without asking the ground controllers anything.

Tabasco-hot pride surged through Marshall. Shouting "God-damn, that makes it official, I'm an ace!" he jerked the controls to shift his sights to the next plane, flying straight and level, still unaware that the Sabres were on top of it. As the pipper covered the MiG, Marshall squeezed the trigger, and the violent concentration of hits blew parts from the aircraft, slowing it as if it had thrown an anchor overboard.

As he screamed, "That's six!" his aircraft shook with a jarring thud like a motorboat hitting a submerged log.

"Red Leader's hit!" he called as his power fell off and eye-watering smoke from burning oil and hydraulic fluid poured into the cockpit from his pressurization ducts.

Retarding the throttle, he threw the stick over, blue sky and green-gray earth swapping places as he went inverted, tugging hard on the stick to enter a steep dive. Looking behind, he could see Menard was climbing away with two MiGs on his tail. Where were Coleman and Fitz?

Leveling off at fifteen thousand feet, Marshall eased the throttle back on and the engine responded with power. As he peered through the oil-smeared canopy he realized with relief that he hadn't been hit after all, that the burning fluids he'd smelled had been sucked out of the debris of the MiG to burn in his engine and to blow through the pressurization system into the cockpit.

Climbing back up to rejoin Menard, he looked for MiGs, Coleman and Fitzpatrick—in that order. His neck was chafed and sore from swiveling, but he didn't see the four MiGs attacking until their cannon shells pounded his fuselage. Half-rolling instinctively, he split-S'd away, sticking the powder-blackened Sabre nose straight toward the green-brown hills below, hoping that Menard or Coleman could come to his assistance.

Two of the MiGs stayed with him. They were obviously honchos, patient, content to have him diving toward the north away from the Yalu and the safety of his own lines, knowing that he was already short of fuel and ammunition.

He rolled level, and the yellow-red lines of cannon fire reached out for him. Marshall half-rolled once more, diving for the deck, no longer worried about having enough fuel to get home, or finding Menard, just concentrating on shaking these two implacable enemies. It was his last dive—he was out of altitude and damn near out of ideas. He headed for the coast, jinking at low level below the ridges, the trees just a blur, throttle to the firewall, waiting for the MiGs to finish him off. A black wall of flak opened up ahead of him, shutting off the horizon like a theater curtain dropping.

A glance told him he was passing over the edge of Feng-cheng, a new airfield stocked with MiGs and studded with radar-directed antiaircraft guns. Flying in a filthy black cocoon of flak, he skipped like an airborne Eliza from one smoky, iron-filled cloud to the next.

"Keep on, one more minute, I'll be out of here . . ."

An explosion like colliding locomotives shattered the airplane, and the Sabre went slack in his hands as life drained out of it. Choking in the black smoke that filled the cockpit, he eased the canopy partially open, trading the risk of sucking flames into the cockpit for enough visibility to see the instrument panel.

His tailpipe temperature soaring into the red confirmed the fire down below; he could blow up in the next second. Where were the MiGs? He looked behind him, then sacrificed some of his precious speed to roll the aircraft steeply left and right to make sure he was alone. The MiGs were gone, either called home, or confident that he was a goner.

Speed leaked from the Sabre like sugar from a punctured bag as he limped along a river at 160 knots, flying nose up, defenseless. His compass spun mindlessly, but the sun told him he was heading west, toward the Yellow Sea, toward the coast where a Sea-Air Rescue Albatross might come to rescue him. There'd be a chance for rescue off the coast—and he didn't want to eject in Manchuria. "As long as the damn thing keeps flying, I'll fly it."

Cannon shells shook the Sabre again as a flight of two North Korean Yak 9s closed behind him. Piston-engined fighters from the Second World War, resembling a cross between a Mustang and a Spitfire, they were far faster than his crippled F-86. Scared as he was, he knew the glee the two Yak pilots felt, sitting there, pumping cannon shells into his Sabre, knowing that even crippled, he'd count as a kill. The F-86 sagged as every emergency light on Marshall's instrument panel lit up. Ahead, the river's delta land looked reasonably flat. He blew the canopy and cut the throttle, deciding to belly in before they blew him up.

Touching down at 120 knots, the nose bulldozed into the river's edge, sending aircraft tumbling end-over-end like a tossed boomerang. With a suction pump squash, it plopped down, disappearing right-side up in a geyser of debris. The F-86 surfaced like a marshmallow in a cup of chocolate, and Bones sat in the cockpit, not certain if he were still alive, hoping that the plane didn't burn, that his ejection seat wouldn't fire.

Reaching up to grab the cockpit side to crawl out, a blinding pain from his left arm told him he was alive and badly hurt. With agonizing effort, he pushed himself upright with his legs alone, steadied himself, then slid over the cockpit side to fall face down into the mud welling up over the wing, wishing desperately that it was a dream, that he was really home in bed with Saundra.

The two Yaks turned in, guns spitting, the ground erupting in four lines, a mud picket fence rising and falling from the muck-sucking explosions of the cannon shells. Bones hugged the wet earth face down, the pain in his arm as excruciating as the terror in his heart.

Satisfied, the victorious Yaks came back one last time, a hundred meters in the lead. Marshall peeked up to see the first Yak do an impeccable victory roll just over his head, the pilot's head briefly visible in the cockpit as it snapped past him. The second Yak pilot, probably an excited kid just out of flying school, came in a little lower on his pass and forgot to keep forward pressure on his stick at the top of the roll. Dishing out at the three-quarter point, he went nose down into the river bed, punctuating the end of his short life with a magnificent explosion of gas, oil, and mud.

Bones let the silence descend for the second time in five minutes, wondering despite his pain if he could claim the Yak as his third kill of the day.

Offutt Air Force Base, Nebraska/ September 22, 1952

"Sit down, Riley. Do you know why you are here?"

General Curtis E. LeMay was only forty-six, but a decade of war and responsibility had chiseled his perpetually unshaven face into a harsh mask. His voice was low and slickly abrasive, a well-lubricated grinding wheel honing every word razor sharp.

"No, sir. Except that I flew with the 27th Fighter-Escort Wing."

"What's that mean?"

"The 27th is a SAC outfit—"

"For Christ's sakes, Colonel, don't tell *me* who the 27th belongs to!" Exasperated, LeMay shuffled some papers on his desk. "Larry Gunter tells me you are a first-rate operator and a fine pilot. Is that right?"

Answers whipped through Riley's mind, and he picked the safest. "Yes, sir."

"Well, I don't need first-rate operators, and I've got a lot of fine pilots. What I need are some wing commanders who'll come in and kick some ass. I've got a lot of outfits that are nothing but flying clubs still celebrating VJ Day. I want hard-nosed, mean sons of bitches who'll get done what I want done when I want it, which is right now."

LeMay's cigar wasn't drawing and he ground it out. He glared up at Riley, then carefully prepared another one, biting off its end, rolling it between his fingers, and lighting it. Riley debated what he'd do if LeMay offered him one. The option didn't arise.

"The biggest problem I have right now is changing SAC over from a piston-engine air force to a jet air force. The B-47s are finally starting to come off the production line, but they're loaded with problems, big problems. Still, we've got four wings converting right now. By this time next year, I want to have ten operational wings and three more in training. You're going to help me."

"Yes, sir, but I've been a fighter pilot all my life."

"Yeah, tell me about it. How about that little probationary stint flying C-54s in the Berlin Airlift?"

"That was an exception, sir."

"Right, and so is this. A permanent exception. Your first job is recruitment. I want you to use your knowledge of hotshot fighter pilots and recruit one hundred of them for me to fly B-47s."

"Yes, sir, but can I ask why?"

"The old days of flying formation for mutual defense are over. The B-47 flies more like a fighter than a bomber, and one of them can carry more destructive power than all the World War Two bombers combined. I want three-man crews who can go in alone to Moscow, Kiev, wherever, and flatten them. I want to infuse the fighter-pilot spirit into my bomb wings. You're the guy who's going to spearhead that infusion."

"When do I start?"

"I'm having orders cut for you to go to Wichita to take the B-47 course. When you're finished there—it'll take about four months— I'll either assign you to a newly equipped bomb wing or drag you back here. I'll let you know. That's all for now."

LeMay picked up another file as Riley saluted and marched smartly out of the room, preoccupied with the assignment. It was only later, when he went to phone Lyra, that a thought occurred to him: SAC guys stay put pretty much; maybe she'll marry me now.

Los Angeles, California/September 22, 1952

The whole process with Peterson—exciting, dangerous, and guilt- laden—had started one week before, when she'd gone to the down- town public library in the hope of finding a book that would tell her how to get out of the rut she was digging for herself. Her business had grown swiftly and then leveled off. She was still just breaking even, just able to meet the payroll for the staff of thirty working for her. Every time her sales went up, so did her expenses. The problem was, she had to pay for the expenses faster than people paid for the sales.

Sales had hit a plateau in Los Angeles, but when she tried to expand in San Francisco and San Diego, there was a negative return—the market simply hadn't developed yet. Her first fervent dreams of a national sales organization were replaced by nightmares of not having enough money to pay the bills. She'd already resorted to things she'd never thought she'd do—postdating checks, "forget- ting" to put the check in the envelope, cashing checks on one bad account to cover another one. If John Stuart Marshall had known what she was doing, he'd have had a fit.

The librarian's eyes had flashed with warning at Saundra's scream of delight at the article she was reading. Embarrassed, she sat down, holding the copy of *Advertising Today* as if it were a tablet from Mount Sinai. The article said that seventeen of the biggest

U.S. cities had Negro populations from 15 to 42 percent, and that the Negro market in the United States was worth over fifteen *billion* dollars—twice as big as the total consumer market in Greece or Belgium. It was incredible; she had no idea of the possibilities inherent in products tailored to Negro needs.

She reread the article again and found a brief squib on the author. His name was Fred Peterson and he lived in Los Angeles.

She walked back to her car, happy for the first time in weeks, wishing that John was there so she could tell him about it. As she put her hand on the car door, she made a decision to write two letters that night. The more important one would be to John, telling him that they could work things out, somehow. She laughed to herself, thinking how pleased he'd be when he got her letter.

The other letter went to Peterson, who called almost immediately to give her the appointment for this morning. Saundra had immediately begun to do research on him and was pleased with what she discovered. According to the dozen articles she'd read about him, Peterson had started his career with a thousand borrowed dollars and unlimited gall. He'd sprung his magazine, *OBSIDIAN—black and sharp,* on an unsuspecting public and had become an overnight success. *OBSIDIAN—black and sharp* had unashamedly taken features from *Life, Time, The New Yorker,* and *The Saturday Evening Post* and converted them to a racy style that reached to the soul of a broad cross-section of the Negro population. Critics sniped that his magazine was a steal from John Johnson's *Ebony,* but the hard fact was that it was a roaring commercial success on its own merits.

In the process, Peterson had accomplished the impossible— persuaded white manufacturers to advertise in a Negro magazine. And he did it by demanding the unthinkable—the use of Negro models to sell their products.

His office was dazzling, perched atop his own four-story building on Sunset Boulevard. He'd arranged parking for her, and a beautifully dressed young Negro woman was waiting to escort her directly into his office. Erupting out of his chair, he strode around to meet her, and she was, quite simply, overwhelmed.

Six feet four and weighing 220 pounds, Peterson seemed to be all angles and power, as sharply dynamic as a Georges Braque painting. She felt herself immediately attracted to the geometric juxtaposition of his face, a square from the eyebrows up, transitioning to triangles of cheekbones and jawbone below. As they talked, she found herself entranced by his almond eyes, constantly moving, changing expression from friendliness to skepticism to conspiratorial understanding, their animation relieving the energy-charged power of his face. His black skin had such a lustrous, wine-colored velvety look that she yearned to reach out and pat his face, to stroke his closely cropped black hair.

They sat on a long leather sofa, sipping coffee as he quizzed her closely on her business and her prospects, asking her incisive questions about sales, marketing possibilities, and her willingness to work. They talked easily, the conversation quickly moving from stiff business questions to an easy informality that implicitly acknowledged their strong mutual attraction. At one point he reached out to take her hand, shook himself, and abruptly got up to go sit behind his desk.

When he sat down he furrowed his brow and said, "Whew, that was close, wasn't it?" She laughed and he asked, "I'd like to try to help your business. Are you married?"

"Yes, my husband's a pilot; he's flying combat in Korea." She told him about John's career as a Tuskegee airman, of his victories in Italy, and his work at McNaughton.

As she talked she watched his expression change from anticipation to disappointment and then to resolution. Finally he said, "Good for him! We'll do a story on him—on both of you—in OBSIDIAN. We need all the black heroes and heroines we can get."

When she left, she knew she'd made a friend. She was afraid that she might have found a lover.

Nashville, Tennessee/September 22, 1952

A storm had moved through the night before, cracking the long spell of summer heat, and making it pleasant to walk by the lake. When the plant had been built, the engineers had designed a combination runoff basin and water storage pond for use in case of a fire. The first year, wild ducks had stopped over, charming Troy so that he'd uncharacteristically invested a few dollars to create a park for his employees. Simple, with some swings, picnic benches, barbecue pits, lots of white pines, and gravel paths, it was always filled on the weekends.

It hadn't been long before a few domestic ducks showed up, abandoned pets or sick animals from one of the local farms. Now the lake had a stable population of cheerfully interbred fowl, ranging from pure white domestic through mottled oyster mixed-breed to genuine mallard, all of them quacking for a handout.

Elsie, wearing an old flight jacket and slacks, handed Ginny a bag of stale bread to feed the ducks. It had been an odd meeting so far, with Ginny desperately trying to talk about something, and never being able to come to the point. Had Stan done something stupid, like confessing to their affair?

Ginny picked her way along the path in her high-heeled shoes, her manner strained. "Did Stan visit the plant before he went overseas?"

"Yes, of course, you know he did. Is that why you're here?"

Emptying the crumbs from the bag into the lake, Ginny turned and burst into tears, moaning, "I needed to talk to someone. Stan and I are breaking up."

Nonplussed but still cautious, Elsie said, "Maybe it's just a quarrel? How long have you been married?" Elsie knew the answer very well—Stan had kept moaning about the best eight years of his life.

Biting back her tears, Ginny said, "Eight years. The best eight years of my life."

Broth-er! Elsie thought, they're a pair, all right.

"And you don't want to break up?"

"No, not because I made one little mistake."

Elsie was instantly relieved. Stan had not confessed; she had misjudged him. Then she asked, "He caught you screwing somebody?"

Ginny lowered her head and nodded.

"Did he know the man?"

"Yes."

"You want to tell me who it was?"

"You wouldn't know him."

Elsie thought she was lying. It's probably Troy, she thought, More power to him, poor man. Or maybe Fitz, Coleman's buddy.

"It doesn't matter. What can I do to help?"

"Elsie, you know that Troy and my father have a special relationship."

"Are you talking about bribery or blackmail?"

Ginny laughed for the first time. "You're terrible! No, I just mean that they have some special understandings about how business works with the government. Is Troy well?"

Elsie's tone was brusque. "No. He's dying of cancer. They've operated twice now, first on his lip, then on his jaw. It's spread to his throat. Troy isn't kidding himself, and I won't kid you. He's probably got six months or a year, but he won't take it."

"What do you mean?"

"Nothing. Go ahead." No longer worried about being accused of being the other woman, her manner changed. She preferred being in command.

"Daddy wonders if you are willing to maintain the same relationship, to keep things going as they are."

"Tell your dad that I've been running the place for Troy for years, and that of course I want to maintain the relationship."

"Will you hire Stan when he comes back from Korea?"

"Sure, why not?"

"You don't think it would be awkward—us being divorced and all?"

Elsie thought for a moment about her last tryst with Stan. She no longer needed the variety and quantity of sex that she used to, and she had just been going through the motions—the old drive was missing. Yet it might be amusing to have Stan around, for as much as she enjoyed Dick Baker as a lover, he was independent—he'd leave in a minute without a thought. That was one of the reasons she liked him.

"Look, Stan's a good man, and I can use him. But he's just an employee. He has nothing to say about the business, about policy. Why would he?"

"Well, he's hurt. He might not want to associate with the family."

Her voice had quivered. Elsie looked at her with new interest. Something even worse than just being caught *flagrante delicto* had happened.

At the mouth of the Yalu River, North Korea/ September 22, 1952

Shattering pain reverberated through Marshall like a struck cymbal; it felt as if his arm were being wrenched from its socket. His scream frightened the North Korean farmers tugging at his sleeve. They leaped back and he heard the question, "Russkie?"

He had been unconscious, and now his eyes were caked with mud. He tried to pull himself together, rubbing his eyes with the back of his hand. One of the farmers plowed through the mud to a ditch at the side of the littoral where he'd crash-landed and brought back a rusted canful of water, extending it to him with a bow.

Marshall's left arm hung uselessly at his side. Even pulling the flight suit zipper with his right hand jarred the arm, causing his knees to sag with pain. He found a handkerchief and dipped it in the water. Forgetting how Korean fields were fertilized, he smeared the handkerchief over his face, the filthy water oozing into his eyes and mouth.

After a second swipe, he looked up and the group jumped back. They were expecting a blond Russian and got a black Marshall.

One of them came forward and extended his forefinger, gently touching Marshall's skin and lightly scratching at it with his knarled, dirt-encrusted nail. There was a hurried conversation and their mood changed as fast as crystal cracking.

"Amerikanski?"

Marshall nodded yes, apprehensive. He had to stall them until some military people arrived, someone who'd realize he should be questioned and not killed on the spot.

The crowd of North Koreans was growing rapidly, surrounding him, the mumbles growing louder like a lynch scene in a B-movie, but no one coming closer. Something was holding them back. Standing as still as possible to minimize the pain from his arm, he realized that he had his issue .38 pistol strapped to his left leg.

The biggest man in the crowd slowly detached himself and came forward to stand with his face close to Marshall's, his breath laden with the garlicky smell of kimchee, the fermented cabbage that was such an important part of the Korean diet.

Marshall smiled again. The man smiled back and moved away slightly, pointing politely at the holster. The gun was worse than useless to Marshall, so he nodded, and the big farmer grabbed it, and stepped back, full of bluster. Raising the pistol straight up, he pulled the trigger. The safety was on, and, embarrassed, he looked fiercely at Marshall, who used his right forefinger to push the safety off. The man repeated the act, this time firing two rounds into the sky. He had assumed control.

Almost an hour later, a North Korean Army truck pulled up, and the big man was still holding off the crowd as Marshall sat slumped on the wing, nauseated and trying to fight off shock. When the truck came into view, his guard had pocketed the gun and disappeared into the fast-dispersing crowd. Marshall saw why—the troops were indiscriminately handing out blows as if they were breaking up a riot.

A small soldier came up and stood at attention, saying in halting English, "You are a prisoner of war. We will not harm you."

A flood of relief welled over Marshall. He had no idea of how wrong the man was.

Suwon, Korea/September 23, 1952

The young pilot stood swaying at the door to Coleman's room in the tar paper shanty, face drawn, fists clenched, his rage as ill-contained as milk boiling over a small saucepan. Anticipating his visit, Coleman had readied his arguments.

"Come in, Menard. I understand you really tied one on last night. I don't blame you. We'll all miss Bones."

The major ignored Menard's flight suit, filthy and still wet where he had wiped off last night's vomit.

"I just heard that you claimed two MiGs on that mission, and that Fitzpatrick confirmed them."

Coleman skittered like a water spider across the surface tension of military courtesy. "That's right; that makes six for me. It's a great feeling to be an ace at last. But I want to compliment you on the way you shook the MiGs off your tail. They were honchos, for sure."

Menard wasn't having any. "Bones Marshall got those MiGs, Major, and you know it. What the hell is going on?"

Bristling like a cardsharp questioned on his deal, Coleman shifted to his superior officer role, the last refuge of the insecure.

"Are you accusing me of making a false claim, Lieutenant?"

"Maybe I am. Can I see the gun camera film?"

"The gun camera film showed two MiGs going down. It's already been sent forward to Fifth Air Force. But you can ask Fitzpatrick."

Coleman knew that Fitzpatrick would back him up—Fitz had been the one to destroy Coleman's gun camera film immediately after landing, telling the armament troops that he had to do it because it showed they were violating Chinese territory near the Feng-Cheng air base.

"Damn convenient. I won't talk to Fitzpatrick, but I will call my buddy at Fifth headquarters and get some independent verification."

Coleman was silent for a moment. Menard had just raised the ante a lethal amount. Then he barked, "Lieutenant, that's enough of your insults. If Captain Marshall got two MiGs, we'll put in a claim for them. But you went off and got snockered last night before anybody could debrief you. How the hell am I supposed to know what went on in your flight? You were his wingman—you should have kept him from getting shot down."

It was the killer point, driving Menard's reaction. Bones's death was his fault, no question—that's why he'd gotten drunk. The young pilot was suddenly embarrassed and confused. He had no idea what had gone on in Coleman's flight. He'd seen only Bones's two MiGs go down. After he'd shaken off his own attackers, he'd made his way back to K-13 alone. Maybe Coleman had scored then.

Contrition flooded him. "Jesus, I'm sorry, Major. I've made a fool out of myself. I apologize."

Coleman quickly adopted a fatherly tone. "Don't sweat it, son. I know you are upset. It's tough losing an old friend like Bones. Tell you what, are you up to flying?"

"Yes, sir."

"Best thing to do after something like this is to go up and do a little hassling around in the sky. I'll call down and schedule a proficiency flight, just the two of us. When we come back you'll be fine. You can put in the claims for Bones then."

Twenty minutes later Coleman grabbed Menard by the arm as they walked out underneath the stylized pagoda on the flight line that was inscribed THIS WAY TO MIG ALLEY. Now his voice and manner were totally different.

"This is more than a practice flight, Lieutenant. You were flying wing on one of our best men, and we lost him because of you. I need to see if you've got what it takes. I want you to stick with me, no matter what I do. If you can't hack it, maybe this isn't the place for you."

Stung by the sudden change in manner, Menard saluted and turned toward his airplane, flooded again with guilt. Coleman was right—if he'd done his job, he wouldn't have lost Bones, the best friend he'd ever had. Maybe he didn't deserve to be there, after all.

Forty minutes after they were airborne, Menard conceded that Coleman was a master pilot. They had started with simple formation, then some light maneuvers, wingovers, pullups, some easy rolls all done at 2 Gs or less. Then Coleman had gotten serious, pulling 3 Gs, then 4 Gs, tightening the turns, doing quick reversals; it took all Menard's concentration to hang on, and as the level of difficulty increased, his enjoyment rose and resentment decreased. Coleman was teaching him something, he didn't know what, but the flying was therapy for him.

They were in a tight 4-G turn when Coleman swung outside, reversed, so that they were canopy to canopy, then dropped back.

Coleman, his tone still harsh, barked, "Not bad. Now let's do a little rat-racing. Stay with me."

The silver F-86 rolled and split-S'd. Menard followed, mind and body fused in concentration, Marshall and the hangover forgotten, aware only of the airplane dancing ahead of him against a revolving green background. The controls were heavy in his hands as he caressed the stick to bring the two-plane embrace even closer. The Sabre filled his windscreen; he could read Coleman's name stenciled beneath the canopy. Unable to chance a look inside his own cockpit, he was indifferent to speed or altitude as long as he stayed glued in position. He became Coleman's shadow, trusting him completely, pledging to stay tied in no matter how Coleman maneuvered.

Coleman climbed on turns to the right to give Menard ground clearance, his Sabre outlined clean against the bright blue sky. On turns to the left, Coleman's airplane was a silver blur against the flash of green, rice fields at first and then craggy scrub-covered foothills.

After a hard 360-degree turn that he spent scanning the empty sky, Coleman darted into the half-mile-wide mouth of a familiar valley, hurtling down it in a gentle climb as the floor rose and the walls narrowed, Menard tucked in tight to his right rear. Coleman led them at four hundred knots toward a ridge line where a two-hundred-foot-long catenary dip linked two gigantic rock outcroppings. In an instant, Coleman had passed through the right side of the dip, as Menard merged with the rocks.

. . .

At the debriefing, a badly shaken Coleman told Ostrowski what had happened. His voice broke as he told how Menard had been flying perfect formation when he suddenly rolled, inverted, and dove to the ground.

"It looked like he started a recovery. He"—Coleman stopped to pull himself together—"didn't quite make the pull-out."

Everyone knew that the accident investigation would be useless. All that was left at the site was the circular impression of an explosion, and a rockslide mixed with oily, burned debris. After two days of sifting they would find the only evidence of Menard, the blackened Swiss Army knife he carried on a lanyard.

Fitzpatrick dropped by Coleman's room after the debriefing session.

"What really happened?"

Coleman looked up at him, his face impassive.

"You heard me—we were in formation and he suddenly rolled over and went in, didn't say a word. Must have been hypoxia."

"You lousy fucker, you dragged that kid off like an ape peeling a banana. You murdered him."

Coleman poured a drink, his shaking hands clinking the bottle against the glass. "Bullshit, the kid couldn't hack it. He lost Bones one day, killed himself the next. Shit, it happens all the time."

"Around you it does. What the hell's happened to you, Stan?"

Coleman wearily wiped his hand across his face. "Fitz, give me a break. Haven't I always taken care of you?"

"Yeah, just like Ruddick's taken care of you."

"You're right, you've put your finger on it. I'm sick of depending on that smart-ass Ruddick. I want to make it on my own. I'm an ace now, and that'll help."

"Make it on your own? For Christ's sake, Stan, you're an ace because you claimed two victories from Marshall. You're talking nonsense."

"Don't give me that, Fitzpatrick, you confirmed those victories yourself. All that matters is that I'm an ace and Ruddick had nothing to do with it."

Fitzpatrick stared at him. It was incredible, but the man believed what he was saying. Stealing the two kills and dragging off Menard meant nothing to him; they were just means to his ends.

"Well, screw you, buddy, I'm fed up with it." Fitzpatrick whirled and left the tent, disgusted with Coleman, despising himself.

Coleman sat, heavy-lidded eyes defiant, rugged jaws working. He knew that Fitz couldn't get along without him; he'd long since have been court-martialed if he hadn't been protecting him.

Coleman really couldn't expect Fitz to understand how he felt about still taking Ruddick's help even after catching Ginny and that big black bastard in bed. He'd never told Fitz about that, or anyone else either, not even Elsie.

Fitz would come around. If not, he'd find somebody else to be his number two. He was an ace now, and his career would begin to move. On his own terms. Screw Fitzpatrick. And screw Ruddick, too!

North Korea/September 25, 1952

His arm aching with the same fierce intensity of a freshly broken tooth, Bones almost passed out, not sure where he was or how long he could go on. Since the North Korean Army truck had arrived, he had been shuttled from one headquarters to the next, unable to tell if it was because he was a prize or because they couldn't determine what to do with him.

Even in his pain the fundamental poverty of the country came through to him. The roads were mere graveled slits gouged out from the rocky cliffs, edged by hovels where a tin roof was a luxury. The countryside was free of debris, for at every hut the detritus of war—food cans, bits of canvas webbing—served as homemade household goods.

My God, he thought, what a colorless country—it's like a black and white film. The rough landscape, its near horizon blocked by sharply angled mountains, was a muddy shading of brown and gray, with only an occasional slash of dirty green. On rare occasions, one of the village huts would have a red tile roof, overlaid like everything else with a thick grouting of dust.

Even the people seemed made of stone, their faces impassive, overcast like their clothes with the same ugly coating that covered trees and buildings. He saw no interest in their eyes, no hope; they seemed as inanimate as the rocks and the shrubs.

He heard an explosion of rage inside the command post, and a Korean officer came roaring out.

"You, get in now!" The Korean pointed to the filthy truck and they began an agonizing ride back toward his aircraft.

Unable to understand the sudden anger, Bones tried to calm himself, arguing that if they were going to kill him, there was nothing he could do. Yet the degree of his fear bothered him; he thought he'd been frightened before, flying in combat, but it was nothing like this jellylike capitulation of strength and bowels to utter helplessness and certain punishment. At times, he almost appreciated the insistent reality of the pain that distracted him momentarily from his wild apprehensions about the future.

At the crash site they were met by Colonel Kim, a large man for a Korean. His frothing rage impaired his English, but Marshall gathered that a soldier had blown his hand off in the cockpit of the F-86.

"Sabotage! Sabotage! You did this on purpose."

Marshall realized that the poor soldier must have tried to remove the IFF box, which had a self-destruct detonator built into it.

"No, sir. Not sabotage. You must keep your people out of the airplane. The ejection seat is armed."

The colonel paid no attention to him at all, playing to the crowd that had gathered around, screaming at him in Korean. Marshall was so inexpressibly weary that tears kept forming in his eyes. He hated to show weakness, but he couldn't control himself.

An older man, a retired official of some rank, judging by the people clustered around him, detached himself from the crowd and climbed into the F-86's seat.

Marshall wearily raised his good arm and said, "Dont'! Tell him to get out of there."

Colonel Kim was repeating a favorite phrase, "Those is not relevant," as he turned in time to see the ejection seat fire and catapult the unfortunate Korean into the air. In mid-flight, the victim separated from the seat, falling like a sack of rice into the mud. The seat's trajectory carried it through a crowd of farmers, a huge square bowling ball obliterating human pins. Marshall learned later that three had been killed and six injured.

Berserk, Kim turned and struck Marshall across the jaw, knocking him to the ground, screaming with pain. His face contorting with hate, Kim reached down and deliberately twisted Marshall's left arm. The stabbing flood of agony shocked him into unconsciousness.

He awakened hours later, delirious with pain, stretched out in a stake-bed truck, his body penned in by fuel drums, two morose guards watching him.

After a long wait, they drove into the collection of mud huts that passed for a North Korean field hospital. The largest one had a power line running to it; Marshall found out later that it was for X-ray. They took him into the examining hut first, and a short, bespectacled doctor carefully checked him over before sending him to the next hut. He was apparently getting the same care given wounded Chinese and North Korean soldiers and was grateful just to be sitting quietly and not bouncing across the primitive Korean roads.

Bandaged patients either stumbled out of the operating room or were carried slackly by their arms and legs—he hadn't seen a single stretcher. After an hour's wait he was taken into the surgery and immediately, without any preparation, given ether as an anesthetic. He knew he had to have his arm set, but as he began to fade, he wondered if they would interrogate him. He was starting to protest when the blessed night took the pain away.

Santa Monica, California/September 25, 1952

The telegram lay crumpled on the floor beside her. Saundra slowly sagged into a chair as its full import hit her. John had been missing since the 22nd, shot down in a dogfight.

The message was infuriating—it didn't say what the circumstances of his loss were, what the chances were that he was alive, or when she would learn anything else.

She began sobbing, bitterly aware that he wouldn't have received her letter, that he might have died thinking they were through.

Her hands shaking, she went to the refrigerator where John had put a bottle of gin months before, poured a cold syrupy inch into a jelly glass and drank.

Maybe he was a prisoner of war. He could have ejected and been captured. She wondered how the Koreans would treat a Negro.

The telegram also said that the personal affairs officer from George Air Force Base would be getting in touch with her. Maybe he would know something.

There was a knock at the door. Her heart leaped, for she knew it would be Fred Peterson. She wanted to see him desperately, to draw on his strength as she had always drawn on John's. And she knew that she must not, not now, not ever; as much as she like him—as much as she wanted him—it would now never be more than strictly business.

Nashville, Tennessee/September 27, 1952

Elsie McNaughton walked naked down the crooked narrow aisle of Baker's trailer, swiveling her hips to move between cases of beer and chairs piled high with old clothes and cardboard boxes. The oil stove wasn't on, but the damp air hung heavy with the smell of kerosene, dirty laundry, and booze. They had just made love, but the deep sense—and scent—of his primal presence excited her again.

"A pig wouldn't live here, Dick. Can't you clean up that bathroom sometime?"

Baker rolled over on the bed tucked into the far end of his thirty-two-foot-long TravelKing.

"Bring me a beer, sugarbaby, then you go clean it up. Do a good job, I'll be checking on you."

It was the answer she expected—and wanted. Her excitement rose as she obediently complied. She hadn't done any housework of her own for years, but Baker's demands gave her a perverse pleasure.

He was fat, none too clean, totally inconsiderate, and unquestionably dangerous. Yet beneath his crudity, Baker had a rollicking sense of humor; he had made her laugh more than any man in her life. When Troy was out of town, they occasionally went out to dinner or a movie. Then Baker was a different person, kind, considerate, gallant, even. But here in his own domain, their little "sex palace" as he called it, he played to her need for mastery, dominating her completely.

As she swabbed the shower vigorously with Lysol, trying to make a dent in the mildew, she contrasted him to the fastidious Stan, so conscious of his manners, so immaculately clean, so anxious to please, so humorless. Baker *stirred* her, got her excited with just a phone call, and knew exactly what to do to satisfy her—if he chose to. Usually, he let her satisfy him first, then wait on him all day in a sustained heat, but before they parted he would make love to her with a powerful energy that left her totally fulfilled.

She knew, too, that she loved him in part because he treated her exactly as her first lover, Bruno Hafner, had. Bruno had often been brutal, sometimes pleasant, very rarely tender, but always dominant. She liked that in a man, and she rarely found it. Most of them were flowers and candy guys; she craved pretzels and beer and an occasional rough shove if she got out of line.

"Come here, doll, I want to talk business with you."

She ran back gladly and slithered under the sheet. He jerked the sheet away, cocking his hairy leg across her thigh.

"You know Troy ain't going to be with us long."

Staring at him like a child, she nodded. Troy was effectively dead already, as far as the business was concerned. He no longer came to the office—he hated to be seen wearing the dressings on his face and neck—and she kept him informed only of the positive things happening, like being awarded the modification contracts taken from Roget Aircraft.

"Well, that'll make you a widow. What say we get married?"

To Elsie, sexual slavery was one thing, business was another. "Are you crazy? Why would I marry a swine like you? I'm never going to get married again."

"Come on, Elsie, you need me. We'd be a great team. Besides, if you don't marry me, I'm going to cut you off."

"Be the best thing that ever happened to me."

"You know you can't live without me. Now roll over on your stomach, I'm going to teach you to be nice to me."

As she rolled, he slapped her ass, barking, "Move it, bitch."

While the two of them were romping, Troy McNaughton had summoned the strength to drive himself to the little park he had created on the far side of the airfield. In the last few months, he had enjoyed the park more than any of his other possessions, even the plant that had delighted him so long.

His chauffeur usually drove him, bringing along a sack of the dog chow the ducks liked better than bread. The park was deserted in the evenings, and the ducks amused him with their pecking order feeding, reminding him of board meetings he'd held.

This evening, he had only a coffee can of chow, and he sat on the pier, carefully tossing the food so that the smaller ducks got their fair share. For the hundredth time, he saw that duck society was no different from his own—the bigger ducks greedily ate up all they could, shoving the smaller ones aside, turning to chase them away, plucking viciously at their tail feathers. There was one little mallard that he identified with, calling him Lumpy, because he had a swollen open sore on the side of his head.

"Come here, Lump—looks like your tailfeathers are all gone, poor guy. Just like me."

He made sure that his favorite got a full ration, luring the larger ducks to one side with a few chunks, then tossing a handful out for Lumpy to sluice greedily out of the water.

When the can was nearly empty, McNaughton took the last three pieces and tossed them to his favorite, using Dick Baker's favorite phrase: "All gone, kid, if I'm lying I'm dying." Then he stretched out on the pier, his head protruding over the side. He placed his .45-caliber Colt automatic under his chin, positioning it precisely where he felt the pain gnawing so relentlessly. He hesitated only a moment, as a brief feeling of regret passed over him that he hadn't gotten the flying wing into production. Then he pressed the trigger, blowing his cancer and his brains into the water. The frightened ducks flew away, quacking. Lumpy left with the rest of them.

Pyoktong, North Korea/October 10, 1952

Bones slept in all his clothes, bright blue cotton jacket and pants over the canvas outfit they'd given him after he crashed. Frozen stiff as freezer beef, the cold congealing his very marrow, he grudgingly awoke from a poignant dream of a forgotten time. He hadn't thought of it in years, but in his sleep he had re-created a rainy warm afternoon when his father had told him about the British surrender at Yorktown, when the redcoats had marched out to the tune, "The World Turned Upside Down."

Yesterday a chance meeting had turned his world as a prisoner upside down. Walking with his guard back from the benjo, the filthy slit-trench toilet fifty feet from his mud hut, he met a white man and a Negro soldier.

He thought he was hallucinating when the white man said in an English accent, "Good evening, I'm Alan Burkett; this is Sergeant Taylor. You must be Captain Marshall."

They shook hands. Marshall peered at him, thinking how warm

the quilted jacket and the big waterproof boots must be. The man's broad red face was peering from a Russian-style fur hat and a wide checkered scarf wound around his throat and face like a snowman's.

Bones stole a quick look at the guard, who was ignoring them, obviously afraid of the Englishman.

His high voice filtered up from his well of cosseted warmth. "I'm a correspondent for the Liverpool *Daily News*. Sergeant Taylor was with the 1st Division. How are they treating you?"

Marshall was on his guard at once—the man was too friendly, the situation too strange. He answered by asking, "Sergeant Taylor, how are they treating you?"

"You know how it is, Captain, they treat us Negroes as good as they can, while they feed us all this shit about racism in America. We eat about as good as they do, and that's bad enough. No sense in starving to death."

Marshall nodded as if he agreed with the words.

"Have you met any other pilots?"

"No, sir, they keep the white pilots locked up and starving. They beat them up pretty bad."

Burkett broke in. "Nonsense, Taylor, that's just hearsay. I damn well know for a fact that they treat them well."

Taylor raised his eyebrows. It was enough.

"Captain Marshall, I'd like to come over and interview you some day, if I may?"

"I don't know what the rules are about that. I'd appreciate it if you'd get word to my wife that I'm alive."

"Certainly." Taylor raised his eyebrows again, and they walked on, leaving Marshall deep in thought.

Breakfast had been the usual—a tin GI cup of tea, a large bowl of rice with some kimchee, and a small bowl with some roughly chopped squares of meat, boiled to a gray-white hue and spiced with red pepper. Marshall considered it a starvation diet until he saw how enviously the guards looked at it.

Normally, he forced himself to eat everything to keep his strength up for an escape, but today he placed the food aside.

His watch had been stolen at the crash site; timepieces were obviously in short supply, for he had not seen any Korean below the rank of colonel wearing one. For the most part he ignored the hour, content to plot the day's monotonous course in the ruthless busy-work of prison routine, the guards changing and the bugles blowing. But he always knew when it was precisely ten o'clock, for that was when Colonel Kim came in, ostentatiously looked at his wrist, and began his interrogation.

After the blowup at the airplane, the colonel had been scrupulously correct, even friendly. Each day, he would pull out his little black notebook to ask the same questions of Marshall. At first Marshall told him his name, rank, and serial number and nothing more. In time, Marshall found it was smarter—and easier—to eat up the interrogation time by talking at length on any subject except military matters. Kim seemed to enjoy it, especially when Marshall spun out the plots of movies and books, improvising when he didn't remember, telling him fantastic stories about American motion picture stars or baseball players. In time he exhausted all he knew, and made up stories freely, combining the plot of *Gone With the Wind* with *Snow White*, or *Frankenstein* with *Dawn Patrol*. Kim loved them all, but as the time grew to a close, he would again ask him how many aircraft were in his unit, and where various Air Force units were located. Marshall would decline to answer, and Kim would put the notebook away, shrugging.

Toward the end of the session, Kim would bemoan the unfortunate lot of the Negro in the United States. It was bad propaganda, straight out of *Uncle Tom's Cabin*, and Marshall could have given him much sadder, more blatantly unfair examples if he'd chosen to. Instead he told him extravagant lies about his father and mother, and how fortunate they were and how well they lived. Kim had routine intelligence information on Marshall, but he tried to be subtle with it, asking Marshall innocuous questions about his background and utterly refusing to believe that his father was a minister and actually owned his own automobile.

The session always closed with Kim giving the same short lecture on the importance of confession in "rehabilitation," and the fact that there were some unfriendly ways to get cooperation. The threats were softened by smiles, as if it were a pro forma speech, something he had to say but that they mutually understood would not happen.

This day, as he rose to go, Marshall reached out and grabbed his arm. "I demand to see my fellow pilots. I will protest to the UN if you don't end this solitary confinement. I demand to be treated exactly like white pilots are treated."

Kim stood up, perplexed and obviously transfixed with horror that Marshall had touched him. Mumbling, he used his favorite expression, "No, this is not relevant."

On impulse, Marshall picked up his tin cup of tea, cold now, and poured it down the front of Kim's pants. "I demand to be placed with my fellow officers!"

His face blank with incomprehension, Kim turned and ran from the room. Marshall never saw him again.

Washington, D.C./October 25, 1952

There were few satisfactory places in Washington to bring a European to eat, but at Harvey's, the beef and the seafood were always good.

Harvey's had another advantage—your privacy was respected. No matter which of the regulars were there—Congressman Dade, J. Edgar Hoover, whoever—none would do more than flicker an eyebrow in recognition.

He'd asked for a table where they could talk without fear of being overheard. Josten had a shrimp cocktail and a T-bone steak; Ruddick ordered the same. They drank scotch before, beer with, and cognac after.

Milo was pleased with the man. He was doing well at the McNaughton plant and still covertly maintained his contacts in Germany with other art collectors. To his surprise, Ruddick had found that the large portfolio of paintings by Hitler was proving to be the most valuable Josten had sent to him, serving a double purpose. To the collectors, they had an immense intrinsic value. There was apparently no price they would not pay. More important, the paintings were a very powerful tool when used as a gift, or a reward, with certain of the most powerful figures he was dealing with on Klan matters. They were almost as potent a political symbol as was the Blood Flag—a treasure for the future.

With coffee and the Dutch Master cigars, Milo guardedly began to talk business as Josten cradled the cognac glass in his hands.

"With Troy dead, things are a little uncertain at McNaughton. You'll have to stay there for a few months, but then I'll have some other tasks for you."

Josten sniffed the cognac, nodding, his eyebrows raised. "What do you have in mind?"

"I need your help in revitalizing the Klan. It's become a redneck debating society run by beer-drinking bullies. It needs to be stripped of the old rituals and given a new purpose. I want to rename it, get rid of the stupid costumes, and narrow the focus of interest."

Josten's face was impassive. "How will you narrow it?"

"Concentrate only on the Negroes and the Jews. Catholics are no longer an issue."

"So. And what will you call this new organization?"

"I'm not sure—it has to have a catchy acronym. Right now, I'm thinking about the National Order of White Workers—NOWW. And I'd like to use your party's old slogan, 'Awake.' "

Josten considered this a moment. "And what am I supposed to do?"

Milo leaned forward enthusiastically. "You have great organizational ability; we can use that. But I really want you to inspire the Klan, to tell them what was done in your country. You have no idea how they would look up to a Luftwaffe colonel, a real Nazi."

Josten's scarred face twisted into a grin. "A real Nazi. Oddly enough I was never a Nazi, never belonged to the Party. I thought that Hitler was crazy. I loved Germany, of course, and did all I could to win the war."

Ruddick looked at him, appalled, and Josten went on. "After the war, confined for months to a hospital bed, I realized how wrong I was. Everything Hitler had predicted came true, from Russian rapes to Negro music blasting on the radio, the country in ruins. I should not have betrayed him."

Mind racing, anxious to show his sympathy, Ruddick said, "It's just like Hitler himself, after the first war. He was gassed, you know, and hospitalized, just like you were."

Josten nodded slightly, amazed by Ruddick's insight. He was absolutely correct—his belief in Hitler had begun to grow in the hospital, too late for it to benefit Germany.

The American went on. "Do you see the similarities in Hitler's policies and what I'm trying to do with the Klan?"

"Of course—you're using the working class to put across an ideal. He tried that and failed because of people like me."

There was a silence and Josten asked, "Do you intend to win elections, or make a revolution?"

"Neither. The Communists have fostered a growing liberal tide in this country. That's why the military services were forcibly integrated, against the advice of all the generals and admirals. It was a desperate attempt by Truman to gain votes."

"Ah, but it worked, for him, and for the Negroes. How does Eisenhower stand on the issue? He is a general's general."

Ruddick snorted in frustration. "I don't know, but I doubt if even he could do anything to reverse integration in the military. But it won't be long before the Jews will be advocating other craziness—integrated schools, open elections. The blacks outnumber us in the South—they will simply swamp us. That's what the Jews want."

"What do you want your organization to do?"

"Create a backlash. I want my people to do so much violence to the Negroes that they will rebel. I want the Negroes to come out of their houses, out of their subservience, and demand their rights. But I don't want them to do it peaceably. I want them killing whites."

"Presumably the other whites will then rebel themselves?"

"They always have, they will again. We need Negro-led race

riots, whites dead in the streets, white houses burned, white churches blown up. Then this liberal nonsense will subside."

"Why not have your own people do it and blame it on the Blacks?"

"Do you think someone stupid enough to wear a white sheet and a megaphone on his head could be that subtle? No, I'll have to harness their natural instincts."

Josten carefully tapped his cigar against the ashtray, as Ruddick went on. "The sad thing is that, stupid as they are, their natural instincts are correct. If they still had the power, and the tacit support of the government, they would soon sort out the Negroes and the Jews. But the Klan has become a laughing stock, a magnet for the screwballs."

"Screwballs?"

"Means eccentric, weird, crazy. But I must work with what I have, trying to change them over time, giving them better direction, better goals."

Josten shook his head. It seemed bizarre, but so had the Nazi party to many people in 1923.

"Do you work alone?"

"No. Many people, most of them far more affluent than I, think the same way I do. I have contacts with very wealthy people in twelve states who are sympathetic to my aims and who are members of the Klan."

Josten went to the heart of the matter. "How powerful is your group? Could you force a confrontation now?"

"No, absolutely not. I've just begun the process. Give me five years. I need you to help me. But I've done all the talking. Tell me about yourself, about life in the Luftwaffe. You weren't in the SS, I know, but tell me what you know about it."

Josten stirred uneasily. It was not something he liked to talk about. Could Ruddick be recording the conversation?

"It's late. Let's leave the Luftwaffe for another time. I have too many painful memories of our failures with our jet fighter. And while I wasn't in the SS, I can tell you that it has been badly misrepresented. It was primarily an elite fighting organization, idealistic, dedicated to our leaders. The SS got all the nastiest jobs, all the worst fighting in Russia and in France. But people remember only the concentration camps."

He was silent and Ruddick said, almost wistfully, "I believe you had experience at Nordhausen, did you not? Tell me about it."

Josten stared at him; the man was a true believer, no mistake, but this was something he didn't want to talk about. He stood up, saying, "Excuse me for a moment. Where is the toilet?"

A few minutes later, Josten stood looking in the mirror as he washed his hands, thinking about Ruddick's proposal to join him. It was not a bad offer. With the flying wing dead at McNaughton, there was really no reason for him to be there, and, with his disabilities, it wouldn't be easy to find employment elsewhere. Why shouldn't he use this corrupt fool Ruddick, as a tool? He could work for him, building up his Klan while he recovered his strength. Then, perhaps, he'd be ready to see Lyra and Ulrich.

His eyes misted as he thought of them. She had been so cruel to take Ulrich away from him. He had not gone to see her because he was not yet fit—not yet potent. It would be unendurable to approach her again and not be able to make love to her. Perhaps in another few months . . .

Outside, the weather had turned cold, a front had switched off like a lamp the past two days of Indian summer. Erich Weissman sat in a Chevrolet sedan, its engine running, the heater and the wipers working. He'd stolen the car weeks ago from a new shopping center, where the owner had obligingly left the key in the ignition. The theft made him feel guilty as an assassination never did. Weissman had kept it garaged until tonight. He had the window cracked, the gun in his lap, and was grateful to have found a parking spot within good shooting range.

Weissman was still debating with himself the ethics of killing an American, even though he knew Ruddick was one of the most influential opponents of arms sales to Israel. He had nothing against Ruddick; his real target should have been the man he was dining with. If the intelligence was correct, Josten was the sort he hated most, an officer who pretended to despise the Nazis, while doing everything he could to help them win the war. He didn't know if Josten had ever beaten a slave laborer or sent a Jew to a concentration camp. But he did know that he had masterminded the installation at Nordhausen where slaves built jet engines for the Luftwaffe. Weissman knew that he would never have seen him there— the neatly uniformed Luftwaffe personnel rarely came down into the depths of the tunnel. But Josten was even more guilty than the guards who actually cracked skulls and broke bones. They were just brutes, unthinking animals. It was people like Josten who made their work possible.

Yet of the two, Israel had designated Ruddick as the primary target, the real enemy. Well, if the state of Israel had existed in the twenties, perhaps Hitler and Himmler would have been deemed enemies and been executed. Many millions of lives would have been saved. As the Germans always said, orders were orders.

He started each time the restaurant door swung open, bringing the gun up to window level. There had been only false alarms so far.

A light rain began to fall, shimmering against the windows of the jewelry store to the right. He tensed as he saw Ruddick emerge, holding the door for the slower man behind him. Ruddick continued to hold the door open while a couple, laughing, heads down, ran down the street in the rain.

The two men turned right and Weissman fired twice. Both dropped as the bullets ripped into the jewelry store window, an Atmos clock blowing up among the avalanche of glass cascading into the street. Weissman gunned the car out of its space, then roared down 17th Street, cursing himself. He should have concentrated on Ruddick; he knew he had missed them both.

Josten asked, "Are you all right?"

"Yes, I'm surprised my reflexes are still so good. I don't know what that was about, but I've made a lot of enemies over the years."

"They weren't after you. They were after me. It's the Jews."

A black and white patrol car materialized out of the air, and two officers emerged, guns out.

"Freeze. Put your hands up."

Ruddick smiled at Josten, now his comrade-in-arms. "They think we smashed the window to grab some jewelry."

Wichita, Kansas/October 26, 1952

The news commentator had just finished the fifteenth repetition of Eisenhower giving his "I will go to Korea" speech, and Ulrich switched the channel to "The Cisco Kid."

"How much television are you going to let him watch?"

"As much as he wants. He's a smart boy."

They'd been married one month, bought a new station wagon, moved two thousand miles, rented a furnished apartment, got Ulrich into school, and not yet had their first argument.

Bayard Riley stretched out on the couch, one arm around Lyra, one around Ulrich. "It's great you're so adaptable."

She looked at him with surprise. "Let me tell you something. Traveling across the United States in a Chevolet is much better than riding to Berlin in an ox-cart. How many times did we get strafed on Route 66? Not once." She kissed him. "You don't know how nice it is to open a refrigerator and choose what to eat. You don't know how nice it is just to have a refrigerator!"

As if on cue, Ulrich ran in to the refrigerator and pulled a Milky Way out of the freezer compartment. As he came back he rubbed his stomach appreciatively. A good kid, Ulrich had protested a little about leaving school in California, but by his third school day in Wichita, he was perfectly happy.

Lyra asked, "But how adaptable are you?"

Bear looked at her with surprise. "What do you mean? I'm the most adaptable guy in the world."

"So? Will you adapt to flying a bomber instead of a fighter? Will you adapt to have a crew reporting to you? Will you adapt to having a baby?"

He grabbed her. "Honey, are you pregnant?"

"Yes, two months. It turns out we would have had to get married, even if we didn't want to."

Bear rolled his eyes at Ulrich, absorbed in "Ceeesco's" antics.
"Don't be prudish. He's got to live in the real world."

"Lyra, this is great! And we'll have lots more."

"Perhapszz." When she was excited, a trace of her accent returned. "If you live long enough. I wish you'd get a job where you didn't have to fly."

He pulled her to him, ignoring the familiar Air Force domestic argument, and she pushed him away.

"There's more. I got a call from Helmut."

He rolled his eyes at Ulrich again.

"Ulrich knows that his father is in this country. Helmut knew all about us—when we were married, where we were going."

"What was his attitude?"

"Bitter. Very bitter. He didn't exactly threaten me . . ."

"Do you want me to confront him? I can be in Nashville in a few hours."

"No—he'd like that. I just want to avoid him. If he comes here, that's different. I can't believe that he'd hurt me, but he might try to take Ulrich away. I don't know what he'd do to you."

"Let him try. Does he know you're pregnant?"

"No. Do you think I'd tell him before I told you?"

"No. But tell me how you feel about him."

"Profoundly sorry. He was once a good man and I loved him very much. The war changed him; it changed me, too. If I could help him, I would, but no one can."

Salinas, California/November 4, 1952

The day had started well. Bandy and Patty went to the polls early, where for the first time in their lives they didn't cancel each other's votes. After McCarthy's violent attack, they'd become straight-ticket Democrats, even though Bandy liked Eisenhower better than Stevenson.

But everything turned sour when they returned to their factory. It was hell to see something they'd built up so quickly and so well disintegrate. Half the work force had already been laid off; the rest would go when they finished the work in progress. No more airplanes were waiting on the ramp—now they were being flown straight to McNaughton's Nashville plant.

The Air Force, reacting to pressure from Congress, the public, and Milo Ruddick, had shut off the contractual spigot. There would be no more airplanes coming in for refurbishment.

Hadley had been waiting for them in their tiny conference room.

"First of all, Bandy, how did it go with Varney?"

The general had called Bandfield back to Washington the week before. "I offered to resign my commission, but he wouldn't let me. He's sending me to Boeing, to try and help out on the production problems they're having with the B-47."

"Well, that's a concession, anyway. I'm surprised, I thought sure this was it, that Ruddick had put the squeeze on you to get you out." Roget turned and asked, "How bad is it with the banks, Patty?"

"Well, I never should have tried to buy this place; the banks offered to build it and lease it back, but I figured we were good for four years of war work, anyway. My fault."

Roget shook his head vigorously. "No, it was the right thing to do. What's it mean to us now?"

"Well, we can't keep it up. I'm going to try to go back to the banks and sell it to them, then rent or lease it back. We'll lose our shirt, but we'll be out from under the payments."

Bandfield said, "Maybe we can just rent half of it back; we wouldn't need the whole facility at first."

"Let me talk to them. I'm not sure I want somebody else in here—if we sell as many executive planes as I think we can, we'll need the space. If somebody else comes in and does well, they'll want to run us out."

"Patty's right; if we can hold on to the whole place, let's do it. And if we start making B-17s into water bombers, we'll need all the space we can get."

Roget had already dismissed his anger against McCarthy and

Ruddick. If he could have gotten his hands around their necks, he would have cheerfully strangled them, but they were unassailable, and now the problem was there in Salinas, just like always—how to wring a living out of aviation.

Pyoktong, North Korea/November 23, 1952

Demanding to be treated as the other pilots were treated turned out to be a worse idea than pouring the tea on Colonel Kim. John had lost track of time since the rapid-fire events of that morning, but it no longer mattered. He knew he was going to die.

Each day brought him closer to breaking. Time was passing in a blur, just black moments between the beatings and the solitary, yet there were rare moments of great lucidity. A few days before, as he was being walked to a new slit trench, Marshall had turned a corner in the crooked street and had suddenly looked out on a sublime scene, the first element of beauty he'd ever seen in Korea. The sun had broken through and was gleaming off the fresh snow blanketing the mountains that arced around Pyoktong, their white edge sharply defined by the deep blue of a huge lake. He'd been aware of the mountains but never knew until that moment that the lake was nearby. Startled, he hesitated momentarily and the guard clubbed him to the ground. Reflexively, he curled into a ball as the guard beat consciousness from him with his rifle butt.

Now, an unknown number of days later, still confused from the beating, he was told he would meet Colonel Kim's replacement. After a long wait in a cornstalk-lined mud hut, he was jerked to his feet and the viperous Colonel Choi entered his life, a short, sallow-skinned Korean who tapped a strip of bamboo against his hip like a riding crop.

Through Marshall's throbbing head came the thought: This guy looks like the villain in a Jap war movie.

Choi leaned forward, his brow beetling over thick, Coke-bottle-bottom glasses.

"Captain Marshall, I'm Colonel Choi. I will be interrogating you in the future. You will cooperate." He spoke without an accent.

He sensed his question coming, knew he should not ask it, and plunged on anyway. "Colonel Choi, haven't I seen you in the movies?"

Marshall heard the crack of bamboo before he felt it slice into his cheek. Raising on his toes, Choi rained blows on both sides, quick precise taps that cut flesh but left him conscious.

"Sit down, Captain Marshall. That's just a taste of what you'll get from me if you show any sign of disrespect. You will cooperate."

Marshall sat down carefully.

In the days that followed, Choi's questions were routine, but each carried the implicit threat of quick, sharp punishment. Once he said, "I'll never beat you beyond your endurance, Captain Marshall. I'll just push you to your limit of pain and hold you there until you tell me what I want to hear."

He kept his word, as aware of Marshall's physical limits as a physician, metering punishment out carefully, knowing that fear was as debilitating as the actual punishment.

His blows and threats were coupled with mind-numbing diatribes on the superiority of the Communist system and the certain downfall of capitalism. As Marshall's strength and mental acuity gradually returned, he drew comfort sometimes thinking what his own little capitalist, Saundra, would have had to say to Choi.

Choi differed from Kim in another respect. Someone was funneling him accurate information on racism in America. When he came in each day, he had fresh—and reasonable—statistics on Whites versus Negroes in employment, education, conviction rates, prison sentences, lynchings, percentage of Negro officers—anything that adversely reflected on the system. Choi didn't demand a reaction—he just fed the material, contrasting it sometimes with the harmony of ethnic relations in the Communist system. Marshall was sure that someone had provided Choi with the phrase, but he would conclude each of his race lectures with, "Remember, Captain Marshall, that Communism has no prejudices about color.

And remember, too, your Air Force has forgotten you; to your Air Force you are just a nigger."

Irritated by the term nigger, knowing that it was true for some, like Coleman, Bones had declared a private war against the interrogator. The rules were weighted so that Choi must inevitably win—but he knew also that he would never surrender, never break. Choi could kill him—and he had given some thought to killing himself—but he would not give him any of the limited military information he had, nor would he ever admit to the unspecified war crimes he was supposed to have committed.

His biggest challenge was to remember the lies he'd told before, for Choi was obviously working from the papers Kim had prepared. Once Kim had asked him to describe the F-86; Marshall had spun out a long line of technical misinformation, most of it taken from material he'd read about the MiG, liberally laced with "secrets" from the Avia he'd flown—a millennium before?—in Israel. Kim had been ecstatic, and he forwarded the material with relish. When Choi repeated the question, with Kim's report in front of him, Marshall's weakened state made it difficult to recall exactly what he'd said.

Bones had discovered immediately after Kim's departure how very special his rations had been. Now all he got, twice a day, were wooden bowls of cold water and *chook*, a watered, gummy rice that every fourth or fifth day might also contain a fishhead or some garlic buds. Either was very welcome. Before, he felt as if he were starving; now he really was and knew that his nickname had never been more appropriate.

The first serving came before dawn. There was not much time to eat, yet he always saved the bowl of water to rinse the chook bowl, a spoonful at a time, to make sure he got every dreg. The second came at the midpoint of the evening, when the interrogators broke for their own supper. Then he had a little more time and would carefully space his bites, chewing each one until every trace of it, even the barely perceptible flavor, had entirely disappeared. When he was finished he would scrape the bowl with the spoon, as if he could express nourishment from the wood.

There was no way to tell the time, but judging by the appearance of his interrogators as they tired, he was being questioned from about six in the morning until one or two the next morning. The interrogators grew progressively more exhausted and ill-tempered, even though they took turns and often absented themselves, one or two at a time.

The prayers his dad had taught him were sustaining him mentally, but there was nothing he could do about his physical deterioration. There were no mirrors, but he could see his spindly limbs and feel his bony ribs. Sleeping on the hard-packed dirt floor was an agony. After eighteen or twenty hours in the interrogation cell, he'd collapse on the frigid floor and fall into a dreamless sleep for an hour or two until the insistent pain from his arms and bony hips would awaken him. He'd massage himself for a few minutes, then drop back into exhausted slumber like a stone falling into a well, repeating the process until the guard kicked him awake.

Marshall had already decided that the kicks, like most of the Korean brutality, were not aimed at him specifically; they treated each other the same way, and it was only natural that he would be low man on the kicking pole. The nine guards lived in the same hut with him, all in a room not much larger than his own four-by-eight-foot space. He watched their crude domestic arrangements—patching each other's socks, the tattered rags still on their feet; studiously picking lice out of seams; interminably reading, or pretending to, from Communist textbooks. They shared their frugal rations, and they stole from each other and everyone else without remorse. The lowest man in the guard's pecking order, evidenced by the fact that everyone kicked him and he kicked no one but Marshall, was U Eun Chur. U didn't kick him as often as the others did, and he had once given him a small frozen potato to eat, a gift from God. When the other guards were out of the room, U Eun Chur would come over and point to his skin and to Marshall's, then make a kicking motion with his foot. Marshall assumed he meant that they were both dark, that they were both maltreated.

Yet everyone in Korea was maltreated—and didn't seem to know it. Even field-grade officers lived animal-like lives, five or six dossed down in a room with only a rough canvas tarpaulin as a blanket, eating coarse, ill-prepared food, and entertaining themselves by studying Marxist doctrine. Women had achieved true equality— they lived under the same primitive conditions, sleeping under the same tarpaulin. There were no signs of any sexual relationships.

On one of his trips to the slit-trench, he saw a little Korean boy, no more than three, run outside into the subzero weather totally nude, relieve himself, spend a few moments casually examining some refuse in the snow, then scamper back into his mud hut. They were hardy people—no wonder they were so tough to fight.

In some mysterious way, Choi's merciless pounding was strengthening him like a blacksmith tempers steel. In recent days Marshall had undergone a miraculous transformation for which he was supremely grateful. He was no longer afraid; the quivering jelly feel in his belly was gone, even when, like yesterday, Choi was raging, "I'll kill you, but that's not all. I'll go to the United States; I'll kill your wife and your family!"

The week before, the threat would have terrified him. Now he snarled back, "You blind gook bastard, you couldn't find the United States if it was tattooed on your ass. Shut up and let me alone."

Marshall wasn't sure what had given him this new courage. It still hurt just as much to perch on the interrogation stool for hours, or to lay bent up on the frozen floor, or to take the casual blows and kicks, but the fear was gone. Analyzing it, he realized that lack of sleep and agonizing hunger drove fear away by making death seem attractive.

In the end, he became almost grateful for Choi and his continual threats of punishment and death because they gave him strength to hate so much. And he even learned a lesson, when Choi began to talk with obvious relish of tortures to come.

"Captain Marshall, things have been easy for you so far. If you do not confess to your criminal actions, I will have a hose inserted in your rectum, and force water into you until your stomach is flushed out of your mouth."

"Go ahead! I haven't committed any criminal acts. I hope you do flush me out, it will kill me. And when the war is over, you will be a

war criminal, and you will be hung like Tojo. And I will meet you
in hell and kick your fat Korean face in!"

The Koreans hated and feared the Japanese; Choi jumped at the
mention of the feared wartime premier. He gathered up his notebook and left the room, appearing as hurt as a suitor whose offer is
rejected. Marshall realized that he still had some negotiating room
left, that threats they didn't understand might scare them.

They didn't understand much. They seemed to have no feeling
for the military situation, for the potential power of the United
States. The questions they asked him were repetitive. Where were
American units located? What radio frequencies did they use? They
were all things that they must have known from their own sources.
Marshall sensed that the psychology was to get him to admit anything, no matter how trivial, and then more important things would
follow. While still denying knowledge of anything important, he
gave them lots of material that sounded technically accurate without
having any bearing on the F-86. He made it as complex as he could,
so that they would ask him to repeat, to spell out what he was
saying, and thus eat up the interrogation time. When he had more
energy, he'd launch implausible digressions that they copied as
faithfully as they did his technical jargon. He racked his brain for
American slang and randomly tossed in catchphrases from old radio
programs: "Do you want to buy a duck?" or "Inka-dinka-doo" or
"Monkeys are the cwaziest peoples," little bombs that turned the
interminable translating process upside down. Only a few of them
spoke English well enough to conduct an interrogation, so that both
questions and answers had to be translated.

Yet he knew that the cruel conditions of the interrogation would
ultimately kill him, and he was not sure how long he would last.
The process was routine to the North Koreans and Chinese who
spent their days questioning him, sucking down countless cups of
tea and smoking foul cigarettes. They would lead him up a flight of
stairs to a dank, gray eight-by-ten room, moisture oozing from the
walls. Twelve interrogators, mostly Chinese, would be crowded
around a table, facing a small wooden stool. A single unshielded
lightbulb hung from its cord. The stool was low, so that he had to sit

with his knees up almost to his face. They did not allow him to move, even to stretch; either brought sharp, painful blows or, worse, a rifle barrel prodded deep into his back. After the first few hours, his legs were asleep, and only the gnawing pain from his hipbones grinding against the stool kept him awake. His swollen feet looked like eggplants, purplish-black, and pus drained from his toenails. He could no longer tie the tops of his canvas shoes together.

The interrogation room had a sole saving grace. Looking up from his stool at the interrogators, his eyes could go beyond them to a small window through which he could see a single tree branch, arched like a scene from a Japanese screen. Early in the interrogation process—a month before? he could not say—the branch had held four leaves. He'd watched them fall one by one, rooting vainly for them to hold on. They were all gone now, but yesterday he had seen the little bumps of this year's buds gently outlined in the falling snow, an image more beautiful to him—and more strengthening—than anything in the Louvre could have been.

As soon as Marshall entered the interrogation room, he saw that today was going to be different. Besides the usual dozen interrogators, there was a suitcase-sized recording machine with a bespectacled Korean beside it. The stool had been moved in closer to the table, and Colonel Choi was standing next to it.

"Sit down, Captain Marshall." He gave the technician a head movement that would have made Toscanini proud, and began: "Yesterday you said that you did not know what criminal offenses you have been charged with. Today I will tell you, and I expect your confession. Listen to this."

The recorder creaked and moaned. There was static, then a wavering voice, so slowly paced that it had to be deliberate.

"I . . . am . . . Lieutenant . . . Dick . . . Jameson . . . United . . . States . . . Air . . . Force. I . . . confess . . . that . . . I . . . have . . . waged . . . biological . . . warfare . . . against . . . the . . . people . . . of . . . North . . . Korea."

Obviously pleased, Choi nodded and the technician quickly rewound the tape and changed the reel.

"Because Lieutenant Jameson has confessed, we have identified him as a prisoner of war. He will return to the United States when the war is over. Unless you confess to your crime of dropping biological warfare agents, you will not."

"Colonel Choi, first of all, I have not waged biological warfare, and neither has Lieutenant Jameson, and you know it. Secondly, are you telling me that I haven't been reported to the United Nations as a prisoner of war?"

Uncustomarily direct, Choi answered, "You have not. And you will not be unless you cooperate. As far as the rest of the world is concerned, you died in the crash of your aircraft. Your wife thinks you are dead, your family thinks you are dead. In fact, you are dead—unless you confess."

An overwhelming sense of isolation engulfed him; maybe Choi could win after all. Saundra wouldn't know if he were dead or alive—neither would his family. Somehow, he imagined that as a prisoner of war, some vestige of the Geneva convention might protect him, that he might have some value in a prisoner exchange. Was Choi right? Was he forgotten because he was a Negro? Did the Air Force not care about him?

The interrogation began to heat up; Choi stated that canisters of germs had been found in his F-86, that four people in the crowd had died of the disease—his catalog of sins went on and on.

Marshall gazed out at the tree branch, gathering himself, realizing that he somehow had to gain an advantage, to score even a small victory, to punish them for kidnapping him and treating him like this.

The questions reverted to their familiar turn—frequencies, call signs, the usual innocuous questions that they obviously hoped would be the thin edge of the wedge in getting him to respond. Then Choi asked, "Are there any newly formed units in Japan, Captain Marshall?" He'd asked the question a dozen times before, but this time Marshall answered, "No, not unless you count the Japanese divisions and squadrons."

Choi and the other members of the board who could speak English seemed to explode and a riot of translation followed as fear stalked the table.

Choi was unable to keep his voice steady. "What Japanese divisions?"

Marshall saw that he had struck a nerve. "We Americans admire the way the Japanese ran Korea. We are re-forming the first seven divisions from the old Imperial Japanese Army, using men with experience in Korea. And six squadrons of B-29s."

Choi's mouth moved but no words came out; a confused fear showed in the eyes of every man on the board, but the North Koreans were obviously far more frightened than the Chinese. More than thirty years of occupation had taught them to hate the Japanese with unbridled passion and to fear them even more.

Marshall went on, "I'm only a captain, but even I know that by next year they'll have ten more Japanese divisions fighting in Korea. And, of course, they are designated to be the occupation troops, too."

Choi waved his arms in dismissal and the guards pulled Marshall to his feet. As Marshall left, he called over his shoulder, "The Japanese secret service is already here in Korea, taking names."

In his cell he felt a giddy joyous triumph swirl with concern that he may have gone too far. But he was left undisturbed till the next morning, and his evening ration of chook had *four* fishheads in it. He saved two of them for the morning.

7

Pasadena, California/January 1, 1953

He bulled his way through the crowd, Saundra following in his wake like a canoe behind an ocean liner. She didn't know who was playing in the Rose Bowl but she knew who was watching them— everyone in the stadium. The procession to their fifty-yard-line seats was causing more eyes to turn than the parade had earlier in the morning.

Tapping him on the shoulder she asked, "Are the natives hostile, Fred?"

Peterson smiled his big grin and nodded. "They're not hostile, Saundra—just observant. They see that times have changed when Negroes can have such good seats."

Moving as confidently as Caesar setting up a battle line, Peterson told his party of twelve where to sit, passed out the programs, made sure that the ladies had blankets and the men had silver flasks, doing everything with the absolute assurance of a man who had made millions already and was preparing to make millions more.

She felt he handled his wealth well; nothing in his speech or his manner ever referred to money. Instead, the whole focus of his life

242

was on accomplishment, on self-improvement—and on improving the status of the Negro. That's why he'd brought his twelve biggest clients to the Rose Bowl—to show them off.

Today his guests were mixed—also unthinkable in the past—three Negro couples and three white couples. Saundra shifted her attention to her new friends. The Negro couples were overdressed and somewhat formal; the white couples were trying hard to be friendly. After a few minutes she noticed something else; the white men would talk to both Negro men and women; the Negro men would initiate conversation with the white men only and be quietly deferential responding to the white women. The reactions among the women were more gender than race related; the more attractive of them spoke to everyone; the less attractive talked mostly with each other.

She tried to plumb her own feelings; she related to the Negro women easily, of course. And she understood the white men quite well—they were businessmen, first and foremost. But the white women were different; their movements, and their language, were different than what she was used to with Lyra and Patty. They seemed artificial, at once defensive and aggressive. It would take some time to figure them out.

"Always thinking, eh?" Fred squeezed her arm. It was not a romantic gesture, but once again she was strangely stirred by his primal power. For a moment, she wondered, wistfully almost, what she would do if he changed his manner and really tried to seduce her, then forced herself to think about his motives for having the various couples there today.

"Tell me about your friends, Fred." He turned away from the game to smile at her. "Later I'll tell you all about them. Right now let me just say that each man here has business with a counterpart; I'm the link between them."

Linkage had been the key to Peterson's financial success, but that alone didn't satisfy him. He was now seeking promising Negro businessmen—and women—and throwing his influence behind them.

Saundra was glad she was one he was trying to help. He had

provided immediate financial support, as well as the services of his accounting and advertising departments. All without charge. And he had treated her with sensitivity, from their very first meeting when their chemistry had almost boiled over. Peterson had remained the perfect gentleman, respecting the fact that she was married and her husband was overseas. When she first told him that John was missing in action, he was totally sympathetic. Later, he added, "I'll never interfere in your life as long as you are married. But I am not going to step aside and let you forget me. I guarantee that I will never make a romantic move—or let you make one— until you find out what has happened. If your husband is alive, I'll simply be a friend to you both. If he is dead—and I hope he is not, truly—I'll be here."

She grew to depend upon him; he was strong, like John, like she would have wanted her father to be, if she had ever known him. They spoke every day, on the phone or in person. Once, as Peterson was driving her to dinner, the usual planning-her-business strategy had evolved into a discussion of their personal feelings.

"Fred, this isn't a fair situation. I can't go on accepting your help and not offer you anything in return."

"I'm helping you because you are a smart businesswoman. A smart *Black* businesswoman." *OBSIDIAN* was promoting the use of *Black* instead of Negro; Peterson used it invariably in the magazine, despite the controversies it ignited.

"What do you get out of it?"

"First of all, if you are a success, you'll advertise in my magazine. That's the first return. Second, if you are a success, other Black women will imitate you. It's like building a bridge, one stone at a time. You're an important stone in my bridge to equality."

"I don't want you to feel that I'm exploiting you."

"I wouldn't let you. And I'm protecting myself, just staying in touch." He paused. "Besides, I have a favor to ask of you. A business favor."

"Anything."

"There's no way for you to know, but I'm providing financial support to a number of social rights activists around the country."

"I'm not surprised."

"No, but it's potentially poison to my business. I've got to be very careful not to support anyone who could upset my customers."

"Why would they care?"

"People are worried about the Communists; if they think the Reds are supporting a Black leader, they'll be angry. That's why I want you to become a front for me, to take my money and convey it to the people I designate."

She was silent for a moment.

"There's nothing illegal about it, Saundra; I'm not trying to get any tax deductions, nothing like that. I'm simply taking my money and giving it to them. But if one of the people I support makes a wrong move, or gets in trouble—or really is a Communist; there's no way for me to know—then I could lose a lot of business—white business—that I've spent years cultivating."

"You know that I'll do it. I'm not sure that it's enough."

"Ah, back to the primary subject. Let me tell you what you really mean. You're concerned that we're not making love, as if you should be repaying my patronage in bed."

She looked away; he was right as usual. She wanted to make love to him; she felt she could not while John's fate was unresolved. Yet she felt the attraction constantly, especially in the moments when his polite manner could not conceal how much he wanted her.

"You're right. I'm ashamed of myself, but that's the way it is. But I can't betray John, not now, not knowing what's happened to him."

More than a little angry, he barked, "Well, what you're saying is that you want me to take the decision out of your hands, to force myself on you. It would ease your conscience."

She blushed. He was exactly right, and it was horrible—*she* was horrible.

"Well, I won't. I put in my time in the last war; I'm not going to poach on someone's wife in this one." Then, in a kinder tone, "Don't worry about me, and don't worry about my love life—I'll tell you straight out that I'm no monk."

She knew that and it hurt, and she was angry with herself because it did.

He drove another block, then pulled over to the curb. Reflexively, each of them leaned back in the corner of their seat, as far apart as the Cadillac's body would permit.

"Saundra, here's the real scoop on what I believe. I think fate plays a hand in situations like this. If we're supposed to get together, we will; if we're not, we won't. In the meantime, I'm going to see to it that your business is a big success. You know what I mean by 'big success'? I mean you're going to be a millionaire, have a house in Beverly Hills, have a house in Europe, drive Cadillacs."

She shook her head. "I don't need all that. And you've already done too much."

"Hardly. Just look in the next issue of OBSIDIAN. I'm running a full-page blowup of that little advertisement you sent me. I've got my promotion people developing five more. I'll run another one every month for six months. At the end of that time, I'll start charging you full rates—and you'll be able to pay me."

He'd left her that evening turbulent with emotion, a mixture of satisfaction and frustration. She wanted her business to succeed, and Fred Peterson could make that happen. She hadn't betrayed John, and although she knew she had been vulnerable, and that a lesser man than Fred would have taken advantage of her, it made her want him all the more.

Three weeks after they'd watched USC slip by Wisconsin, 7 to 0, Saundra took a day off to take stock of her very complex life, her growing depression—and her growing guilt. She was increasingly attracted to Fred and wanted to spend every minute with him, just to enjoy the strength of his personality. It was not how the wife of a missing pilot should behave.

Eisenhower's inauguration day gave her a perfect excuse for a holiday. She found it impossible not to like Eisenhower's irrepressible grin, irresistible even in the grainy black and white of television. Unfortunately he didn't say the thing she wanted most to hear, that the war in Korea would be over soon. He'd gone there as he had promised, but he hadn't returned with a solution.

Later the same day, she'd driven out to George Air Force Base and talked to Bones's old squadron commander. He was immensely sympathetic and gave her the honest opinion she had asked for.

"It looks like Bones and Dave Menard, his wingman, were jumped by a flight of MiGs. Menard was driven off. The last time he saw Bones, he was diving straight for the ground, smoke pouring from his aircraft. Then the next day, Menard was killed in an accident."

"Did anybody see John bail out?"

"No. No sign of an ejection or a parachute."

"Then he's probably dead."

"No, don't count him out yet. He might have crash-landed. Bones was a hell of a pilot."

"Where did he get shot down?"

A curious look passed over the C.O.'s face. "Don't ask me that. I'll tell you after the war, okay?"

She knew at once what it meant. John had always said he'd go across the Yalu to get the MiGs if he had to. Except that they had gotten him.

She thanked him and went away unwilling to believe the worst. On the long drive back she realized how lucky she was that Fred had not taken advantage of her; she was now totally convinced that if she were faithful to John, he would come back. The only thing important to her was John's survival; when he came back, she would forget about her business, forget about Fred, and just take care of him, make him well again. And she would not even think what might happen if he didn't return.

Manpo, Korea/February 28, 1953

Marshall knew he was dying, and he was not afraid. Contrary to his fears, as his bodily strength declined, his willpower increased. He had recently been shifted to Manpo—he never knew why the switches were made, or why new interrogators came on duty. Detained momentarily in an outer room, he was shocked at the sight of himself in the first mirror he's seen in all of North Korea.

The mirror, old, cracked, and tarnished, was a metaphor for both Korea and his appearance. He had known he had lost weight, but the reflection was of a corpse—protruding cheekbones, werewolf eyes sunk back in his skull, lips split like cracked ice, his hair almost completely gray. Marshall felt pain at this squandering of his youth and health, yet took a bitter satisfaction that as bad as he looked he still lived and could still fight back.

He tried to detach himself from his suffering by making a military contest of his starvation. He would lie on the dirt floor and imagine wonderful meals—steaks and lobsters, and always when he was feeling homesick, neckbones, sauerkraut, and Bavarian dumplings. Then he would marshal the imaginary nourishment, an army of calories, and march it to different parts of his body. He always sent most of it to his brain, where he had identified a little compartment called "will." The neckbones always went to will because he needed strength to battle the man he hated. He prayed all day, reciting every prayer his father had taught him. Each night he prayed for a painful death for Choi. His father hadn't taught him that, but he would understand.

Now he was waiting for the thirty-fourth day of his latest round of interrogations to begin. The hut was just like every other one he'd been thrown in, walls of mud-packed cornstalks, no furniture, not even a straw mat on the floor. A few rough boards supported a thatched roof where he could always hear and often see rats running. As he thought of Choi he flexed his muscles, making them work against themselves, trying to stay strong enough to deal with his enemy. All the vicious processes of his imprisonment—the traveling about, the starvation, the freezing cold, the questions—had been distilled into one evil constant: Colonel Choi. Hating Choi kept him alive. He even took a perverse pleasure in the endurance of his pain, for it proved that Choi had not yet won completely.

Almost two weeks elapsed before the furor of his hoax about the Japanese divisions had finally died away, and now Choi was back with his bamboo stick and his blustering threats.

Marshall wanted to use his remaining strength to get him. He'd toyed with the idea of taking a gun from the guard, but he knew he was too weak to overpower anyone, and there were always three or four in the room next to him. But there had to be a way.

Alan Burkett, muffled as usual in wonderful warm clothes, had visited him two weeks before, bringing some cigarettes and chocolate wrapped in an old handkerchief. Burkett had also given him an American government issue ballpoint pen and a small notebook, telling him to write down his impressions of his captivity. He said that he would return in three weeks with some other treats, to pick up the notes.

That evening, on the way back from the slit-trench—he had a bowel movement only every six or seven days now—he found a dead rat, frozen stiff. He picked it up and stuffed it in his jacket, thinking of it first as food, then realizing that this rat was a way of striking at another one. When he entered his cell, he shoved the rat into a hole eroded in the mud wall where it would stay frozen.

The next four nights he squatted on the floor, using the dim light flowing under the shoji screen that separated his cell from the guard shack. With a splinter of plastic broken from the ballpoint pen, he carefully worked individual threads from the fabric of his cotton jacket. So cold that he had to put his filthy fingers in his mouth to warm them, Marshall wound the threads into slender cords and made a tiny parachute harness complete with shroud lines.

He spread Burkett's dirty handkerchief out on the floor, frozen slate-hard. Bearing down on the ballpoint pen, he carefully marked the handkerchief USAF on both sides, then drew a single large skull and crossbones in the middle. Then, for sentiment's sake, in the corner where the shroud line attached, he drew a tiny picture of Banjo, the dog Saundra had when they'd married. Next, he tied the harness around the frozen rat to make him a stiff, four-legged parachutist.

His artistic skills hadn't deserted him; even the printing looked authentic. The next time Choi asked him if he had conducted biological warfare, he would give it to him. It would be better than a cup of tea down his pants.

The next morning he was on his feet before the kicks, and the two guards marched him through the morning darkness to the interrogation center across the street. A fit of common sense took hold, and he tossed his labor of a week, the paratrooper rat, into an ox-drawn cart lumbering past.

The center was another mud hut, lacking a window. Like many of the huts it had newspapers pasted to the walls, including a few London *Daily Workers*. Even though they were old and spouted the Communist line, they offered him a diversion as he waited the customary thirty minutes while the interrogators assembled and discussed the forthcoming session. He was glad that he'd thrown the rat away—Choi might have beaten him to death on the spot. But just planning the joke had been worthwhile, sustaining his courage for a few days.

The interrogation process went on, implacable, interminable— question, translation, answer, translation, threat; question, translation, answer, translation, threat. He was weary, unable to summon the strength even surreptitiously to massage his folded arms with his suppurating hands.

At midday, there was an unexpected break. When the interrogators left for their luncheon, instead of being left guarded in the room with nothing to eat or drink, Bones was ushered into the adjacent building. Alan Burkett, engulfed in his uniform of argyle sweater and baggy brown pants, sat at a table loaded with food.

"Sit down, Captain Marshall, and join me for lunch."

Bones couldn't believe his eyes—there was rice, some boiled meat, fish roe, and dried squid. He wanted to fling himself onto the table, face down in the bowl, but he forced himself to sit down slowly and to wait. He knew he had to pace himself or he'd throw up.

"Have some tea, Captain. I thought you might like to be brought up to date on the peace talks."

Marshall nodded his head as he took the first spoonful of rice, letting it fill his mouth with a heavenly warmth and comfort, as different from chook as champagne from sewage. Like vibrations from a tuning fork, whole symphonies of sensation radiated from the rice. Lost in unbelievable pleasure, he sat perfectly still, his eyes closed and growing moist as Burkett went on, "Are you aware that peace talks were resumed at Panmunjom?"

Marshall slipped a piece of meat in his mouth—dog, probably, but he didn't care. The flavor welled over his tongue, and he could feel strength funneling into him like sunlight down a well, suffusing his pores, his veins, his nerves, his marrow.

"I'm glad you're enjoying your food. Did you hear what I said about the peace talks?"

Marshall nodded absently, chewing slowly, eyes closed again.

"Well, perhaps we'd better just eat, then talk."

In twenty minutes it was all gone; with each bite Marshall felt strength return and resolve wilt; instead of pacing himself, he stuffed everything in sight into his mouth.

Burkett was pleasant about it, eating little, and presenting Marshall tidbits from his side of the table. Marshall took the cigarette he offered, saving it to bribe a guard.

After a few sips of tea and some preliminary throat-clearing, Burkett assumed a grave-digger's air. "I'm afraid I have to tell you that you are in serious trouble, Captain Marshall."

Made reckless by the food, Marshall said, "I'm dying of starvation, being beaten senseless, and you tell me I'm in serious trouble? I've had more food at this one meal than I've had in the last three months. I'm living on chook—that rhymes with puke! Look at this!" With a groan, he pulled his leg and lifted his swollen pustulant foot level with the table's edge.

Burkett gagged. He looked away, lit a cigarette, then went on.

"No, I'm quite serious. The North Korean government has formally charged the United Nations with conducting germ warfare. They already have confessions, as you know. If you don't confess today, I can tell you that you will be dead in forty-eight hours."

The single meal had allowed fear as well as hope to creep back, and Marshall felt his stomach go into spasm.

"I won't confess. Let them shoot me."

"They won't shoot you, nothing so pleasant. But they will kill you, and it's absolutely pointless. The North Korean government wouldn't make a formal accusation like this unless they had proof. I believe them. If you sign a confession, they'll see that your wife and family are notified that you are alive, and when the war is over, you'll go home."

"Out of the question!"

There was an uproar next door, and Burkett excused himself. Choi burst into the room.

"So, Captain Marshall, you say the United States does not wage biological warfare! Look at this!"

With a sweep of his arm, he plopped a canvas-wrapped object on the table. He pulled at the folds to reveal Marshall's rat, still stiff in his parachute.

"Look at this, they found it in a cart at the inspection point."

Marshall kept his face impassive, trying to see if Choi was really taken in or if this was just a prelude to a beating. The whole thing was ludicrous; they could not possibly take it seriously. Then with a dawning horror he realized that the Koreans were so cut off from the world, so terribly impoverished, that even an educated man like Choi could see only the symbolism, the fulfillment of his dialectic, overlooking the sheer stupidity of the concept.

There was no mistaking the colonel's joy.

Marshall went the next step, hesitating, then saying slowly, "All right. I'll confess that I parachuted rats out of my airplane. This is proof, I can't deny it anymore."

They escorted him back to his room, talking excitedly in Korean. Choi had a table and chair brought in, along with lined white paper and two pens. Marshall began to write, trying to be funny enough for American readers, but serious enough for Orientals.

"I, Captain John Stuart Marshall, confess that I dropped measles-infected rats by parachute from my F-86 Thunderjet."

The "Thunderjet" was the F-84, not the F-86, and no Sabre pilot would ever admit that he'd flown one.

Choi leaned over. "Say where you dropped them."

Marshall added "from 40,000 feet, at 600 miles per hour, over defenseless villages in North Korea." Any American would see how absurd a concept it was; rats would freeze and parachutes rip apart under those conditions.

"Scratch out 'defenseless.' "

Marshall complied.

"Now write it over on the other sheet and sign it."

When he had done so, Choi snatched the paper and ran from the room toward a waiting truck. A guard handed Marshall a thin cotton blanket, the first he'd had in North Korea. He gave the guard his cigarette on the spot.

At midnight, Choi burst through the shoji screen of his cell. Marshall, curled on the floor in the minimal comfort of the blanket, groggily heard the screaming, then awoke in time to recognize Choi and see the boot arcing toward his face.

"Nigger! I will kill you tonight!"

Choi grunted with each kick, cursing him alternately in Korean and English.

"Nigger! You made the parachute!"

Marshall's body, inert as a rolled rug, offered no resistance, torn flesh and broken vessels absorbing the kicks. Bleeding and unconscious, one eye bulging from its socket, his magnificent lunch spewing bloodily from his mouth, he lay in a black void, insensible to cold and pain.

Gathering his strength, Choi kicked again. "Now, Captain Nigger, you'll never lie to me again!"

Marshall lay there, his shattered defense mechanisms flickering as his broken body made spasmodic last-ditch efforts to sustain his ebbing life.

Exhausted from his efforts, Choi stood over him and spat out, "Nigger! Nigger! Nigger!"

He reeled out of the room, as certain that Marshall was dead as he was that his own career was ended. The guards watched him go, then went back to sleep without even looking into the cell.

Little Rock, Arkansas/February 15, 1953

Stan had started divorce proceedings as soon as he got back to Little Rock from Korea, but Milo Ruddick had intervened with his usual directness.

"Stan, don't be a damn fool. You will *not* divorce Ginny. If you do, I'll hound you out of the Air Force and out of aviation. You know I can do it."

Coleman, intimidated as always by the man, fought back. "How would you feel if you came home and found your wife screwing a nigger? A servant?"

"She was raped, Stan, you know that!"

"Raped, my ass; if any raping was done, she did it!"

"It's all been hushed up; Nathan's moved away, nobody knows but us. Are you going to go into court and make a fool out of yourself?"

"Yes, I am, and you, too. It'll look great that you've got a whore for a daughter, out fucking whoever comes along."

Ruddick's voice was like chilled steel. "Shut up. I want you to stop and think for a moment. Do you believe that I would permit things to go so far? That I would allow *you* to put me in such a position?"

The contempt in the word *you* and the quiet menace in Ruddick's voice were convincing.

Then the familiar, throaty politician's coo returned. "Now, I don't want to be rough. If you go along with me on this, I guarantee that you'll become a general. You know I can do it. And then there is the estate—I'll see to it that you participate in its proceeds. And we can alter my will so that you'll get a one-third share after I die. Ginny's already agreed to this."

Coleman winced as he realized that either the threat or the bribes would have been enough. Putting them together had been an overwhelming argument.

"I can't live with her, not after this."

"Sure you can; half the successful marriages in this country are make-believe. You can live your own life, have your own women—just don't get a divorce and screw up your career."

A residual flame of defiance flared in Coleman. "And yours, too!"

"That will never happen, I assure you. If we gloss over this little untidy business, you and Ginny can both have good, productive lives. I'll see to it that you get the best jobs in the Air Force, promotions, and good contacts with industry when you retire. I can do that, you know I can."

Stan hung his head, hating himself for allowing Ruddick this ascendancy. There was no sense to it. He was a better pilot than most, a good officer; yet he still chose to depend upon this miserable man. He wanted to stand up and smash Ruddick, to send his fist smashing against that well-shaven jaw. Yet he looked at the floor, knowing that a deal had been made. Ruddick knew it, too, but he added, "If you don't cooperate, I'll be very unhappy—and so, my friend, will you."

Nashville, Tennessee/March 6, 1953

Elsie loved to walk the aisles of the plant on Friday—payday. Everybody felt good, there was a general air of expectancy, and she was sure to get some nice compliments, rendered respectfully from the foremen.

It must have been like this in the old days in the South, she thought, all the field hands looking on, the overseers paying their respects.

Elsie had their respect, in truth. Troy McNaughton had always been a mercurial sort and held himself distant from the workers on the floor. Elsie toured all the time, keeping her fingers on the pulse of the place. If somebody had a complaint, they could confide in her, confident that she wouldn't tell on them, believing she would help if she could.

The huge B-47 center sections and inner-wing panels were moving down the line, glistening in the sheen of their protective green paint. The subcontract was immensely profitable, for the terms had been computed on the higher wages paid in Seattle. In Nashville, McNaughton was making a killing.

But the parts were anonymous; they never moved down the line to assume the personality of a complete airplane to be flown away. Instead, they were sealed in long cocoons and shipped by rail to Boeing in Wichita or to Lockheed in Marietta, Georgia, where B-47s were completed.

She much preferred trooping the refurbishing line, where old airframes were given new life, and at the end of the process engines sputtered, props spun, and an airplane took off. She had asked Dick Baker to meet her there, and he was late as usual.

McNaughton's suicide had no impact on the plant's operation. Elsie couldn't truthfully say that she missed him; in the last years of his life, even before his illness, he had been difficult to get along with. For some reason, missiles had taken his fancy, and it had bothered him that none of his missile programs got off the ground, literally or figuratively. And after he learned he was dying, he was impossible.

"Yo!"

It was Baker. God, if she could only bring herself to get rid of him! He'd slipped into being familiar with her in public, no matter how many times she'd reproached him for it. But that was nothing. She'd been going through some purchase orders at random—an old habit of hers—and had found out that Baker had authorized the purchase of some critical B-47 attachment bolts. Called "milk bottle pins" because of their shape, they were used to attach the inner-wing panel to the fuselage center section.

"Who the hell authorized you to get into the parts-buying business?"

"We already talked about that, honey. If I'm lying I'm dying! I told you I could improve on some of the prices and you said, 'We'll see.' Well, take a look. I got those parts for sixty percent less than we were paying before."

"What are they made of, putty?"

"No, this is first-rate material, and a first-rate producer. He's just hungry, wants to buy into the business. I had our quality control guys check it out real good."

"Don't ever do it again. Let me rephrase that. *If* you ever do it again, I'll fire you on the spot."

His voice dropped, threatening. "You'll never fire me, babe—you need what I've got, as often as I'll give it to you. And don't you forget it."

She shuddered, knowing he was right.

Salinas, California/March 9, 1953

"Damn, Bandy, we haven't argued like this for twenty years! Seems like old times."

"Don't old-time me, you silver-haired bastard! We're strapping these JATO bottles on whether you want to or not." Bandfield had installed the battery of two JATO bottles on each side of the amphibian's fuselage.

Roget slammed his fist against the hull of the Catalina. "Come on, be sensible. Weight is critical on this old dog."

Bandfield put down his wrench; the temptation to crack Roget on the head with it was too strong.

"Look, you con me into spending two weeks of my leave to fly this thing, and then you won't let me do what I think is right. It damn near doesn't make sense—you keep telling me weight is critical when you're going to be scooping up tons of water?"

Roget growled, "Of course we're going to scoop up tons of water—that's the whole idea."

Bandfield wasn't convinced that it was safe. Roget Aircraft had converted seven Lockheed Lodestars to executive aircraft, cleaning them up and selling them as "Roget Rockets"; they had a backlog of nine orders on the books. But Roget had acquired six Grumman TBMS, old torpedo bombers, two B-25s, and a gorgeous C-54—all intended to be made into water bombers for firefighting.

"Hadley, I think you're getting us in over our head, tying all this money up in inventory and development costs. The market just isn't there yet, and you know the Forest Service won't buy anything they haven't developed themselves."

"Yeah, yeah, yeah, you're always too conservative. The Forest Service is fiddling around trying to drop water from crop dusters—hell, you can't get a decent load in a little Stearman! I've been running some tests, and unless you can get two hundred gallons out in one drop, it's not worth it. They're bound to come around, and when they do, I'll be ready."

Bandfield shook his head; it was a familiar melody, one he'd heard for twenty years, all his adult life. The strange thing was that Roget was always right—it was just that he was always years ahead of his time.

Now Roget was looking five years downstream. Fighting forest-fires with water bombers was going to be a tough job. The amount of water even a C-54 could carry was limited, and the planes would have to be precisely positioned to drop at exactly the right spot, or else the whole load was wasted. And most of the time would be spent flying back and forth from the fire site to an airfield where they could retank with water.

That was the reason for their current experiment. Roget was determined to cut the turn-around time of the airplanes. He'd rigged the Consolidated PBY Amphibian with two scoops that dropped down on each side of the hull, snorkles in reverse. The plan was for the PBY to drop its load, then go and make a quick pass along a lake surface, touching down under power. The scoops would lower and open, water would be crammed into the tanks, and the PBY would be back over the fire site in minutes. Figuring conservatively, he estimated that his system would quadruple the utility of a fire-fighting airplane—if it worked.

Bandfield stepped back up on the stand and continued bolting the

JATO bottle holder onto the fuselage. "Well, old man, I'll tell you what's really critical, and that's power. This old clunker hasn't got any. In the service it used to take off at eighty knots, cruise at eighty-five and land at eighty—I don't know what it'll do after you stuff it full of water."

"You're worrying about the wrong thing. It's the water scooper I'm concerned about."

"Don't worry about the scooper, pal, just worry about whether this tub has the oomph to get back off the water. If it doesn't we're going to wind up in the trees at the edge of the lake."

After a week of intensive work, they were ready for the first test of the system. Roget insisted on going along, overriding Bandy's objections.

"I may be a geezer, but I can still take care of myself. It's my idea—if something's wrong with it, I'm the guy who needs to see what happens so I can fix it."

"I'd rather have you in a boat at the lake, ready to fish me out if we go in."

"Don't worry, I've already made arrangements to have some of our people out there in a powerboat, if we need it."

Lake Sutherland was a 3,600-acre water management lake northeast of Salinas, nestled in a shallow ring of hills, with an adequate north/south approach and departure axis. Bandfield made two low practice passes, uncomfortable because he had only about ten hours in the airplane. Speaking through the intercom, he called, "Hadley, I'm going to try to put it down this time. Ready?"

"All set."

Bandfield skirted the lake's edge, wishing he had time to admire the blue-green contrast of trees and water at the edge of the pebbled beach.

His landing attempt was bad; trying to minimize the impact forces, he kept on too much power and shot across the lake's surface without ever getting low enough for the scoop mechanism to engage.

Embarrassed and annoyed, Bandfield growled, "I'm just going to drop this sucker in like it was a normal landing, Hadley. As soon as I touch down, you punch your buttons."

Taking his time, Bandfield made a long, low approach over the scrub pine and manzanitas that lined the north side of the lake, the first growth after the forest fire of two years before. He touched down a hundred yards from the shore and yelling "Scoops out!" applied full power.

Roget's scoops lowered and the bright-blue water cascaded inside, staggering the big amphibian as if an anchor had been thrown out. As the weight built, Bandfield felt the sloshing water shift the center of gravity back and forth, bucking the airplane like a rocking horse.

"Gotta have more tank baffling . . ." Now the PBY was staggering nose high, the rear of its hull dragging the surface, airspeed dead-stopped at eighty, just below the point he needed to get airborne as the opposite shore loomed up.

"JATO coming on." His fingers stabbed the switches and, after a second's hesitation that lasted a lifetime, the rockets fired, lifting the PBY majestically into the air, water dripping from the hull.

Nothing was said on the way back. When they'd landed, Roget crawled forward and said, "Told you we needed that JATO. By God, I guess you'll learn to listen to me."

Frederick Air Force Base, California/ March 12, 1953

The B-47s sat on the ramp like acres of gigantic insects, their long slender wings drooping, sleek fuselages cocked nose high on the bicycle undercarriage. Each of the three squadrons of the 103rd Bomb Wing (Medium) were equipped with fifteen of them—and each bomber could carry more explosive power in its bomb bay than an entire wing of B-29s armed with conventional bombs.

The B-47s cost $3 million apiece and were the hottest airplane in the air, faster than most fighters. They were the backbone of the

Strategic Air Command's evolving war plan, demanding of their crews—but trouble-prone and dangerous to fly.

Lieutenant Colonel Stan Coleman's assignment as commander of the 445th Bomb Squadron suited him perfectly. His experience in fighters made the transition training at McConnell Air Force Base easy, and he had quickly mastered the B-47. The fact that he had less flying time in bombers than anyone in the outfit was more than offset by the fact that he was an F-86 ace from Korea. Both the base and the command had been the first of Milo Ruddick's payments in kind.

Ginny had stayed in Little Rock. The story was that she was there to help manage the estate and no one cared enough to question the argument.

Coleman was a realist. He knew he had been lucky in F-86s and felt he'd earned the chance to relax a little, with a copilot to back him up and a radar-observer to navigate. He found that his salesman's personality fit into the general scheme of things at Frederick. The 103rd was run by a Colonel Williams, a World War II B-29 pilot who liked a good time and took care of his people. Guy and he had hit it off instantly—Williams loved to party, and the two of them would put on civvies and cruise the bars up and down Route 99. Coleman bowled the country girls over, and Williams was more than content to pick up on his rejects.

Now things were looking even better. Fitz had finally gotten over his anger about the Menard accident, after Coleman had persuaded him to for weeks—and bailed him out of two jams. When Fitz graduated from Wichita later in the month, he'd be his copilot. He was a perfect choice—skilled and discreet.

Manpo, Korea/March 13, 1953

U Eun Chur had come hesitantly into the room on the day following the beating, expecting to find Marshall dead. Yet his heart still beat in his frozen, broken body, and his breath came in rasping grunts. U brought in two armloads of thatching and a sheet of canvas; he lifted Marshall from the floor and laid him on it.

The next morning he checked again—the man was still alive. U Eun Chur brought in a bowl of warm water, washed Marshall's face and hands and sponged his lips. That afternoon he went to the kitchen as usual for the prisoner's chook ration. It was given without comment.

It was two days before Marshall, responding to a primitive urge for survival, was able to swallow the diluted gruel without even gaining consciousness; he lingered on, scarcely breathing. U Eun Chur undertook his care by default—no one else knew what to do. To his surprise, he found that he was no longer bullied and given the worst tasks to do. Instead, like the prisoner, he's simply ceased to exist.

In the camp there had been little reaction to Colonel Choi's beating of the American; prisoners were often beaten to death. But this man refused to die, becoming an embarrassment to all but U Eun Chur, the only Korean who'd shown Marshall compassion. If he had died, they would have known what to do—shovel him into some common grave. If he had been an ordinary prisoner, they might have taken him to the hospital. But as a prisoner who had ruined an officer's career, Marshall was an enigma, too dangerous to help, too threatening to kill, so his existence was ignored.

U was sitting by Marshall's side, puzzling about the rising tide of fear that permeated the camp. Joseph Stalin had died the week before and the entire Communist structure seemed to be reeling. The door to the hut creaked open and a North Korean captain stood before him with a pistol in his hand.

"Where is the Negro American?"

U pointed to Marshall, blood crusted around his nose and mouth.

The captain studied Marshall for a few moments, then screamed, "Get this man to the hospital. We need him for an exchange of prisoners." In that instant, Marshall's life had assumed value. The captain ordered U to stay at his side.

At the hospital the doctor gave him transfusions and intravenous liquids from captured American stocks. On the second morning, Marshall awoke to look into U Eun Chur's frightened eyes and slurred, "Where is Colonel Choi?"

U Eun Chur understood only "Choi," and he shook his head vigorously and pointed out the door. Then he ran to get the doctor.

Pine Bluff, Arkansas/June 30, 1953

It was a pleasure to see Josten work. The rough crowd that made up the Klan—mill hands, truck drivers, laborers—listened respectfully as Josten told them how close Hitler had come to winning, and what he would have done to the Jews and the nigras in America if he had not been betrayed by his army generals.

Pine Bluff was surrounded by thousands of acres owned by the paper companies, who harvested the timber. Most of the land was totally vacant, leased out to hunters, and dominated by clouds of savage mosquitoes. The Klan meeting was held on acreage Ruddick owned near the Arkansas River. Armed Klansmen blocked the access roads to keep out unwanted visitors, while the state police looked the other way. It was one of the many signs of Josten's organizational skills.

They were hanging on his words—his talks were really rewards for undergoing the tough discipline and training he demanded. As terribly injured as he had been, Josten now had the strength to work them all into the ground, roaming the drill fields, supervising rifle practice. They tolerated his brusque instructions, totally convinced that they were now working with "the real thing."

The German had done his homework. His speeches were studded with references to the Confederacy, to all the great fighters of the

South; Lee, of course, and Stonewall Jackson—but also the irregulars like Nathan Bedford Forest and Quantrell. Listening to him one got the feeling that Lee had been Hitler's right-hand man, that Stonewall Jackson had led the thrust through France, that Rommel had charged at Gettysburg, and that Quantrell could still be found in the Alpine Redoubt.

He mesmerized them, speaking in cascading sentences, words piled upon words, emotions lashing emotions, the torches casting flickering shadows across his lean face, seeming to send sparks flying from his demonic eyes. He painted a clear picture, one they believed and understood, of noble white men defending their women against raping nigras led by grasping Jews. He never said nigger or Negro—always *nigra*, and with a Germanic snarl he turned Jews into *Juice*.

Ruddick nudged Dixon Price in the ribs as Josten moved toward his conclusion, his hoarse voice brittle with intensity, saying, "Let me tell you a story, my comrades. In Munich, in 1923, a little band of men led by Adolf Hitler were shot down like dogs by the reactionaries of the German government. Yet only ten years later Hitler came to power in a new Germany!"

Josten let the facts sink in, saw the crowd grow tense with excitement, with the idea that they could gain control, be somebody.

"When Hitler began to expand the German armed forces, he brought with him the flag that had been with him at Munich, a flag that was stained with the blood of his comrades. It was called the 'Blood Flag of Munich,' and he used it to consecrate all of the banners of the newly formed units of the Army, of the Navy, and of the Luftwaffe."

Josten looked about, knowing that *consecrate* was a big word to use with this group of idiots.

"He blessed the new flags with the Blood Flag."

There was an audible gasp of comprehension.

Josten turned, and a case was handed to him.

"In this leather case, I have the original Blood Flag of Munich. And with the same flag that Adolf Hitler used to consecrate the flags of the German armed forces . . ."

He turned and a huge silk flag carrying the Klan insignia was presented to him.

"So in the spirit of creating a new Blood Order, I consecrate the flag of the Pine Bluff Klaven—the first Storm Klan's flag!"

For a moment there was a shocked silence so profound that he could hear the sounds of frogs croaking on the river bank. Then there came a guttural roar from the crowd, a swelling joyous scream of approval that echoed across the field.

Josten carefully replaced the Blood Flag in the leather pouch, gave the raised-hand salute of the Nazis, and left the podium, going directly to a car where Ruddick and Price were waiting to take him to the next meeting, outside of Little Rock.

"Helmut, this Storm Klan idea is working like monkey glands on the old guard."

"Yes, but there's not much we can do with the older members; they're too set in their ways. The only way to rejuvenate the movement is with new recruits."

Driving slowly through the admiring crowd, some of whom pressed their faces against the glass to get a closer glimpse of Josten, Ruddick said, "Recruitment's not a problem now. We could sign up a thousand men tomorrow. You've got the people excited!"

"You all had me going, I swear I was ready to jine up myself." Excited, Price had dropped his usual crisp accent, lapsing into his native Texas drawl.

Josten responded, "Let's not be hasty. I'd rather keep the numbers low for a while. Let's insist on high standards of physical fitness, perhaps even require a high school diploma for eligibility to become a Storm Klanner."

Ruddick nodded quietly to Price, then said, "Helmut's created a new initiation ceremony, one like the SS used. We'll give the candidates ceremonial knives; at the initiation we'll slash their fingers and have them touch them to the flag."

Dixon slapped his thigh, laughing. "That'll get 'em. Why is it that blood and knives appeal so much?"

"They appeal to brutes, and brutes are what we want."

Ruddick drove swiftly on the two-lane road, delighted to see his idea taking shape, pleased that Josten and Price were getting on well.

Price asked, "What about the older Klan members? Can we still use them? Aren't they jealous?"

Josten nodded to Ruddick to speak. "The older men are jealous, but we'll keep them, even let them wear the robes to cover their fat bellies. But the young ones, we'll give them spiffy new uniforms."

"Like the SS?"

Josten shook his head. "No—too provocative. We'll take the Arkansas State Trooper uniform and dress it up. The Storm Klan will have a white band around the hats and arms—signifying purity, of course—and silver-colored insignia. We'll make that close to the SS, use an S and a K, done like lightning bolts."

Ruddick chimed in, "And they'll have short hair, like the troopers wear."

Tired, Josten leaned back in the seat. "No, even shorter. We'll crop it to the skin, like the German students used to do."

They came to a railroad crossing where an L&N freight train rattled by. Ruddick turned, saying, "Helmut, these ideas are too good. Dixon and I don't think we need to wait. We'll lose time if we don't expand the Storm Klan as soon as we can. Who knows how long we can keep them interested?"

Josten shook his head.

"No. Let the word spread first. It will make the Storm Klanners seem so immensely desirable that you'll have to turn hundreds away." He was quiet for a moment, then went on, "Let's get the Storm Klan completely indoctrinated, ready to die for the cause. They'll become the elite SS while the Klan will remain the SA. I don't want to dilute the results by expanding too fast."

Ruddick gave in, as he realized he was beginning to do in every instance to Josten. He was going to have to talk this over with Dixon. The caboose passed, the gates lifted, and they drove on in silence.

Little Rock, Arkansas/July 4, 1953

Ruddick was sitting with his hand over the receiver when Dixon Price came in, red-faced, collar soiled with sweat and tie askew, strutting like a banty rooster.

"It's the governor. As usual." The governor got uneasy when Price wasn't immediately available and kept tabs on his whereabouts by phone.

Price rolled his eyes and took the phone while Ruddick went over to the weathered leather couch; if it had been a client, he would have left the room, but he and Price went back too far for such niceties. As he listened, he watched Price closely.

"Yes, Governor, I understand what you mean. But if you'll recall, I told you that I was working on that, and I'm going to talk to Milo about that just this minute."

Price was five-feet four-inches tall and had weighed the same 125 pounds since he was in high school. His thinning white hair covered his sun-pink bald spot like a thin smear of frosting on a strawberry cake. Small but mighty, Ruddick thought. In thirty years of politics, Price was the smartest, toughest man he'd ever met, and he was profoundly grateful that they'd always been on the same side. After the war, as soon as the oil business had come off, Price had come to Little Rock and set up his own law firm. He'd never run for political office himself, but he'd insinuated himself into state politics from the start. He'd been the primary reason the governor had been elected, and for the past two years he had practically run the state.

Price shook his head as he listened to the governor. After a while he let the receiver dangle, spinning on its cord; Ruddick could hear the governor's droning voice. Price flipped the receiver to his hand, mumbled, "Uh uh, uh uh, yes, sir," and then cut in. "Governor, ah don't want to interrupt, but remember, you've got a meeting in the Capitol building in two minutes. With the folks from TVA? Remember? Yes, sir. Good-bye, sir."

"The governor's on his usual rampage?"

"I tell you, Milo, I have my hands full keeping him on track. He's the most capricious man I ever met."

"What does he want now?"

"Well, he's not satisfied with just having the Klan and the National Guard supporting him on segregation. He's upset about the progress the Air Force is making with integration on Little Rock Air Force Base. Wants you and me to go out and straighten out the base commander."

"Stupid move; the base commander doesn't owe him anything. He's not going to ruin his own chances for promotion, just to butter up the governor."

"Well, you know how he is, he gets an idea, he holds on to it like a tick in a hound's ear. I told him the best thing was to let me work on a local level. There are some people out there I can talk to, Southern boys, maybe we can get some token support. But that's not why you asked me to come in."

"No, I wanted to get your take on Josten. I'm worried that I've let him go too far, that I'm losing control over him."

"I don't think so. You've let him have his way, you had to do that to get the kind of enthusiasm he has. But you can get rid of him tomorrow. I think letting him run things is to our advantage. If something goes sour, we can walk away from it, point our fingers at him."

"He's a clever bastard. Mean as a snake, too. That's why the Klansmen love him."

"Yes, but without us, he's got no financial support. He sure as hell couldn't run the Klan by collecting dues. Besides, I don't think he's out to take over the Klan. He's got something else on his mind, something personal. I get the feeling that this job is just a holding action for him, something to keep him busy while he sorts things out."

Ruddick relaxed and went to the side bar. "Damn. No wonder you're running the state, Dixon, you've always got the take on things. Let me fix you a little drink—you've earned it."

Pyoktong, North Korea/August 15, 1953

Since asking his first question about Choi, John Marshall had not said another word, fearing more interrogation. There had been none; instead he had been isolated, in contact with no one but U Eun Chur. The guards did not speak to him, even in Korean. Yet in the last few weeks, his treatment had vastly improved; he was allowed to bathe once a week, and the last two times there had been a sliver of brown soap. His rations had increased to two bowls of rice a day, along with some kimchee and about two ounces of the amorphous, indefinable substance that passed for meat. He ate it greedily.

As he sat dozing in the spot of sunshine at the door to his hut, the routine noise of the camp was suddenly broken with blaring march music and the sound of cymbals and drums. A ragtag procession of Chinese soldiers and Korean natives was marching through the center of the camp, carrying large pictures of Comrade Mao and Comrade Kim Il Sung.

"Good show, eh, Marshall?"

Alan Burkett was standing beside him, dressed in the same un-made-bed outfit of baggy brown pants, plaid shirt, and argyle sweater that he'd worn to their lunch.

Burkett sat down and offered him a cigarette. Marshall put it away as guard bait.

"Well, when are you leaving?"

"Don't joke with me, Burkett. They'll never let me out of here."

"*Au contraire*, my friend. The war has been over since June; you're one of the last captives. They'll be shipping you out as soon as you are fattened up a bit."

He felt a flash of anticipation, automatically suppressed it, and repeated, "Don't joke with me, Burkett."

"No joke at all. You'll be going to Panmunjom in a few days, and then it's over the border to your brothers-in-arms."

The Englishman seemed genuinely pleased to relay the news.

"And I'm glad to tell you that I was able to inform your wife and family about the happy news. I sent a wire this morning. They probably already have it."

Marshall sat, unwilling to believe. The last time Burkett had been with him, Colonel Choi had almost beaten him to death.

"Do you know where Colonel Choi is?"

"No, old chap; he just vanished."

"Well, I'll find him, come peace or war, hell or high water."

Washington, D.C./September 1, 1953

Erich Weissman walked out the prison doors, contrasting the last ten months of relative luxury with the years he'd spent in concentration camps. To call this a prison, with three good meals a day, a bunk, a library, even medical care.

But it was good to be out. He'd been picked up a week after the attempted shooting, still driving the Chevrolet. The police had not made the connection between the assassination attempt and the car theft, but he'd drawn a year's sentence.

An old friend was waiting outside for him. He got in the car—a Chevrolet, not unlike the one he'd stolen, and Jacob Goldberg, tall, thin but board-hard, arms folded over the wheel as if he were clutching the reins of a team, said, "Welcome, Erich. How was it?"

"Better than Dachau, worse than Coney Island."

Goldberg sat for a moment pulling on his thin driving gloves; Weissman had never seen anyone do that before. Goldberg adjusted the mirrors carefully, checked his tie in the process, then carefully moved out into traffic. He was a fashion plate, a regular Adolphe Menjou, Weissman thought, but a neatnik.

"They want you to rest for a while, take it easy. We have less stressful work for you in Chicago."

Weissman whirled in his seat. "Am I being punished for missing my targets?"

Goldberg smiled. "No, anyone can miss. They just want you not to be conspicuous for a while."

Silent for a moment, trying to quiet his resentment over Goldberg's patronizing smile—the man had been born in New York,
lived in the United States all his life, what did he know?—
Weissman said, "You had me shooting at the wrong man. I should
have concentrated on Josten—we are fellow alumni from Nordhausen. I want another chance at him."

He could see that Nordhausen didn't mean anything to the man.
"Perhaps . . . but not for a while. You recuperate, investigate some
records for us. Then we'll see."

Weissman stared straight ahead, pursing his lips. He would go
along with this for a while. If they didn't give him a new assignment, a new try at Josten, he'd go off on his own. It's a free country.

Pyoktong, North Korea/September 15, 1953

Dangling his legs off the wooden table, Marshall surveyed his battered body with some contentment. No doubt about it, he had put on some weight and most of his wounds were healing.

"Ready?"

He nodded and looked away, concentrating on the white medical table with its array of chipped enameled bowls, bottles of red and blue fluids, and the neat kit of surgical instruments marked U.S. ARMY, wondering why they all looked unusual, then realizing it was because they were serving their intended purpose. Almost everything else in North Korea was improvised and make do: boards torn from railway cars to make buildings, stoves made from truck fenders, clogs made from tires. No wonder Dr. Liu seemed so proud of his office.

"Hold still." Then, to distract him from the pain, "You friend Burkett coming today."

Apprehension shot through Marshall, as cold and cutting as the scalpel slicing away the proud flesh from the wounds in his side. He winced, even though the pain from Liu's blade was not great.

"He's not my friend, Dr. Liu. You're my only friend here."

Burkett's past visits had marked turning points in Marshall's prison life. The first time, Choi had almost beaten him to death; the second, he was told he would be freed. It had been six weeks since their last talk, and things had continued to change for the better. They'd hauled him back from Manpo to Camp 5, by the beautiful lake, then on to this empty main prison camp on the Yalu. It had been in turmoil when he was here before; now it was strangely quiet, as charged with memories as a dead parent's home.

They still kept him isolated, but now there were no other prisoners to be seen in the distance, to yearn to talk to. Silence muffled the camp like a cloak of wet felt; bugles didn't blow, the loudspeaker no longer crackled its malevolent signals of bad news; there were no soldiers herding prisoners along the crooked streets.

His personal treatment had improved tremendously. Dr. Liu, who had examined him at Manpo, now saw him every day, treating his wounds with sulfa drugs and giving him vitamin pills. The doctor was learning English—and perhaps surgery, judging by his eagerness to practice on Marshall at every opportunity.

"How you bowels?"

"Still sick, much diarrhea."

The word was difficult for Liu, and he repeated it several times. "Diarrhea, diarrhea, like dysentry. Well, you try this, good medicine. You say."

Liu shoved the box in Marshall's face, who read aloud, "Sulfaguanidine."

As Liu tried unsuccessfully to repeat the word, Marshall regarded the package with suspicion. It was obviouly from American stores, but he couldn't be sure what the medication was, or what it was good for. Still, he knew he had to gain strength, to convert the better rations he was receiving into flesh on his bones. In the past he'd been given only a noxious mixture of ground charcoal and tannic acid that didn't cure the diarrhea and made him violently ill. He decided to accept it unless Liu wanted to administer it with a hypodermic—he was still unwilling to submit to that, afraid that they would give him some sort of truth serum.

"Shot?"

The doctor's smile was genuine. "Drink!" he said, and, wiping a tin cup carefully with his dirty handkerchief, shook the sulfa into it, filled it with cold tea, and stirred it with a spoon he had tied on a string around his neck like a stethoscope.

Three hours later, when he saw Burkett shambling toward him, Marshall felt strangely strong and comfortable. For the first time in months, his knees didn't tremble or his stomach convulse with the need for instant release.

"Burkett, you Commie bastard, I'm going to live! I'm going to get out of here."

Burkett, his face puffed and swollen from drink, leaned against the entrance. "Of course you are, dear boy, and soon, too." Marshall hated his affected accent.

"What have you heard?"

"You're to be moved south to the so-called 'Freedom Village.' That's where most of the transfers have taken place. But do come along, I've arranged for you to go to the cinema."

Somehow it didn't surprise Marshall—after months of brutality, he had food, medicine, and now, entertainment.

They went inside a hut that once had been an orderly room, judging by the notices still pinned to the wall, and a derelict desk and chair. At one end of the room a sheet of white cloth had been hung as a screen; at the other was an ancient 16-mm film projector.

There were no lights to turn off, but the shutters on the one window were pulled and, outside, a generator was started. In a few minutes the projection light snapped on and the opening titles flickered, first in an Oriental script, then in English. He felt his stomach clench as he heard the words "United States Air Force Captain John Marshall confesses to germ warfare." The voice was unmistakably Alan Burkett's.

When his image appeared on the screen, Marshall was appalled at the way he looked, furious that he had been filmed without his knowledge.

"How did you do this, Burkett?"

"Simple, old chap. They shot through a hole in the wall. Too bad there's no sound track for your comments; I believe you are in the midst of your famous 'Wanna buy a duck?' routine."

Marshall scanned the screen closely, hoping he could see his lips move, so that later the film could be slowed down and his lips read by someone, but the shot had been taken from the side. The film switched to show some damaged drop tanks and a native funeral procession, with Burkett's voice coming in loud over the squeak of the projector's take-up reel, droning on about germ warfare and its cost to innocent civilians.

Marshall couldn't believe how poorly it was done; he glanced at Burkett, smiling at the screen with pleasure as he heard himself say, "And so Captain Marshall, having confessed his complicity in germ warefare, signs his confession."

On the screen his shattered body slumped on the chair. God, how bad he looked, hair almost white, knobby elbows protruding. A guard stepped forward and prodded his arm, and he signed the papers placed before him. The lights flickered brightly, and Burkett turned the projector off.

"We'll have that edited and be releasing it throughout the West just about the time you get home."

"Burkett, why are you doing this to me? You're an Englishman! You know that it is all lies!"

"I don't know anything of the sort. I know you confessed, and I know that your precious United States Air Force will make you pay for doing so."

Marshall swung at Burkett, his arm looping ineffectually. The reporter moved back, laughing.

"Don't do anything foolish, my dear Captain. You'll be home in a few weeks, and then you'll see how your friends treat you. Maybe some of the things we've tried to teach you will sink in then."

"No one will believe I confessed; you know the sort of garbage I wrote."

"They'll find ways to believe, Captain. As the late Colonel Choi used to say, you are only a nigger to them."

Despite his fury, Marshall pounced on the word. *"Late? Late?* Is Choi dead?"

"As dead as that little rat in the parachute you made for him. He was sure he'd killed you—"

"So was I."

Burkett nodded impatiently; he liked to do the talking. "So after he left you he went on a monumental drunk; he shot another officer, and someone shot him. End of story, end of Choi."

Marshall tried to press him for details, but Burkett wouldn't say more. As he was about to leave he took off his hat and rolled it in his hands.

"I say, Marshall, I do have another bit of news for you. Bad news."

His mind still churning with pleasure at the thought of Choi's death, Marshall looked blankly at the reporter.

"You've noticed that we've been doing a bit of intelligence work on you. The other prisoners, too, of course, but we've concentrated on you. I'm sorry to tell you that your parents were killed in an automobile accident."

Marshall's legs went rubbery and he flopped down on the floor.

"No, it couldn't be."

"I'm sorry, I thought it would be best for you to know. It happened a month ago, on August fifteenth, according to the Cleveland newspaper."

"You're lying, Burkett, you lousy bastard."

"No, I'm not. I don't know any of the details. But what I'm telling you is true. I'm sorry."

The next few days passed in misery. Marshall's emotions rocketed up and down, one moment hoping that Burkett was lying about his parents and the next certain that the news was true. In time he became convinced that they were in fact dead. As he prayed for them, adjusting to his sorrow, he realized that he had overlooked an important element of Burkett's message and began to worry that he might be considered a traitor for having confessed to a pack of nonsense.

The Pentagon/September 16, 1953

The cleaning staff had just departed, leaving the polished tile and wood paneling gleaming under the bright fluorescent lights of the office of the Air Force chief of staff. The room was empty except for a four-star general prowling impatiently, examining the paintings he'd seen a dozen times before. It was an unusual situation for LeMay; normally he called other people on the carpet. Not tonight.

The door to the chief's office opened and a voice, chilled-steel cold, said, "Come in, Curt, let's get this over with. I want you just to sit down, shut up, and listen. For a change."

The two men might have been brothers. Both had similar blocky builds, with strong faces, dark bushy eyebrows, and jutting chins; only Nathan Twining's fine white hair stood in contrast to LeMay's shock of silvered black.

"Mind if I smoke?"

"Yes."

LeMay boiled quietly. Usually soft-spoken, Twining had a reputation for being kindly, a regular Mr. Nice Guy. But he'd had a piece of LeMay before, back in 1945 when Twining had replaced him as C.O. of the Twentieth Air Force.

"There's nothing personal in this—we go back a long way. But you're a special case, Curt. You've been bullying and blustering your way for years. Poor old Van couldn't handle you."

The just retired chief of staff, Hoyt Vandenberg, was terminally ill with cancer.

"But I can. And I want you to listen hard to what I'm telling you, because I won't tell you again."

LeMay nodded.

"As vice-chief, I worked hard to get the Air Force into the best position it's ever been in in regard to budget share. But now we're in a three-way squeeze—old 'Engine' Charlie Wilson is hacking at the budget with an axe, the Army's trying to grab control of strategic missiles, and the Navy's going for nuclear submarines."

LeMay cleared his throat, ready to speak and Twining said, "Be quiet. I don't want to listen to you—I want you to listen to me.

Curt, you've been fiddling around with the B-47 for six years now. You've only got about six bomb wings ready—and the airplane's still full of bugs. Right?"

LeMay nodded. If the fucker didn't want him to speak, he wouldn't say a word.

"Now I've got a hotshot young brigadier named Bernie Schriever—"

It was too much. "I know Schriever—he's your fair-haired boy. He—"

"Shut up, Curt." Twining savored the silence. This was how the military survived, on ground-in discipline even at the highest levels. He said shut up, and even Curt LeMay was silent.

LeMay's hand moved instinctively to his pocket for a cigar, then returned to his lap as Twining continued. "I'm going to put Schriever in charge of the Atlas missile program. I've got faith in him. It's going to be a damn expensive business; we don't even know how much it's going to cost ultimately, but we've got to have it."

Twining's desk was immaculate, but he reached forward to adjust a folder, letting LeMay stew over the idea of missiles coming to the fore.

"Curt, you know that no matter how big a share of the budget we get, there's only so much money in the pot. I don't have to tell you that I've been a big supporter of jet aircraft, everything from the F-86 to the B-52. I've tried to make this an all-jet Air Force, even though Congress thought we ought to stick with piston engines."

He stood and leaned forward. "But I'm telling you, if you don't get the B-47s fully operational, ready to go to war, I'm going to cancel them. I don't mean ready to go in an emergency, and I don't mean one-way missions. I mean an operating command, with decent serviceability percentages and a good safety record."

LeMay stared at him, stony-faced, aware that no one had talked to him like this since flying school.

"And get this, if I cancel the B-47s, I'll cancel the B-52 program, too, and spend all the money on Atlas missiles."

LeMay shot to his feet and leaned across the desk, his face inches from Twining's, brows knotted together, mouth twisted. "You'd be a fool to do that, Nate! The Atlas is in R and D—no one knows if it'll work or not. If you cancel the jet bombers, and Atlas doesn't work, we'd be defenseless."

Twining raised his voice. "Goddamn it, that's the point! The goddamn B-47 *isn't* working right now. The ramps are covered with an aluminum overcast of grounded B-47s; the accident rate is high and the crews are scared. We'd be better off keeping the B-36s and B-50s in the fleet until the Atlas is deployed."

Straightening, he held up a finger to silence LeMay, and went on, his tone moderated, "Unless you can prove me wrong. I was behind the B-47 from the start, and you sold me on the B-52— but by God, I've got to have some results. And I want them this year, not in '55 or '60! Now what the hell do you say to that?"

"General, I'm going to prove you very wrong. I'll have the B-47 program in shape by the end of the year."

"You're dismissed."

LeMay exploded from the office mumbling, "Dismissed, eh, dismissed like some fucking second lieutenant. I'll show that son of a bitch. Wait till I got ahold of Riley."

Seattle, Washington/September 17, 1953

Bandfield had never been to Seattle, but Boeing Field was familiar from the hundreds of photos he'd seen over years. The two parallel north/south runways were bordered on one side by tatty-looking factory buildings and on the other by a line of green hills overlooking the farther runway. It was here that they'd rolled out the prototype B-17, all shiny silver and covered with the Plexiglas blisters that made it a Flying Fortress; and it was here that endless lines of bombers had poured out the factory doors during the war.

Boeing hospitality was legendary for being frugally adequate; last night they'd taken him to dinner at Ivar's Acres of Clams, and this morning a battered station wagon had picked him up at the Windsor, a hotel run-down just enough to be affordable on a government per diem and still be respectable.

He was waiting at the Boeing Field security desk, where a professionally cheerful young man was making out a pass boldly marked "Escort Required," when Riley walked up.

"Glad you're here early, Bandy. I just had a royal ass-chewing from LeMay himself. He's under the gun from the chief, and when LeMay's under the gun, everybody suffers." He grimaced and went on. "I need to give you a little prebriefing before our nine o'clock with the Boeing brass."

Riley's pass permitted him to escort Bandfield up the circular stairway, past the glass-block foyer, and into a paneled room.

"We're secure here, Bandy. We've only got about twenty minutes, so let me level with you."

Bandfield poured them both coffee from a silver vacuum flask and sat down. "Shoot."

"First thing—LeMay is spooked. He says the whole B-47 program is in jeopardy; the chief might stop production tomorrow and shove all the dough to the Atlas program. It would wipe out the B-52 as well."

"Holy Christ, who knows if the Atlas will work?"

"That's it. And Bandy, I want you to know that we're not talking just about the Boeing B-47—we're talking about Weapon System 100A."

Bandfield shrugged. "What's the difference?"

"The difference is in the spread of the problems we've got to solve. The B-47 alone is an enomous task; the weapon system is everything—the airplane, bomb-nav systems, gunnery, maintenance, bombs, spares—all designed for this aircraft. There are problems everywhere."

"So what's new? Every airplane in the past had the same components, the same problems."

"No, it's a change in management philosophy; instead of plugging standard equipment in, everything is specially designed. It reflects how advanced the airplane is—most equipment from the past is too big, or too heavy, or too slow to work in the B-47. Bandy, this is one hot son of a bitch—it's a world-beater, if we can just get it operating right."

He glanced at his watch. "Let me just rattle off the main problems, so you can track the meeting. First, the airframe. We've got four main contractors working—Boeing, Douglas, and Lockheed actually building the airplanes, and McNaughton building big components, center sections."

Bandfield snorted at the name McNaughton.

"Yeah, you said it. Then we've got a shit-load of changes, more than two thousand major engineering change proposals. It's driving the quality control and production planning guys crazy."

Bandfield stretched and looked closely at Riley. The man was obviously tired, with dark circles under his eyes. "How are you handling it?"

"Just like World War Two—pump them off the production line into modification centers, and there they sit, mostly at Grand Central in Tucson."

"Looks like a procurement foul-up."

Riley rubbed his eyes. "Exactly. LeMay is going off his rocker because the components to build the airplanes—radars, gunnery systems, ejection seats—are all out of phase with production."

"But from what you say, the airframe and the engines are on schedule? No problems with them?"

"I wish! The damn thing's gross weight has crept up, and that's just for starters. The canopy's not safe, already taken one poor guy's head off, and you can't bail out of them."

A feeling of weariness swept over Bandfield; this sounded worse than the early days of the B-29 program, and the stakes were even higher. Then it was a question of bombing Japan; now it was a question of deterring Russia from atom-bombing the United States.

"What about the ejection seats?"

"The early planes don't have any; the E models just coming off the line have them built in, and we're going to try to retrofit the early ones. But for the time being, we're just doing without."

Bandfield whistled. "Christ Almighty, that must make the crews happy! What else?"

"Fuel leaks! This thing gets so cold at altitude that the metal shrinks and it leaks like a sieve. There's a problem with fuel boil-off, too; we're losing thousands of gallons out the vents."

"Maybe Twining's right—maybe they ought to just cancel it."

Riley shook his head vigorously. "Hell no, it's the hottest thing around, Russian interceptors can't touch it. And it can carry the H-bomb. Right now the Air Force has ordered almost two thousand of them—when they're in service, the Commies won't be able to do a thing. If they make a move anywhere, Europe, Asia, wherever, we'll bomb them right back to the Stone Age."

Meditative, Bandfield poured more coffee, then said, "Yeah—if we can get any of them off the ground."

"Ah, we'll do that, Bandy, you and me, and a bunch of other guys. But it'll take work. One thing, the Boeing guys are first rate—they're trying as hard as we are. Part of the problem is that they're too good—they designed an airplane with more capabilities than the Air Force knows how to use right now."

Bandfield went on probing, trying to see if there was a central issue, something they could focus on first. "Eisenhower's cutting the Air Force back to a hundred-twenty wings—what's that going to do to the program?"

"Could be the killer. We could wind up with an Air Force without any strategic bombers."

There was a knock on the door and the Boeing team came in, arms laden with charts. A big man in a Western-style sport coat led them, his string tie and turquoise clasp contrasting sharply with the inexpensive suits and drab, neatly knotted ties of his teammates. Their breast pockets were crammed with pencils, and each man carried a leather-covered slide rule at his side like a gunslinger's holster.

Riley smiled and said, "Just one moment, gentlemen; I want to finish up with my colleague, then we'll get busy."

Whispering, he said, "Bandy, the problem is in the management. We've got systems to manage, but no management system. You and

I are going to go down to Los Angeles and talk to Bernie Schriever and hammer out some new techniques. I've been working on some ideas for years—I call it 'systems management.' I want to brief you on it later."

Bandfield nodded. "Sounds good. Listen, Bear, you and me, we'll make it work."

Nashville, Tennessee/October 2, 1953

It wasn't really cool enough for a fire, but Baker, too fat even for his old sweater and sweat pants, took a special pleasure in enjoying all the luxuries of Troy McNaughton's house—and he had some papers he had to burn.

"Sure beats my trailer, don't it, hon?"

Elsie lounged on the long, low-backed sofa, eyes closed, her soiled white terry cloth robe open down the front, drawing deeply on a homemade cigarette.

"I sort of liked the trailer; it was cozy. Here I expect to see Troy coming around the corner anytime."

"The only corner old Troy's turning is in hell. Give me a drag on that."

"It's good. See if you can get some more tomorrow; we're about out."

Baker snorted—there was half a pound of marijuana in the humidor in the library and Elsie knew it. She was a greedy about it as she was everything else.

"You love that stuff, don't you?"

"Yeah, it makes even you tolerable."

Baker didn't answer as he bent over the fire, carefully feeding it with invoices, cancelled checks, and inspection rejection notices, thinking, When we get married, I'll never have to fool with penny-ante stuff like kickbacks from vendors anymore.

She watched him with amusement. He was so shallow, and so predictable. She already had microfilm copies of everything he was burning tucked away in her safety deposit box. Yet he was always there; he eased the loneliness she so often felt.

"I've heard about cooking the books, but this is the first time I've ever actually seen it."

He shrugged and asked, "You still going to see that head doctor?"

"None of your business!"

"That means you are. You ain't nuts, honey, you're just selfish."

Indignant, she left to get something to eat. As she pawed through the refrigerator, she thought about what her psychiatrist had told her. By letting Baker—she'd even given his name—stay around, she was acting compulsively, deliberately humiliating herself. When she told him Baker was stealing from the company, the doctor advised her to make the break, to get rid of the man and then get herself involved in some new projects.

Elsie came back with a yellow bowl of cold fried chicken. Baker picked up a drumstick and they munched, staring into the fireplace where the mass of paper wasn't burning well. He stirred it with a poker and they watched the sparks leap up.

She sat up suddenly. "Oh, shit, I forgot the anniversary."

"Anniversary? Hell, we ain't even married, how can we have an anniversary?"

"I mean Troy. It was a year ago on the twenty-seventh that he shot himself. Poor man. I should have put some flowers on his grave."

"Poor man? The son of a bitch lived like a king all his life, treated everybody like shit, and you say 'poor man.' "

"He wasn't all bad, and I was with him a long time."

"Yeah, and you were fucking other guys the whole time—Coleman, me. God knows who all. You try that on me, and you'll regret it to *your* dying day. And if I'm lying—"

"Yeah, if you're lying you're dying. You're always lying and you never die. And why would you care? The only thing you want out of me is my money."

Baker quietly rolled another cigarette and handed it to her.

"Elsie, you're lucky to have me. I know what you want, and I give it to you. You don't give a damn about Troy, or the plant, or nothing."

Elsie snorted. "That's not so. I cared for Troy, and I like the plant. The workers like me. You know that."

"Maybe, but they won't like anybody if we run out of work. The modification line is gone; this B-47 business won't last forever; and we've got nothing in the pipeline. That's Troy's fault; he let things go to pot when he got sick."

"You can do better? You wouldn't know a good airplane if one fell on you. At least Troy grew up in the business; you've been nothing but a mattress-sniffing private eye all your life. If it wasn't for me, you'd be working as a house dick in some two-bit hotel."

Baker laughed. "Well, if I was, I'd probably be running into you a lot." He reached over, took the cigarette from her fingers, inhaled deeply, then went on. "But you ain't so wrong at that. This is my big chance to be somebody."

"Don't kid yourself. I'm going to sell out and move a million miles from you. You can go back to following wayward husbands and peeking through motel windows."

"You'd go nuts in a week." He poked the fire again and turned to her. "Listen to me, Elsie. I've got some ideas. The great thing about the airplane business is that if you have money, you can hire the best. Companies are always going under; guys are always looking for jobs. We could hire a team to develop new products. Look what that old fool Roget is doing out in California, making a ton of money building corporate planes."

"Don't knock Hadley, he's all right." Elsie stubbed her cigarette out. "Do you really mean this? I didn't think you were interested in anything but siphoning off dough from the subcontractors."

He didn't even blink at the charge. "No, I've been thinking about this a lot, reading the trade papers. Martin's laying off a bunch of guys, and so is Curtiss-Wright. We could have our pick."

She stood up, wrapping the robe tightly about her. She could do what the doctor said, but maybe just reverse the order. "That might be fun. They'd probably have some ideas about what to build, and maybe some contacts, too. That's the big problem."

"And you're still in bed with Ruddick, aren't you, so to speak? You got him on the payroll still?"

"Yeah, so to speak. And he'll be as interested as we are in digging something up. I'll call our personnel guy in tomorrow, and get started."

Baker reached across and gave her an affectionate hug; it was unlike him and she moved away, suddenly wary. Maybe this is a way out, she thought. I'll get some new projects going, bring some decent people in, and rid myself of this man.

Baker sensed her movement and smiled. "Getting touchy, eh? I think it must be that weed—you always act funny after you've smoked a little. Never mind. Call the personnel guy on Monday. Right now, it's time to watch 'Ozzie and Harriet.' "

She knew that beneath his coarse manner, Baker was lonely, too: he had a strong domestic streak, and she liked that. Snuggling closer to him, she thought; I'll miss this more than the sex.

San Francisco, California/October 15, 1953

He'd been able to pick out Saundra's upturned face from the crowd even before his ship docked that morning. Except for a long interrogation about his confession, the Air Force had kept the entry problems to a minimum. There had been a very short briefing for the press, and then they'd brought the two of them to the VIP quarters in Fort Mason. Now he lay deep in a tortured sleep, Saundra watching over him.

Marshall rolled over and groaned, eyes fluttering open.

"It's all right honey, I'm right here." Saundra's voice was soothing, warm. He lay still as the comfort hit him, the clean sheets, the smell of her perfume.

"Sorry—just a nightmare, a dream within a dream. I thought I was back in my cell, dreaming about you."

He rolled into her arms and felt her hands glide over his body, her fingers gently following the contours of his wounds. "My poor baby, they treated you so badly."

"You should have seen me before—I gained twenty pounds on the trip over."

Marshall brought her hands to his face and kissed them. "I'm sorry about this afternoon—I was just too eager."

"Me, too, baby. Don't worry about it, we've got a long time to get readjusted."

They'd fallen into each other's arms as soon as the door had closed behind them, tearing their clothes off as they struggled toward the bed. It had been frustrating—Marshall had ejaculated almost immediately, even before he was fully erect, and he hadn't been able to make love since.

"I'm wide awake now—want to talk some more?" She snapped on the light and nodded. "Where was I? I told you about going down to Panmunjom? The Chinese gave us haircuts and a shave and issued us new towels, new clothes, everything, even candy, some kind of rice paper sweet—it was delicious. Then they drove us down to Freedom Village."

Marshall closed his eyes and felt once again the tension of the trip, the sense of disbelief that the long imprisonment was actually ending, the fear that it was just another ploy, like the mock executions, the beatings, the solitary, just a trick to make him talk.

"The Reds had motion picture cameramen all the way; I thumbed my nose at them every time. Then I heard it—American music from a military band. I started crying. I never used to cry. Now I do it all the time—when I see the flag, or hear the national anthem. I bawled when I saw you on the dock. Nerves, I guess."

She stroked his head. "After what you've been through, you deserve to cry. Being a prisoner was bad enough, then losing your parents on top of it. You can cry all you want, and I'll join you."

He kissed her and went on. "The truck came to a stop, and I stepped down. All of a sudden a crowd of Air Force guys surrounded me, shaking my hand, slapping me on the back. They hustled me into an ambulance. I was free."

His voice broke as he repeated, "I was free."

"You don't have to go on . . . we can talk tomorrow."

"No, I want to tell you everything." He lay on his back, and the memories spilled out—the first hot shower, the first American food, the clean sheets in the hospital. "That's where I wrote my first letter to you." He gulped and said, "Then there were the reporters, wanting to know what they fed us, how they beat us. Nobody asked anything about the confession, and I was glad."

"Why did they send you home by ship? You rated a flight back home after all you went through."

"They said it was to give us a chance to get our health back. They were right, and it gave me a chance to get used to the idea of Mom and Dad being gone. But things changed on board ship. The nearer we got to the States, the cooler everybody was. The last day out they really grilled me about my confession—it was almost like being a prisoner again. I told them how I'd faked it, made it ridiculous, but it didn't seem to matter. I think I may be in real trouble."

"Oh, Bones, don't say that! They know how they tortured you, and you didn't tell them anything that made sense."

"I know, but I can't get that across. Tomorrow I've got to write out another complete statement. I already gave them one on the ship. It's like they're comparing it, to see where I'm lying. I wouldn't be surprised to see Colonel Choi tomorrow, threatening me."

She felt him shiver in her embrace.

"Honey, they're just trying to find out what happened; the problem is you feel guilty and you shouldn't. Nobody could have put up with all you did. Nobody."

"I don't know. I really didn't break, I thought I was making fools of them; I thought anyone back here could see that."

"They'll see it, sweetheart."

"Did you hear that Dave Menard crashed the day after I was shot down?"

"Yes, they told me."

"Well, you can be damn sure that wasn't an accident. He was

flying with Coleman, rat-racing. Coleman probably flew him into the ground to keep him from talking."

She looked at him with pity. This was more than anxiety, it was paranoia. "Oh, honey, I don't think that could be true. You're just overstressed."

He was upset for a moment, then realized that she couldn't know how well Menard flew, how careful he was with his equipment—nor how evil Coleman could be. She spoke to him again. "Now you try to get some sleep."

"In a minute. Come here, let me see if I can't do a little better than this afternoon."

They kissed for a long while, until he fell asleep again. She lay with her hand on his chest, trying to will strength into him, uncomfortable in the role. She had always found her strength in him; it was strange to have their roles reversed.

Frederick Air Force Base, California/October 23, 1953

"Colonel Coleman's compliments, sir. He regrets that he's unable to be with you this morning—had to go to sick call with a touch of the flu. But he's asked me to give you a demonstration flight."

Bandfield reached out to shake the major's hand; he was short and chunky, a fireplug in a flight suit.

"Haven't we met before?"

"Yes, sir, at the McNaughton plant once—I was just visiting with Stan, and you and I had some coffee together."

They walked down to the personal equipment section, where technicians were standing by with an array of flight suits, oxygen masks, and helmets. After they fitted him up, Fitz took him to another room.

"We've got an ejection-seat trainer in here, sir."

"Call me Bandy. Think we'll need it?"

"No, the B-47's a good bird, but there's a local regulation that requires that we use it. It's just a procedure trainer, just to give you confidence in the seat in the airplane."

"Doesn't give you much confidence in the plane, though. How long have you been flying B-47s?"

"Not quite a year—but I've got three hundred hours time. Stan's been working me hard as an instructor." He checked Bandfield's expression and grinned. "I think you'll be safe."

Bandfield grinned back. "I'm not worried about you, Fitz, but I'm a little spooked by all the stories on the airplane. You know, the jazz about critical approach speeds, getting into the 'coffin corner,' where there's only a couple of knots difference between a high-speed stall and a low-speed stall—stuff like that."

"The coffin corner is just bullshit—you'd really have to work to get yourself in a pickle like that. The B-47's like any airplane. If you fly it right, it'll treat you right; if you abuse it, it'll bite you. The approach speed is critical, but it's easy to be precise with this airplane, and hell, that's what they pay us for."

They spent the morning flight planning, then drove in a staff car out to the flight line, past the long rows of B-47Es. Coleman and Williams were waiting at the airplane, along with Birch Matthews, the radar observer.

After the usual courtesies, Coleman said, "The wing commander and I pre-flighted it for you, Fitz—pretty good service. Colonel Bandfield, how much time do you have?"

Bandfield looked at him closely; Coleman might have the flu, but it looked more like a hangover to him. Williams didn't look much better.

"I'm at your disposal—all the time in the world."

"Fitz, I know you've flight-planned to go over to Tonopah. Why don't you show Colonel Bandfield the new toss-bombing delivery technique we've been working on?"

Fitzpatrick flushed. "This is just a demonstration flight, Stan— I'm not sure we want to overload the colonel."

"No, I know this man, Fitz. Give him the works." He turned to Bandy. "You won't actually be dropping a bomb—it's electronically scored."

Once he'd gotten used to the tricky ground handling of the bicycle gear layout, Bandfield began to enjoy himself. The takeoff was long, but climbing at 310 knots was exhilarating—not many airplanes could go that fast in level flight. At altitude, the airplane handled beautifully. In the backseat Fitz was a perfect instructor, anticipating Bandfield's questions, talking him through the fuel management routines and demonstrating how the airplane flew in various configurations.

"This thing could grow on you, Fitz."

"Yeah, I'd go to war in it tomorrow, if I had to. We've burned off enough fuel now, Bandy; let's go down and let me demonstrate the bomb drop Stan was talking about."

Fitz got clearance from the Tonopah range—the controller was clearly unhappy about being worked on a Saturday. Fitz called, "I got it," and dumped the drag gear; the B-47 began a four-thousand-foot-per-minute descent at 290 knots.

Bandfield watched the earth rushing up to him, heard Fitz and Matthews run the checklist and call the range.

"Tonopah, this is Nectar Two One, we're approaching the initial point." Then, to Bandfield, "Okay, you got it, we're level five hundred feet above the ground. Bring the speed up to four hundred twenty-five knots."

Bandfield shook the wheel and advanced the six throttles. The airspeed stabilized at 425 as the desert floor whipped past, the sagebrush turning into long blue-green blurs.

"Bandy, maintain this heading. When I say 'now' start a two and one-half G pull-up and stay with it. Keep positive Gs and do an Immelmann turn off the top and then I'll take it."

Wondering what he'd got himself into, Bandfield concentrated on course and heading as he heard the bomb release system tone button come on. The airspeed was surprisingly easy to maintain; only the ailerons were stiff, locked tight by the speed.

"Now, pull back, not too hard, just two and one-half Gs, nice and steady."

Bandfield checked the G-meter as he pulled back on the wheel and advanced the throttles; the B-47 eased back into the first half of a loop; there was a sharp crack of the quick-opening bomb bay doors, and Fitz called "Bombs away!" as the tone signal cut off.

The airspeed bled away in their high, arcing zoom that flattened on the top so that Bandfield saw the ground beneath his canopy and the horizon as a crazy inverted line ahead of them. He rolled the airplane level.

Yelling, "I got it!" Fitz pulled back on the power and lowered the nose. Within minutes they were roaring across the desert floor in the opposite direction of the bomb run, airspeed nudging 450 knots, wings stiff as a board.

"That's it, Bandy—we just lobbed an H-bomb in on Moscow."

Fitz called Tonopah. "Ah, Roger, Tonopah, how did you score that last run?"

"Nectar Two One, that was a shack, right on the target. Will you be wanting another?"

"No, thank you, Tonopah, don't want to press my luck."

That night Bandfield called Riley from the BOQ.

"Bear, the airplane's a jewel, but I'm not too sure about this toss-bombing idea."

"LeMay isn't crazy about it, either, but it's about the only way to get a B-47 in with an H-bomb and not fry the crew with the radiation."

"Yeah, but you're flying the airplane right at its limits—if the pilot got a little nervous, or if he hits some turbulence, he could exceed the G limits easy. What then?"

"Well, then the fucking wings fall off—you know that. The crews will just have to practice enough to get proficient."

"Easy to say, especially with new airplanes. What happens in five years when they begin to wear out, when fatigue and corrosion gets to them?"

"We'll just have to watch it. You got any better ideas?"

Bandfield's voice went up a notch. "I sure as hell have. It'd be a lot better to put a parachute on the bomb, let it float down and let the B-47 just make a normal bomb run."

"LeMay doesn't like the idea. Not accurate enough—it's been tried."

"That's just bullshit, Riley. We're not dropping darts, you know, we're dropping H-bombs that can flatten a city. How accurate do you have to be?"

"You want to work up a test program on it?"

"Absolutely. Talk to you tomorrow; I'm going to do some figures tonight."

"I warn you, Bandy, LeMay probably won't okay it."

Bandfield slapped his forehead with his hand, Goddamn it, he may have four stars but he doesn't have all the answers. If the wings start falling off B-47s all over the place, he'll be the first one screaming for a solution.

"Tell you what—I'm going to L.A. next week to talk with Schriever about systems management. I'll be going to Dayton from there to the B-47 weapons systems office. Why don't you meet me there, and we'll get some people working on a parachute-retarded system?"

"Can we get any dough to fund it?"

"Trust me, Bandy. If I can't get a million or two squirreled away for this, I've lost my touch."

"See you in Dayton."

Los Angeles, California/October 30, 1953

Patience had never been Saundra's long suit, and John's suspicious attitude was beginning to wear on her.

"Look, honey, I asked you to come along; I won't be gone for more than an hour."

"All I know is my wife is going off to meet some strangers from Georgia. How am I supposed to react?"

"Two of them are ministers; one is a woman lawyer, or so I'm told, from the NAACP. You ought to just come along to see for yourself."

"How come it's not NAABP, National Association for the Advancement of Black People, now? How come Peterson can't just give them the money himself?"

She ignored the first question; he'd asked it a dozen times before. "John, don't be like this, I've told you why three times—he's afraid he'll lose business if his advertisers know he's backing the civil rights activists. And if he loses business, he won't be able to help them anymore. Come along, see for yourself."

"No. I disapprove of what you're doing."

"How can you disapprove when you've been treated worse than most Black men?"

He thought she was using the term deliberately, knowing he hated it. For most of Marshall's life the worst insults a white man could give a Negro involved the word *black*—"you black bastard" or "you black bitch" were fighting words. Now Saundra and her friends insisted on using Black as a term of honor—they wouldn't use Negro or colored anymore.

He snapped the television set on and she stood, clutching the big purse in her arms. It was filled with money; she didn't know how much, but it made her nervous to have it.

"I'm your wife, and I'm carrying a lot of money. Don't you want to come along to protect me?"

They were exactly the right words. He sprang to his feet.

"Honey, you're right. I'm coming along."

On the way over she told him what she was supposed to do. "We'll attend the prayer service. Afterwards, they'll meet us in the children's Bible-study room."

"Sounds crazy. How do we know if they're the right people? You could be handing it over to a total stranger."

"No, Fred's arranged a little code." She saw him wince at the name Fred.

"What is it?"

"They'll say 'Judge not' and I'll say 'Be not judged.' I'll give them the money, and we'll leave."

"Honey, this is just stupid. What else would anybody answer to an opener like that? Peterson's being theatrical, that's all. Did you look in the purse?"

"No, why?"

"Are you sure it's money? Maybe it's dope. We might be running heroin for your friend."

"Don't be silly. Look for yourself—it's not locked."

He snapped the purse fastener open; the purse was filled with hundred-dollar bills bound in neat packets of ten. He dug through them; there was nothing besides the currency. He tried to estimate how many thousands of dollars it contained and could not.

The prayer service was in what once had been the fashionable St. Luke's Episcopalian Church. The neighborhood had changed, and now it was the Western Concord Baptist Church.

The service was just beginning as they walked down the frayed carpet of the aisle to the front. For Marshall it stirred poignant memories of his father's old church; it had not been so grand, but the hymns were familiar, as were the words of the first minister to speak.

The difference came at the end, when one of the visitors was asked to pray. A young man stood up, his broad smile slowly fading as he surveyed the crowd. He began to speak, his voice deep and powerful, and Marshall sensed the congregation suddenly fuse together, as if the electricity in his voice had melded them into a single conductive unit.

He glanced at Saundra—she seem transformed; her eyes were shining, her mouth open. The purse had slipped from her lap to the floor. He nudged her elbow and she did not respond; he picked the purse up and held it at his side.

After the speaker concluded, the congregation swarmed to the pulpit. They slipped away to the children's Bible-study room, examining the drawings pinned proudly to the wall.

The door opened, and a young woman walked in dressed in a

choir robe, followed by a white man they hadn't seen before and the preacher who had electrified the group. The woman smiled and said, "I'm May Nuttley, and I'm supposed to say 'Judge not.' "

Saundra said, "I'm Saundra Marshall and this is my husband, John. I'm supposed to say 'Be not judged.' "

The woman smiled. "The code seems sort of silly, doesn't it? Let me introduce Reverend King and Alan Loeb." They all shook hands with John first, then turned to Saundra, who stood looking at the minister, still clutching the purse to her bosom.

King extended his hand and smiled. "I noticed you when you came in. You seemed to be very worried about something."

Saundra held on to his hand, visibly moved. "I enjoyed your sermon, Dr. King."

He let her hold his hand, a quiet smile on his face, his eyebrows slowly edging up. John nudged her, and she said, "And I'm supposed to give this to you." She handed the purse over; King passed it immediately to Loeb; both men nodded and left the room.

Outside, Marshall said, "Glory be, Saundra, there must have been fifty thousand dollars in that purse, and we don't have any idea who we gave it to."

She didn't answer at first, still carried away by her religious exaltation. "I heard him speak—that was enough for me. The man is a genius, I can tell."

"You can't tell anything from one sermon. We should have asked for some identification. We have no idea if we gave the money to the right people or not."

"John, he's the right person, for now and forever."

As they walked back to their car, Marshall felt inadequate. He was physically weak, the Air Force had put his career on hold while he was being investigated, and his wife's "friend" could afford to give a fortune to strangers. Saundra was silent, still wrapped in her emotions.

He grabbed her arm. "What if we were followed?"

It took her a moment to understand what he was saying. "Who would follow us? Nobody knew what we were going to do but you and I and Fred."

"The FBI, that's who. What am I going to say if they ask me where I got all that money? They'll think I'm on the take from the Russians."

She started to laugh until she saw the fear in his eyes. It should have inspired pity; instead it made her dislike him.

Santa Monica, California/November 6, 1953

His head whirled to the phone when it rang. She forced herself to sit still, telling herself that she loved him despite the profound changes in him and in her she didn't yet understand.

When John had returned, they tried to make everything seem the way it was when they were first married. But he was too ill, perhaps even too frightened, though he wouldn't admit it, and now she knew that nothing would ever be the same. Being a POW had turned John into an angry man, haunted with guilt, burning for revenge, afraid of the future. Worst of all, he was incapable of seeing that she, too, had changed dramatically. The phone rang again, insistent in the silence.

"Go ahead, get it; it's your boyfriend."

Saundra rose, and for the tenth time that week said, "He is *not* my boyfriend. He is my business associate."

Dishes clattered as he banged his cup down and leapt up from the table; in a moment she heard the outside door slam. She simply didn't register with him anymore, not as a real person, not as she was; for him she had been frozen in time and place while he was in

Korea. He simply couldn't understand anything about her business, about her interest in the movement.

Saundra picked up the phone. "Fred? I'm sorry to keep you waiting. He's being difficult again."

"No wonder, after what he's been through. Shall I stop calling?"

"No, we can't stop now. We've damn near got this deal completed. He's just going to have to bear with it."

"Good. The lawyers from the investment firm say they've almost completed their due diligence search; there were some questions about the way you value your inventory, but I've got it squared away. They've lined up some potential backers, and think they can take Love's Products public in the fall."

Peterson's voice, earnest, eager, droned on; she understood only half of what he was saying, giving short yes and no answers to his questions. Peterson was handling it for her, and that was enough. At any other time she would have been hanging on every word, asking questions, prodding him for information; now she was too emotionally drained by the changes in John, by the shifts in their relationship.

"Well, as I said, Saundra, it looks like you'll wind up with fifty-one percent and enough capital to expand nationally. And it's time to bring some decent managers who'll take some of the work off your shoulders. I've got three people here who would be perfect."

"Whatever you say, and thanks for everything. I'm sorry this is taking my time and attention away from the movement."

"Well, it has to be first things first. The people I'll send to you will give you some time to help me." His deep voice shifted abruptly from its usual clinical business crispness to conspiratorial. "And there are some people coming into town that I want you to meet—they are leaders for the future, believe me. You met one of them at the church the other night. Can you be in my office tonight about seven o'clock? You and John, both, I mean."

"He'll never go. The business with the purse full of money upset him terribly. And now, I couldn't go without him."

"Look, it may be hard to believe, but this is even more important to him than to us. I'm going to come over and talk to him, to see if I can't persuade him to come."

Her tone shifted. "No. You can't do that."

There was a long moment of silence and he asked, "Saundra, are you there?"

The phone had slipped in her hand as she stood staring into the mirror that revealed John leaning forward with his ear pressed against the door. He was as frail as his reflection, his hair nearly white, his tortured body fragile. For a brief moment she remembered him when they were first married, lean, muscular, virile, and full of life.

"I'm sorry, Fred. We can't see you. Just prepare the paperwork as you see fit and I'll sign. Right now I've got a problem here."

She walked quickly into the next room and threw her arms around her husband.

"John, baby, you don't have to listen at doors. I'm not doing anything wrong, just business. We'll get another phone, you can listen in on all the calls, there's nothing going on."

John Stuart Marshall—ace, test pilot, survivor—burst into tears.

"I'm sorry, honey, I'm so goddamn jealous I can't stand it. I know you must have gone to bed with this guy; for all I know you're still going to bed with him. I wouldn't blame you, he's a big success, he can give money away like water, and I can't even get along in the Air Force."

She pulled him to the couch and they sat with his head cradled against her breasts. "John, John, John, what am I going to do with you? I've never gone to bed with him, or anybody else but you, never, not in my whole life. You know that. And you haven't received an assignment because the war's only just over; they're demobilizing people. The Air Force knows you need rest. They'll find a job for you, just give them time. Or better still *don't* wait for them. Get out, come to work with me, I need help."

He didn't even hear the offer; instead, his mood switching with ferocious intensity, he struck his fist into his palm. "The goddamn newspapers are to blame. Nobody will leave it alone, they think we're all traitors."

"It'll pass. The stupid television coverage got them excited, that's all."

Two weeks before a clip of Alan Burkett's newsreel had appeared on the Douglas Edwards show. Edwards had commented sensitively on how obviously badly treated Marshall had been, but his remarks left the clear implication that Marshall had confessed to charges of germ warfare. There had been a deluge of requests for interviews from newspapers and radio stations for almost a week, along with some crank calls and poison-pen letters, most with a racial twist. Saundra had declined all the interviews for him.

Marshall shook his head wistfully. "You may be right. If they'd just send me some orders, get me back to flying, I'd be okay. It's the waiting around, getting paid for doing nothing that's killing me."

"Darling, you always told me that to get anywhere, you had to make things happen."

He nodded. "I used to say that."

"It's still true. You've got to start picking up the pieces, physically and mentally. You've got to get your mind off the way the Air Force is treating you—or the way you think it's treating you."

"How, by being a big civil rights worker like you?"

"Don't sneer at me; I do what I can while I'm making a living. And it's not a bad idea, the movement needs heroes like you. And you've got to start working out, to build your body back up. They hurt you, but they didn't kill you; you can come back."

"Any other advice for me? I'm just a poor nigger captain, I need all the help I can get."

"Your daddy would really be proud of you for saying that."

He half-turned and sat down on the sofa. "I'm sorry; I'm just feeling sorry for myself. Be still for a minute."

She sat next to him, quietly watching him compose himself. After a moment, his hand reached out and he said, "Saundra, you're absolutely right. The first thing I've got to do is get back in shape. I'll start today, exercising, running a little; and I'll begin to get active in the movement."

The phone rang again and they both sat still. He smiled and said, "Thanks, honey—sorry I was angry about Peterson. I guess I just don't like rich guys . . . You get the phone, it's probably for you."

He watched her move to the phone, as tiny and as beautiful as always, her little bottom as appealing here in Los Angeles as he had imagined it in prison in Korea. Yet as much and as often as he wanted her, he was not yet performing well. Another reason for exercise.

"Yes, he's here. I'll get him."

He knew from her voice that it was trouble. Putting her hand over the receiver she said, "John, it's somebody named Frazier. From the Office of Special Investigation."

Frederick Air Force Base, California/ December 7, 1953

Standing in the back of the darkened room, Stan Coleman watched the briefing, talking softly with Fitzpatrick.

"You should have been at the O-club Saturday night, Fitz, it was a riot."

"Yeah, I heard the Brit was really bird-dogging Williams's wife."

Coleman laughed. "The hell he was, it was the other way around; everytime she went past him you could hear the whistle of her bloomers dropping."

"It never fails—British accent, strange uniform, the broads go crazy."

In the front of the room, an obviously miffed Colonel Williams snapped off the overhead projector as he finished the pre-flight briefing for his British visitor. Wing Commander Penrose yawned broadly and said, "Well, that's all right, then. Looks like flying the B-47 is much like flying our Valiant."

Williams laughed. "I hope not. You crashed the first Valiant, didn't you?" Whirling on his heel, he growled to Fitz, "Take the wing commander out to the airplane and get him strapped in. I've got some paperwork to do."

Coleman followed Williams into his office.

"What's the matter, Guy, is this limey cocksucker getting your goat?"

"You mean that two-bit David Niven in there? Thinks he's so fucking superior! The RAF doesn't have a decent airplane in its inventory and he acts like the B-47 is a piece of shit. Well, I'm going to show him just how good it is."

"Too bad you didn't plan a toss-bombing run; he'd probably toss-bomb his cookies."

"I'm going to do better than that. I'm changing the flight plan to include one now, and I'm going to stick his ass in the aisle when I do it."

The B-47's crowded crew compartment was connected by a narrow aisle that ran along the left side of the fuselage from the emergency gear extension installation to the radar compartment. Rightly called the "black hole" it was cold, dank, and hard; no one rode there unless they had to, except instructors, or pilots desperate to earn their flying pay at the end of the month.

Williams settled the Englishman in the front seat and Fitz in the aisle, and Penrose thawed as he began to appreciate the B-47's superb performance. They'd taken off lightly loaded, staying in the pattern to shoot a few landings before rendezvousing with a KC-97 tanker to refuel. Three hours later, after simulated bomb runs on San Francisco, Williams called out, "Fitz, would you swap seats with the wing commander? I want to show him some new tactics. I'm beginning a descent."

Ignoring the whirlwind noise of the descent as the drag gear came down, Fitzpatrick first safetied the ejection seat with red-flagged metal pins—parachute harness had a way of grabbing the ejection seat handles—then helped Williams struggle out of the cocoon of his lap belt, headset, and oxygen connections. It took another two minutes to strap him in on the chill metal floor. By the time Fitz got himself hooked up in the relative warmth and comfort of the front seat, he heard Williams calling.

"Roger, Tonopah, Nectar Zero One, we'll be entering the bomb range shortly. Request clearance for two low-level toss-bombing runs, with a climb to altitude after the first drop."

The nasal voice of the controller at Tonopah came back, "Cleared on to the range, Zero One, give me a call inbound and at your Initial Point."

In the aisle, Penrose fumbled for his mike button and called, "I say, Williams, you didn't brief me on a toss-bombing run. I'm glad you're going to show me." He didn't sound glad.

"Happy to do it, old chum."

As he removed the pins from the ejection seat, Fitzpatrick felt ill at ease at Williams's violation of procedure and courtesy. They never flew with a fourth crew member on a toss-bombing run unless it was an instructor for the radar operator, and to put a visiting dignitary at risk in the aisle was insulting. He comforted himself that he'd made more than thirty of these runs at Tonopah, and knew every sagebrush and fence line on the way in; he would be able to judge how things were going. But each run held its own hazards, and the aisle was no place to be in an emergency.

"Tonopah, Nectar Zero One inbound, five hundred feet, four hundred twenty-five knots indicated; say winds and weather." Williams surged with elation; the airplane was flying beautifully, 170,000 pounds of streamlined power totally at his command. He'd show the limey bastard what a real airplane was like.

"Roger Zero One; winds variable, three hundred thirty to three hundred sixty, gusting twenty to thirty knots. Visibility forty miles."

Williams keyed his intercom. "Now, WingCo, you might want to hold on down there, this is apt to be a little rough."

Penrose clicked his mike button in acknowledgment as the B-47 flashed its swept-wing shadow across the desert floor, past the initial point, turbulence buffeting it as it hurtled down an invisible corridor marked only on the radar screens in the Tonopah scoring shack.

Fitz was nervous—Williams should have started the pull-up. He delayed another two seconds, and then said, "Start your pull-up!"

"Roger that!" Annoyed, Williams overcontrolled as he yanked

back on the control column. The B-47's nose rose rapidly in a swell of G-forces and Fitz yelled, "Watch the G-meter . . ."

Fitz's hands were already going through the left-right sequence of the ejection seat handles as the excess Gs multiplied the weight of the B-47 by three, then four, flexing the long slender wings upward like the arms of a ballerina till the relentless forces pulled them from their fuselage roots, metal arms from metal sockets, to explode the now vertical B-47 like an overripe melon. Fitz's seat blasted out of the ball of fire, briefly hurtling parallel to the desert floor. Kicking free from the tumbling seat he felt his parachute deploy automatically, the canopy blossoming an instant before he slammed into the ground. He lay on his back, amazed to be alive, watching the pieces of metal rain down from the black-red ball of fire in the sky that had once been a B-47. A huge piece of a nacelle struck the ground fifteen feet away, bouncing to glance off his helmet before landing across his legs. Unconscious, Fitz didn't feel the misting drizzle of unburned drops of fuel.

Tonopah, Nevada/December 7, 1953

Riley had flown down from Omaha in a T-33; Bandfield had come up from Albuquerque in a B-25. Now they sat side by side in a Sikorsky H-19 helicopter en route to the crash site, shouting over the deafening roar of engine and rotor blades, deliberately avoiding any speculation about the crash.

"LeMay happy with your new systems management scheme?"

"He's never happy, but the program office is working better. They've cut down on a lot of the communication problems. It may just be that the system's maturing, anyway, but most of the big problems are clearing up, one by one."

"I wish I could say the same about putting parachutes on bombs. The goddamn things either rip right out of the harness, or else they drift off the range. We haven't got the right opening technique for them yet."

"Stick with it. They treating you all right at Kirtland?"

"Like a champ. They've got a lot of practice shapes there; all we have to do is fit a parachute package on them."

The intercom clicked on and the pilot told them to prepare for landing.

"How's things otherwise, Bear?"

"Well, the kids are great. Ulrich's doing well in school, and Gracie is darling, a wonderful child. Lyra loves Omaha and the Air Force, but says I'm away from home too much." He paused, as if hesitant to go on. "But she's absolutely paranoid about Helmut coming to steal Ulrich."

"You think it's possible?"

"Christ, no. He has legal redress—he could get visiting rights, all that, and he hasn't even done that. Why would he do something illegal?"

"Isn't that what he mostly did for you?"

Riley looked hard at Bandfield. "You think he might do it?"

"Hell, I hardly know the guy, but Lyra's no hysteric, even after all she went through during the war. She knows him a hell of a lot better than you do."

They were silent until they clambered down out of the chopper, instinctively ducking their heads beneath the whirling blades as they ran across to the checkpoint. Panting, they showed their IDs to the guard controlling access to the crash site.

"Have they located all the bodies yet, Sarge?"

"Not yet, sir. They think they may have parts of two men, but they won't know until they get back to the hospital. So far they're just finding the usual bones, teeth, and hair."

Bandfield flushed. "Sergeant, this is no joking matter. You may be hardened to it, but the families are not."

He walked over to the Air Police truck and came back talking to the NCOIC, a burly master sergeant who was obviously totally pissed off with Bandfield and the sergeant.

"You're relieved here, Sergeant. Come with us. Maybe you'll learn something."

The three men, the sergeant trailing along looking hangdog,

walked toward the center of the field, where the largest single surviving portion of the wreckage, the tail section, lay.

Riley whispered, "He's just a kid wising off, Bandy. Don't let it get to you."

"I know. It's just that I've done this so damn often, and it gets worse every time. I'm not going to be rough on him; I just want him to see some of the bones, teeth, and hair he was spouting off about."

The SAC crash investigation team was already at work. A harassed young captain was running the operation, with papers and manuals spread all over his Jeep while a crew set up radio antennae. When they introduced themselves he groaned.

"Great! I need a flight surgeon and I get visiting brass. Look, don't touch anything. If you find something of interest, mark it so we can find it again and come tell me." The "sir" he added was a clear afterthought. Both Riley and Bandfield understood; the last thing he needed was a couple of bird colonels and a sergeant poking around.

They walked first to a little rise in the ground to survey the wreckage. Riley shielded his eyes from the glare as he surveyed the area. "A real Pearl Harbor Day present, eh? Look at the way this shit is scattered."

They talked to the other searchers as they met them. A tech sergeant, smeared coal black from plunging through the burned brush, said, "I was off-duty at the radar site. Saw the whole thing. It didn't look no different than the regular runs, until the wings bent up and it exploded."

Bandfield shook his head. "It's a miracle Fitzpatrick got out alive; he must have been sitting with his hands on the ejection seat handles."

"Yeah, and that's not like him—he's usually pretty relaxed. He must have seen something coming."

"Well, we knew all along that it's a dangerous technique; the damn airplane was never designed for it. And if you don't do it right, it'll bite you."

Subdued, they moved slowly through the blackened debris that covered the desert floor in a two-block-long oval pattern. Three fire trucks from Tonopah were battling a raging brushfire, the firemen choking in the acrid smoke from the burning sage. They tramped the area carefully, trying to get a picture of the distribution of the fallen parts. An arroyo, shallow at the west end, deepening toward the east, ran through the crash site, and they tramped it together. Riley stopped to point to a patch of sage overhanging an oblong lump. It was about two feet wide and four feet long, charred so black its outer surface was flaking.

"Look here, Bandy. What do you think?"

"Might just be a parachute, but it could be a torso; too badly burned to tell. Come here, Sarge, I want to show you something."

Bandfield reached his gloved hand out and gently brushed at the blackened fabric. It tore away, and there was a gleam of blood-stained khaki underneath; a sudden smell of roasted flesh rose up, overwhelming the pervasive odor of burned jet fuel. His hand jerked back and he felt the flood of futile helplessness, the sense of total waste that a crash site always brings.

"It's the Brit."

The sergeant turned to the side, vomiting.

They walked back to report their find in silence; as they approached the Jeep, Bandfield said, "What a hell of a note, to come all the way to California to have some jerk kill you."

"Pure pilot error?"

"Sure. At least I hope so. If it's not, the B-47 fleet's in worse trouble than we thought. I want to talk to Fitzpatrick as soon as possible."

At the Jeep Riley tapped the captain on the shoulder.

"Sorry to bother you, Captain, but I think we found the Englishman's body. Part of it."

The captain pulled his headset off, turning to look at him, white-faced, uncomprehending.

"I said I think we found a body."

Without a word, the captain handed him a message he'd just copied down from the radio. It was barely legible, hard pencil against a yellow tablet, and Riley squinted as he read it to Bandfield.

"86th BW B-47 broke up and crashed, Pinecastle, Florida."

"Holy shit, what the hell is going on?"

"I don't know, but we better find out before we lose another airplane—and before LeMay has our ass for breakfast."

Little Rock, Arkansas/January 15, 1954

Ruddick was uneasy as he led them into the privacy of his inner office. Looking sour, Baker threw himself full-length on the couch and lit a cigarette. Milo bustled over with an old-fashioned ashtray shaped like an elongated bowling pin and weighted at the bottom so that it couldn't tip over. "Excuse the way the place looks; I don't allow the cleaning staff to come in here."

Elsie stood by his desk, dabbing at her nose with a Kleenex. "Do this for me, Milo, and I'll clean your office up myself."

Ruddick seated himself behind his desk. "Tell me what it is, and if I can do it, I will."

"I've got to get Dick out of sight for a while." Maybe for good, she thought.

"Because of the B-47 crashes?"

"Right. The Air Force is investigating the last two crashes—both the same thing, wings pulling off. The plant reps in the factory are going crazy, checking everything twice."

"I'm sure they're doing the same thing at Boeing and the other plants. Standard procedure. What's this got to do with Baker?"

The big man bridled, rising half out of the red leather chair. "It ain't got fuck-all to do with me. It's not my fault if the goddamn Air Force pilots can't fly."

Elsie whirled on him. "Shut up! There's no time for your stupid whining." She turned back. "I'm sorry, Milo, he knows we're in trouble, and he won't stop blustering. He took a kickback on some critical parts and lined his pockets. I'm not sure that's what caused the crashes, but I think so."

Ruddick turned his gimlet eyes on Baker. "How much did you take out of this? Come on, tell me!"

Baker's finder's fee had been twelve thousand dollars. He looked down at his shoes. "About three thousand."

"Well, Elsie, he probably took a lot more than that. It's too bad he didn't just ask you for a raise." Turning to Baker he said, "You stupid ass! For three thousand dollars you've risked the lives of God knows how many men. What was the part? How many airplanes are involved?"

"It's the attaching pin for the wing-fuselage juncture, a twelve-piece kit. I bought two hundred of them."

"How many were installed? Can you identify the airplanes they were installed in?"

Elsie leaned forward. "That's the problem, Milo, we don't know how many are in the fleet. He screwed up the paperwork as he went along, just for camouflage. We did dump all the ones that were still on hand, more than a hundred. But we don't know how many were installed, or which airplanes they were installed on. Some might have been shipped out as spares."

Milo made a fan-shaped motion with his open hands. "Don't panic. How do you know Baker caused this? Has the Air Force accused you?"

"No, it just seemed probable."

He stared at her for a moment. She seemed to be putting on weight, her makeup was smeared, and there was a funny look in her eyes. "Holy Christ, Elsie, this isn't like you. Did you check out the serial numbers of the aircraft? Did McNaughton even make the center sections on these airplanes?" He whirled on Baker.

"When did you start this—no, when did the first parts you bought arrive?"

"About a year ago."

"Well, for Christ's sake, check to see when the two airplanes that crashed were built. They might not even have McNaughton parts in them."

Baker brightened and looked at Elsie. "He's right. We might be home free."

Ruddick exploded. "Shut up, both of you! You've really screwed this up. Now if they see that some of the paperwork is missing, they'll be suspicious, even if it's not your fault."

He tapped his fingers on the desk. "Look, Elsie, you've got to do some retroactive paperwork of your own to get some stuff in the files. Backdate it to last summer. Make it look like you gave Baker more duties—made it legal for him to buy parts, and give him a title, like 'Space Manager' or something. Baker, you fake records on how much you've thrown away. Make it seem like you really cleaned house, indiscriminately, everything went out, the baby with the bathwater. Can the two of you handle that?" Contempt registered in his question.

They nodded.

Ruddick went on. "Then, Elsie, you discover what Baker's done, and you fire him."

"All right, that sounds good. But is there any chance you can get the investigation stopped?"

"That would be the worst thing I could do. I'm going to do just the opposite. You're going to hear me calling for heads, at Boeing, at Douglas, at Lockheed. We'll spread them so thin they won't be able to do much at McNaughton. I'll head up a team at Boeing myself, scare the hell out of everybody."

"I still want you to take Baker off my hands. I figured you could hide him somewhere in your little organization."

Baker muttered, "Stop talking about me like I wasn't here!"

Ruddick glanced at him, then back at Elsie. "What organization, the Defense Department?"

"Milo, I haven't got time to be coy. You've got Josten running things for you with the Klan; he can use Baker as an assistant."

Milo reached out with his fingertip and rolled a pencil back and forth. It was inevitable; more and more people knew about his sympathy for the Klan; there was even talk about it on the Hill. But years of gathering dirt and saving ass had left him well positioned; he had the goods on so many people that he wouldn't be attacked, not for something like sympathy for the Klan. He was hardly alone in that. Even Drew Pearson knew about the Klan business—and knew better than to say anything.

"You want me to hire this slob to work with the Klan?"

"Hey—"

"Shut up, Dick. Yes, Milo, I want exactly that. I want him off my payroll and on yours."

"But why me? Why the Klan? You could set him up in a little office somewhere, subsidize him. Hell, I'll help subsidize him myself, I'd rather pay to keep him away than have him around."

Baker stood up. "You guys are real cute, ain't you? Talking about me like I'm not here. Well, I'm here, and I got enough on you both to send you both to jail for a long time."

Elsie said, "Well, Milo, that's one reason. Another is that you can keep an eye on him here; if we set him up in California or New York, he might do anything."

"Let me think about it." Ruddick reached into his desk and pulled out a bottle of Vat 69. Absent-mindedly, he poured a short drink in the water glass on his desk without offering any to them and put the bottle away. Josten had been complaining that the work with the Storm Klanners was tiring his legs, that he couldn't keep up the pace anymore. Maybe Baker could work for him, do most of the running around. Or maybe . . .

"Christ, I'm getting to be a retirement home for McNaughton rejects—first Josten, now you."

Ruddick turned to Baker. "What do you say? We can't force you to do anything."

Baker nodded. "You're damn right you can't." Then, more conciliatory, "But I'm flexible, I can play ball when I have to."

"Can you work for Josten?"

"I don't want to, but I could. He's a sour kind of a guy."

Ruddick walked to the window and gazed out over his beloved Arkansas, feeling laden with guilt. He'd always done the best he could for the services. Now, if Baker's parts turned out to be as bad as he seemed to think they were, he might be putting some aircraft in jeopardy. He just didn't see any alternative. Baker was a loose cannon that had to be controlled or eliminated.

Speaking over his shoulder, not turning to look at them, he said, "Tell you what, Elsie. We can't be too obvious about this. Baker's going to have to disappear, just drop from sight. The sooner the better. He can go to work for Josten, I'll pay him the same as you were paying—but no records, no social security, no taxes, none of that. We'll figure out a way to cover that. It's not much of a shield, but at least I'm not directly connected with him."

"Thanks, Milo. Do you need to talk to Josten first?"

"No—he'll be grateful for the help. And he can handle Baker."

He turned to look sternly at the bigger man. "You're going to have to change your appearance—dye your hair, grow a beard, lose some weight. We can't afford to have you tracked here."

Baker nodded. The idea of the changes was oddly appealing to him.

Pine Bluff, Arkansas/February 2, 1954

He pushed the plate away, wondering how the Americans could make such wonderful cars and airplanes on such a rotten diet! Josten, thinner now than when he'd left Germany, glanced out the window at the hills that reminded him of his Luftwaffe flying school days. He'd been stationed at Halle, on the river Saale, quartered with a family who ran a little delicatessen. When weather put a stop to the flying, he'd always been glad to go home to the big ceramic stove and feast on good rye bread and thick slices of sausage. This stuff! Abominable.

He hated cold weather now; it ate into his bones and made walking even more difficult. They'd just finished an overnight exercise with the Storm Klan; it had been miserable, his legs had ached, and the scars of his burns felt as if they were on fire again.

When he'd been there alone he had not minded the isolation; now he had to endure Baker's company, cheek by jowl in this rustic hovel, with its plain plywood walls and linoleum-covered floors. But the man might have his uses.

Years before Ruddick had looked for an area where the "Invisible Empire" of the Klan could hold their meetings undisturbed. He had enough influence to induce the big paper company to sell him an old farm that included an abandoned Boy Scout camp. Over the years he had refurbished three of the larger buildings. One was a meeting hall; the second an armory; the third was the old camp headquarters, where Josten now lived, a rough wooden building heated by two gasping kerosene stoves.

Across the table, Dick Baker's big hand smeared a rubbery piece of white bread in circles on his plate, spreading the bright orange yolk and the red catsup into rainbow arcs. He'd dyed his hair and started on a beard, but his weight had gone up instead of down.

"You going to eat that piece of Spam?"

"No, take it." Josten watched with disgust as Baker forked the Spam onto his plate, cut it in two, dabbed it daintily in the catsup-egg mixture, and wolfed both pieces down.

"You're sure no one knows where you are?"

"No, I told you that, nobody but Ruddick and Elsie. I just cleaned out my desk, packed my suitcase, and left. Elsie had a trucking outfit come in and haul my trailer away, took it out west and dumped it. I left no forwarding address, no nothing. I did keep a Post Office box I'd set up a year ago. I'll use that when I file my taxes."

"Any reason for anyone to track you? Besides the Air Force, I mean."

"The Air Force ain't going to track me, nor anybody else, either. Why should they?" Baker still insisted, as a matter of practice, that neither he nor anyone else had done anything wrong. It was his story and he stuck with it, no matter who the audience.

"You'd know that better than I. How are you taking the isolation here?"

"I'm going buggy and I ain't been here two weeks yet. But I'll find something to do."

"Don't find it in Pine Bluff or in Little Rock. We stay clear of those two places. If you have to have some excitement, in a few weeks you can go to Dallas, or to New Orleans."

"No problem, I can stand it."

"Do you mind cold weather?"

"Hate it. This place gives me the creeps. Want some hot water for your tea?" Josten shook his head no, watching with morbid fascination as Baker carefully dunked his teabag several times, dropped it in his spoon, then squeezed it dry by wrapping the string tightly around the bag.

"How would you like to take a little trip?"

"Send me to Florida, or better yet, Havana."

"No. I want you to go to Omaha."

"Holy Christ, it'll be a zillion below in Omaha."

Josten slapped the table with his hand. "You're going to have to learn to do what I ask immediately, without question."

"Don't give me that shit. You think I'm one of these dumb Klan guys, walking around in stupid sheets or dressing like they're state troopers, playing soldiers in the freezing rain? What a bunch of jerks."

"Ruddick didn't tell me you were an expert on uniforms, too. What would you suggest for the Klan?"

Baker settled back, always happiest when giving advice. "The old guys, let them keep their robes. You ain't never going to get much out of them, anyway. For the new guys, I'd train them in old GI fatigues, stuff you can crawl around in the muck with. But if I was trying to create a political force—that's what you're doing, isn't it, trying to keep the niggers in line?"

"Something like that."

"Well then, hell, I wouldn't put them in uniform at all. No, I'd let them all be plain-clothed guys, so nobody knows what they're thinking. In time, get them on the school board, make them deputy sheriffs, have them join the Guard, stuff like that, so they'd know what's going on and have some influence."

Josten stared at him in disbelief—here was an idea, a good one from this idiot—and it worked with Dixon's ideas about recruiting some people at the Air Force Base.

"I see what you mean. Not bad. Let me think about that— perhaps we need to have a small force like you describe."

"Sure. 'Course I'm a plain-clothes guy myself, so I'm biased—but think about it. Who's going to pay attention to somebody in Klan robes? It's a joke. And unless you do an awful good job, the Storm Klanners won't be much better. Look what you have to work with."

As Josten thought this over, Baker prodded him. "Now about this trip. I'll go to Omaha, but I want to go by way of Las Vegas, lay over a couple days each way. Okay?"

"You can do that. My wife is in Omaha, with my son. I want you to go and see where they live, where he goes to school, what time he comes home."

"Are you going to snatch him?"

"He's my son; it's not kidnapping."

"That's what you say. What are you, another fucking Bruno Hauptmann? Want me to go up there and make a wooden ladder and drag the kid—"

There was an instantaneous explosion as Josten's pistol fired a bullet into the wall behind Baker's head. Rising, Josten slapped his Smith & Wesson down on the table.

"Shut up." He was leaning forward, his eyes slits, his mouth in a grimace.

Baker squirmed. "I'm sorry, I was just lipping off, just talking. I'll go. You tell me what you want me to do."

"Just what I said. Find out exactly where they live, which room in the house my son sleeps in, what time he comes and goes, what their schedule is. I am his father. I have rights."

"Sure, sure, boss. I understand."

Josten scuttled into the next room while Baker, still shaken, slurped his tea; until the moment of the pistol shot, he had despised Josten as an ugly cripple. Now he thought he could work for him.

Offutt Air Force Base, Nebraska/February 9, 1954

Leaving the World War II factory building that now held SAC Headquarters always reminded Bandfield of the old sunken submarine movies, where the crew put on their Momsen lungs and bubbled their way to the surface. The air seemed to get fresher and the lights brighter every step away from LeMay's office.

"Spending ten minutes with that guy is like going ten rounds with Rocky Marciano."

Riley nodded. "He's brutal, but he's getting the job done. It's his style that makes systems management work." Riley rubbed his eyes, sunken and dark-shadowed. "What do you think of the accident investigation team's reports?"

"One of them's right—one may be wrong."

"Which is which?"

"I think that Williams just jerked the airplane apart; that's what Fitzpatrick says, and he's a professional pilot, no matter what else he is. But the other airplane, at Pinecastle, I don't know. It may be pilot error, too, but it might be material failure. I'm going to go down and have a look at the wreckage myself."

Both accident investigating teams had come up with the same conclusion: pilot error. At Frederick, Williams had simply placed too much stress on the airplane in the toss-bomb maneuver. In the Pinecastle accident the report said that the pilot had stressed the airplane beyond its design limits by making a high-speed high-G turn at low altitude.

Bandfield stopped to tie his shoe. "I thought they might recommend dropping the idea of toss-bombing."

"They can't—the War Plan calls for fusion weapons that can't be delivered any other way and have the crew survive the radiation. They've even got a new acronym for it—LABS, for Low Altitude Bombing System. Your guys are going to have to come up with something pretty fast with the parachute-retarded bombs."

"We're about a year away, I think. The AEC is hell to deal with, and the problem is a hell of a lot more complex than it looks."

"What ain't?"

Pinecastle Air Force Base, Florida/ February 14, 1954

Bandfield followed the line-chief's instructions, letting the T-33 nose-wheel edge around the yellow stripe that marked the parking slot, his eyes squinting in response to the glare from the acres of concrete ramp bleached white in the Florida sun. As he shut down he was furious with himself—on his way to investigate an accident, and he was almost one himself.

The problem was preoccupation—between trying to get the parachute-retarded bombs to work, help Riley with the investigations and keep Patty happy with an occasional visit home, he worried that Hadley had gone off the deep end with their fire-bomber program. In the past year they had re-manufactured six old TBM torpedo bombers, modifying them to carry both borate and water—and couldn't sell a one. Now they had a B-17 nearing completion, and no takers for that, either. The PBY sat in a corner of the hangar, flyable, but with no demand for its capability. Hadley tried to get the Forest Service let him give a demonstration, but they weren't interested—they were developing their own system.

But none of this excused the sloppy way he had planned the flight, nor the poor execution of his penetration. He'd arrived over McCoy with his tanks running dry; if Orlando Approach Control hadn't noted the urgency in his voice and given him an immediate clearance, he'd have had to declare an emergency. Then, in the descent the canopy had fogged up, and despite the bright Florida sun he'd had to have a GCA to help him on to final approach, like leading a blind man across the street. What a balls-up!

The 86th's Flying Safety Officer, Major Darby, was overage in grade and none too happy to see him; all crashes immediately reflect on the safety officer's past work, and he didn't feel any good could come of Bandfield's visit. The decision was pilot error and he was satisfied with that, especially since the pilot had just transferred in, and no blame was going to attach to Darby.

The B-47's wreckage was in a secured hangar; the charred and battered parts were laid out as closely as possible to the way they'd been when the aircraft was whole.

"Thanks, Major Darby. No sense in you hanging around; I'll be poking around for a while, and then call Base Ops for a ride back."

The last thing in the world Darby was going to do was let this s.o.b. from out of town run around unsupervised. He snorted, "No, sir; I'll stay here in case you need me. Or in case you find something."

Bandfield methodically checked the charred wreckage of the aircraft as if he were pre-flighting it, moving from the mangled cockpit around the exterior in a clockwise manner, threading in and out of the jumble of parts. Some, blown clear by the explosion, were only moderately damaged; others were so burned beyond recognition that only an expert could have guessed what they were.

After one circuit of the wreckage, Bandfield homed in on the fuselage center section. The wings extended in stubs from either side, broken off about ten feet from the fuselage.

"Major, is there any way we could pull the access plates on the wing-fuselage juncture?"

"I'll get someone in, Colonel, but why? That's about the only part that held together."

"Just a hunch. Do you mind?"

Bandfield wandered around the wreckage as they waited; it was hard to believe that something so potent as a B-47 could be reduced to rubbish like this in an instant. After about forty minutes, a truck with two crew chiefs and their tools showed up. They were eager to please, but it took almost two hours to shore up the fuselage center section safely enough for them to work on it. Once they got the fuselage secured, it took them another forty minutes to pull away enough panels for Bandfield to inspect the wing-fuselage juncture. He straddled the center section like a cowboy riding a horse and, using a big six-cell flashlight, peered into the triangular openings.

"See anything, sir?" Darby's tone clearly implied that there was nothing to see.

"I don't see anything that might be connected to this crash,

Major, if that makes you feel better. But I'd like you to have your men pull both the milk-bottle pin assemblies from this aircraft, tag them left or right, and send them both to me."

"Colonel, that's a *lot* of man-hours you're asking for."

"Do you want me to have General LeMay ask you for them?"

"Ah, no thanks. We'll get them to you by the end of the week at the latest."

"Thanks."

Omaha, Nebraska/April 12, 1954

"Bear, wake up! Listen to that noise!"

Riley sat bolt-upright. "Goddamn it, Lyra, don't do that to me. You must have been dreaming. I got a quart of adrenalin circulating now; I might as well get up."

"Shush. Don't talk to me like that. Just be still and listen."

He waited patiently, then he heard it, a soft scraping sound, coming from the kitchen or the garage.

He slipped out of bed, put his shorts on, then crept down the hall to Ulrich's room. Ulrich was sleeping, and Bear picked up his stepson's baseball bat.

The old floors squeaked badly, and he moved down the hallway next to the wall, one foot in front of the other, finally easing through the open door into the kitchen. There was no one there.

A small utility room connected the kitchen to the garage. As he moved forward, the bat caught a mop hanging on the wall, knocking it to the floor with a clatter.

Riley heard the side door of the garage open and the sound of someone running. He burst through the door in time to see a big man lope around the corner and out of sight. When Riley reached the corner, bare feet freezing in the snow, there was nothing but the sound of a car pulling away.

Lyra was waiting at the door with a robe, slippers, and a glass of bourbon; he took them in reverse order.

"Let me call the cops—then we'll talk about it."

"There's nothing to talk about. Helmut's behind this. I know it."

At seven the next morning the Omaha police called.

"Colonel Riley, we have a suspect we caught a little while ago. Can you come down and identify him?"

"Sure, what's he look like?"

"Ah, he's a little spade, really dark, maybe five-foot-six, one hundred thirty pounds."

"Couldn't be the man who broke in, Officer. I saw him, and he was well over six feet tall and must have weighed two hundred and fifty pounds."

"Ah, well, sorry to bother you. We'll have to find somebody else to prefer charges against this guy."

10

Los Angeles, California/March 26, 1954

"If old Sinatra can win an Oscar, I can get back into flying. If old Sinatra can win an Oscar, I can get back into flying."

Marshall repeated the phrase as he pounded along the beach, breathing hard and bathed in sweat, trying to think positively, to focus on anything but his investigation. He liked the linkage with Sinatra; both were outcasts from their profession. As Maggio, Sinatra had fought his way back to an Oscar for *From Here to Eternity*; Marshall would fight his way back to flying, one way or another.

He ran four miles a day now and usually worked out in the gym for two hours. When he read, he squeezed a spring-powered hand exerciser. He did a lot of reading, for there were no Air Force duties except to report in once a day to a little office in Space and Missiles Systems Office on El Segundo. Every Friday morning he met with the investigator from the OSI in a searching interrogation that seemed endless.

Fortunately, there were some major differences from his questioning in Korea—he always came in well rested and well fed, and the room, dreary as it was in its two-tone war-surplus green paint and muddy-brown asphalt tiles, was a thousand times better than the cornstalk and mud walls of a North Korean hut. The investigator didn't torture him, and he didn't have to worry about what was happening to Saundra.

But there was one tremendous difference favoring the brutal questioning in North Korea. There he didn't feel guilty—here he did. Fortunately the physical training was hardening him physically, just as the questions were hardening him mentally.

The interrogator had gotten off to a bad start when he asked, "Did you know any other prisoners of war who might have cracked under the North Korean questioning?"

"I don't know anything, they kept me in solitary. But that's a hell of a question to ask—you want me to be a stool pigeon for guys who suffered like I did."

Daniel Frazier, the investigator, was sympathetic to him. "No, no, come on now. We're just trying to get the facts." Yet he continued his routine of asking the same questions over and over, like Colonel Choi but without the brutality. Frazier inquired about every detail of his imprisonment, trying to construct a day-by-day record. The investigator, of medium height, with sand-colored hair, had a good sense of humor and was obviously not out to crucify him—but he wouldn't let go. None of the answers Marshall gave fully satisfied him. Finally Marshall realized that there was a method in Frazier's self-fulfilling madness, for the more he prodded, the more Marshall remembered of his months in North Korea, mostly things he'd prefer to have remained forgotten.

"Tell me, Captain Marshall, can you remember just when you were taken to Manpo?"

"Danny, you know I didn't have any calendar—I didn't even have anything to mark the days going by. They moved me about so much, I couldn't have kept track of it anyway."

Frazier took off his glasses to wipe them carefully. "Let's change the subject, shall we? How do you think the Air Force treats Negroes?"

"Is this official? I mean is this part of my interrogation?" Frazier nodded. "I used to think it was pretty good; after all, I was flying in an integrated outfit the whole time I was in Korea. And most bases are integrated today." The image of Coleman crossed his mind. "Of course, there were some diehards who were still prejudiced." He straightened the crease of his uniform; he could have come in civilian clothes, but he always made a point of being in uniform, with his ribbons and his wings.

"You say, 'used to think'?"

"Sure, until I came back from being a prisoner of war and got treated as a traitor."

Frazier, quietly methodical, just shook his head. "No one's treating you as a traitor, John. You signed a confession that you engaged in germ warfare—that puts the Air Force in an embarrassing position."

"I signed a confession that I parachuted measles-infected rats out of an F-86 Thunderjet at forty thousand feet; it was an obvious joke, a way to stop them from killing me."

Frazier was relentless. "A joke, maybe, but the Communists are making use of it. Besides the Douglas Edwards show, the film clip of you signing has been shown around the country on dozens of other programs. And, of course, there are certain implications in your actions."

Marshall felt as if he were standing tiptoe as a pool of guilt washed up higher and higher around him; he resented it because he knew he was innocent—yet there it was, a clammy accusatory rising tide.

"What implications?"

"Like what is permissible to say, and what is not; what and how much a person is supposed to endure. This investigation isn't out to get you, John; it's part of a bigger program to establish a code of conduct for the future."

"And guys like you, sitting four thousand miles behind the battle line, working forty hours a week, wearing civvies, eating high on the hog, sleeping warm with your wife every night—you're going to decide?"

"Not me, John, but the top leadership."

Marshall pushed his chair back. "Let me tell you something. You put the top leaders where someone starves them for weeks, keeps them awake for maybe four or five days at a time, tells them they are going to die every other day, puts pistols"—he was screaming now; he stopped to get control of himself before going on—"puts a pistol against their heads and pulls the trigger—it's a blank but for one hot minute you don't know it's a blank, you don't know if you're dead or alive, until they laugh."

He knew he was too excited, but he went on. "Ask the brass to put up with stuff like that for a year, and then let them make a code of conduct."

Clearly taken aback, Frazier waved his hands and said, "Let me get you some coffee."

"Can I leave?"

"Not right now. Let's take a break, then I've got a few other questions to ask you." Frazier fixed him a cup and left the room.

Marshall used to drink his coffee black; since he came back it was double cream and sugar, for he never wanted to miss another calorie. He sipped the coffee, thinking of the fetid water that had been his usual drink in Korea. He was sorry that he'd lost his temper just now, but glad he'd said what he did.

When Frazier came back he was smiling. "I understand how you could get emotional after all you've been through. But I've got to get back to the basic question. How do you feel the Air Force treats Negroes?"

An irrational urge swept over him; he couldn't stifle it. "Wanna buy a duck?"

"What's that?"

"Monkies is the cwaziest peoples."

Frazier smiled. "Okay, John, I get it. You're giving me the same business you gave the Koreans. Point well taken. But, come on, tell me, how do you feel about the Air Force?"

"I love the Air Force. I just don't like what it's doing to me. I shot down three planes in Korea, I'm an ace, and nobody believes me. Think about it, I'm the first Negro ace, and nobody gives me the time of day. They won't let me fly; I don't even have a job in the Air Force, except to come in here and let you pick my brains."

Frazier was persistent. "I can't comment on the ace business, out of my field. But how do you think the Air Force treats Negroes in general?"

"Compared to what?" It was a rhetorical question and he went on. "Compared to towns in the Deep South, it's terrific. Compared to the Army or the Navy, it's good. Compared to how it should be, it's lousy."

"Give me some specifics."

"Let's do it next time, when I can think about it. Right now I'm too pissed off to comment."

"Well, I've got to finish a report a week from tomorrow. Would you give it some thought between now and then, jot down your ideas, and bring them with you for the next session?"

Marshall went home, churning the idea over. Oddly enough, most of the information he had on the Air Force now came from Saundra, material she'd gotten from her activist friends. From what he could gather, integration had gone pretty well at most bases. The real rub was off-base relations—in many places, North and South, there was as much segregation as ever.

He picked up the phone and began calling, with Lockbourne first. It was like a chain letter; every place he called gave him some information, then referred him to someone else. He gave up everything but his running to stay by the phone, not worrying about the phone bill, trying to call Negro friends still in service, getting suggestions from them on who to call next.

Many of them were suspicious at first, but he was gratified to find out that his name was well known, and that they would talk frankly to him.

The results surprised him. Two of his old buddies from the 332nd at Lockbourne said that integration had sold them out—that they had a chance in a segregated outfit, but were strictly out of luck in an integrated unit. He talked to two others who said just the opposite, that they had a better chance in an integrated unit.

He felt he'd hit the jackpot with a sergeant in personnel at Scott Field who had access to the statistics that indicated what sort of opportunity a Negro had. The sergeant told him that only twenty-two of of 2,085 aviation cadets were Negro, a little over one percent;

there were 1,356 officers in flight training, and only *eleven* were Negro, less than one percent. And as far as living conditions, things were worse in the South, predictably enough. At Keesler, the base commander had forbidden base teams to play with local teams that would not play against Negroes; yet off base, in Biloxi, there was not only total social segregation everywhere from restaurants to poolrooms to whorehouses, but everything was substandard or worse. At Maxwell Air Force Base in Montgomery, Alabama, he found that segregation was just about eliminated on base, but not entirely, because white civilian chaperones at dances sometimes tried to keep Negroes out. Off-base housing was still miserable for enlisted Negroes, who had to live in a shantytown.

But on the whole, and to his surprise, it was heartening; time after time he got back reports that the ice had broken, that jobs were opening up, that people were getting used to the idea. The only really outrageous thing he found was that Little Rock Air Force Base, an elementary school built with federal funds and intended exclusively for Air Force dependents, was segregated because it was located on Pulaski County property, and the local school board rules applied.

He gave the report, six pages, single-spaced, to Frazier the next Friday.

"Jesus, John, I only wanted an opinion, not a thesis."

"This is no thesis—but it's a pretty good capsule survey of the Air Force and integration. The Air Force is doing a better job than I thought."

"Does that make you feel better?"

"Some. There's been progress, but not enough of it. When I get back to work, I'm going to see what I can do to help. But that's the big question—when are you going to be finished grilling me? When am I going back to flying?"

"I'm finished, and it was a pleasure to work with you. I understand you'll be getting orders in a few days. I hope they are just what you want."

That night John had a shaker full of martinis waiting when Saundra came in. They kissed and she asked, "How did it go?"

"Honey, I knocked him on his duff! He couldn't believe the information I had in that report. I couldn't believe it either—things seem to be looking up."

Saundra stood, unsmiling, a folded *Los Angeles Times* under her arm. "Tell me more."

"He says the investigation's over and that I should be getting orders pretty soon. I'll probably be back in the cockpit this time next month."

"That's great, I hope so. But you might want to take a look at this."

She flopped the newspaper in front of him, tapping at an article in the first column of the front page. The headline read RUSSELL RAILS AGAINST TRAITORS and followed with a letter printed in full from Senator Richard Russell of Georgia to Secretary of Defense Charles Wilson.

Marshall read it out loud. "My views may be extreme, but I believe that those who collaborated and the signers of false confessions should be immediately separated from the services under conditions other than honorable." The letter went on for several more paragraphs, but John dropped the paper to the floor. "Conditions other than honorable"—it was impossible.

"This may not mean anything, Saundra. It's just a letter from a die-hard Southerner. The services still have their say."

She took his face in her hands and whispered, "John, John, think about it. The Air Force won't even let you put in your claims for your victories. Maybe they won't discharge everybody. But they'll probably have to sacrifice some."

"Saundra, they couldn't. I never told the Commies anything useful. And before we went into combat, when the intelligence guys briefed us about capture, they never told us we had to die! Sometimes they said, 'Tell them only your name, rank and serial number' and sometimes it was 'Tell them anything they want to know.' But they didn't give us any poison pills, or anything. Besides, most of us didn't know anything the Communists didn't already know."

"You don't have to convince me, John, you just have to convince a board of white officers who probably already think you're a trouble-maker because you're claiming to be an ace. Damn it, think about it! Will they pick Langford Uppercrust the Third from Harvard to be a sacrificial lamb, or will it be poor John Marshall, a jigaboo from Cleveland?"

He sat with his head in his hands. The prospect of a dishonorable discharge was too much.

"Okay. You're right. I'll resign my commission."

She hugged him, saddened at the thought that this, the smart thing to do, was going to make him unhappy for the rest of his life.

Little Rock, Arkansas/April 1, 1954

Baker ran his hands uneasily over the DeSoto's chrome and plastic steering wheel. "You realize we could get arrested for this?"

Josten snorted with impatience. "For what? Sitting peaceably in a car?"

"Loitering in a car by a schoolyard. If some old woman reports us, the cops'll be down in a minute, figuring we're waiting here to flash our weenies at the kids."

Josten sulked as Baker put the car into gear, turning down the first street away from the schoolyard.

"I just wanted to see where my son will go to school."

Baker glanced at Josten in troubled silence, uncertain how to handle Josten's growing schizophrenia. More and more it seemed as if he were working with two totally different men. One was a brilliant planner, a leader who inspired the Storm Klanners, rational, courteous, sometimes even pleasant to get along with. The other was a man hurtling toward madness, obsessed with the idea of reclaiming his wife and his child.

With an abrupt gesture, Josten stuck the clawed fingers of his hand under Baker's nose and launched into a tirade that had become familiar in the last few weeks.

"See these burns? I spent many months on my back in a hospital, not knowing whether I'd live or die, whether I'd ever walk again.

The one thing that sustained me was the thought of my son, that I had to live to take care of him. Do you think I'm going to let some stupid American pilot take my place, to serve as his father?"

Baker eased into the parking lot of a drive-in root beer stand. When these moods struck—and they did with increasing frequency—their conversation fell into a pattern: Josten's complaining, and Baker trying to calm him. "Look, Helmut, you're not the first guy whose wife divorced him and took the kid. It happens all the time."

Nothing impaired Baker's appetite, and he ordered two hamburgers, french fries, and a root beer float for himself, a coffee for Josten. Eating methodically, licking his fingers between bites, Baker said nothing, contemplating the situation. As long as he still needed cover, he'd have to put up with Josten's growing craziness. The Air Force inspectors had torn McNaughton's paperwork apart, and Elsie performed exactly as Ruddick had instructed her to, preferring charges against Baker with the local district attorney. It satisfied the Air Force, which backed off to concentrate on getting McNaughton's production procedures straightened out.

He enjoyed working with the Klan, feeling superior to most of the members, and seeing many ways that he could profit from it in the future. His duties for Josten were light, and he liked the entertainment he found in the bawdier sections of New Orleans, going down for a week or two at a time, feasting on oysters before nosing around the red-light district, looking for new young girls just in from the bayous.

While he ate, the other man watched him with amused contempt, realizing that Baker could have no inkling of what it was like truly to love some one, or what it meant to have your son stolen from you. He looked on Baker as his senior non-commissioned officer, a good sergeant who did what he was told. It didn't matter that he was a pig—uncultured, ill-mannered, unread—for he did not want him as a friend. He needed him only as an instrument, an extension of his own crippled arms and legs.

As Josten slowly regained his composure, he realized that he would have to say less about his feelings for Lyra and Ulrich—he was giving too much away, and while Baker might be a good worker, he had no illusions about his loyalty.

As they drove back to Pine Bluff in silence, Josten realized that he was better far off here than at McNaughton. The work with the Klan suited his own needs perfectly, giving him time to recover his health, and to plan for his reunion with Lyra. He already had his first objective well in hand, making the Storm Klan into an elite unit. In a way it was his apology for his disloyalty to Hitler. There had been too many men like himself, who had not supported Hitler at the most crucial moments, when the war might still have been won. Now half of Germany was occupied by Russian peasants, the other half by predatory Westerners who bled the country dry. Negro music rang in the dance halls, German girls were bearing half-caste babies; it was exactly what Hitler had predicted—the degradation, the "nigrification," of Germany.

Now Josten was beginning the expansion of the elite Storm Klan concept to other Klan "Realms," as the state organizations were called. In its decline, the Klan had splintered, disintegrating into local, autonomous chapters. The Kleagles—organizers—enjoyed their power and had been suspicious of previous suggestions that they cooperate. But in the past few weeks, Ruddick had brought several of them in to see how well things were working in Pine Bluff, and now there was even talk about affiliating to create a United Klans of America. From there it would be but a step to a political party.

The idea of a party made it essential that he create a plainclothes force, and he had recently spent days interviewing likely Storm Klanners, trying to see which ones would have the intelligence and the presence to insinuate themselves into responsible positions in the community. It was tough going—most of the Storm Klanners were Neanderthals, much more willing to fight with a club or fists than with their brains. But there were a few who made good candidates, and they were recommending more. One was already a deputy sheriff in Pulaski County, and another was on the school board. Several were in the National Guard. It was a start.

But more important than anything was planning his personal mission. He would not allow someone else to take his rightful place. No one else had any right to Lyra and Ulrich.

Wright-Patterson Air Force Base, Ohio/ April 15, 1954

The giant base spilled like an upset Monopoly board along the Erie Railroad and the Mad River, extending from the old Fairfield Air Depot over ten miles of farmland to the runways at Wright Field. Bits and pieces of logic were evident in those few acres where streets were laid out in nice rectangles, and sweeping drives approached handsome headquarters. But most of the area was filled in with a crazy quilt of buildings, some ugly because they were quickly and cheaply built, others strange-looking because they had unusual test functions to fulfill.

At the core of the complex was an array of bureaucracies acting as its central nervous system, fulfilling the age-old military needs of procurement and supply. These civil service fiefdoms, replete with manual calculators, file cabinets, and endless serried rows of clerks, labored on through the years, growing quietly, layering the paperwork into an immense, inedible baklava of rules and regulations.

Dependent upon this core were the many engineering divisions, experimenting with materials and processes, creating new test procedures, guarding the established standards. The engineering divisions provided a stability and a continuity to the field and had strong, productive contacts with its civilian counterparts. This layer grew, too, at a faster pace than the central core, but not so swiftly as the new stars of the expanding Wright-Pat galaxy, the Weapon System Project Offices, products of new management needs that had to keep all the many facets of a modern weapon system coordinated. There you found the bright young officers, the advocates who identified their careers with the complex systems they managed and took weapons from the cradle of inspiration to the grave of obsolescence.

Bandfield's first memories of the place went back to 1934, a simpler grass-field time when he'd flown the losing entry in a twin-engined bomber competition. He hadn't done too well then— he wondered how he'd do today.

"Riley, this place reminds me of a coral reef; always growing one new organism, one on top of another. An organization is created for a new project; it matures over time and becomes part of the foundation while a new outfit gets superimposed on it."

Riley laughed. "Yeah, it's been a real alphabet soup—AMC, WADC, WADD—always changing with the Air Force mission, with the weapons."

They walked down the shining corridors, so worn and polished that wood knots gleamed like voyeurs' eyes through the linoleum that dated the building to wartime construction. Bandy noticed it, and reflected how floors signaled when a government building was built—hardwood in prewar, linoleum in wartime, and asphalt tile in postwar, a downward spiral of aesthetics. The route took them past dozens of glass-walled partitions, which transmitted some of the light and all of the noise, toward the B-47 WSPO—the Weapon System Project Office.

"You satisfied with how things are going with the B-47?"

Riley took two steps and clicked his heels. "Christ, I'm happy as a clam because LeMay is happy. We'll have nineteen operational B-47 wings by December, and twenty-seven a year after that. The in-commission rate is good and getting better, and we've finally got a handle on the engineering change proposals. LeMay attributes it all to the fact that the WSPOs are working so good, and he thinks Bernie Schriever and I are geniuses for setting them up."

"What's the secret? You're working with the same people."

"The real reason is LeMay—people know he wants the system to work, so it does. It has what I call lateral leadership; the project officers can cut across the usual chain of command to get something done. You get a hotshot young captain cooking in here, and he can make things happen."

"Well, Bernie Schriever made brigadier last year—when are you due?"

Riley looked genuinely surprised. "Me make general? Are you kidding? There's more chance they'll court-martial me than make me a general."

He walked along, pensive. "Seriously, Bandy, I've never thought about it before. Hell, I haven't done any of the right things, gone to any of the right schools. They'd never even consider me."

"All you've done right is get next to LeMay and straighten out the B-47 program. You should ask LeMay to be the B-52 WSPO director—that should do it."

"We'll talk about it later."

They turned the corner, threaded their way through the battered and ill-assorted desks, some still wearing the NRA tags they came with during the Depression, to a series of offices lining the wall. The glass partitions here went all the way to the ceiling and the offices were reserved for lieutenant colonels and above. At the end, one office had been called a conference room; it was identical in size to the other four offices along the wall, but it had a long conference table, straight-backed chairs, and an overhead projector. Sitting around the table, faces long, were representatives from the various Wright-Patterson divisions—Engineering, Procurement, even Flight Test. In the center of the table, tagged like toes in the morgue, were the milk-bottle pins Bandfield had pulled from the Pinecastle B-47 crash the previous February. Next to them was a black three-ring binder, the kind school kids use.

Bandfield studied the men for a moment before Riley introduced him. This was exactly what Riley had devised his systems management and the WSPOs to overcome—the dogged inertia of the usual civil service hierarchy. He looked at them with a mixture of anger and sympathy. They were a classic Wright-Pat civil service team—five GS-12s, in rumpled suits from Sears, their stained birthday-gift ties worn and frayed, each man with a forest of pencils in his shirt pocket. Together they constituted an engineering Greek chorus, ready to back up past decisions or defer new ones.

Most of the engineering at the complex was a mere ratification of the manufacturer's proposals; a very few individuals, one or two in each office, were aggressive enough to stick their necks out a little to do some engineering on their own. More than anything else, they were skilled in a thousand ways to cover their asses.

The team leader came in a little late, a tired psychological ploy to show how busy he was, how unimportant he considered this meeting compared to his many other duties. Bandfield immediately pegged him as a GS-13 hustling for GS-14.

"I'm Chuck Baleske, and I'm chairman of this august group."

Baleske paused, clearly savoring his moment in the sun. Bandfield knew the type well, gunning for position, staking out a claim for the future while being fiercely defensive about the past. Baleske was sleekly vulpine, hair slicked back with too much Vitalis, the odor dominating the room. His round Santa Claus cheekbones contrasted strangely with his long, strong jaw that moved in chewing motions when he wasn't speaking.

"Colonel Bandfield, we appreciate the effort you went to to have these milk-bottle pins pulled, but after a great deal of analysis, we have concluded that the accident investigation report was correct, and that these parts had nothing to do with it."

He handed Bandfield the black binder, who looked at it and said, "I didn't say that the accident investigation was incorrect or that the milk-bottle pins had anything to do with it. I said that they had deformed, and that a similar condition might cause an accident in another airplane."

The men around the conference table leaned forward as one. This was clearly what they were waiting for.

"Colonel, every part in the B-47 went through long analysis here before the airplane was built; we subjected the milk-bottle pin to hours of testing, under all conditions. We know that is strong enough for its function."

"Did you check these *particular* pins? Did you analyze their material?"

"We didn't have to. They were purchased from a qualified vendor, who built them to military specifications; they were inspected by McNaughton quality control. We aren't in the business of tearing every airplane in the Air Force apart and inspecting its individual parts." Baleske looked to his group, who laughed dutifully.

"This isn't every part, and it's not from every airplane. These are specific parts from a specific airplane, and they're deformed. My question is, what caused the deformation?"

"Who knows? The violence of the accident, the temperature of the fire?"

Bandfield wasn't surprised at the animosity in his voice, a feeling that everyone in the room except Riley seemed to share.

Sitting at the left rear of the room was a tiny gnome of a man, with a great bulging bald head; his chin seemed to be resting on the table. In a voice as high-pitched as nails across a blackboard he said, "Colonel, I'm Roy Palm, and I was in on the structure of the B-47 from the start. I can't tell you how many hours we put in studying this particular kind of fitting, but I can tell you that we decided that it's plenty strong enough. Just a look at the wreckage confirms that—they held together while the rest of the wing broke off."

Bandfield saw his mistake at once—he had challenged the years of effort they'd put into the airplane. They'd approved the milk-bottle pin once—they couldn't consider reexamining it without casting doubt on everything they'd done.

Bandfield shook his head as he leafed through the report, which addressed the accident only. Finally, he looked up, saying, "Gentlemen, thanks for coming. You didn't answer the questions I asked, I don't agree with your conclusions, and I predict that we will be in this room in a few months or a few years from now, discussing another accident."

"Colonel, you can use your crystal ball to predict what you like; we're engineers here, and we deal in facts, not theories." Baleske's voice was triumphant; the home team had won again.

Bandfield didn't speak until they were passing through the bronze double doors at the front of the building. "Bear, I'm sorry I brought you down here. Those bastards don't want to see a problem because they've rubber-stamped the design in the past. I just hope your WSPOs can control them."

Riley was shaking his head. "I don't know, they'll just have to chip away at it."

"Good luck. I've got a gut feeling we've got massive trouble with this milk-bottle thing, and it's just a matter of time before it breaks loose."

"I hope you're wrong; if you're right, we could lose a lot of crews."

"Can't you do anything?"

"I'll talk to LeMay about it, and see if he can't beat up on the bureaucracy. But believe it or not, he's got even bigger worries on the operational side; that's why he's assigning me to a different job."

"The B-52 WSPO?"

"I wish. No, I'm supposed to start running ORIs, Operational Readiness Inspections, on a few selected B-47 wings."

"That's an important job, but there's a lot of guys who could do it. I wouldn't stand for it if I were you."

"No, this one's a little special. I can't tell you about it now—but you'll understand, I think, when it finally comes out in the open."

Santa Monica, California/May 18, 1954

She felt the usual sense of deprivation when Fred Peterson left, as if a vital current in her life had been turned off. He was eternally radiating energy, spinning off ideas as he walked, calling for improvements, making suggestions; he was, in short, exhilarating—and exhausting. Especially when he was as excited as he was today.

He had done so much for her; he was a financial genius. The public issue of stock in Marshall Products, Incorporated, had sold out within a few days, much of it, she knew, to Peterson and his friends. Now she had her own factory building on 26th Street, red brick, with two floors of well-lit offices above the cosmetic factory itself. Fred had already rented the second floor to a commercial land development company; the monthly rent almost covered the mortgage on the building.

He had reserved the third floor for her own offices and the laboratory for developing new products. Never again would she have to stir her stainless steel vats of face cream; now there were high-speed mixing machines that blended hundreds of pounds of materials a day. And never again would she experiment in the kitchen with new fragrances for her Love Potions, using fresh herbs and spices to try to develop something new. She wasn't sure she was entirely glad that this was so.

The new people he'd sent over—two men and a woman—were proving to be perfect. She'd made the woman, Martha, her personal assistant and put one of the men in charge of production and the other sales. For the first time in years she felt free.

It was almost five-thirty, time for John to come by and pick her up. She hoped he'd be in a decent mood. The Air Force had at first been reluctant to let him leave, as if it had some sort of plan—a bad plan certainly—for him. Then, two weeks ago, his resignation had been accepted, he'd gone to March Air Force Base to be processed out, and he was a civilian again.

And, once again, out of work. They'd talked again this morning about him coming to work at the plant; she knew she'd be in for an argument tonight.

It started the minute the car pulled up. He kissed her and opened with, "Let's not even discuss it, Saundra, it's just not my kind of life. I can't sit at some desk, barely knowing what's going on, and watch you be the big executive."

They headed up Pico Boulevard and he almost hit a truck.

"Keep your eye on the road, John. That's just stupid Black male pride, and you know it."

"It's not Black and it's not male—but it is pride. I'm not going to work at a job just because you own the place. When you start an airline, then I'll work for you."

She said, "Maybe I'll just do that."

And he replied, "And maybe you won't have to. I got a job today."

Relief swept through her. "Doing what?"

"Flying, what else? Old Hadley Roget wants me to come up to Salinas and test his airplanes—he's building water-bombers to use on forest fires."

"Is it safe?"

"Safest thing in"—he jammed on the brakes to let another truck pass—"safer than driving in Los Angeles, anyway. I start next week."

"Where will you stay? What about us?"

"I told him I'd work forty hours in a four-day week; I'll be home on Thursday night, and leave Monday morning, As busy as you are, you won't even know I'm gone."

It was true enough; by the time she got home at night she was exhausted.

"I'll go you one better. You get a little place up there, and I'll come up on alternate weekends. I'd like to spend some time with Patty again, anyway."

"Great! Only one way to celebrate—Mexican food!"

They went to the Red Onion and ordered the house specialty, a huge platter of enchiladas, tacos, and chile rellenos, along with a pitcher of margaritas.

"It's still amazing to me that we can sit here, just like white folks."

She nodded, mouth full, then plunged in. She no longer tried to avoid talking about Fred Peterson; he was a vital part of her business life, and John had to get used to it. "Fred was by today. He was all excited about the Supreme Court decision."

Marshall was feeling too happy to be upset by the mention of Peterson's name. "What decision?"

"The Supreme Court has ruled that segregation is illegal in public schools. No more 'separate but equal'—no more segregation."

He spooned salsa over his beans and rice. "I'll believe it when it happens." He hesitated, hating to ask, "What does Fred think it means?"

"He says it's a landmark decision, that only a liberal like Earl Warren could have gotten it through the court. From a business point of view it won't have any effect for four or five years, but after that, look out!"

"Why four or five years?"

"It's sort of arbitrary—he thinks we won't feel the effect until kids have been integrated in high school for four years—the same with college."

"Well, your Mr. Peterson is a mighty smart businessman, but you can tell him from me that he's off by about ten years. No matter what the Supreme Court says, segregation is going to be around for a long time. There'll be blood in the streets before there will be Negroes in the classrooms in the South."

Willow, California/August 13, 1954

A pall of smoke hung like a great gray jellyfish, long tendrils of white smoke whisping down to the fires dotting the state. Forty miles from the Willow airport, the whirring cicada-like murmur of bark and leaf rubbing together broke the stillness of the supercharged afternoon heat, the arid crackle signaling how little moisture remained in the foliage of the vast Mendocino forest. One hundred thousand acres hovered at flash point, the deciduous trees fluttering millions of brown distress flags in the growing westerly wind that spun red snakeskins of bark from the manzanitas. The scrub brush—"light fuel," the Forest Service firefighters called it—was so dry that limbs snapped at a touch. Above the scrub, evergreens towered in frowsy lines, the dust covered needles drooping, resin oozing, ready to turn from tree to torch with a spark.

On the flight line, the local Forest Supervisor, Joe Dasmann, felt his nerves grow taut. He was exhausted from two days of parceling out his slender resources to fight a dozen fires, and now he had to get rid of these volunteers and get back to work.

"Mr. Roget, we appreciate you and Mr. Marshall coming up here, believe me. We're all for using airplanes—been using 'em for years to drop supplies and smoke jumpers. Just today I dropped a whole mess of gear in to a crew we've got fighting a vicious fire on the side of Copperhead Canyon. And we're getting ready to experiment with aerial tankers, too. There's a line item in the budget for it next year. We're going to convert a Stearman crop duster for experiments."

Marshall winced as Roget barked, "Damn it man, you already done that! You don't need no budget item to test this—I'm offering to demonstrate it to you for free!"

"I appreciate that, really. I just don't have any authority to let you do it—but if you crash, I'd have all the liability. I'm not going to take that chance. Besides, I've got my hands full right now fighting little fires, trying to keep them from becoming big ones."

Marshall put his hand on Roget's arm. "We understand, Mr. Dasmann, and we'll be on our way. I would appreciate it if you'd just take a look at our airplane, and let us tell you what we're thinking."

Dasmann walked with them toward the bright orange TBM Avenger parked at the side of the runway. Built by General Motors for Grumman during the war, the ex-torpedo bomber sported a 1,700-horsepower Wright Cyclone engine beneath its gleaming cowl. Roget had replaced the rear turret with a sleek fairing, then spent hours preparing it as carefully as if it were a racing plane.

"Man, that's a big bird! Looks better than any I ever saw in the Navy. How much water will it carry?"

"Six hundred gallons. We cleaned up the airframe, tore out the military equipment, bulged the bomb bay and sealed it into one big water tank. We can drop it all at once, or in two passes, three hundred gallons at a time."

Dasmann eased himself up on the wing to peer in the cockpit.

"Go on, get in, I'll show you the gear we installed to drop the water."

Twenty-six tired and thirsty men met at the bottom of a steep draw in Copperhead Canyon, sixty-two miles from Willow. Their faces were blistered underneath the dusting of chalky charcoal ash from the fire they'd just contained to the sloping mountainside, their throats as dry as their canteens, hacking and gasping from inhaling too much smoke as they clung to their spades and axes as weary Roman legionnaires clung to their swords.

The foreman, Warren McCarley, reminded them, "Don't wet your boots." Most were veterans and knew better. The young ones might pour water on their thick-soled boots, hot from the scorched earth they'd been working, and get their feet scalded by the steam.

McCarley was pleased; there had been only one flame front. It has been rough work stumbling on the mountainside, eased by the fact that the fire was burning downhill and not up and because the brush thinned out lower down, among the rock outcroppings. Another quarter-mile and it would have hit the stand of old rotting logs and a heavy ground cover of pine needles and branches. Then it would have raced down to where the canyon settled into a densely packed quarter-mile-wide floor, full of tinder-dry foliage that would have started an uncontainable blaze. McCarley squinted up at the clouds gathering overhead—they held at least the promise of rain along with their threat of lightning. Even a small shower would help cool down the vegetation and slow down the spread of the next blaze.

A ham radio operator, McCarley was delighted with the new radio he'd been issued and, tired as he was, methodically stretched the antenna in the best direction for a report back to the base station at Willow. He glanced at his watch—4:21—enough time to report, walk the men back to the trucks, and get home in time for dinner.

"Willow Operations, this is McCarley, over."

The Willow operator came back loud and clear. "Hey, Warren, how you doing? Got all your marshmallows toasted?"

"Yeah, thought we were going to lose it about halfway through, had some rolling logs come tumbling down. A little draw caught one and it stopped the others—" His voice was drowned out in a crack of thunder that reverberated though the canyon.

"Holy Jesus, Warren, what happened?"

"Bad news, Willow—looks like multiple lightning strikes down the canyon, less than a couple of miles from here."

"Did it start a fire?"

"It had to—that lightning looked like a scene from a Frankenstein movie. And if there is one, we're in deep shit."

McCarley's voice came on again, now tinged with fear. "I can see the smoke already. We've got to get moving, Willow, and try and beat it out of the canyon."

"Can you stop it?"

McCarley didn't bother to unplug the radio. They couldn't stop it and there was no way to pack the radio out.

Dasmann was slinging his leg over the polished cockpit side when a woman raced out of the operations shack, waving a sheet of paper.

"Joe, we got a problem up in Copperhead Canyon. A lightning strike started a big fire downwind of McCarley's crew."

Dasmann glanced at his watch; it read 16:23. "Did you tell them to get the hell out of there?"

"They didn't need no telling; Warren said he could see the smoke already."

"Did he say how far he was from the road?"

"Nah, but I took a look at the map—figure it's three miles, maybe more."

"Wonder what the winds are?"

"Don't matter; if a fire goes down that canyon, it'll make its own winds. I've been in there; it's thick with manzanitas and scrub pine that'll burn better'n matches."

Dasmann turned to Marshall and Roget. "How about a demonstration, right now?"

Marshall said, "You got it. Climb in the backseat there and tell me where to go."

Roget hopped off the wing to get the fire extinguisher, yelling "Clear!" as he ran.

. . .

None of McCarley's men needed to be told what to do—their lives depended upon reaching the road before the fire reached them, and they dumped everything to lighten the load for the steady jog eastward.

From above, the fire looked like a blossoming Rorschach inkblot, spreading slightly to the north and south, contained toward the west, but racing in an all-consuming flame to the east, licking down the canyon in great leaping arcs of flame, throwing firebrands ahead to spot new fires. The lightning had struck little more than two miles from McCarley's crew, but the wind was advancing it eastward at eight miles an hour. An invisible balloon of heat rolled ahead of the flames, roasting the foliage, stripping it of every molecule of moisture so that it exploded into flame when the first spark reached it. The canyon, now changing into a chimney, pulling heat and flames up to ignite the sides, was burning like a dynamite fuse, a snaking, rustling stream of fire aimed at the small fire-fighting party racing toward safety.

The twenty-six men strung out in two parallel files, forcing themselves along the paths they'd cut to get in that morning. McCarley had a good eye for time and distance, and they'd covered the first mile in a little over twelve minutes, not bad for tired men in rough terrain. But he knew the fire would be doing better, striding with long tongues of flame, never stumbling, never falling, never short of breath.

One of the young firefighters fell in step beside him; McCarley couldn't remember his name even though he knew his father.

"Think we'll make it, Warren?"

McCarley knew almost certainly they would not, that unless the wind died down—unlikely given the self-generating venturi effect of the canyon—that the fire would overtake them somewhere before the sanctuary of Eagle Pass, a slit in the mountains now just a little less than two miles away. There the rocky ground inhibited growth, and they'd have a chance to outdistance the flames, to make it to the trucks and safety.

But he knew they'd never reach it. It was like a high school algebra problem—the fire was traveling at eight miles per hour and accelerating; they were doing five and slowing. The old Western movie "head them off at the pass" cliché came to mind—they were going to get headed off at the pass, and more.

"No problem, son, but we've got to keep hustling. Can't fool with Mother Nature, you know."

The boy dropped back, reassured, as McCarley, heart pounding, increased the pace.

As Roget strapped Dasmann in the backseat, gave him a rudimentary briefing on using a parachute and bailing out, and showed him how the intercom worked, Marshall started the big Wright engine. They were off the ground quickly, the ungainly landing gear folding up inside the Avenger's thick wing as they climbed westward.

"Mr. Marshall, did you ever do any water-bombing before?"

"We've had a lot of practice sessions, getting the rig to work. But I've done lots of other kinds of bombing—I think I can handle it."

"Let's try to drop as low as we can—fifty feet or so—we'll lose less by evaporation, won't we?"

"No, it looks to us like about one hundred fifty feet is best—you get a maximum dispersion, without dissipating the hit."

Dasmann had given him a westerly heading, but their course was soon no problem, for they could see the convection column of smoke from the Copperhead Canyon fire climbing up three thousand feet before merging with the cloud deck. To Dasmann it was a good sign; the fire had not progressed to a fire storm yet.

Marshall had shoved the prop, throttle, and mixture forward, and the old torpedo bomber groaned along at 240 mph.

"Walk me through this, John. We're doing four miles a minute, and they're only about forty-five miles away now. That puts us over them in about eleven minutes, right?"

"Right."

"They're probably not making more than three miles or four

miles an hour over the rough ground they've got to cover. It's 16:28 now. That means we should be there by 16:39. If the fire is moving as fast as I think it is, they're goners."

John was figuring with him as he eased the power farther forward, coaxing another thirty miles per hour out of the old bomber in their slight descent. "Too close, Joe, too close."

Just over forty miles ahead the twenty-six men were strung out in long uneven lines, the younger men forging ahead now, the older ones gasping for breath as they struggled on. The scrub at the bottom of the valley had been the major beneficiary of the little moisture that had fallen that year and had grown into an impassable tangle that forced the men to climb up the canyon wall to edge through it. The older men felt the stress, and neither the buzzsaw crackle nor the lashing hot breath of the fire behind them could drive their legs faster.

McCarley, breathing hard, head pounding, was in the middle of the pack. He stopped and let the others stream by him as he listened to the ugly turbine-like roar of the fire heading toward them, the throaty growling punctuated by the sharp explosion of trees bursting into flame.

McCarley felt the hot wind gusting and realized it was hardly worth making the effort. He felt a tug on his belt—it was the kid.

"Come on, Warren, you said we've got to hustle. Let's do it!"

Ahead he could see the sun glinting against the sharp line of granite outcroppings that marked Eagle Pass. The terrain beyond the entrance to the pass was nothing but spilled rocks from past floods for over a mile; if they could make it there, they might have a chance. He glanced at his watch and couldn't read the ash-coated dial. Rubbing it clean, he saw that it was 4:40, just as the roar of the TBM's engine broke through the crackle of the fire rushing behind him.

In the Avenger, Dasmann saw the foliage of the canyon floor melting away at the inferno's edge like a sheet of paper thrown into a fireplace, tendrils of flame first browning then igniting the scrub.

"There they are—about a quarter-mile from the pass."

Marshall was checking the terrain, remembering how he felt only a few years ago, checking out a Korean valley in his F-86. He mumbled, "At least there's no flak" into the intercom and Dasmann yelled, "What?"

"Nothing, I'm going to make the first run-in from this heading, no time to set up; I'll make two drops. the first one right at the end of the line of firefighters."

"Get with it, John, the fire's almost on them."

Below the twenty-six men were running now, flogging the last reserves of energy from their desperately tired bodies as the fire roared only a few hundred yards behind them, the point of the flame cone-shaped on the valley floor, its flanks extending back up the canyon wall. A heart attack dropped one man, two others stopped momentarily to help him, then left him to press on knowing they could not save their friend, could not save themselves, as the horror howling behind them accelerated.

Marshall put his landing gear down and then lowered his flaps, slowing to 140 mph; he lined up carefully, checking the wind, his wingtips no more than forty feet from the sloping canyon wall. When the last man disappeared from view beneath his nose he toggled off the first drop, calling "Water away!" as he poured power to the Avenger, pulling up his gear and flaps and climbing straight ahead, the TBM bucking in the smoky turbulence above the fire.

McCarley was amazed to see the water blossoming from the plane's belly, a great white balloon that expanded until it hit the ground behind them with a rush, bouncing up to meet the fire in a massive hissing embrace. The fire suddenly sagged, recoiling upon itself, as if it were regrouping for another attack. McCarley turned and ran with the rest of the men, racing for the pass, where the rocky floor now gave them a chance to live.

As soon as Marshall cleared the lip of the canyon he turned back for another run.

"Good drop, John. Can you put the next one right at the fire's edge? If we can give them another couple of minutes, they might be able to make it to the trucks."

Marshall clicked his mike in response, lowering the TBM into the canyon again. "This time I will drop to about fifty feet, and just bowl the water along the center of the canyon."

McCarley was standing at the entrance to the pass, his arm swinging in encouragement to the last of the men stumbling toward him. The TBM passed low overhead, the pounding of its engine reverberating against the canyon walls.

Ahead the fire was moving forward, slower now with less dense growth to fuel it.

Marshall used two rivets on the cowling as a primitive sight, lining them up with the fire's leading edge. He was lower and slower this time, and he dropped just as the fire apparently moved between the two rivets, calling again "Water away."

There was no one to see the three hundred gallons of water hit the ground, then rise up like a wave cascading into the surf, a sheet ninety feet high and forty feet wide that fell across the fire's edge like a huge wet blanket, blunting its rush.

There was no time for celebrations when they got back to Willow; Dasmann quickly organized another team of firefighters to go in to contain the Copperhead Canyon fire and try to recover the body of the man who had died.

"John, are you ready to make some more drops?"

"As fast as you can turn me around—but I need one forty-five/one fifteen av gas for this dude."

"Already sent for a truck. I can't promise you'll get paid a dime for this, not even expenses. You know Uncle Sam."

Roget bridled, but Marshall put his fingers to his lips and laughed. "Joe, listen, Uncle's screwed me before. Don't sweat it; I figure I'm learning a trade, right, Hadley?"

Roget grinned broadly. "Hell, I hadn't thought about it that way. Sure, Bones, if the goddamn government won't buy these airplanes, we'll go into business for ourselves. We ought to be able to rent them out, follow the fire season around the country."

Marshall shook his head in agreement. "Yeah, maybe we'll even find a use for that old water-scooping Catalina of yours."

Little Rock, Arkansas/December 18, 1954

Sitting in the high-backed chair, under the all-seeing eye of his wife's portrait, Milo Ruddick pretended to be absorbed in his newspaper as Ginny walked in. It was two in the afternoon, but she was still wearing her orange satin robe and fuzzy slippers.

He turned a page as she opened the liquor cabinet door and gave a little gasp of surprise.

"Daddy, where's the booze? I want a little drinkie."

Ruddick folded his paper. There were few things he couldn't control—Ginny's drinking was one of them. It was time for a change.

"There's no liquor in the house, Ginny, and there won't be. You've got to pull yourself together and do something with your life."

As expected, she stormed out of the room. Ruddick began reading again; there was a long editorial on the Senate's censure of McCarthy. Damn fools, he thought. McCarthy's one of the few patriots in the whole damn government.

He heard her sidle back in and sit down. He didn't look up.

"Daddy, don't be mean. You don't know what I've been through."

"No, I don't, not anymore than you know what you've put me through, first with that business about Nathan, then having Stan leave, now your drinking. Where is it going to end?"

"Do you want me to leave?"

"Yes, when you're ready—when you're able. But you've got to stop drinking first."

"I don't want to—it's the only way out I have."

"Wrong. Let me tell you a way out. First of all, you've got to forget about this business with Nathan. I don't know why it happened, but it's over. Now you've got to get a job, get back into the mainstream of life."

"I don't have any skills, can't even type. Who'd have me?"

"Well, the governor, for one. You don't have to type; he'll take you on as a special assistant."

"What could I do?"

"Just be nice to him, see that he's taken care of."

"What do you mean 'be nice'?"

He looked at her and shook his head. "Do you think I'm pimping for you, that I'm selling you into white slavery? For Christ's sake, Ginny, you're my daughter! I mean, be pleasant, be helpful. The governor owes me a lot of favors; giving you a job is just one way of paying me back. You can work with Dixon Price over there, he'll keep you busy."

Ginny had moved back to the liquor cabinet and was staring wistfully at the bare shelves.

"Did you throw all that stuff out?"

"Of course not, I took it to the office. I'm not quitting drinking just because you have to."

"How do you know the governor will hire me?"

"Because I told him to. You start two weeks from Monday; I want you to get dried out, get yourself a new hairdo and some clothes, and do me proud. You understand?"

Ginny walked from the room without answering. She needed a drink, and she remembered she had a half-pint bottle of Old Forester tucked under her mattress. She'd think about her daddy's offer after she had a drink.

Nashville, Tennessee/December 25, 1954

It was a lonely Christmas Day, and Elsie had turned on all the lights, upstairs and down. She was playing her new high-fidelity record player at its peak, trying to force life into the house Troy McNaughton had built for her.

She'd left a lot of men in her life and a few had left her. She missed only two, Bruno Hafner and Dick Baker. Under the stress of the crash investigations, she had been glad to see Baker go, but now she missed him. As troublesome and cantankerous as he had been, as shamefully as he had taken advantage of her, she still wanted him back. It was perverse; she knew it and liked it. Baker had the perfect mix of dominance and domesticity—he knew exactly how to handle her. It struck her that she would have liked to have had a child by him.

But she also knew better than to try to seek him out. He'd given her his post office box number and combination, promising to send her an address as soon as he could. She checked the box every week, and he had not even sent a card.

It was the smart thing to do. Ruddick had advised them to keep totally apart for at least a year, to see what happened. The Air Force had apparently lost all interest in the case as soon as she indicated she would be willing to sell out if the price was right. A few weeks ago, she'd convinced the district attorney to drop the case against Baker, and she thought that the heat was off. Yet she couldn't be sure, and the last thing she wanted was to lead anyone to Baker. And that meant she couldn't let the trail lead to Ruddick, either.

Baker had left a paperwork nightmare behind him; the only reason McNaughton had any contracts at all was the Air Force's desperate need for B-47s. They had doubled up on the quality assurance inspectors and brought in a tough new plant representative. Worse, they'd made her to take on virtually the entire management staff from Vanguard, while insisting that she take no part in the management. Technically she wasn't barred from the plant, but whenever she visited, one of the quality assurance guys was detailed to be with her the entire time.

She was desperately lonely; she'd even gone to the plant a few times for personal reasons, trying to find a companion among the workers there. The word must have gone out, however, for while most of the men on the floor were as friendly as ever, no one responded to her overtures. Baker's departure had created an emotional vacuum, and it was proving to be extraordinarily difficult for her to summon the energy to find a new companion, a new lover. Her whole life had revolved around the plant, and she hadn't cultivated any other friends.

Part of the problem and most of the solution was the marijuana Baker had introduced her to. She smoked it regularly now, half a dozen times a day, and it softened the edges of her ambition even as it honed her various appetites. She gained back twenty pounds, which she'd lost in her long pursuit of Stan Coleman, and couldn't summon the initiative to go out and shop for new clothes.

Dick Baker wouldn't have cared that she'd grown fat again—he wouldn't even have noticed, not as long as she took good care of him. She wondered who was taking care of him now? Ginny was still in Little Rock, but Baker was not her type. And Milo would want him to keep his distance.

Even as she reasoned with herself, a current of envy tore through her. That was it! It would be just like Baker to get next to Ginny— and just like her to let him. She made up her mind to go to Little Rock. She could handle Ruddick—and he could put her in touch with Baker. As soon as they cashed her out, she'd be on her way.

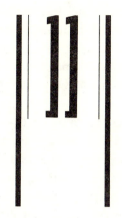

Chicago, Illinois/February 28, 1954

The elevated train shook the ancient building with a rumble like artillery fire, lending credibility to the article Weissman was reading about an Israeli attack on the Egyptians in Gaza; a nostalgia for the frantic days of 1947 swept over him, recalling how he'd help bolt the Messerschmitts together, working with the eager Negro, and the other dark American, the one named Riley.

The incidental reading was the only compensation for the interminable analysis and filing—the rest was tedious cross-referencing, trying to knit individual atoms of information into a molecule of intelligence. Yet it was valuable; his service had brought in innumerable snippets of data on the Ku Klux Klan, and he had found out that his old enemy Josten, of Nordhausen days, was working with them in Arkansas.

It was a natural alliance, Nazi and Klansman. At first he didn't understand the Klan's ineptitude, their failure to capitalize on the strength of racist feelings in America. He saw all around him signs that Negroes—"Blacks" they called them now—were as hated as the

Jews had been in Germany. It had taken only a fanatic minority to begin the pogroms there. What was holding the Klan back?

Bit by bit, the files revealed the secret: lack of leadership. There was no longer any meaningful national Klan apparatus; instead there were local Klans, more vindictive Rotary club than terrorist, run by shabby, mean men who milked the organization for a small living.

There was a very short dossier on Josten, confirming what he had already known. He had been an ace in the Luftwaffe and spearheaded the drive to get the jet fighter. When jet engines were vitally needed, he collaborated in using slave labor to build them at Nordhausen. My alma mater, Weissman thought. Josten had been burned in a crash and came to the United States legally, ostensibly part of Operation Paper Clip, but apparently in repayment of some postwar service he had done. His wife had divorced him and had also come to America. She had been in the Resistance. Interesting. Maybe that was the cause of the divorce. He'd have to see where she was, too. Josten didn't sound like the sort of man who'd give up his family willingly.

Weissman had already raised the issue of becoming active again. Goldberg had told him to wait. They'd even given him a nickname, "Weissman the Marksman." Very funny. As far as he knew, none of the others, including Goldberg, had ever been in prison, had ever tried to kill a man. Who were they to ridicule him?

Frederick Air Force Base, California/ March 24, 1955

The cavernous maintenance hangar sang its own songs, creaking with every change of temperature, rattling in the wind, sighing as clouds formed and rained beneath its ceiling during humid weather. It had been built to accommodate the B-52s that would be arriving next year. Now it was packed with B-47s, their swept wings tucked together like gears in a watch to conserve space. Sergeant Greg

Larson had just crossed from the yellow hydraulically lifted platform to the slanting wing and fuselage intersection of 51-5214, careful as a man on a tightrope, balancing a toolbox in one hand against the electric drill in the other.

Two hundred feet away, Lieutenant Colonel Kosanovich looked at his watch and cursed—5214 had a mission in six hours, and it was past time to get it out to the refueling pits. He walked rapidly over and called "Hey, Sarge, how long you going to be? This plane has to fly this evening."

"I'm not sure, sir. There's a tiny crack on the underside of the wing that I just stop-drilled, and there's another one up here. I was going to pull a couple of panels off and see what was happening inside."

"Look, we've spent too many man-hours on this inspection already. I want you to sign it off and get it towed out to the refueling pits."

"Colonel, you know what the tech order says—we're not supposed to let a crack like this go without fixing it. At least let me stop-drill it." Stop-drilling was a technique as old as metal airplanes—when a crack appeared, the mechanic drilled a hole at its terminal point, which slowed, but often did not really stop, the spreading fracture.

Kosanovich forced himself to stay calm—first-rate mechanics like Larson were overworked and underpaid, and it was bad policy to lean on them. But when the C.O. had asked about this airplane's status, he'd told him it was ready to go.

"Sarge, I told Colonel Coleman this bird was in commission. Tell you what. It is going back to Boeing in Wichita at the end of the month to get the new heavyweight landing gear installed. I'll write up this crack before it goes, and they can fix it there. I'd rather have them replace the panel than have you just stop-drill it. Now get your ass in gear and get this airplane ready to go."

The mechanic shook his head as he carefully climbed back off the airplane to the lift. That was the service—never any time to do anything right, but always lots of time to do it over.

Frederick Air Force Base, California/
March 25, 1955

Curtis LeMay's primal presence soaked the Strategic Air Command in a sweaty mixture of fear, respect, and admiration; he was Billy Mitchell, Patton, Rommel, Churchill, Rockne, and Ziegfeld all rolled in one. Apocryphal stories blossomed about the hide-blistering profanity with which he chewed ass, about airplanes not daring to blow up when he smoked on board, about colonels turned into quivering tureens of jelly at his briefings. Most of them were true.

On the other hand, LeMay labored mightily to get the best living conditions for his people, fighting for quarters, and improving the mess halls by sending cooks to hotels to learn their trade. In the process, LeMay had turned SAC into one vast competition, pitting crews against crews, squadrons against squadrons, wings against wings. The single standard was perfection—anything else called for immediate explanation and then practice until perfection was achieved. If a pilot dinged a wingtip in California on Wednesday night, he was explaining why to LeMay personally in Omaha on Thursday morning. If an airman got drunk and ran his car into a ditch, LeMay was on the horn to the airman's boss, wanting to know why he let it happen.

There were two sweeteners in LeMay's program. The most important was the sense he inspired of being on the first team in the world's best air force; the second was his spot promotion program for the crew members who did well over a sustained period of time. LeMay had secured the authority to promote an individual on the spot, without regard to seniority, giving him the pay and rank of the next grade. The hottest of the hotshots had spots on spots—some young captains were wearing the silver leaves of lieutenant colonels. LeMay gave and LeMay took away—if the crew member stumbled anywhere along the line, the promotion was gone, often not only for him, but for his crew as well. The spot was a sizeable carrot to match the forceful stick of LeMay's personality, and it was having a positive effect throughout most of SAC. Under a lesser man, the competitive system could have simply become nonproductive tyranny. LeMay made it work—most places.

No one outside of SAC had any idea how hard the crews were trying, how fully each mission was packed with requirements to accomplish and be measured. A typical SAC bomber flight might begin with a celestial navigation leg, which could include gunnery and ECM practice, followed by an in-flight refueling, practice radar bomb runs, a practice low-level mission, followed by another refueling and another celestial navigation mission. After eight busy hours, the tired B-47 crews would wind up back at the field to shoot instrument approaches and touch and go landings for an hour before shutting down. Then they had to face the long debriefings with maintenance and operations, for LeMay's rules required that the crews had to record how well—or how badly—they did on every aspect of each mission.

A few weeks after the B-47 crash at Tonopah, Coleman succeeded Guy Williams as wing commander, and he let the crews know that he wanted top scores in everything—no matter how they got them.

The crews Coleman inherited were led by veterans of the Second World War, somewhat jaded and not impressed with LeMay's gung-ho competitiveness. They had found the peacetime Air Force to be a good life and stayed in for the flying, which was even more enjoyable because they weren't being shot at. There were few college graduates in the group—most were products of the egalitarian Aviation Cadet program, and most were making more money than they'd ever dreamed of. As soon as they understood what their new commanding officer wanted, they began to figure out ways to beat LeMay's system. Most of their tricks were easy to do and hard to discover. It became common to use visual assists on the radar bombing runs and to help out the celestial navigation legs with radio fixes. Within weeks, the wing had developed a variety of other gimmicks that saw to it that most missions received perfect scores, with just enough screwups to provide credibility.

Basically good crews, they had to cheat only a little to look like world-beaters. For the most part, the crew members regarded the whole process as little more than a high school prank, a joke on that stern principal, Curt LeMay.

Frederick Air Force Base had begun life as a primary training base in World War II, and the H-shaped wing headquarters building was the usual wooden shack, upgraded with shiny pine plywood panels and industrial-grade carpeting. In the glassed-in conference room adjacent to Coleman's office, Major Fitzpatrick was immersed in a mound of paperwork. A table on his left had all the reports on the last month's missions, with piles of Form 1's, maps, navigation logs, and the mission debriefing logs. On his right was the ground school work—war plan briefings, code of conduct, special weapons training, any one of the dozens of courses that were going on all the time. He was enjoying himself, ignoring Coleman's hovering presence.

"This ain't easy, pal, but I'm getting there. There's only so much fixing you can do with the paperwork. It's a damn good thing the crews are doing as well as they're doing legally."

Fitz, as always in a flight suit—Coleman wasn't sure he even owned a uniform—and still the incorrigible con man, the loner with a heart of stone, was in his element doctoring mission reports to improve the scores. He kept an array of pens and pencils at hand to match whatever the crews were using and had a forger's facility with handwriting. The ground school work was relatively easy; just a few pencil strokes were enough to raise the recorded grades.

The flying reports were another matter. Even with the best cheating will in the world, crews often failed to put down the near-perfect numbers required to make them competitive in the race to be number one in SAC. Some of the mission elements— radar bombing or electronic countermeasures, for example—were scored by the ground, and unless the crew found some way to cheat in the air, there was no way anyone, not even Fitz, could falsify the results. Actual practice bomb drops couldn't be fixed—there was no disputing the call from the ground on those. But other elements of the mission were fully controlled by the wing—the number of refuelings, the amount of fuel transferred, celestial navigation legs, nuclear weapons training—and these Fitz could improve as the situation demanded. His main problem was to make sure that any changes he made were kept coordinated with the rest of the reports on the mission. You could not, for example, record an in-flight refueling of forty thousand pounds of fuel, immediately followed by pilot proficiency work involving touch and go landings. The people reviewing the paperwork at Headquarters would know the aircraft would have been too heavy to land and immediately smell a rat.

"Listen, boss, we've got a real problem in covering maintenance. We're falling further and further behind, and just pushing a pencil doesn't fix the airplanes. Sooner or later, there's going to be an accident."

"What's bothering you?"

"Well, you got the maintenance officer signing off on the periodic inspections. We don't know how many airplanes have problems that have just been passed over."

"Look, these airplanes are almost brand-new—they can skip a few inspections and nothing will happen. Don't you worry about it."

Although they were equally good pilots, Fitzpatrick was much more attuned to airplanes. Coleman flew them and forgot them; Fitz became absorbed in them, understood all the complex systems, knew where failures could occur.

"You're a funny guy, Coleman. It used to be you always thought that your luck was running out, that you had to ration everything out to yourself. Now you act like there's no tomorrow, that you can cheat day after day and never get caught."

Coleman stared at him as old fears and memories stirred.

Fitzpatrick went on. "Just don't say I didn't warn you. We've got no idea about what corrosion or metal fatigue might do on these monsters. They're not built like the old-style airplanes, and they fly in a totally different flight regime."

Coleman was disturbed; Fitz normally never gave a damn about anybody or anything, just as long as he got forty or fifty hours flying a month. He frowned. "They should be better than the B-17s and the B-29s; look at all the experience behind them. Don't sweat it."

Holding up a red pencil to check its hue against the marks on the paper he was working with, Fitz shrugged and said, "We've been playing this little game now for over a year, and it takes more fixing everytime. The crews are getting lax. I don't know how long you can keep a lid on this—it's the old pitcher to the well bit."

"Don't talk like that. We only have to keep this up till the fall, when the list for brigadier general comes out. If I can keep this wing number one till then, I'm home free."

"What if the guy who takes over after you looks into the paperwork? What if the guys tell him what's been going on?"

Coleman felt his confidence return. "First, the guys aren't going to say diddly—they're in this as deep as I am—as we are. Second, there's not going to be any time for a new guy to learn the job and look over the paperwork from the past. All anybody will see is that when Coleman left, things went downhill fast. And that's how I want it to look."

Fitzpatrick went on with his work, and Coleman said, "Besides, who do they have who's as good a con man as you, Fitz? They'll never figure out what you've done."

Fitz nodded in agreement; the only reason he was doing it at all was just to beat the system.

Santa Monica, California/April 11, 1955

John never felt comfortable in Saundra's plush offices, so much nicer than anything he'd ever had in his life. And it was worse because Prosperous Fred was there, dressed in his five-hundred-dollar suit and hundred-dollar shoes, face shiny as a bowling ball, oozing wealth at every pore, and so nice to them both. Marshall was jealous of him, and he resented that fact as much as he resented the man.

"Now listen, you two, old Fred's going to give you his last word on this crazy idea. I think you are nuts to get into the firefighting business, John—there's no proven market for it and it's got to be as dangerous as hell. And of all the businesses you could go into, there's none where being Black would make it more difficult for you. You'll be dealing with rednecks in every part of the country— and I don't think they'll want to deal with you."

Marshall was rested and well, his body hardened by the tough training he'd imposed on himself. Mentally he'd bounced back from the rough treatment the Air Force had given him, charging it off as just one more example of government racism. Now he spoke in a civil but determined voice.

"You've said all that before, Fred. You may be right. But I'm going to do it, whether Saundra gets involved or not."

Saundra turned in her tall-backed red leather chair, bristling. "I *am* getting involved—you both know that. I can afford to back you for a couple of years, if you start small. After that, we'll see."

Peterson shook his head and smiled. "All right. But you've got to set up a separate corporation, so that your liabilities can't hurt Marshall Products. John, it looks to me like you're going to be vulnerable to a lot of liabilities. What happens if one of your pilots gets killed flying your airplane?"

"We shouldn't lose any pilots; I'll train them myself. Besides, I'll have them sign a waiver when they're hired. Believe me, there's enough pilots looking for jobs that I won't have any trouble picking and choosing."

Saundra waited until he was finished and then spoke to Peterson sharply, something she never did before. John wondered if it had anything to do with the fact that Peterson had married two months before. Or that he'd married a white girl.

"Fred, we've been through all that. We'll set up a separate corporation, and I'll invest one hundred thousand dollars in it to get it started. That's settled."

"No, it's not. Since you insist on going ahead, I'll come in with you, on a couple of conditions. I'll add a hundred thousand to the pot, for a quarter interest—I think that's fair."

Marshall felt a grudging respect for the man. Peterson had argued vigorously against the whole idea, and now he was willing to put up as much capital as they—as Saundra—was putting up.

Saundra was pleased, not so much by the money, but by his support. "What are your conditions?"

"Well, as I understand it, you're going to buy six of these TBM planes from Roget, are you not?"

"Yes, three this year, three next."

"Okay. My first condition is that I buy one of Roget's converted bombers to use as a flying headquarters. I want it fitted out with the best radios and whatever you use for flying in bad weather. And I want it to have couches that convert into beds, a full bathroom, no damn bucket in a closet, and a complete galley, everything. It won't have to carry a lot of people, three or four, but I want it to be able to carry them in comfort. I'll put up the money for the airplane and lease it to you for a dollar a year."

Marshall felt uncomfortable; he couldn't tell where this was leading. "We don't need anything like that, Fred. We could use the money better to buy more equipment. And one of Roget's airplanes is going to cost at least six hundred thousand, maybe more."

"John, don't try to tell me how to invest my money." Disdain dripped from his voice; he spent more on clothes each year than John had earned in the Air Force. "I'm telling you that you *do* need it. When the season starts and you start following the forest fires, you'll be heading into the Southwest and the South. You've got to have a place to stay; I can't have you sleeping by the side of the road if you're responsible for so much of my money."

Marshall flushed. He'd never even thought that he might run into discrimination in this business. Peterson was thinking ahead—maybe that's why he had so much money and John had so little.

Peterson went on. "But that's only part of it. I really want you to have an airplane capable of flying some of the Black leaders around the country on a moment's notice. When the airplane's not actively being used in fighting fires, I want to be able to use it as an executive transport for some very special people."

Saundra looked pensive. "I don't want to sound negative, Fred, but does this make sense? Wouldn't it be better just to give them the money to fly commercially?"

"It would if they weren't being watched by the FBI. Hoover has his eyes on them; he thinks they're all Communists. I want to use the airplane to give them free access to all parts of the country without being followed."

Marshall, remembering his own concerns, laughed too loudly. "Come on, Peterson, you're being paranoid. You think the government's shadowing some poor Negro ministers around?"

Visibly angry, Peterson snapped, "For Christ's sake, John, they let you rot in prison, didn't credit you for your victories, and hounded you out of the service because you were Black! And you don't think they'd watch our leaders? What the hell is the matter with you, anyway? Sometimes I think flying's turned you into an Oreo."

"An Oreo? What the hell's an Oreo?"

"He's a nigger who's black on the outside and white on the inside. You've got to wake up, John."

Saundra stared at them. Peterson had never used the word *nigger* before in her presence; John had never heard it said without taking violent exception to it.

Things were changing.

Wichita, Kansas/May 14, 1955

Seven hours before, 51-5214 had left Frederick Air Force Base on a standard SAC training mission. Now it swept along at 39,000 feet, stars glittering above it, the ground below masked by billowing thunderstorms glowing incandescent with lightning.

"Wichita, this is Nectar One Nine, over your station at thirty-nine thousand feet, request clearance for an approach and landing at McConnell."

"Roger, One Nine; you're cleared for standard jet approach to McConnell. Be advised that there are thunderstorms in the southeast and southwest quadrants."

Nectar 19's mission was to end at the Boeing plant in Wichita, where a more rugged landing gear was going to be installed. As its mission ended, another of SAC's 1,200 B-47s would be starting another. At any given moment as many as five hundred of them were in the air, practicing their war plan strikes against the Soviet Union.

The pilot acknowledged the transmission and pressed his intercom switch. "Radar, you painting those storms?"

"Roger; looks like they're all over the area; he must only be picking up the big ones."

"Keep your eye on them. Copilot, Before Descent Check List."

They went through the familiar fifteen-step ritual carefully; dead tired after a seven-hour flight, throats parched and sinuses throbbing from breathing the arid oxygen, no one wanted to make a mistake.

The copilot read off the second-to-last item. "Gross Weight one-hundred-twenty thousand, Best Flare Speed one hundred forty knots." It meant that the pilot would have the airspeed at exactly 140 knots the moment they crossed the edge of the runway, poised to touch down.

"Roger, one-forty, gear down."

The pilot called "Wichita, Nectar One Nine departing angels thirty-nine."

At 305 knots indicated airspeed, the landing gear came down, effectively doubling the aircraft's drag, and the B-47 edged into a four-thousand-foot-per-minute rate of descent.

Four minutes later, Nectar 19 entered the thunderstorm at 23,000 feet, immediately encountering a steadily growing turbulence.

"Lookit that! St. Elmo's Fire."

The pilot looked out to see the greenish-gold tracery of the lightning's discharge dancing the length of the swept wings, covering the edge of the engines in a shimmering neon glow, perpetually moving over surfaces being swept by winds faster than any hurricane.

"Holy Christ, look at the wings!"

The wingtips were flexing up and down through an eight-foot arc; a few feet closer in to the fuselage, the outboard engines were writhing up and down in a twisting motion, as if they were screwing their way through the air.

The pilot frowned; a four-or-five-foot flap of the thin swept wings was normal; he knew that in ground tests the wings had flapped through an arc of seventeen feet without failure. Still, this was too much for comfort and he called, "Radar, it's rough as a cob in here; I'm going to slow down to two-fifty. What's the best heading out of this mess?"

"Try steering about one-forty for two minutes."

The B-47 turned to the southeasterly heading, which carried it through the center of the thunderstorm, into the line between two cells. One was a mass of violently rising warm air, carrying within it the scent of the fields below; the other was a dump of cold wet air, plummeting down headlong like a runaway elevator to burst out on the ground with cyclonic force.

"What's that . . ."

The sheering winds forced the swept wings to flex near their limit, bending upward not in a simple U shape but in an undulating wave that began in the center of the aircraft and moved in a washboard ripple out to the tips. The flapping caused an alternation of pressures, a squeezing and relaxation that deformed the milk-bottle pin fittings holding the wings to the fuselage, weakening them as they elongated.

Within the wing-fuselage juncture, the tiny flaw discovered four months before was stressed with each flap of the wing, lengthening a bit at a time, creeping inexorably toward the milk-bottle pin like a crack in a dropped mirror.

As Nectar 19 passed through 22,000 feet, the aircraft shuddered in the increasing turbulence, sending the wingtips flapping through a ten-foot arc, each cycle moving the fitting imperceptibly upward. Suddenly the crack spurted forward, relieving the compression that held the milk-bottle pin tightly within its grasp. At 21,000 feet, the pin popped out of its socket like a champagne cork from a bottle; instantly the immense forces of the storm tore the left wing from the aircraft like a sheet of paper from a phone book. The rest of the airplane rolled violently to the left for three-quarters of a turn before disintegrating in a massive explosion that illuminated the thunderstorm brighter than lightning. The last words of the aircraft commander, inadvertently transmitted to Wichita radio, were the last words of most pilots in most crashes—"Oh, shit!"

Frederick Air Force Base, California/June 20, 1955

"This is a hell of a way for two hot pilots to arrive." Riley and Bandfield were in a rented Chevrolet, waiting in line in the morning rush hour to go through the gates at Frederick.

Riley laughed. "Well, LeMay wanted to keep this as quiet as he could, involve as few people as possible. I didn't want to spook anybody by filing a flight plan here. I'm sure Coleman's on the lookout for visitors from Omaha."

"What's our first stop?"

"We're going right to the Air Police headquarters; I'm going to requisition twenty APs and have them shut down the wing headquarters and every squadron operations office. Then we'll have them vacate the place and you and I'll start checking their bookkeeping."

"God, I hate this, Bear! Why didn't LeMay just call Coleman in and ask him what's going on?"

"They've lost two B-47s from this wing in the last year—and they're supposed to have the best flying and maintenance record in SAC. I've looked at the records for the last airplane that went in, and something stinks."

The major running the Air Police squadron was reluctant to cooperate at first, wanting to call Coleman to find out what was going on.

"You go ahead and call him, Major, and I'll be calling General LeMay at the same time. You saw my orders—I expect you to cooperate."

Thirty minutes later the doors to the wing headquarters and the three squadron operations offices were closed; outside each one an Air Policeman stood guard, with orders not to let anyone in or out.

The two men burst into Coleman's office without knocking; he jumped up, spilling his coffee.

"Bandfield! Riley! What the hell are you doing here?"

"Colonel Coleman, we're here to go through your records. Something phony is going on, and you'll save a lot of time if you just tell us what it is. If you don't, I'm putting in a call to SAC headquarters, and I'll have fifty eager young officers down here with fine-tooth combs, figuring out just what your game is."

Coleman staggered, put his hand up to the wall and knocked a picture clattering to the floor. His mind whirled like a wheel stuck in a snowbank, spinning helplessly, unable to think. Finally he waved his arm at the door to his conference room. "In there."

In the glass-walled room next door, Fitzpatrick had already risen from his chair. He spoke to Coleman first. "Well, Stan, I guess our luck's run out." Then he turned to Bandfield and Riley. "I wondered when you guys were going to catch on. Lemme show you what we were doing."

The following morning, Coleman, his three bomb squadron commanders, and Fitzpatrick were gone from the base, their resignations processed.

"Those guys should have gone to jail, Bear. I thought LeMay was such a tough guy."

"He's tough, all right, but he got his instructions straight from the White House. The word was 'Let them resign.' They're going to clamp a lid on this, Bandy, just like I thought they would."

"It's not right; this wasn't just some kind of fraud, this was murder. If they'd inspected that B-47 the way they were supposed to, they might have caught the crack in the wing."

"You think LeMay likes it? His hands are tied; somebody got to the President."

"Somebody? It was that bastard Ruddick, for sure, taking care of his son-in-law again."

Little Rock, Arkansas/August 1, 1955

Ruddick was alone in his office, doing some damage assessment. It could have been a lot worse. Coleman's stupid boneheadedness would have gotten him court-martialed if he hadn't been able to intervene with the President. But now time was running out. He could fight off comments on the Hill about being a Klan member—hell, half the congressmen in the South backed the Klan. It looked like things were quiet on the McNaughton front, but the rash of crashes might cause it to blow up anytime. Getting Stan off had cost him the last of his political chits at the White House, and more.

The whole business was unraveling because of sheer stupidity—the venal Baker jeopardizing the whole scheme for a few thousand in kickbacks; Coleman cheating like some schoolboy. Neither needed to have done it. He'd have paid them to keep their noses clean. If Elsie hadn't been a trooper, keeping her mouth shut about the whole business, he might have been going to jail.

The only thing good about the mess was the timing. He had been planning to leave Washington at the end of the year anyway, to come back to Little Rock and take over the Klan from Josten, who was running it as if he were the Fuehrer himself. Everything Josten had done so far was positive—but he needed to be controlled. The mess with McNaughton just moved his decision up on the schedule.

He glanced at the clock; it was after six. Walking to the buffet, he put two cubes of ice in a glass and filled it halfway with Wild Turkey. He'd been drinking more lately, but he needed it. He sipped the drink slowly until six-thirty, then gulped the rest of it down. He carefully rinsed the glass and chewed on a peppermint. Ginny was coming over; she'd stayed on the wagon, and he didn't want to remind her of her drinking problem.

Sending her to work for the governor had been a masterstroke; she'd wheedled her way into a position of influence in no time at all, and he wasn't asking how. She'd arranged an appointment with him tonight, here in Ruddick's own office, telling the governor only that it was "a private matter, one that had to be kept secret."

The door opened and she skipped in, looking ten years younger than she had only a few weeks ago.

"You're looking mighty happy."

"I should; I've been promoted. I'm going to be the governor's personal assistant."

"How personal do you have to be?"

"Daddy, don't be nasty. The governor's taken a fancy to me, I'll admit, but it's strictly professional."

Their eyes locked in mutual understanding; she was doing what was necessary, and he approved. It was just business.

"The governor"—she rolled the words around her mouth—"will be here in a few minutes. He was hesitant about meeting here at first, but finally agreed. I hinted that you wanted to talk about the Klan. Dixon will be coming with him."

Ruddick and the governor had never been friends, but he had worked with him for thirty years, contributing regularly to his campaign chest. The door opened, and they came in, the tiny Price skittering in front like a sparrow. The governor, tall and painfully thin, was the picture of a country schoolmaster in his rumpled seersucker suit, thinning blond hair combed over his bald dome, iron-rimmed glasses perched precariously on his great Roman nose. Behind the glasses his eyes were bright and searching. Physically, Ruddick and the governor were similar, but the way they clothed and groomed themselves was totally different. The governor was a man of the people—Ruddick was a suave operator from the military-industrial complex.

"Hello, Mr. Congressman. I want to thank you for sending your beautiful daughter to work with me."

"Governor, I've always been willing to do my part for the great state of Arkansas—and I'm sure my daughter will do hers."

Dixon broke in. "We haven't got a lot of time, Milo, but he wants to talk to you about the Klan."

"Dixon's probably told you that it's been rejuvenated, Governor.

It's not the half-baked collection of nitwits it was ten years ago. And it's gathering strength." After thirty years, he knew better than to call the governor by his first name—the man was an egomaniac.

"It better. There's lots of pressure on me to integrate the schools and end segregation. I'm going to need some signs of popular support; I can't do it by myself—and I can't associate myself directly with the Klan."

"You don't have to—you'll have the Klan's support, count on it."

"Will there be violence?"

"No, of course not."

Price broke in. "That's not what we want to hear, Milo."

Ruddick smiled. "I was jesting, speaking for the record. Between you and me there'll be as much violence as we can create. We want the niggers in the streets, fighting mad."

The governor was startled. "You want the niggers violent? I meant the white folks, the rednecks, our guys!"

"Sure—but just in reaction, defending hearth and home, preserving the virtue of their women. We've got to get the nigras to strike the first blows, to blow up a school, do something that'll bring down the righteous wrath of the white man on them. A rape would be good, a child molestation better."

Sensing Price's agreement, he said, "That's a twist, Milo. Get the nigras violent, eh? That's what's always been feared, the slave rebellion, the black man up in arms. You're sure this is the right way to go?"

"Of course. You can't make a move today without some pinko newsman from the North down here writing things up. Let's let the nigras do the dirty work, get some sympathy in the press."

The governor looked nervously at Dixon, then back at Ruddick. "Didn't you keep a bar here? Can't a man get a drink?"

Ruddick went to the bar and, grinning, Ginny said, "Just a little one for me, Daddy."

He poured three healthy drinks and one ladylike, well diluted. The governor sat quietly, sipping, turning Ruddick's idea over in his mind as Price made a phone call.

"Let me understand this. Can you provide violence on demand?"

"Yes, sir. Give me twenty-four hours notice, and we'll give you a riot. Give us forty-eight hours, and we'll give you a rebellion."

"What's this Dixon tells me about some Nazi being in charge of the local Klaven?"

"He's not a Nazi, just thinks like one. He's doing a hell of a job."

"You running him, or is he running you?"

"Governor, you've known me a long time—do you think I'd let some crippled-up German come in and take over my territory? I'm using him, and when I'm finished, I'll get rid of him."

"Good. But be ready. I don't know when we're going to have to act, but it'll be soon. Then we've got to beat it down."

"Right; I'm your man, just like I've been for thirty years. But I'm thinking of leaving the federal government—and I may need a hidey-hole."

"You're in trouble?"

"I might be; some foolish business about contracts, a problem I had nothing to do with, really, but I may have to take the fall."

"What can I do for you?"

"Well, I was thinking that you might need some consulting services for the state—you know, looking into rural education, poverty, civil rights, things like that."

"Maybe, but what would it cost?"

"Let's talk first about what it would get you. I've been supporting the Klan for many years now, and my well is run dry. Old Dixon will confirm that for you. We're running out of money just when you're going to need the Klan most."

"I have some discretionary money, but that wouldn't be enough."

Price hung up the phone and swigged the last of his drink—he reminded Ruddick of the little toy birds that bobbed their heads up and down in a glass. He wiped his mouth, and said, "Milo, do you still have that little construction company over on Whipple Street?"

"It's inactive, but I could get it cranked up again."

"Well, Governor, I think we could find some money for contracts for some construction, don't you?"

"Sure; that's probably the way to go. There's always a bridge needing repair or some roads to be built out in the hill country." Ruddick smiled with relief. "I knew I could count on you." The governor turned to Ginny. "Now you said something about making a homemade dinner for me. Is that still on?"

Ginny nodded, the shot of Wild Turkey giving her face a glow.

Chino, California/August 15, 1955

Even in the early dawn, the airfield looked as if World War II had mugged it and left it to die; sprinkled around the edges of the runways was every kind of fighter and bomber, most in disrepair. Edging the field was a line of hangars put up during the war, in varying stages of dilapidation. Outside the fourth from the end—if you didn't count the two pads where the remains of burned-out hangars lay—Marshall and Roget were standing by a sign that read:

MARSHALL AVIATION

AERIAL FIRE FIGHTING

AGRICULTURAL AVIATION

CHARTER FLIGHTS

FLIGHT INSTRUCTION

SIGHT-SEEING

Marshall spoke. "Okay. We're ready to go now, but I've still got to do my run and my exercises. If it's all right with you, we'll leave at ten sharp."

Looking admiringly at him, Roget punched him lightly on the arm. "Whatever you're doing, keep it up, Bones. You look like yourself again. When are you going to let Saundra dye your hair? Make you look ten years younger."

"The day after you let her dye yours, Hadley."

Roget laughed, nudged him, and said, "Give it to me straight, John, you making any money yet?"

Sighing, Marshall walked over and leaned against the door of their operations shack. "You know I'm not; all Saundra's money is already long gone, and I'm not letting her sink another dime in it. We've been hauling Fred Peterson's people around, two, three times a week; it's the only thing that lets me meet the payroll. My new partner, Corky Frost, calls it our 'Back of the Bus Airline,' and he's about right."

"How are you feeling about helping these people? I don't mean to pry"—he hesitated, knowing that John knew he wanted to pry, always did, couldn't help it—"but Patty tells me that Saundra's gone off the deep end and it's causing you problems. Is that right?"

"Yeah, it's screwy. Saundra's letting her staff run the business, and she's spending more time and money on the movement than she can afford. The funny thing is, I am, too. It's hard to explain to a white man, Hadley, but this man King is right! Something's got to be done in the South—hell, all over, for that matter, look what the Air Force did to me. The time's coming, and I'm going to support it. I—"

"Whoa, pardner, you don't have to convince me, I'm on your side. But what is it doing to you and Saundra? That's what worries me."

Marshall looked off in the distance. "I'm not sure. It's like she's had a religious calling. In a way, I understand it; King is a real leader, I'm under his influence, too. But . . ."

"Is it a romantic interest? Is she in love with him?"

Bones turned and looked him in the eye. "No, I think I could handle that. But this is a religious thing, a kind of exaltation."

"What do you think about it?"

"I hate it. I want to support the cause, just like she does, but not at the expense of my own family. But we've had such rough times since I got back that the worst thing I could do would be to try to interfere."

"Look, if it's any comfort, you're not the only one having problems. Patty and Bandy are fighting all the time over the kids, and Lyra's driving poor old Bear Riley nuts."

"What's the problem?"

"She swears her husband is going to try to do something, hurt her or kidnap the children. Bear half-believes her, but it's making their life tough."

Sensing Marshall's unease, Roget abruptly changed the subject. "Back of the Bus Airline, eh? That's pretty good. Where'd you meet this guy Frost?"

"He's an old desert rat, got a face like a bulldog, been around the airport for years, and funny as hell."

"What'd he invest to get to be a partner?"

"His name and his white skin. I let him be pilot-in-command for any trips down South; that way I don't have to worry about them dumping water in the fuel tank of an uppity nigger's plane."

"What's he think about Fred's friends, and all that civil rights business?"

"He could care less—he's so happy to be working a regular job he'd haul rattlesnakes if he had to."

The two men walked out to the converted Lodestar that Peterson had purchased for the new firm. "How come you didn't want to take a TBM, Hadley?"

"Tact, my boy, tact. My specialty. They're going to be running another test of their little Stearman today, and I thought it would be poor taste to bring a TBM in."

"What the hell's the matter with them, anyway? They're not going to be able to prove anything with a Stearman that we didn't prove last year."

"It's the government—they got their way of doing things and that's it. They'll run the tests on the Stearman, and then maybe they'll buy something from us next year."

"Will you be there to buy from next year? How's your business?"

"No problem. I've sold almost a dozen of these fancy Rockets, and it looks like I've got orders for maybe another dozen more coming. Oilmen love them, and even Mike Todd down in Hollywood is buying one. And I haven't advertised, got no salesmen, this is all drop-in business. I'm sitting pretty, John, but I'd like to sell the TBMs and that old Catalina I got sitting on the line. That old Cat would make the TBMs look sick, but I can't get anybody to listen."

"Bandy says that you're always ten years ahead of your time."

Roget interrupted, "Twenty, but who's counting?"

"Well, I sure hope he's wrong about that with water-bombing."

"No, I think what we're going to have to do is put in one season for free, just follow the fires around, volunteering our services. It'll be expensive as hell, but not as expensive as never getting started."

Marshall whistled. "I don't know, Hadley, that'll be tough. I'm not sure if even Peterson could afford to subsidize an operation that size."

"Lemme see what I can do with our banks. Maybe we wouldn't go all the way, just do one section of California. But I'd like to get the Catalina up to Canada; I think I can do some business there, and it ought to be good for Florida, too. They had a big fire in the Everglades and couldn't do anything about it. With all those lakes and canals, it would have been perfect for the Catalina."

"Maybe next year?"

"If either of us is still in business."

12

Salinas, California/November 19, 1955

Bandfield woke to the almost forgotten sounds and smells of Patty making coffee. Groaning, he tried to roll over; he was stiff as a board, every joint and muscle aching from the long trip back from Washington in a T-33 the previous afternoon. The T-Bird was fine transportation, but the seat was a torture chamber after a couple of hours. He'd rented a car in Los Angeles and didn't even remember the drive to Salinas; he had continually dozed off, awakening sharply to the drum of tires signaling his drift to the side of the road.

Easing himself to the side of the bed, he flexed his toes and stretched his muscles, aware for once of the care Patty had taken in decorating their home, imprinting her personality on it with the colors, the pictures, the things he called clutter and she called collectibles. She always said she wanted the home to be cozy and comfortable rather than a work of art. He realized how well she'd succeeded, when he compared it to the clinical austerity of the anonymous BOQ rooms he'd been leaping in and out of for the past six months, all done in early Cheap Motel. Between following up on Coleman's debacle at Frederick and the B-47 accident investigations, he'd been on the road more than three-quarters of the time, often working so late he couldn't even call home. No wonder Patty had given him the freeze last night.

The kids were glad to see him, though. Charlotte was seventeen and as beautiful as Patty. George was almost fifteen, big for his age, and built like Bandy's father, blocky but still able to move well, sort of a thin Jackie Gleason. Both children were readers, and when he was on the road, Bandfield tried to read the same books and the same authors, to be sure they had plenty to talk about when he was home. Right now George was devouring all of Kenneth Roberts's books, while Charlotte had discovered Agatha Christie. The music was something else; there they had no common ground at all.

Patty came in as he loved her best, no makeup, hair down, cloaked in a white terry cloth bathrobe, and, he knew, nothing else. She carried a tray bearing two mugs of black coffee, the morning paper, and dog biscuits for their mutt, Maya, now snuggled companionably at the foot of the bed.

"I'm sorry about last night, Bandy. I should have been more welcoming, but you came in, gulped down two big drinks, drank half a bottle of wine while you gobbled dinner and then fell asleep in the chair. Not exactly the Cary Grant treatment."

He pulled her to him and kissed her. "You're right—but I was wiped out. Now I'm feeling frisky, and won't take no for an answer. Where are the kids?"

"They're in town, decorating the gym for a dance tonight."

"Great! Then let me boot Maya out the door, and I'll try to make up with you."

"The coffee will get cold."

"That's okay, just so long as you don't."

Later, they lay in each other's arms, content. She snuggled against his chest and said, "Bandy, remember the old days, when you'd come in after a long mission, all hot and sweaty in your flight suit, and we'd make love right away? It was so earthy, so good; now you're always showered and shampooed, sticky with deodorant. Where's my old animal lover?"

"Growf. Right here. Tell you what, I'll work like a horse all day today, and tonight you can have me au naturel. But you have to do the same."

She agreed, and then he said, "But since we've had a little romp this morning, could I get a raincheck until tomorrow?"

"A raincheck? Like making love is some shopper's special? Bandy, you've gotten to be a mood-ruining expert. But, okay, a raincheck, and no showers."

Then, more hesitantly, "Bandy, how much time do you have in the service now—you must be pretty close to the magic twenty-year mark, aren't you?"

"I can tell you exactly—I had it checked out in August. With my cadet time, I've got eighteen years and eight months."

"Are you going to retire at twenty?"

"I don't know—I don't know what I'd do for a living."

"Don't be foolish—Hadley and I need help. But I'm thinking about the kids. You're never around, and they're at a stage when they need you, particularly George. He's so big now, it's tough for me to discipline him."

"You think I should get out at twenty?"

She sat up, leaning on her elbow, pulling the sheet across her breasts. "Let me put it to you differently. If you don't, I'm getting a divorce."

He checked her eyes to see if she was kidding; she was not.

"Understood. What if I'm in the middle of something, like these accidents?"

She turned away from him, not saying a word.

"Right, twenty it is. Now go let Maya in."

En route to Montgomery, Alabama/ December 8, 1956

It was in that lovely ephemeral time just before dawn, when the colors of the eastern sky reach out in long fingers toward the aircraft, and the ground below grudgingly sheds its gray camouflage, giving up its shapes to shadow. The cream and green Roget Rocket was cruising slightly nose down at seventeen thousand feet; they'd burned off most of the fuel coming from Los Angeles, and the two Pratt & Whitney radial engines were throttled back to a comfortable low grumbling hum. In the cabin, Saundra lay asleep on a leather couch, covered with cashmere blankets that bore the monogram FP.

Frost ran his fingers admiringly over the radio console. "This bucket has everything! Old Hadley really did a job on it."

Frost's comments broke in on Marshall's jealous doubts.

"What's that? Yeah, it's sensational. And for the first time in his life, he's making money selling airplanes."

"No wonder he named it 'Rocket'—with a three-hundred-mile-per-hour cruise and a thirty-five-hundred-mile range, this is one going Jesse."

Marshall smiled to himself. Frost probably had no idea that "going Jesse" referred to Jesse Owens, a Black man like himself, a natural leader like the man they were flying money to in Montgomery.

Grateful to have his worries interrupted, he responded, "Yeah, Roget really pissed Lockheed off; they said he could never get this kind of performance out of a Lodestar. It sort of made them look bad when he did, like they didn't do it right the first time."

Frost's laughter seemed to boom across the cockpit. "I'll bet! But it's a whole different deal, customizing one plane at a time instead of turning them out like cookies on a production line. Did Roget have any help with it?"

"Well, Bandy, of course. They'd worked on their first Rocket back in the twenties. And they got Gordon Israel, the racing pilot, to help, knew him from the races at Cleveland. Israel's like Roget, not much for degrees but inspired and with lots of common sense. They cleaned up the whole airframe, changed the wing profile, smoothed out the cowling and nacelles. Then they added a lot of nice touches—flush mounting all the windows, carrying the flush riveting all the way back to the tail, stuff Lockheed couldn't take the time to do."

"I hear Roget went nuts cutting weight and drag."

"Yeah, he went over the entire airplane, all of it, feeling it with his hands, not just trusting his eyes to see something that might cause drag, but sweeping it with his hands like a sculptor molding a statue. It paid off."

Marshall was glad Frost liked the airplane. The man was a natural pilot, one of the few Marshall had ever met, and he handled the Rocket as if he'd flown it for years.

Frost put his finger to his lips as he responded to an inquiry from air traffic control.

"We'll start our descent on the hour, Bones. Now what's the drill?"

"We'll land and taxi over to get refueled. You get off and go into the ops shack to file our clearance for the flight back. We don't want to spend any more time on the ground than we have to. I'll handle the refueling. They won't mind a Black guy doing that. You do the paying, though."

It occurred to Marshall in passing that he was calling himself Black now, just as Saundra and Peterson did. Funny—it was a word he would have refused to use a year ago.

"When we're done, Saundra will get out and walk over to side entrance to the operations shack. Somebody will be there to meet her with a car."

"How about her luggage?"

"She'll take the one bag with her. When you come back out, I'll hustle her bags over to her. I'd like her to get out without anybody seeing her, if I can."

Frost nodded that he understood. Then he leaned over and asked, "Has this got anything to do with the bus boycott down here?"

Marshall liked Frost and trusted him; he didn't feel he could ask him to make flights like this without knowing what was going on.

"Corky, I'll level with you. They didn't even tell me what this is all about. But Fred Peterson wouldn't ask Saundra to make a trip like this unless it was important. I suspect she's carrying some money for the local leadership."

"Where does this guy Peterson get his dough?"

"He's a hell of a businessman. When he bought this airplane

Roget was suspicious because of all the gyrations Peterson went through, with one company owning the airplane, another financing it, another leasing it—but when it was all done, Roget had a check for seven hundred grand in his hand."

"You know, you ain't got no money, you ain't never gonna get any; you got money, you can't stop gettin' it."

"Looks like it. Me, I'm one of the 'ain't got no' types. Let me go back and wake Saundra, so she can clear her ears on the way down."

He slipped back into the cabin and stared at her for a moment. Even though she was so tired, worn-out from trying to do too much, she was still so beautiful. Yet she'd become so remote; they no longer had a marriage in the real sense. They were faithful to each other, and sometimes they still had sex, but he could tell it was just conjugal duty on her part, all the old fire was gone. They no longer enjoyed themselves on the rare occasions when they went out to eat, or to a show. Paradoxically, the only time they became close was when they talked about the thing that was pulling them apart, the civil rights movement.

The problem was that he loved her so, even though she clearly had a new mission in life. Only a few months ago she'd been consumed by her business; now she'd virtually turned it over to her managers, spending as little time with them as possible. She was totally committed to working with the small group of Black leaders from Atlanta that Peterson had introduced her to.

He stroked her head. "Saundra, wake up. We're almost there. Be sure to keep your ears clear on the descent." He kissed her and went back to his seat.

She sat up and began combing her hair. She wore very little makeup now—it didn't seem appropriate, even if she was in the business.

Clearing her ears carefully as they descended, it struck her that it was the first time she'd ever flown with John, and that she'd paid no more attention to him than if she'd been on a commercial flight. It was natural, she had faith in his ability. She wished she could have the same faith that he would understand what was happening to them, that he would approve of her being called to a vocation.

Yet as much as she tried to convince herself that it was purely a
religious calling, she was aware that it was also a part of her endless
search for a father figure. That's why she'd been so attracted to John
at first, and then, when he was gone, why she'd been drawn to Fred.
Now, when she had proved herself in business, when she was
financially independent, another cause—and another man—had
come along. She was still groping for a way to explain her feelings to
John when she heard the squeak of the wheels touching down on
the Montgomery airport runway.

They taxied past the line of hangars to the fuel pit, where the
transfer went off easily. Marshall had flight-planned to arrive just
before dawn, and the sleepy line boy was more than glad to have
him help with the refueling. While John kept him occupied, Saundra flitted out from the airplane like a ghost; the line boy didn't
see her.

Twenty minutes later John carried her two bags over to where she
was waiting. He put the luggage in the trunk of a tan 1941 Ford
sedan; the two men in front nodded to him but did not speak.

"Saundra, are you going to be all right? Have you got a place to
stay? This whole thing is beginning to scare me."

"They'll fix me up with some family in town. I'll be fine, and I'll
call you in a few days."

He kissed her, and she said, "John, this is important. You know I
wouldn't leave you, leave my business, unless it were."

"I know it's important. I just hope it's not more important than
me, than us."

She didn't answer; instead, filled with a nameless excitement, she
gave him a little wave, then slipped into the backseat of the Ford.

Nashville, Tennessee/January 26, 1956

Elsie McNaughton, mink coat almost dragging on the ground,
moved slowly through the guesthouse, talking to the U.S. marshal
with her. He was friendly but businesslike, assigned by the court to

make sure that she took nothing but personal belongings from the property.

She had lost the guesthouse forever, just as she had lost the house Troy had built for her and the old farm that Henry Caldwell had given her. All the properties had been wrapped up in the complex financing of McNaughton Aircraft, and the settlement she'd made took them all away from her. In exchange, the government had arranged a sale that gave her more money than she'd ever dreamed of. It was more than a good deal; it suited her new attitudes, her new habits. Once a fireball of energy, she now was relaxed and easygoing, content to enjoy herself.

She felt that the government had been rigorous but fair. As both a stockholder and a chief executive, she was considered responsible for the installation of the defective milk-bottle pins, even though she had denied any role in the coverup. Because the plant was essential to B-47 production, she was given a choice of criminal prosecution or divesting herself of her interests in McNaughton.

It had been an easy decision. So many things had changed. Troy was dead, Baker was gone, and the nature of the business was so different. McNaughton no longer made aircraft, and she'd found no enjoyment in subcontracting to other manufacturers. In the past year, the new management she'd brought in had tried to diversify— they were making canoes and buses now, along with metal cabinets, barrels, and other totally boring products, and making money on none of them. The canoes were three times as expensive as a standard canoe, and the buses broke down with monotonous regularity. It was time to take the money and run. Surprisingly, finding a buyer had been easy; Congressman Dade had seen to that. It had not been difficult for him to get financiers interested; they knew that his hinting of a whole series of juicy contracts was better than another man's promise.

The Air Force had been as anxious as she was to consummate the deal and shut down the investigation. They had shown no interest in trying to find Baker, and if they had tumbled to the Ruddick connection, they had declined to pursue it.

"I never really liked this place, you know—the first guesthouse we had was just an old farmhouse, but it was cozy."

The marshal nodded; the woman drove him crazy with her endless palavering, but he had instructions to be nice to her.

"Will you be doing some traveling now, Mrs. McNaughton?"

"Some. I'm going to Elkhart, Indiana, first. They make good trailers there, and I'm going to have one custom-made just for me."

"To pull behind your car?"

She couldn't restrain herself from mischievously running her hand up his arm; he jumped, startled. "No, silly, to live in. I'm going to get a nice, big comfortable trailer, set it up on a big lot, and just have fun."

Backing away, he asked, "Here in Nashville?"

"No, I think I'll be going to Alaska. Always wanted to go there."

It was easy to see that he wasn't a live one, and there was no point in telling him that she was going to Little Rock, to see some friends.

Little Rock, Arkansas/March 23, 1956

Locked in an unwilling partnership like a bounty hunter and his quarry, Ginny and Stan sat sipping coffee in the sun-room of the old Ruddick home. He was slouched in one of the well-worn wicker chairs, nursing another of his monumental hangovers while she read the Gazette's latest account of the racial turmoil sweeping the South. She encouraged Stan's drinking and enjoyed his hangovers; looking at his red eyes and puffy face strengthened her own resolve not to drink anymore.

"Good! Listen to this, Stan. They found that jumped-up nigger preacher, King, guilty! That'll teach him to go around organizing boycotts."

Coleman didn't speak, gazing morbidly out at the leaf-filled fish pond in the garden. Once the grounds had been immaculately kept—by Nathan. The image of Nathan and Ginny came to him again, as fresh as the day it happened. He should have strangled her on the spot.

"And look at this, some little colored girl has been admitted to the University of Alabama. Well, it won't happen here, the governor won't let it. And neither will Daddy!"

Stan buttered a piece of toast and forced himself to eat it. In an hour he had to be in uniform to be picked up by his driver.

"Now, Stan, don't be sullen. I know you hate me, but just remember, if it wasn't for Daddy, you'd have gone to jail. I don't know how you could have been so foolish to try to do a stunt like that, when he would have gotten you promoted to general on his own."

He would have hated her less if she had not said it every day and if it had not been true. He'd encouraged the cheating at Frederick because he wanted to make brigadier general on his own terms, without any help from Ruddick. Then, when it all blew up, Ruddick had quashed the court-martial charges and instead had him brought into the Arkansas Air National Guard as a special liaison officer to the governor! It made his abrupt resignation from the Air Force look like a planned move. The governor had infuriated the commander of the local Air Guard unit by giving Coleman the rank of brigadier general. It couldn't have been done in the regular Air Force, but the Guard was totally politicized, and what the governor wanted, the governor got. Yet Stan was a little distressed—the careful way Ruddick kept his promises made Coleman believe he'd keep his threats with equal fidelity.

"Ginny, I've got a surprise for you. Your old boyfriend is back in town."

"Don't try to pick a fight, Stan, you always lose."

"Yes, after all his college education, and the tricks you must have taught him, he's working in a tire shop, mounting those big truck tires. Of course, he'd rather be mounting you."

"Shut up; that's enough."

Enjoying himself, he went on, "Does your current boyfriend know about your affair with Nathan? I'll bet he'd be proud to know he was following in a Negro's footsteps, so to speak."

She folded the paper carefully, put it down on the table, and looked him in the eye. Unconsciously, her hand wandered to the back of her head, searching for the single strand of hair. When she stopped drinking her old compulsive habit had returned. Her voice was icy.

"By current boyfriend, do you mean the governor?"

"Yes, I mean the governor—unless you're bumping somebody else on the side. What would he say about Nathan? Maybe someday I ought to tell him about your little experiment with colored men."

"For your information, my relationship with the governor is purely professional." Exasperated, she banged her coffee cup down. "Stan, I wonder what Daddy sees in you. You don't even know how to threaten properly."

Coleman was immediately defensive. "I'm not threatening you."

"Sure you are. You just go ahead and tell the governor about Nathan. I'll tell him Nathan raped me and you wouldn't defend me. Do you think he'll believe you instead of me? I even know what he'd call you—a poltroon."

Imitating the governor's deep voice, she said again, "Poltroon! That's what he'd call you. Even Daddy wouldn't be able to stop him from firing you, and then what would you do? Poor baby, you've never gotten a job on your own. You'd wind up toting groceries at the A&P."

He got up and strode out of the room, furious with himself because he knew she was right. As he passed the buffet, once again lined with decanters, the doorbell rang. Thinking that it might be his driver, early, he answered it, and found Elsie McNaughton.

"Stan, honey, aren't you going to invite me in? Where's Ginny?" Turning to the cab driver behind her, she said, "Just bring the luggage in and sit it by the door."

Offutt Air Force Base, Nebraska/April 13, 1956

They sat on straight-backed chairs in the harsh light of LeMay's outer office, a room hacked out of the old Martin Aircraft bomber plant, its windows providing a view of the Omaha stockyards, more suitable for a garage foreman than for a four-star general. A constant stream of staff officers shuttled in and out, clutching their files to their chests, jaws tight; there was no small talk, no jesting, none of the usual we're-near-the-boss camaraderie.

"Friday the thirteenth—we'll be lucky if we get out of here with our lives."

Bandfield was more relaxed than his friend. "Nonsense, Bear. He's probably calling you in to tell you you're going to make general."

"So what are you doing here? You're going to be promoted, too?"

"Not likely. He just knows we've been working together, probably wants me to be here to congratulate you."

"Yeah, LeMay's like that, always trying to figure out ways to make the troops happy. I don't know what you're smoking, but whatever it is, send me a carton."

A glassy-eyed lieutenant colonel popped out of LeMay's office like a cork from a champagne bottle. He steadied himself, looked around, and mumbled, "He wants you two next," and then staggered off.

"Looks like he's in good form today."

They walked in and saluted smartly; the great stone face said, "Sit down, both of you," and went on reading a file, marking it ferociously with a big red grease pencil, grumbling to himself like a dyspeptic dragon. It occurred to Bandfield that he was the only man he'd ever known who could snarl quietly. After a very long two minutes, he turned to them, saying, "All right, Bandfield, what's the bad news on the McNaughton milk-bottle pin fittings?"

"The best guess we can make is that there could be as many as forty B-47s in the fleet with defective parts installed. The problem is you can't tell if it's a bad part or not unless you pull it out of the airplane and analyze the metal in it. On the surface, the damn things look just like a standard unit."

LeMay turned his head, scowling at the wall, rubbing his iron jaw with his hand.

"What kind of audit trail was there?"

"None. Whoever was responsible at McNaughton—we think it was a guy named Baker—did a real job on the paperwork. It's not only the data on the milk-bottle pin that's missing, but he got rid of the paperwork on everything they'd bought for the past two years. When the heat came on, he vanished."

LeMay's lips contorted. "Is the FBI looking for this guy?"

"They were, but they've had no luck at all."

"Well, what're we going to do? Ground the fleet?"

Bandfield knew that wasn't the right answer and put a single sheet of paper on LeMay's desk.

"No, sir. I'm recommending that we restrict the LABS maneuver tactic to a specific number of aircraft to minimize the chances for overstressing the wings." LABS was the acronym for the Low Altitude Bombing System developed for the toss-bombing technique.

"If we equip about ten percent of the fleet with the LABS, and shift the rest over to use parachute-retarded bombs, we'll reduce the impact of the problem considerably. We can earmark the ones we select for extra inspections for cracks."

LeMay nodded unenthusiastically, and Bandfield went on. "They've finally got things worked out at the Special Weapons Command at Kirtland; for most of the units you can get the same degree of accuracy from a parachute-retarded weapon as you can from a free-fall bomb."

LeMay rolled a fresh cigar back and forth between his fingers. "How much time will it take to modify the stockpile of bombs?"

"Two months, three at the outside."

The general lit the cigar, mind racing. "Well, if we have to go to war before then, we won't be worrying about the wings falling off anyway. Okay, I'll go along with that. What's next?"

Bandfield and Riley concealed simultaneous sighs of relief. They'd never thought LeMay would go along with having only ten percent of the B-47 fleet dedicated to the LABS technique.

"When the airplanes go through modification at Boeing for the LABS, they ought to have their milk-bottle pins pulled and new ones substituted. It will be expensive as hell, but I don't see any way around it."

LeMay was scribbling furiously on a big yellow pad. "Okay. I'll try to get authorization to have one hundred fifty aircraft designated for modification for LABS. The rest of them we'll restrict to two G-maneuvers and pray that the wings don't start falling off. Bandfield, you're excused."

When the door had closed he turned to Riley. "Bear, I'm sorry to tell you that you're not going to be on the general's list this year, and probably never."

Riley shrugged. "I didn't expect to be, sir."

"Well, *I* expected you to be, and I'm pissed off that you're not. But you've got a congressman mad at you, and the word's been given to the air staff not even to submit your name."

"What is it, the crackdown on the 103rd?"

"You got it. It's Congressman Dade who's blacklisting you. He carries a lot of weight, and doesn't mind using it. I figure it's his old pal Ruddick who's putting him up to it."

Bear Riley actually felt relieved. Academically he liked the idea of being a general officer; realistically he knew he wasn't cut out for it. It might have been nice for Lyra, as much as she enjoyed the club work, but . . .

"No problem, General, I never expected to be more than a buck-ass major flying the line anyway."

"Me either. Funny how things work out. But let me tell you why I can't go to bat for you like I'd like to. Dade's on the House Armed Services Committee, and I've got this legislative package coming through on improving airmen's housing. I can't afford to antagonize him."

Bear nodded; it made sense. LeMay had done more for the troops in the last five years than anyone else in the Air Force. He couldn't win them all.

LeMay went on. "But at least I can give you a break from this miserable staff work; you're going to take over the 103rd at Frederick. You've earned it."

Riley was stunned. "I'd love to have a wing, General, but how is the 103rd going to react to me? I blew the whistle on them, and fired a lot of their bosses. They'll want my ass on a platter."

LeMay had already shifted back to his stack of files.

"Jesus, Riley, don't tell me your problems, I got enough of my own."

Pine Bluff, Arkansas/May 20, 1954

It was truly a luxurious trailer. Elsie had spent two months at the Elcar factory overseeing its design, incorporating everything she'd liked about the old guesthouse and Baker's little trailer, along with custom touches that had daunted the builders until they were sure that money was no object. They had never built bedrooms and baths paneled entirely in mirrors, and there was a lot of sniggering about it until Elsie personally demonstrated their utility to the general manager one evening.

The whole project almost came to a halt before it started when they told her that what she wanted would be too big to haul over the roads. She remembered how they'd shipped huge parts of airplanes from McNaughton and suggested that they simply split it into thirds, then assemble it on-site. When they finally saw that they weren't building a trailer at all but a modular house with super-numerary wheels, they became enthusiastic.

She'd come to Little Rock knowing only that Baker was some-where in the area—they had not communicated once since his rapid departure. Staying with the Colemans had been just a whim, a way to make sure she learned from Ruddick where Baker was—and a chance to sample Stan again. The first time Ginny left the house he'd willingly leaped into bed with her for his usual insipid lovemaking. It convinced her that Baker was what she wanted out of life.

Ruddick had tried to quash the idea, refusing at first even to tell her where Baker was.

"Elsie, my dear, I reckon we've been friends for a long time, done a lot of business together. Your husband was a good friend, too." They were alone, drinking bourbon and branch water in the study. "But coming here is just plain crazy. What if another airplane crashes, and they start the investigation again? Ah'm not going to be able to help." It sounded like *heallp*.

In harsh contrast to Ruddick's mellow Murrow voice, after two drinks, Elsie lost her cultivated Southern drawl and her Jersey accent cut through. "If that happens it won't make any difference where any of us are, they'll find us. Look on it as a package deal—you took McNaughton for all it was worth when the going was good; now you have to put up with me because things went sour."

"Elsie, you could live high on the hog anywhere, with all your money. You don't need to be here, living with us."

"No, and I won't be for long, not after you take me to see Dick Baker, and we get a few things straightened out."

Ruddick sighed, knowing that at least one of the things she intended to straighten out was firmly attached to Baker.

When he did put her in touch with Baker a few days later, the big man had been delighted to see her—the girls in New Orleans were younger and prettier, but they didn't respond like she did. He immediately began planning the installation of her trailer on part of the Klaven's acreage. Curiously, Josten had been all for it from the start, welcoming Elsie effusively. Later he told Ruddick that he thought it would keep Baker from getting into trouble on his regular trips to New Orleans. The truth was he was just glad to have Baker away from his headquarters, but still close enough to call on if he was needed.

Baker sited the trailer in a valley, buffered on all sides by thick growths of pine. In just a few weeks, he'd sunk a well, arranged to have the septic tank put in, and, with some reliable Storm Klanners' help, built a concrete-block foundation. The three parts of the trailer came together easily, and he handled the installation of the interior himself, not wanting any of the local boys to get a look at the mirrored rooms.

Now they lived like honeymooners, Baker so glad to have her that he reasserted his old dominator role only when they made love, because Elsie wanted it. For the rest, he was like a young newlywed, fixing up the yard in front and, out back, planting a crop of marijuana. Elsie was the soul of domesticity, spending hours with the Sears catalog to get just the right drapes, the right accent pieces.

"Honey, the only thing we need around here is a baby. Too bad we're too old."

"Well, nothing says we can't have pets instead. How about a dog?"

Tears formed in Elsie's eyes. The man seemed to have changed so much, he really was trying to please her. "Let's do get a dog. Two dogs, a big one and a small one. One for you, one for me."

Pine Bluff, Arkansas/May 21, 1956

The relief he felt when Elsie moved out was only one of the things that told Ruddick things were going well. Leaving Washington was the best thing he'd ever done, even though nothing had come of the investigations at McNaughton. He hadn't realized how tired he was of the politicking, of the favor-swapping, the back-scratching. At first, he'd been worried about the double loss of income from his salary and from McNaughton, but the real estate market had taken an upturn and there was a small but constant series of contracts coming from the State House for his contracting firm.

Even so, he'd decided to sell off some of his art collection. Dixon Price had located an agent for him in Los Angeles, who was doing a good job, selling off the less desirable pieces first, the things he would ultimately have sold anyway, and the money was pouring in. The biggest surprise was the Hitler watercolors. He put a few of them on the market and they were snapped up by two Texans, each of whom immediately wanted to buy everything he had. He'd pulled the rest of them off the market right away, because their price was obviously going to skyrocket.

And, best of all, Josten had not proved to be a problem. When he came back, Helmut readily assumed the position of second-in-command, behaving with military deference.

Although he seemed physically strong, the man was intensely

preoccupied about something. Ruddick assumed that his health was bothering him, but Baker didn't agree.

"He's not feeling too good, boss, but that's not his problem. He's nutty about a woman, and it's eating him up."

"His wife?"

"Former wife. She's married to some Air Force guy now, they have a kid, and it's killing Josten. He's sent me to Omaha, twice, just to spy on them."

"Must be going crackers. What's that big blue bus he's fooling with?"

"He may be crackers, but he's still a genius. If he'd been running things in Germany, they would have won the war, believe me. He calls the bus his command post—he's made a real luxury deal out of it—it's just like a trailer home inside, bathroom, kitchen, everything."

"You should be an expert on that subject. How do you like trailer living?" Disapproval dripped from Ruddick's words. Baker ignored it.

"Great! You should come out and see our place. It's not really a trailer, you know, you couldn't hardly move it nowhere. It's got everything."

Ruddick drummed his fingers, falling into the exaggerated drawl he used when he was being sarcastic. "You all don't think it's just a little teeny bit risky, her coming here and you moving in with her?"

"Boss, the FBI ain't looking, or they would have found me. Those guys are good, and I'm not exactly inconspicuous. I don't think the business at McNaughton is a problem anymore. They got rid of Elsie, turned the management over to a bunch of pros—why would they want to look for some poor joker who ordered the wrong parts?"

"And tore up all the paperwork."

"That was your idea, boss, don't forget." Baker smiled; he didn't often win an exchange with Ruddick. On balance, he much preferred working for Josten. Ruddick's Southern drawl, the round-about political way he approached things, his reluctance to use violence, all made him pale in comparison to Josten's no-nonsense approach.

One hundred yards away, inside the converted bus, Josten sat listening to their conversation. Weeks before, he'd taken the precaution of placing a microphone in the wall of his old office—the one Ruddick was now using—and putting a tap on the telephone. He had no basic disagreement with Ruddick, but he wanted the advantage that good intelligence could bring. Baker, loyal swine that he was, could be helpful when he wanted to provide Ruddick with a little misinformation.

His eyes wandered around the inside of the bus. The business of running the Storm Klan was sporadic, for he had to work when the men were available, after hours and on the weekends. It left a lot of time on his hands, and he poured it into finishing work on the bus. It was fatiguing—his hands had not recovered their strength, probably never would—but he enjoyed being deliberate, taking his time. Most of the Storm Klanners were blue-collar workmen, and he had used the most skilled of them for the rough work.

He put a great deal of thought into the design. The bus was powered by a diesel engine, and he had built huge fuel tanks along its perimeter; it had a nonstop range of more than 1,200 miles. It was not fast, he'd drive it no more than sixty, but it was comfortable. There were two bedrooms, one a master suite with a bath, the second with bunkbeds for children. One of the local men had finished the interior in a beautiful walnut, the wood coming from trees felled on the Klaven's grounds. The bus was filled with more conveniences than most American homes had. There was a television set—of no use in the hills above Pine Bluff, but it would be useful on the road. And it had air conditioning—damn few homes had that. He'd had to cover up the windows—couldn't have people peering in—but he'd replaced them with paintings he knew Lyra would like, cadged from Ruddick's collection.

Less obvious was the fact that the bus could keep guests secure comfortably and without danger to himself. The doors could all be locked from the driver's position, and there was nothing, no andiron, no lamp, not even an electric cord that could be used as a weapon.

Helmut knew that the time had come to bring Lyra back. He longed to possess her again, to make her see how wrong she was to have divorced him. He was stronger than he had been for years, even though he had not yet recovered his sexual capacity.

It distressed him that his feelings for Ulrich had changed so much. Yet it was hardly surprising; he had never really known the boy, and now, according to Baker, he was like any American child, no accent, a member of the Cub Scouts. It was difficult to contemplate, but Ulrich might best serve as a means to persuade Lyra to come with him. He would have only a few days with Lyra; they shouldn't be diluted—or inhibited—by Ulrich's presence. Someone would have to take care of him. Ulrich could be the lever, the means by which Lyra could be persuaded to come.

He needed someone he could trust, someone to take care of the boy for the few days he would spend with Lyra. It was too delicate a matter, and far too hazardous legally, to expect anyone to do it willingly. As he turned the problem over in his mind, he realized that it would have to be Baker.

13

Santa Monica, California/January 15, 1957

Tears smeared her mascara as they coursed down her sunken cheeks. "I don't understand it, Fred, you've backed King all along, you've brought me into the movement, even John is convinced, and now you say you're dropping out? What is the matter? What has he done?"

Peterson, obviously shaken, said, "It's this personal leadership thing. The man has a Messiah complex. He's set up the Southern Christian Leadership Conference as a grassroots church organization, and he's going to make himself the head of it, you'll see. The N-Double-A leadership is furious, and so am I. He's a great man, but he's not acting in the interest of the movement!"

Saundra wondered if her obvious admiration for King had influenced Peterson. "Fred, tell me, this is not because of me, because I'm so involved in it?"

He looked at her in a way he never had before. "You're so transparent, Saundra, and so vulnerable, always searching for your own personal Messiah. But don't pump yourself up. This is not between us; it's not about you. It's about what's good for the

396

movement. And my people have serious doubts about Martin Luther King."

She was stunned at this, the first unkind thing he'd ever said to her, the first unkind thing she'd ever heard about King.

He went on. "Don't think you're the only one to fall under his spell; just don't get hurt."

"What are you saying? He doesn't know I exist."

"Believe me, he knows you exist, he knows where the money has come from. Now the real question is, how is this going to affect the way we operate? I'm still going to want to use John and the airplanes, but for people I choose, not for King. If you want to use it for his group, you'll have to pick up the tab."

She nodded, and he pressed on, relentless. "And I know that things are not going as well as they should at Marshall Products. I've talked to the managers I sent over to you, and they're worried."

"Are they your spies?"

"Yes, they're my spies, and your best friends, and you know it. But they can't run the place if you're off in Atlanta or Montgomery or wherever most of the time. It's your business—and if you don't run it right, you won't have any money to support your man with."

Saundra was confused for a moment, not knowing whether he meant John or Martin.

"You've been good to me, Fred, and you've been good to the movement. I know you're sincere, and I respect that. But I'm sincere, too. We'll just have to see how things work out."

Saundra called her husband as soon as Fred left, asking him if he could come home from the airport early.

They met on the balcony of their new house in Malibu Canyon. Marshall had been against buying it, feeling it was obscenely expensive, all glass and redwood, big enough for a dozen people. She loved it, but now she was forced to agree with him; it was probably going to have to go back on the market.

She told him exactly what Fred had said.

"What does he have against King?"

"He says he's going off on his own, that he's trying to establish a personal following that will hurt the movement."

Marshall mixed a pitcher of margaritas, carefully rimmed two glasses with salt, and poured. They sat on a white glider, looking out over the strange mixture of trees that their little piece of the canyon had, left from the time when it had been a botanical garden for an eccentric millionaire.

He sipped and began speaking, very slowly. "I'd like to believe that Fred was right. It would make it easy for me to insist you stop backing him, that you pay attention to me. But I believe in Dr. King's movement, too. It's the only rational way to change things, and he's the leader we've been waiting for." He was silent for a long while, tongue just licking the salted rim of the glass. "I know I've got to have faith in you, but despite all your success in business you are a hopeless romantic. You're immature, always searching for a leader to love. The only thing that saves the situation is that I have faith in King. So I've got to support him."

"I'm glad you're going to support him. It's going to take all our spare cash now that Fred is dropping out."

He flung his arms out. "So what? Sell this place, move back to the little house in Santa Monica, use the money for the movement. I was happier there, anyway." He drank the rest of his margarita and poured another, carefully, to avoid washing salt into the glass.

"Saundra, I survived Korea, and I'll survive this. My gut feeling tells me that I've got to rock along with this until you mature, until you're able to support the movement and be my wife, too."

She reached over and took his hand.

Salinas, California/February 1, 1957

Bandfield felt foolish, knowing it shouldn't bother him, that he should be a bigger man than to worry about something like this. But he'd put twenty years into the Air Force, fought in two wars, shot down twenty planes—hell, been shot down himself a few times, too—and when he retired two days before, there had been only a piddling ceremony in his office at Offutt Air Force Base. In a way, he understood it; he'd always been an outsider, not working his way up through the normal chain of command, neither serving his time as a Pentagon staff wienie nor establishing a reputation in a wing or a squadron. And in the last few years, he'd been in his own office in Omaha so rarely that he scarcely knew anyone at Headquarters.

Still, the Army and the Navy always did things like this better. He hadn't expected a parade, or a fly-over, but somehow he was hurt. There had been a cake, the standard mess hall square white sheet-cake, tooth-numbing white pure-sugar frosting, with *Good Luck* spelled out in a deathly shade of green icing, along with the sour GI coffee-mess coffee, served in stained brown-plastic cup holders with wax-paper liners. A two-star general he'd never even met came in and said a few banal words, shook hands—and that was it. No Bronze Star, no Legion of Merit, just a few crummy certificates and a handshake. He was glad he told Patty not to come up. It would have been embarrassing. LeMay should have done better by him, but he couldn't be pissed at him; he knew how busy the commander was.

And the main thing was the job. He'd seen the Air Force grow from a postwar country club into the most powerful force the world had ever seen; the Air Force alone had the power to destroy an enemy with its bombers. The B-47 was working well now, and he'd done a lot to bring it along. The B-52s were coming in, and in a few years the missile fleet would be ready. Still . . . it would have been nice if LeMay had sent a message or something.

His homecoming had been equally low-key—*downbeat* was a better term. Patty and Charlotte were in Los Angeles, shopping for a few days, and glad as George was to see him, he was all wrapped up in his girls and his studies. There was only one thing to do—get back to work. He'd be sure of a welcome from Hadley, anyway.

Pushing the door to Hadley's office open, he said, "Is Roget Aircraft hiring?"

Hadley didn't look up. "We could use an engineering test pilot. But what we really need is a salesman. Interested?"

"Jesus, don't act so glad to see me. I'm out of the Air Force for good now, old buddy."

"Yeah, swell, big deal. I don't know why I'm asking you, you never were worth a damn in the past, but how about trying to sell some airplanes for me?"

"Christ, I couldn't sell tea to Chinamen. You know that."

Roget rocked back in his swivel chair, cocked a foot up on his littered desk, and said, "Brother, do I! But all you've got to do is sell a few water-bombers to some contractors, forest-fire professionals. Should be a snap."

"How about selling Rockets? That'd probably be easier and more fun."

Roget stopped his kidding, smiled, and stuck out his hand. "Welcome back, little buddy. I've missed you." Then, switching back to business, "We don't need no Rocket salesmen, we got customers standing in line for that little racer. But we got to get rid of them TBMs and the Catalina—the inventory cost is killing us. How about working out a tour, sort of like you did when we was peddling fighters down in South America?"

"Take them out of the country?"

"Well, Canada, maybe, someday. But for now, just plan to take a tour through the Southwest and South. I've been looking at the fire seasons, and I'd say we should start in southern California in August, and work our way across to Florida. Then we could come back and work our way north, sort of following the fires like pickers follow the crops. What do you think?"

"You keep saying 'we.' You mean you and me?"

"The three of us—you, John, me, and maybe two or three mechanics. It'd be fun."

"The real fun will be when you tell Patty that the guy she made get out of the Air Force because he was never home is off on a six-month sales tour."

"Don't sweat it, Bandy, I'll handle it. Your wife is putty in my hands."

Little Rock, Arkansas/March 16, 1957

Dixon Price was the last to arrive, slipping in the side door.

Ruddick had given up his downtown office space, with its beloved view of his land-holdings, and they sat in the old-fashioned living room, the chairs and couches decorated with yellowing anti-macassars crocheted half a century before. Stan Coleman, still in his brand-new uniform, sat sullenly contemplating the portrait of Alma Ruddick, her face and eyes so much like her daughter's. He wondered if her morals had been as bad. Ginny passed among them, offering them cut-glass tumblers of Wild Turkey, with ice on the side and a pitcher of water to mix as they wished. Only Josten declined.

Earlier in the day, dressed in a sweater and jeans, Coleman had dropped in again at the tire-recapping shop where Nathan worked. He could see him in the back, laboring industriously. It gave Coleman some pleasure; Nathan had graduated from college, and this was the best he could do. But the scene of him and Ginny coupling had never left him; he wondered if Nathan ever thought about her, if he ever wanted her, worse, if he ever saw her. Ginny would be capable of meeting him on the sly, sneaking him a screw in the back of her Buick. What if they were getting together again?

Price drank deeply, appreciatively, a serious drinker on his first drink of the day. To give the liquor time to settle in and lend him its warmth, he pulled his handkerchief from the pocket of his new gray flannel suit, patted his lips, replaced it carefully. Ruddick eyed the expensive suit—it didn't come from any shop in Little Rock—and realized that Ginny was taking as good care of Price as she did the governor.

Leaning forward, Price began to speak in a low, conspiratorial voice. "We've got some problems coming up. I have it on good authority that the nigras are going to try to enforce the Brown decision on us this fall and enroll some children in Central High School."

Ruddick shrugged. "It was just a matter of time; maybe sooner's better than later." He turned to Josten. "Are we ready?"

Josten nodded. "We have almost a thousand Klansmen in the area we can count on, and, for the front lines, four hundred Storm Klanners."

Ruddick knew from Josten's accent that he was excited; his English was usually perfect.

Coleman spoke up. "We're not going to need the Klan; Dixon can ask the governor to call out the Guard. I'll make sure the little pickaninnies get sent back home."

Dixon Price had spent years speaking at outdoor rallies, fish-fries, Fourth of July picnics; now his deep voice boomed, filling the room. "Let's not be too hasty. How will it look, bunch a Guardsmen with rifles, fighting a dozen nigras? That's a story every Northern reporter would love. We need to get some sympathy for our side, a few white heads cracked, some blood in the streets." He glanced at Ruddick, knowing he was singing his song.

Baker, ballooning out of a horse blanket–plaid sport coat and too-tight Sans-a-belt slacks, had been uncharacteristically quiet till now. "How you going to get the niggers to fight? All they talk now is nonviolence, this Gandhi shit. Look how they won in Montgomery." He smiled and said, "Excuse me, Ginny, forgot myself."

Coleman flushed, irritated that Baker would speak to Ginny so familiarly—she was probably screwing him, too. "Look, Baker, when we want your opinion, we'll ask."

Josten creaked to his feet, his head and shoulders bent forward, the collar of his suit coat, a Ruddick hand-me-down, forming a little arch behind his scrawny neck. "*Herr General*"—his voice was harsh, the lapse into German deliberate—"I brought Mr. Baker here. He is my deputy and you must treat him with courtesy." The words were ordinary enough, the menace in his eyes was not. Coleman lowered his head as Baker glowed—it was the first time Josten had called him "deputy." He liked it, realizing in that instance for the first time that some things were better than money.

Josten then turned to Baker, and with genuine solicitude said, "Your question is valid; let me answer it. We *make* them fight. Let me march four hundred Storm Klanners through their streets, with a thousand Klansmen following. It will be like the old days in Germany, before 1933, when the Nazis beat the Communists into the ground. We'll drag them out of their houses and break some heads. They'll fight for their lives, believe me."

Price rubbed his hands together. "Then, Stan, you could send the Guard in, break up the riots; next day, we slap the Guard around the school, and don't let any niggers in at all, no janitors, no cooks, nobody, in the interest of public safety."

Ruddick was nodding. "That might work. It's not what I'd like; I wanted to have some clear provocations."

Josten pressed his case. "Could we have the Guard and the Klan battle? We need some gunfire, some casualties."

"I'm not sure which way the public would swing on that, Colonel Josten; it might work, but it might backfire. Let's think about it. Does the Klan have enough guns?"

Josten nodded. "Mostly Springfield ought-three rifles, surplus stock from our friends in the Guard." He waved a claw at Coleman to acknowledge his cooperation. Then, persistent, he asked, "Could not we hire some Negroes to fight? Pay them to cause a disturbance?" Josten looked around the room.

"Too risky—they'd talk, for sure. Why do we need a real disturbance? Can we swear there was one? Do we have any reporters we could trust, who'd write up what we tell them?"

Josten thought of the opening days in Poland again, when SS troops had put political prisoners in Polish uniforms, killed them, then claimed they had attacked a radio station. "What if we paid them to fight, and they were all killed in the crossfire between the Klan and the Guard?"

Ruddick whistled. "Now that has possibilities. Let's work on that; it would take some careful planning."

Baker interrupted. "Unless you killed more whites than niggers, it would backfire."

Price held up his hand. "It's getting too elaborate. I think our German friend's first idea was best. Muster as many Klansmen as we can, march them through niggertown, and make them fight."

Ginny spoke for the first time. "They have to have somebody to fight with; you can't have them beating up women and children and not have a backlash."

Josten spoke. "We have some time. Let me propose a two-step plan." They looked at him expectantly, and he went on. "The first thing is to create tension, to cause incidents where whites and blacks have a confrontation. Anything will do—traffic accidents, shoplifting charges, shovings on the sidewalk. We can get Klan members to handle this sort of thing. But have the Negroes win most of the time, let them get a sense of power."

Coleman was anxious to regain approval. "We could make sure there was plenty of free liquor available; start paying off the nigger drinking holes to make sure that the darky drinkers got enough to cause some trouble."

Josten also wanted to patch up their differences. "Good idea, General!" General with a soft G this time. "And not just the older people, the regular drinkers, let's get liquor and beer to the teenagers. They will be more likely to fight."

"And to rape," Ginny added. Coleman glared at her, wondering if she was conveying hope or fear.

The others were nodding, approving. Josten turned to Ruddick. "We talked in Washington about having some of the Klan members pretend to be nigras and stage a mock battle. I've got some people in the Storm Klan who would be capable of doing it."

Price was shaking his head. "Be very careful with that, Colonel Josten, it would require real security. Specially if any of them got killed and were taken to the coroner's office."

Ruddick chimed in, "Well, the coroner could be persuaded to help. He's a sound thinker. Let's work on it."

Glowing, his twisted face eager with anticipation, Josten said, "We're going to have to force ourselves to wait, and not be premature. We don't want this to happen in a vacuum—we have to get the maximum national attention from it."

Price rose. It was a no-lose situation. If he handled this perfectly, the governor might become the South's presidential candidate. And if things went wrong, the governor would still be reelected. "I agree.

But let me—and the governor—decide where and when we have the confrontation." Then, turning and nodding collegially to Ruddick and Josten, "With your consultation, of course. Keep me posted. You have my private number. Why don't you and Colonel Josten and the general come up with a plan of operations? Make it a real wargame. Then, if the niggers organize, we'll be ready."

Josten, nodding, spoke. "Mr. Price, if I may. I think the school district has been preparing a desegregation plan. It might be wise to make it as liberal as possible, just as if we meant to comply with the Brown ruling. It could provide some good publicity, and raise some Negro hopes. That might make them react to our activities."

Price's eyes lit up. This man was a Machiavelli, in truth. Ruddick smiled, and Josten and Coleman shook hands, acknowledging their uneasy alliance.

Chicago, Illinois/April 1, 1957

Weissman passed through the outer rooms of the tailor shop, the racks and tables laden mostly with dusty clothes that would never be retrieved. In the beginning when customers dropped in, they had reluctantly taken their orders and then farmed them out to legitimate shops in the neighborhood. Now funding money was so short that they were actually trying to make some money from tailoring and pressing. It was absurd. No one would believe how impoverished they were, how much work was being done for almost nothing.

He went into the back room where he'd worked for three years with a half a dozen colleagues. Three were active agents, as he had once been, and they were seldom there. "Active" was their euphemism for being an assassin. Two were mere file clerks like himself, endlessly collating and cross-referencing information, using thousands of three-by-five cards. One was the Chief.

Sitting at his rolltop desk, Weissman stuffed a portfolio with the latest reports on Klan activities. The Klan was clearly fostering a more strident anti-Semitic tone in the South, linking Jewish liberals, Communism, and the growing civil rights movement. Weissman had been monitoring it for more than three years now, and it was evident that Helmut Josten's influence was beginning to extend beyond the Arkansas Klan.

It was enough for Weissman, and he began to tidy his desk. He'd hated his position, supinely collecting information, filing it like some Uriah Heep. And he was tired of being Weissman the Marksman to these oddballs, these cripples, still laughing about his failure in Washington.

That would never happen again; for the entire time he'd been in Chicago, he had practiced marksmanship at the indoor range in a local gunshop. It had been expensive, consuming one-third of his meager salary, but it was worth it. He was now expert in many types of pistols and rifles. If they'd had machine guns, he would have found the means to pay to practice with them as well.

The Chief had the only private office, a twelve-by-ten box with a single window looking out on the airshaft.

"Jacob, I have to have another assignment. I'm tired of this, and I want to become active again." Goldberg crossed his long legs and folded his arms about himself, looking like a daddy longlegs curling up for a nap, somehow managing to do it without a wrinkle. He was the neatest man Weissman had ever known—his desk was clean, waxed, there was nothing in his In and Out boxes. Maybe he didn't do anything to get wrinkled.

Goldberg pursed his long thin lips. "I've been expecting this; I've seen how you attend to your Arkansas file. Perhaps it's just as well; our funds are being reduced, and I'm going to have to cut down on the work here. When will you leave?"

"Today. I'm going to drive down, perhaps pick up some information in Texas."

"Erich, be careful. I know the lads have teased you about the affair in Washington. Don't be rash in trying to make up for it."

"Thank you."

"When you succeed—not if, when—you'll be doing our two countries a service. Good luck, and good shooting, Erich."

Weissman nodded and walked away wondering if Goldberg was being sarcastic.

Little Rock, Arkansas/April 20, 1957

The two Storm Klanners sat in their 1953 Chevrolet Bel Air sedan. The driver was slender, his long nose and chin conspiring to give him the look of a cartoon rodent, evil and none too bright. He had a nervous twitch that moved his head and nose slightly every few seconds, adding to his malicious Mickey Mouse appearance. The passenger was even smaller and his face could have been taken from any of a thousand lithographs of young Confederate soldiers going off to battle—round and slack-jawed, suffused with placid incomprehension. Ruddick had selected them carefully—they were small enough to be unthreatening, dumb enough to do what he told them to do, just smart enough to save their own hides.

"I shore hate to bang this car up; I just got it paid for, and I polished it last week."

"The cunnel say he'd take care of it, reckon he will. Look at this 'un coming."

They were peering down South Central, at a tumble-down shack, roof swaybacked and porch parting company with the foundation, where Negroes came to buy beer or straight shots of cheap bourbon. A 1936 International pickup truck was pulling away, three men in the seat, four others in the back, talking and laughing.

"Remember now, shoot out in front of them, let them hit us, then get out and run."

"I don't like this. What if they run after us?"

"They won't. They do, the cunnel said he's got men standing by around the corner. Here we go."

As the pickup truck turned into Elm, the Chevrolet accelerated in front of it; the truck struck it in the right rear fender. Both vehicles stopped. The doors of the Chevrolet popped open and the two men ran.

The Negroes piled out of the truck. "What happened? Is this ole truck still running? Then let's get out of here!"

The next day the Arkansas *Journal* ran a short story about a hit-and-run accident in which a truck driven by allegedly intoxicated Negroes had rammed a Chevrolet. The two white men in the car had been able to escape; the truck had not been found. There were no known injuries. It was the second incident of the type in a week.

Salinas, California/May 3, 1957

"It's for you, Bandy. Bear's calling from Frederick."

Bandfield, clad in shorts and a T-shirt, picked up the phone. "Your nickel, Riley. What's up?"

"Did you hear the news? Old McCarthy's dead."

"Hallelujah! Something painful, I hope. The bastard deserved it. He caused enough problems."

Riley's voice grew serious. "That's not why I'm calling, though."

"I figured not. You need some help?"

"I will. We're going on that little trip I mentioned to you before, and I wonder if you'd give Lyra a call once in a while, maybe have her up for a bit."

Two weeks before, Riley had told Bandfield that the 103rd was leaving in July on a ninety-day temporary tour of duty in England. It would be one of the last of the rotations, as they were called, in which whole SAC bomb wings deployed for three months to overseas bases. SAC was gearing up for a new concept—a one-third ground alert status, with just a few airplanes overseas.

"Sure, Bear, Patty'll be delighted, and the kids will be, too. Maybe the two of them can get Saundra to come up." He meant it; Patty loved having Lyra there, especially with the children.

"Doubt it; we can't even get her on the phone anymore, doesn't return our calls. Always off, either working or doing her missionary work."

"I guess it's a calling. Say, Riley, how old's your boy now?"

"Thirteen."

"Hell, we'll give him a few flying lessons while he's here, get him ready for his license at sixteen, just like we did for George."

"Great, he'll love it. But I'm calling early so Patty can make the invitation seem spontaneous; I don't want Lyra to know I was worried about her. She's still nervous about Helmut coming back, you know how that is."

"Gotcha, no problem."

"Selling any airplanes?"

"Nah, but we've got a demo tomorrow. I hope we'll do better later in the year, after there've been a few fires."

Riley sounded enthusiastic. "Sure, when they see how bad they need them, they'll pull out their checkbooks."

"We got our fingers crossed. We'll take good care of Lyra. Have a good trip; you got our number if you need anything."

"Good luck, and thanks."

Merced, California/May 4, 1957

It was a perfect day in the San Joaquin Valley; the dusting of early morning fog had burned off and the hawks were soaring effortlessly, their wingtips moving as daintily as a surgeon's fingers as they extracted every ounce of lift for the air. Marshall, streaked with yellow powder from head to foot, stood beside an open fifty-five-gallon drum carefully pouring a stream of yellow aluminized powder into it while he stirred.

Bandfield stood by, dubious. "I knew you were a gentleman of color, John, but this is ridiculous. You look like you've just painted the road to Oz."

"I tell you, Bandy, the problem with these demonstrations is that the customer doesn't realize how much effect six-hundred gallons of water can have. You drop it, it disappears in two minutes, and there is no visual impact. This'll let everybody know."

Bandfield nodded. "You picked a tough case to convince. Old

Ransome Fleming's been running his crop duster operation for years, and he pretty much knows it all about everything."

"Let's call it agricultural aviation—the guys are trying to get away from the crop duster image. That's one of the reasons Ransome's thinking about going into fire fighting." He was grunting as he stirred. "Yeah, Fleming's got to see it to believe it. That's why I'm mixing this sea marker dye."

"Where'd you get it?"

"This stuff's war surplus, but you can buy it at any industrial chemical distributor—it's mostly aluminum powder and dye, with some kind of binder. If it were a real fire, I'd use borate instead, you get some residual retardation. But this is just a demonstration, and I want to make a big splash." He put the paddle down, ladled another bucket of the powder into the barrel, and resumed paddling. "Something we did in Korea, Riley and me, gave me that idea." He told Bandfield about the broad-jumping contest and dumping the adjutant in the Nile.

Bandfield laughed. "Pretty good. I could have used something like that a couple of times in SAC. How're you going to work it?"

"You'll see. It'll be a standard drop, out at Fleming's farm. He's got a big sandy field lying fallow, uses it to train his new pilots how to dust. I told him we'd be over to make a drop about eleven."

"We'd better get cracking."

Marshall had already filled the belly tank with three hundred gallons of water. He pumped the contents of two fifty-five-gallon drums of his sea-dye concentrate into the plane, then topped it off with water.

"Any way to be sure it's mixed?"

"No, I'd like to have an agitator in there, to keep it in suspension, but I figured I'd just do some shallow maneuvers on the way over. Hope you don't get airsick easy."

Fleming's field was twelve miles northeast of the airport, one of the hundreds of farms dotting the fertile valley, which raised everything from almonds to turkeys. He had his own airstrip, with a dozen Waco planes converted to spraying parked neatly along the side.

"Fleming Aviation, this is TBM Zero Zero Three Six, over."

Standing outside his little radio shack, microphone in hand, Fleming's voice came in clearly. "Yeah, Bones, hear you five by five, and see you, too. That big orange bird looks like a fucking parrot's pecker."

A bank teller before he went into crop dusting, Fleming tried to be as flamboyant as his five-foot-five height and 185-pound weight would permit.

Marshall, nervous about the way Fleming talked on the air, came back, "Roger, are we cleared to drop?"

"Yeah, you see the double line of yellow flags? Like I briefed you, that's the approach. Then you'll see a single line of green flags, that's the run in. The double set of white lines making the big X is the target. See how close you can get."

"Ah, Roger, we'll make one pass to look it over, then make a live run."

Bones brought the TBM around in a rectangular pattern, still using the two rivets as a sight. "Bingo, that's where I'll drop."

The next pass he slowed down to 150 knots, flying at 150 feet. When the X was between the two rivet heads he pickled off the water.

A burgeoning cloud of yellow mist clung momentarily to the TBM's belly like a huge chrome-yellow tumor; it elongated as it fell, yellow streamers falling away until it hit, mixing with the sand into a massive mustard-colored explosion that blotted out the double X and a dozen acres of Fleming's field.

"Holy shit, what did you drop, Bones, a fucking lemon atom bomb? You just painted my whole fucking field yellow."

"We're on the air, Ransome, better watch your language."

"Don't tell me about my fucking language, just get that goddamn airplane on the ground so I can buy it."

Marshall switched to intercom. "Well, Bandy, we convinced him; that's one down and five to go."

"Great job, John. As long as we can get the yellow marker, we can sell these dudes."

"Yeah, now I got to find something that washes it off; last time I used Lava and Spic 'n' Span for four days before I got it off my hands and face."

Pine Bluff, Arkansas/July 15, 1957

Baker was glad to be back; he'd missed Elsie and the dogs, and he'd missed Josten, too. He'd never worked for a boss he'd like or feared as much. He'd been touched by how attentive Josten had been to Elsie, seeing that she got flowers sent to her, had a tree planted in their yard, lots of little things. If he didn't know how crazy the colonel was about his ex-wife, he would have worried that he was courting Elsie.

"Well, Helmut, they live in government housing about a half a mile from the main gate at Frederick. It ain't bad; they've laid the streets out in curves, the houses are all one-story, California-style, you know, stucco and sticks."

"No, I don't know. Did you get some photos?"

"Yeah, lots of them, front and back, all around. They're being developed. Riley has one of the bigger houses, looks like it's three bedrooms, maybe four. Probably less than fifteen hundred square feet, but nice enough."

"What about security? Is the compound guarded?"

"It ain't no compound, I mean it ain't got no fence or gate. It's just like an ordinary little dumb-ass subdivision. An Air Police car makes a pass-through every couple of hours during the day, and about every four hours at night."

"Did anyone see you?"

"Nah, boss, I'm a pro. I rented two cars, drove them at different times. But they wouldn't have noticed anyway; the airplanes fly all the time, and there's crew members coming in at all hours. It's real quiet, but nobody paid any attention to a car driving through. I talked to the guys at the filling station, though, and they said it was quiet because the wing just went overseas."

"Where? How long?"

"They're in England, but they drop down to Spain and North Africa, a few planes at a time. Sounds like a good deal. Your man, Riley, he's gone, won't be back till the first of October."

Josten's eyes glittered as he digested this. Perhaps he was impotent because he loved only Lyra; perhaps she could restore him. If anyone could do it, it would be her. He thought of the wild night that had begun on the floor of her apartment entrance; he'd just come back from the front. It was then that Ulrich, his son, his flesh, had been conceived.

"Did you see my wife or my son?"

"Yeah, both of them, and the baby, too. They was coming out to get in their car, they got a green and white Olds 88. I couldn't see much, but she looked nice, he looked nice. Couldn't see much of the little one."

Josten leaned forward. "I've got to take you into my confidence. And ask you to help me. It will be worth your while."

"Sure, boss, do you want me to snatch the kid?"

Josten slammed his fist down hard, jarring the ill-protected bones of his hands. "Don't talk like that." Then, recovering himself, "Sorry, that word bothers me. You can't kidnap your own child, your own wife."

Baker nodded, hung his head penitently.

"But I want to have a few days alone with my wife, here in my bus, away from everybody. Then I can get her to listen to reason."

Baker looked at him reflectively; here was this organizational genius, this hard-as-nails leader, living crazy in a dream world. He was ugly as sin, brutal as a chainsaw, and he was going to charm his kidnapped wife back to loving him. What a bunch of shit!

"Will she come?"

"No. Not unless I force her to, and the only way I can force her to is to bring Ulrich here. Then she'll come along."

Baker was merciless trying to force Josten to be sensible. "Use Ulrich as a hostage? Threaten his life?"

Josten hung his head. It was the first time Baker had ever seen him less than totally arrogant. "Yes. But after a few days alone, if she wants to leave, I'll let her."

"Boss, be realistic. She's going to hate you for this. Why should she want to stay? What are you going to do with the two kids? It's a cinch she's going to care more about them than you, or her new husband or anything else."

"You're not as stupid as you act, Baker. You're quite right about this. But this is something I must do. I cannot help it. I don't expect you to understand."

Baker shook his head. "And I can tell what's coming. You want me to help, and you want Elsie and me to baby-sit for you. Right?"

Josten simply nodded, waiting.

Baker thought for a solid two minutes before speaking. Things were going well here, playing soldier, living a good life with Elsie. But it couldn't go on forever, not with the race thing boiling. He'd like to help Josten if he could, but it was a losing battle. Finally, he said, "I won't help you with the kidnapping, and don't go yelling at me, it's kidnapping, any way you look at it. If you get back here safely with them, I'll take the kids for two days, no more; I'll tell the cops I didn't know what was going on, didn't believe them at first. Then I got to turn you in, to protect Elsie and me. So you got to do whatever you're going to do in two days, then let her go."

"I'm not sure I can manage it alone."

"You can't. That's why I ain't doing it. I'm really thinking about you, Helmut."

Josten, his shoulders hunched like a brooding vulture, murmured, "But I could get some young Storm Klanners to help. I'll tell them it's in the interests of national security; some of them will do whatever I want."

"That ain't right, boss. You're setting some kids up for a term in the pokey, and they won't even know why."

Josten, who had seemed to wilt as they talked, becoming frailer, more vulnerable, snapped back to his hard Luftwaffe colonel self.

He thought momentarily of all the good men who'd died in the
Luftwaffe and snarled, "Well, why do you think I trained them this
way? Do you think it matters if a few of these acne-crusted super-
men go to jail or not?"

Montgomery, Alabama/August 8, 1957

It seemed incredible to her that she could be there, on the steps of
the famous Dexter Avenue Baptist Church, in the company of the
most brilliant men she'd ever met, smarter than John, smarter even
than Fred. The great white capitol building loomed only two blocks
away, its spotlit dome glittering in the night. It was here that
Jefferson Davis had begun the Confederacy, it was here that the
painful battle of the buses had been fought and won, despite the
Klan and the shootings and the bombings. She had worked there
during the boycott, proud of the long lines of Black men and
women stolidly walking to work, ignoring the nearly empty buses
passing by. And it was here that Martin Luther King, Jr., had
assumed the presidency of the Southern Christian Leadership Conference.

For the first time, she was beginning to understand and resent
Fred Peterson's anger. She now saw that the Urban League was
concentrated in the North, that the NAACP had become elitist, and
that CORE wasn't going anywhere. All of them had reached an
accommodation in their style of operation that business leaders,
white and Black, could live with. That was right in line with Fred's
business and he had supported them all. But Dr. King was offering
something new, a mass movement keyed to Southern churches
and nonviolence, and it had to use anti-business methods to succeed. The bus boycott had worked—Blacks and whites were now
riding the buses, freely mixing with no problems. If it worked
on a bus company, who could tell what other businesses might be
boycotted?

Yet King was the only truly dramatic leader on the scene. In his introduction yesterday, Ralph Abernathy had used a word new to her to describe King—*charismatic*; she'd looked it up after the meeting. He was exactly that, charismatic; why shouldn't he have his own style of mass movement?

King's beautiful wife stood in the shadows, obviously tired from the two long days of prayers and meetings. Saundra tried not to envy her. Alan Loeb, white, obviously Jewish, with a hooked nose that seemed integral to his tortoise-shell glasses, had King's full attention. They talked low and earnestly, erupting into laughter frequently. Reverend Abernathy, a little taller than King but similar in appearance, hovered in the background, obviously disapproving of the white man's presence, of his influence.

The meetings had ended with a determination to raise $250,000 to open offices for the SCLC in Atlanta. During the deliberations Saundra had been doing some calculations. It would be difficult for her to provide the entire amount without selling off the company. But she should be able to raise half of it by selling her house and her car. Moving forward, she edged toward their conversation. A large man intervened.

"I'm sorry, ma'am, but Dr. King is tired and we're trying to keep him from being disturbed." She could tell it was a spiel he used often, a mixture of condescension and pity for another lovestruck woman trying to edge close enough to touch King.

"Would you please tell Dr. King that I want to make a substantial pledge toward the new offices?"

"Surely, ma'am. How much were you planning to give?" The light was poor at the edge of the stairs, but he could see that she was well dressed.

"One hundred twenty-five."

The man smiled. "That's a nice gift, but I'd hesitate to interrupt his conversation with Mr. Loeb and Reverend Abernathy for that. You understand, don't you?"

She shook her head. "No—one hundred twenty-five thousand."

The man gulped, took her arm, and steered her to the center of the group. As she passed, she saw Coretta King scowl.

"Dr. King, this lady has a mighty fine pledge to offer."

King turned to her, his face serene, and smiled. "Why I know you, you're Saundra Marshall, the lady who has brought us funds from California and helped during the boycott." He turned and in that warm melodious baritone crooned, "Coretta, this is Saundra Marshall—her husband flew us to Washington in that lovely airplane."

Mrs. King managed a small smile. Saundra realized that given all the funds she'd brought to him, King should have known her, but was flattered all the same.

"Dr. King, I believe I can pledge one hundred twenty-five thousand dollars; I don't have it in cash, I'll have to sell some things, but I can give it to you in a month or two, I'm sure."

His warm eyes were penetrating, comforting. "I've noticed you in the audience, both days, taking notes." His hand touched her arm and she felt a current flow. "You won't be depriving yourself, now, will you? That's a great deal of money. And what will your husband say? John, isn't it? John the Pilot."

Behind him Alan grinned, as if he'd thought of something bawdy to say and was restraining himself.

"No, he backs you strongly, too."

"Then thank you, you've made a difference. I won't forget it."

Little Rock, Arkansas/August 17, 1957

Stan Coleman had not had much to laugh about in the preceding months; he stood at the doorway of the decrepit Twin Beech, chortling with pleasure.

"Fitz, you're a sight for sore eyes. Where the hell have you been, what have you been doing? And where the hell did you get this dog?"

Fitzpatrick, balding and haggard-looking, his flight suit stained with too much sweat and too many sandwiches en route, eased his way out of the oval entrance. "After our unscheduled departure from Frederick, I went into the freight business with a couple of guys. We bought two C-47s and two C-45s. Trouble was there were five hundred other guys out there trying to do the same thing. When we ran out of rent money, we divvied up the airplanes. I flew down to see if you had anything I could do here."

"Hell yes, man, the governor's special liaison officer to the Arkansas National Guard and Air National Guard deserves his own plane and pilot—you're the man."

"Think they'll let me back in the service? They weren't too happy when I left."

"Don't sweat it—the governor's word is law, and he'll be proud to bring you on. You can fly him around, too."

Fitz pulled two B-4 bags out of the doorway. "Stan, this airplane and these two bags are all I got in the world. You're going to have to advance me some dough and find a place I can hangar this dude."

"No sweat, we'll put it in the Air Guard hangar here, get them to clean it up. Does it need any maintenance?"

"The radios are shot, and the engines need top overhauls."

"No sweat, little buddy. Goddamn, it's good to have someone to talk to in this crazy cracker town. We'll have a blast."

Fitz arched his back, stretching his arms. "Sounds good, Stan, but no more double-entry bookkeeping, huh? I got a bellyful of that at Frederick."

"Fitz, old man, that was nothing; wait till you see what we got cooking here. You're going to love it."

Ten days later both Fitz and the C-45 had undergone a transformation. He was outfitted in a lieutenant colonel's uniform, complete with the aiguillette of a general's personal aide, and quartered in renovated farm building less than a mile from the hangar where his Beechcraft had been completely overhauled and painted.

"Stan, you guys are miracle workers. New fabric, new instrument panel, more radios than RCA—you've really made something out of this dude. But is it legal to have it painted like it was a real Guard airplane?"

"It *is* a real Guard airplane, until you decide to leave, anyway. But I'm not going to let you do that. We've got a crisis coming, and I'll want to use this bird as an aerial command post. That's why I've got so many radios—need to talk to the Guard, the Air Guard, the police, the Klan, everybody."

"You think the colored people are going to cause trouble?"

"They better, we're counting on it. Let me rephrase that. Yes, the niggers are going to cause trouble, and we're going to stop them."

14

Salinas, California/September 7, 1957

The three men shared the newspaper with its headlines about the evolving school crisis in Little Rock—the governor turning the schoolchildren away with the National Guard; the mobs chanting hatred at the students, pretty little kids, all nine of them.

Marshall scowled. "I sure don't like my wife being down there."

Hadley looked at him sourly. "You don't like it, why don't you yank her back here?"

"For Christ's sake, Hadley, butt out! John's got enough on his mind without you giving him your cockamamie opinions."

Hadley glowered at Bandfield and said, "Well, how cockamamie is this? Is this a good time for us to go on our Southern tour with John here being a Negro? Don't you think it will be dangerous for him? And bad for business besides?"

Bandfield looked at his old friend, appalled. Hadley had embarrassed him in a hundred places over the years, with customers and bosses, women and children, friend and foe; he'd never made him feel as bad as he did at that moment.

He turned to Marshall. "Bones, I'm sorry. Hadley gets carried away. He doesn't mean anything."

Marshall shook his head. "Hell, I know that. Hadley hasn't got a mean bone in his body, nor a tactful one. He's just trying to figure out what's best for all of us, and maybe he's right. What's our route?"

Bandfield pulled out a folded paper, scanned it, and read, "Phoenix, then Albuquerque, Dallas, Shreveport, Montgomery, Atlanta, Nashville, and Memphis. If we can make any other appointments along the way, we will."

"Well, we'll be okay probably till we get to Shreveport. I've been into Love Field at Dallas lots of times; they know me there, it won't be a problem. But from Shreveport on, they're not likely to take kindly to me with what's going on in Little Rock. Why don't you go on without me?"

Roget, abashed, said, "Hell, you're our chief water-bombardier. Maybe we just ought to cancel."

Bandfield waved his arms. "The hell we will. We've got half a million dollars tied up in inventory; if we don't sell a few airplanes this trip, we'll have to drop the whole water-bomber deal, and then where would Bones be?"

Marshall thought for a moment about his old comrade in arms, Jellybutt Walker, and how he used to get him out of scrapes at Tuskegee. Aware that Roget now felt bad, he nodded. "Listen, I've been down in Dixie before, at flight school, and lately, flying the big-wig Blacks around. I know how to shuffle and drink out of the right fountains, don't worry about me."

Hadley grinned, relieved at the way things had turned out. "Well, we got the barrels of dye all loaded, the airplanes are ready. What the hell are we waiting for?"

"Okay, we'll launch tomorrow."

. . .

Frederick Air Force Base, California/ September 17, 1957

The clouds were slung like a hammock between the mountain ranges, dark but unthreatening, perfect for what he had to do. Josten had drawn the shades on the front windows and now turned to look at her. Even with her hair short she was as beautiful as always. Lyra was graying slightly; that appealed to him, made her more vulnerable. She stood with her long tapering hands on Ulrich's shoulders. His son's shoulders. Their son.

Lyra forced herself to look him in the eyes, trying not to show fear or disgust at his livid scars, more prominent where his uninjured flesh had tanned. Yet his manner was terrifying, as anxious and snappish as a birthing wolf.

"Please don't do this, Helmut, don't ruin everything for me, for the children, for yourself. What we had was wonderful, but it's over. There are the children to think about. Taking us is insane."

He jumped at every sound, moving constantly, his eyes gleaming like a guard dog's in their death-cave sockets, his tiny pupils tight discs of black. It was strange to see him dressed in the coarse denim overalls of a working man, a checkered handkerchief hanging from one pocket. She remembered him as he'd been, so many years ago, in his handsome Luftwaffe uniform, young, full of promise.

"Lyra, everything was ruined for me—ruined for us—when you deserted me with my son."

He spoke conversationally, as if he did not have his revolver pointed at Ulrich's head. Ulrich was near tears, his eyes wide.

"If you do as I tell you, no one will be harmed in the slightest. You will have a little vacation, that's all. At the end of it, I hope you'll want to stay with me. If you don't, you'll be free to leave; I'll arrange for you to fly back."

He ruffled Ulrich's hair with the barrel of the Smith & Wesson. "You're a fine big boy for thirteen, Ulrich. Your father's proud of you."

Ulrich looked at his mother, rolled his eyes and shrugged.

Lyra said, "We won't go. I can't leave my Gracie."

"Gracie is welcome to come with us." He spoke of her as if she were an awkward stranger who'd invited herself to dinner. "But we must go now. If you don't come, at once, I'll kill all of us here— Gracie, too—in the next minute."

Ulrich fought back tears and Lyra's stomach convulsed. She threw up, quickly turning away to avoid soiling Ulrich.

"Clean yourself up, and then we're leaving. Don't try to do anything heroic."

He stood guarding her as she washed. She peered at him in the mirror, realizing that all her fears had materialized, that it was happening just as she feared. Helmut had come for her, as he always said he would, and he was totally insane. His eyes told her that he would kill them all if she refused. She had to go along with him, and wait for something to happen, some way to get word to someone for help. It was the nightmare of war all over again, the bombing, the train, the smell of death.

As always, their neighborhood was quiet; in the entire street, only one house had a light on. Josten herded them into the Pontiac he had rented and drove down Route 99 fifteen miles to where the bus was parked with the Cadillac. He'd selected three Storm Klanners, tough young guards from the local state prison, to come along, swearing them to secrecy, telling them that they were going to foil a Communist plot. They had been swept up by the glamour of it, ex-farmboys from Arkansas on a secret mission with this godlike creature, this Klan-Fuehrer. It was the high point of their lives and they willingly did everything he asked without question, enjoying the trip, relishing the baloney sandwiches they ate as they drove as much as they did the quick meals in the Stuckeys. There was satisfaction in obeying Josten's quick, harsh orders as they saw things they'd never dreamed of seeing in Pine Bluff.

With Lyra and the children secure in the living compartment of the bus, they drove cross-country without stopping, alternating drivers to keep pushing on. Josten hated to be gone during the building turmoil in Little Rock, but Coleman had told him that the showdown would not happen until at least the 23rd. It was the crisis that had made him decide to act; he might not have another chance. Riley being overseas made it mandatory to act.

Forty-eight hours after they'd left Frederick, they were in the refuge of the Klaven outside of Pine Bluff. He had his Lyra back at last.

Montgomery, Alabama/September 19, 1957

"I told you we should have brought some mechanics along."

Hadley Roget was grumbling as they buttoned up the cowling on the TBM. It was the third straight day that they'd had to change the front row of plugs, and they were getting sick of it. They had just sprawled in the shade under the wing when the line boy came running up. "You Mr. Bandfield? Your wife's on the line in the ops shack; she says it's urgent!"

Bandfield ran to the edge of the flight line with the customary parental adrenalin rush of images of children hurt in car wrecks. George already had one speeding ticket, and Bandy was pretty sure he was doing some beer drinking, too. Gasping, he grabbed the phone. "What is it, Patty?"

"Something's happened to Lyra and the children. They're gone. It's just like she always said."

The relief that swept through him that his kids weren't in a wreck was immediately replaced by concern for Lyra. "Where's Bear?"

"He's on his way back from England, should be here in a little while. I'm sure it's her first husband; she always said he'd come after her."

"Did you tell the police that?"

"Yes, the neighbors had told them, too. From the newspapers on the porch, they figure she's been gone for two days."

"For Christ's sake, didn't anybody notice?"

"No; the next-door neighbor, Polly, you remember her, she thought Lyra was visiting us. That's how I found out, she called to check."

"Anything I can do?"

"No. Bear will want to talk to you, I know. Where will you be?"

"Depends on when he gets back. They cancelled us out in Atlanta, so we'll go straight to Memphis tomorrow, be there a couple of days. We're not having much luck—the government's practically giving surplus airplanes away, and the contractors are converting them themselves. But you can reach me at Beeler Aviation there, that's where we'll get our service. Be staying at the nearest Holiday Inn. I'll call you as soon as we get there."

"Bandy, do you think he'll hurt her?"

"If he's nutty enough to kidnap her and the children, he's apt to do anything. Riley knew him back during the airlift, said he was mean and crazy then. God help them."

Patty simply repeated, "God help them," and they hung up.

Back at the airplane he recapped what had happened. "When Riley calls me, I'll have to respond, no matter what. Until then, I suggest we go ahead with our demonstrations."

"Might as well, Bandy. This is the last hurrah; if we don't sell any on this trip, I'm going to dump these for whatever I can get."

"You can't beat the government prices if they're giving them away for a few hundred apiece."

"Yeah, but the operators don't know how much it costs to convert them, and to get them reliable. They'll spend more doing it themselves than if they bought from us. But the thing that bugs me is the Catalina. It's different; the scoopers are working good. Why don't nobody like it?"

Marshall tried to ease the tension. "Don't sweat it, Hadley. Its time will come. If not, we can just take the wings off, hang an outboard on the back, and use it as a houseboat."

Little Rock, Arkansas/September 20, 1957

As much as he had hated the clerical work he had done in Chicago, he could not shake the habit, and Weissman spent almost every morning in the Little Rock public library going over the newspapers of the past two years, gleaning information bit by bit from it about the Klan and, by inference, about Josten. It was easy to see how tension had been building, how feelings were hardening. The letters to the editor columns two years before had rarely mentioned racial topics; now more than half dealt with the issue of race. Some made him wince, for they called for concentration camps for the Negroes as a solution.

There were a number of routine references to Klan meetings and to the half-dozen cross burnings that had occurred in the state. But the past few months showed something else that was almost certainly Klan activity, although the Klan was never alluded to in connection with the incidents. There had been a series of confrontations between whites and Negroes—fistfights, traffic accidents, shovings, all petty things, but all with an unusual twist. The Negroes seemed to come out on top in almost every case, and there were no arrests. He thought he understood the pattern, but he was not certain.

It surprised him how the governor was handling the crisis—fulminating to his own constituency as if he were a new Jefferson Davis, but then apparently delighted to be seen meeting with the President, shaking hands with Negro reporters, grinning into the cameras. And Eisenhower himself! For a man with a good German name he certainly vacillated.

The afternoons were equally profitable and more enjoyable for Weissman. After an early lunch—he skipped breakfast, unable to handle the standard Little Rock fare of greasy eggs, bacon, and grits—he would drive to the hills surrounding Pine Bluff. He'd found an abandoned barn and parked inside, carefully replacing the broken door so that his car wasn't visible from the road. Then a stiff climb straight up over the hill behind the barn let him infiltrate the Klan compound. The lack of security was pathetic; there were always guards at the main gate, and a fence ran around most of the compound, but there was nothing to keep a determined visitor out. Most of the Klan members worked during the day. During the week there wasn't much activity until after six in the evening. Weissman found a spot in a dense grove of pines only a hundred yards from his quarry. He had already seen Josten twice, both times entering a large converted bus that, judging by the array of antennae, served him as both a home and headquarters.

The problem was that it was a difficult shot, even if he was now, after all his practice, truly worthy of being called Weissman the Marksman. He'd brought a special hunting rifle and telescopic sight with him. But Josten inevitably drove up to the bus in his car, parked it, and hopped the few short steps to the bus. He was vulnerable for a brief interval as he unlocked the door, but it only took him a moment, and a tree limb impeded Weissman's view. He considered chancing a shot through the car's windshield as it drove up, but was reluctant to do so—if he missed, Josten would be too wary, and he'd never have another chance—or be able to face them back in Chicago.

It was evident that there was someone important inside the bus, for Josten had on both occasions brought presents of some sort—flowers, boxes with ribbons. It was as if he had Rapunzel in there, with her long hair. Who could it be? His lover?

He found the answer and a great deal more information by accident when he went through the contents of the trash barrel outside the bus that night. Waiting until eleven, he had crept to the barrel and rifled through it, packing the smaller pieces of paper inside his coat, leaving the boxes and wrappings. When he got back to the car, he used his flashlight to see that he had two basic kinds of documents: receipts and draft orders for the Klan. Josten seemed to be calling it the Storm Klan.

"Wonder where he got that from?" Weissman thought, as he scanned the receipts first—clothes, makeup, toys, even some lingerie. Josten was clearly buying for a woman and two children. And he was planning, in great detail, a riot for the morning of September 23rd, a joint mission between the "Storm Klan" and the National guard. Interesting! The details were there, some things left unspecified, the names of some of the Storm Klan units left blank, but it was evident that there was going to be combined action against the Negroes. In Germany, they called it a pogrom. What was it here? A lynching party?

. . .

Saundra weltered in discontent. Here she was in the thick of things, and the leadership she had supported with virtually her entire wealth was nowhere to be seen. Instead, it was the NAACP leading the fight, and doing it well. She found herself helping the people Dr. King called reactionary and too tied in with big business. She was beginning to wonder if Fred Peterson had not been right all along.

She turned to her hostess, Lucy Tate, whose stepdaughter was one of the nine students being kept from entering Central High School by the National Guard. The house was tiny, two rooms; they shared a bathroom with the family next door. Yet Lucy kept it spotless, the worn furniture dusted and polished, pictures of family in frames on the wall. It was much like the home Saundra's mother had kept for her years ago, except Lucy exuded a cheerful hopefulness her poor mother had totally lacked.

"Lucy, what happens now that the governor has pulled the National Guard out?"

The older woman looked at her quizzically. This pretty woman from the West was mighty generous with her money, but she didn't seem to have a hold on things. It was as if she were *playing* believer instead of *being* one.

"Lordy, I don't know. In a way I was happy they was there, they kept the mob happy by keeping the children out. Now, widdem gone, who knows, who knows."

Lucy poured coffee into thick china mugs, cracked from long years of restaurant use. She looked at Saundra closely, forgetting her own problems for the moment. "You're mighty unhappy; want to tell me about it?"

Saundra drew her legs up under her on the tired old couch, its plaid upholstery covered with a cottonball-tufted throw. "I'm not sure what I'm supposed to do here. I thought the Southern Christian Leadership Conference would be in the forefront of the fight."

Lucy took out a package of cigarettes, looked at them wistfully, and put them away. "I'm giving up smoking till my stepdaughter is enrolled." Reaching out, she gently took Saundra's hand. "Honey, this business doesn't suit Dr. King's style; he reckons he's better off to stay in the background. First of all, this here's a legal fight, and that's what the N Double A does best. But it's a fight that could get bloody in the next minute, and that's not for the good doctor." Her brow furrowed and she went on, "He's smart, because they's things going on I don't like; the white folks are getting ready to trick us somehow."

"Why do you say that?"

"Little things. They been baiting us for a few months now, dangling things out, letting us win a few little battles. I 'spect we'll see why soon. But Dr. King wants to be the only one in the spotlight; he can't do that here, not wiffout crowding the chillun out."

Saundra sipped her coffee, knowing that much of her discontent was in being sent here without a real job to do; she had contributed a large sum of money, probably larger than anyone else in the movement—she expected to be in Dr. King's outer circle, at least, if not at his side. Instead she was operating almost on her own, even disbursing her money to the NAACP people.

"Honey, you're not setting your cap for Martin Luther King, is you?"

Lucy's tone was kindly, but firmly inquisitive. She repeated, "Is you?" and Saundra felt compelled to answer truthfully.

"I think maybe I am—I know I shouldn't, but I can't help myself."

Lucy Tate locked her arms across her huge bosom, shaking her head and groaning. "Uh-uh, you listen to me, child. He's a mighty powerful man, and he's got a mighty powerful way with women. Lots of women want to be his woman. But he's got a mission, and no woman is going to stop that. You married, ain't you?"

Nodding, Saundra realized that Lucy was a warrior, engaged in the fight; she had to be listened to.

Relentless, Lucy went on. "You got you a good man, he's working hard, doing things, don't you go fooling around eyeing Dr. King. Dr. King, he's got a mission—and it ain't you."

Saundra hung her head, wondering if she could be as totally foolish, as totally misguided as she felt at that moment.

Fitzpatrick had just finished installing another UHF radio set in his now-pristine C-45. With the whirlwind energy a military outfit always throws into an illegal but worthwhile project, the National Guard crew had changed the engines, painted the plane in Air Guard colors, reupholstered the inside in a soft gray leather the governor liked, and even painted the tires like whitewalls.

"This thing's got more radios on it than the *Columbine.*"

"That's exactly right; when the governor visited Eisenhower in Newport last week, Ike told him to get all his airplanes outfitted with radios so he could be reached at all times."

"How long is this school business going to go on?"

"Until the niggers stop trying to integrate, simple as that. But I think we're going to see some action in the next day or two."

"That stupid Klan business?"

"It's not so stupid, Fitz. These guys aren't like the guys in sheets you saw in the old newsreels. I hate to say it, but Josten has them better trained, better disciplined than the Guard."

"What the hell's going to happen?"

"You be at the house tonight at nine o'clock sharp. We're having a briefing on the next three days' activities. You're going to see some real action."

Dixon and Ruddick were worried about the governor. The meeting with Eisenhower had gone badly, with the President accusing him of being the first man to use the armed forces of the state to oppose the federal government since the Civil War. The governor had come back raving about a federal plot to have him dragged off in chains and put in jail.

Now the two of them were waiting for Josten to arrive. Ruddick didn't want to believe the rumors he'd heard from Baker that Josten had somehow gone across the country and kidnapped his wife and was holding her at the Pine Bluff Klaven—and that three of the young Storm Klanners had disappeared. If it was true, Josten would have to go, and soon—but it couldn't be until after the showdown.

He felt more comfortable with the intelligence his own people had gathered. For a few dollars, he had been able to get loyal coloreds to go to where the Negroes were meeting, nose around and see what was happening. There was some surprising news—one of the women leaders, who was supposed to be passing out lots of money, was named Marshall and was married to a Negro pilot back west. It had to be the same person; there wouldn't be two nigger pilots named Marshall. He was the man who'd caused the trouble in Cleveland, right before Bob was killed, who'd made Bob so mad that he raced when he shouldn't have. Now he had to find out if the man was here, too, with her, and where they were living. When the balloon went up, he just might be able to get some revenge.

Josten came in, eyes sparkling, sweating, wringing his hands. Ruddick surveyed the room; of the people there, only Ginny and this new man, Fitzpatrick, seemed to sense that anything was wrong. The rest, including Stupid Stan, as he'd come to call him privately, seemed as excited as if they were at a high school prep rally.

Ginny had supplied Dixon Price with a drink. He gulped it down, signaled for another, and said, "We're going to have to implement our plan on the morning of the twenty-third. The governor's going to distance himself by going to a conference at Sea Island. He wants everything to happen while he's gone. He's got to have some space to maneuver if things go wrong."

Price looked around belligerently, as if someone might question him; instead he got a series of nods, for it made sense.

"Remember, we want a big riot, lots of heads broken, white and black. But the governor wants me to control how it goes." He turned to Coleman. "Stan, have you got a radio that can reach him at Sea Island?"

"Is he going down in his C-47?"

"Plans to."

"Fine. We have ARC-21 radios in the C-45 now. We can talk to him direct, if he's in the airplane, or his pilots can relay what we say by phone. Will that do?"

"I'll check with him. I want you and Colonel Josten here airborne, over the scene, so that you can stop it if things get too rough. I'll be on board with you, so I can talk to the governor."

Josten interjected. "Things might not get rough enough."

Price grinned, a rare sight. "You're right, that may be the main problem, if they don't resist. In any event, we've got to have enough blood shed to let the governor come back, declare martial law, and shut down the schools if he has to."

Ruddick resented Price telling Josten to be in the airplane—his rightful position. "I was planning to be in the airplane, Dixon."

His old friend shook his head. "No, Milo, I want you on the ground, with your eyes on things close up. You know our people better than anyone, and you may have to have some of them rough up some white people, too, just to get the blood."

Appeased, Ruddick said, "Well, I've got a panel truck fitted out with radios. You and I can stay in touch."

Ruddick felt the new plan was satisfactory, much like they'd been thinking about all along. But somehow he'd hoped to have better people to execute it with. Josten had been a jewel until the past few weeks. He'd become progressively more preoccupied, more fatalistic. What would he be like when the chips were down? And Stan . . . the man was at least consistent: he never failed to disappoint.

Coleman had a large map of the city pinned to the wall and a telescoping aluminum pointer that he toyed with constantly, pulling it in and out. Now he tapped the map authoritatively.

"Colonel Josten, please feel free to jump in at any time. We've simplified the plan since our last meeting. It was just too dangerous to have the Klan and the Guard facing each other, with the niggers in between. We are going to form up here"—he tapped a large red A located just northwest of Adams Field, the commercial airport—"this is the old football field on the edge of darkytown, where the Storm Klanners and the Klan will muster.

"When the signal is given, the men will march out, going from house to house, pulling our Negro brothers out into the street. We won't hurt any of the women or children, unless they make us—some of those black bitches can be mean—and we'll do the minimum amount of property damage. We'll march these six blocks"—he tapped them off with his pointer—"where there will be four companies of the Guard, in uniform, to control things, keep them from getting out of hand. Then the Klan will disperse."

"What do you think, Dixon?" Ruddick asked.

He was obviously relieved. "It's a much better plan than before, much simpler. Let's have it look like a civil uprising, the Klan leading it, the citizens following. Exactly when will it happen?"

"The troops and the Klan will be transported in civilian trucks to the area at six-thirty in the morning; they'll move out at seven, and should be finished by eight. The trucks will pick them up here." His pointer tapped a big blue B.

Plainly pleased with himself, Coleman asked, "Any questions? I'll be overhead, in the new airplane"—he turned and smiled at Fitzpatrick—"that my friend has provided for us."

There were no questions, but Ruddick had reservations about the leaders, Josten and Coleman. But it was too late now. No one but Ruddick noticed that Coleman had kept tapping the map with his pointer at the spot where Nathan lived, Marny's house, halfway down the first block the Storm Klanners were going to invade. His eyes met with Coleman's in agreement. This would be the time to silence Nathan for good.

Pine Bluff, Arkansas/September 21, 1957

Lyra looked at the hands of the electric clock, sweeping endlessly around. It was past nine, and Helmut had not returned.

She had long since ceased weeping; now she was totally focused on surviving, day by day, waiting until something happened that could free her children, if not herself.

Helmut's planning had been excellent, real German General Staff–caliber work. The bus was as comfortable as a hotel room, but there was not a single thing in it that she could use for a weapon, not a soda bottle to break, not even a pencil to jam in his eye.

She had steeled herself to make him welcome when he came "home," enduring his kisses and the caresses of his scarred hands, which felt like the scales of a fish being scrubbed across her. She felt toward him exactly as she'd felt toward Goebbels so many years before—a sense of utter revulsion that she had to mask, to keep under control. She talked to him constantly about how things were when they were young, trying to instill some sense of remorse in him.

Despite his terrible wounds, she felt no pity for him, this animal who had once been her lover. If she could have killed him with a thought, he would have been long dead. But she knew that keeping up his hopes that she might return to him was essential; the instant he realized that it was impossible would be her death warrant, and the children's, too.

Her days as a prisoner in Germany helped her endure. And it was more comfortable here, with plenty of food and water. He was never brutal with her physically and had brought her to see the children twice. Ulrich was behaving like a champion; he understood the situation perfectly, and he was bearing up. Gracie, at four, was too young to understand; she obviously missed her mother terribly but was taking her stiff-upper-lip cue from Ulrich.

Josten had introduced her as his wife to the slovenly woman, Elsie. She seemed to be in a daze, but was genuinely taken with the children, who did not appear to be frightened of her. Now she seemed to offer the only chance for help. If Elsie became aware that Helmut was going to kill them, she might help them escape, or at least go to the police. But Helmut was always along, and Elsie seemed—or pretended—to believe that Lyra and the children were there voluntarily, trying to work out a domestic problem. In the meantime, she was spoiling the two children dreadfully.

There was a timid scratching at the door. It couldn't be Helmut, who had the only keys. She waited, unable to open the door from the inside, wondering if it were someone who might help.

Slowly a piece of folded white paper threaded itself through the crack at the bottom of the door. She picked it up and read: "This is a friend. I'll try to get help. Knock on the door three times if you are Josten's wife—former wife. Destroy this note."

She read it again, wondering if it could be Helmut trying to trick her. It didn't matter, she had to take the chance. She knocked on the door three times. There was nothing but silence.

An hour later, puffing as he sat in his car, Erich Weissman contemplated his options. If he called in the FBI, he would never get a shot at Josten. And if the FBI was not careful, Josten might shoot the woman before they took him. There was really no need for the FBI; if he killed Josten, no one else would intervene, except perhaps the big man the children were living with.

Yet if he waited too long, he might not get a shot at all, and Josten might kill this woman anyway. There had to be another way—if he could get some help, just one or two persons. He fumbled in his crowded briefcase and pulled out the file he'd brought from Chicago on Josten. He read through it again, looking for a note he'd scribbled in the margin of the paragraph on Josten's former wife. Squinting under the Plymouth's dim dome light he made out "Married to Colonel Bayard Riley. Living at Frederick Air Force Base."

Frederick Air Force Base, California/ September 22, 1957

Exhausted, Riley sat on the couch in his living room, desperate with fear, as the team investigators from the OSI and the FBI went over his home. He'd been in the air in his B-47, en route to Sidi Slimane, when the call came through that his wife was missing.

SAC headquarters had done the mission planning, and he'd turned to fly nonstop back to Frederick, refueling three times on the way.

His family had been missing three days before anyone checked on them; he told the investigators that it must have been Helmut Josten. They didn't seem convinced, but assured him that they would find his family.

A young major came in, smooth-cheeked, deferential; he asked Riley if he could come down to the command post to get an important message that needed an immediate response. He left, and in the car the major said, "It's a phone call about your wife, sir, but the caller specifically asked that you be the only one informed."

At the command post, Riley raced down the stairs, past the guards, into the familiar room filled with maps, telephones, and plotting tables. They had the phone ready, a message pad on the desk. The major handed him the receiver, saying, "The guy was calling from a phone booth, and running out of change. We had to call him back, so we know he's in Little Rock. He's on the line, he'll talk only to you, and he told us not to tell anyone else."

"This is Colonel Riley."

"I knew you long ago in Israel. You were Moshe Niv; I am Erich Weissman."

Bone-tired, head pounding from his sixteen-hour flight, Riley hardly recognized the names at first. Then he said, "Weissman! The mechanic."

"Now Weissman the Assassin, as I promised you. I've located your wife and children. They are alive but in great danger. Your wife's first husband, Josten, has them, and he is crazy."

Riley mumbled, "I knew it."

Weissman's voice was stern, emphatic. "Do not tell anyone else about this; Josten will kill her if the FBI comes. We don't need the FBI, all we need to do is kill Josten."

"What about the children—aren't they *with* Lyra?"

"Yes. They are all being held in a converted bus. But I don't think they will be in danger if we kill Josten. Once he is gone, no one else will care. I don't think many people are even aware that he's kidnapped them."

Riley bit his lip, trying to clear his head. Hell, Weissman was the man on the spot, he knew where they were.

"All right, I'll leave for Little Rock right away. I won't tell anyone. How will I find you?"

"When will you be here?"

Riley's eyes blurred as he looked at the big Breitling chronograph on his wrist. He forced himself to think—two hours to get an airplane ready, four hours en route. "I'll be there six hours from now."

"I'll be outside the main gate at Little Rock Air Force Base in a green Plymouth sedan. Bring two sidearms and a big crowbar—really big. We may have to tear the door off the hinges, or go in through the air-conditioning vent. But I hope we can just take the keys after we kill Josten."

Riley turned to his deputy. "Bob, will you get a crew and B-47 prepared to launch as soon as possible? We'll be landing at Little Rock—I'll go in the crawlway and try to get some sleep."

"Boss, you forget, all your B-47s are in England except the one you flew in on, and it's down for parts. But I've got a KC-135 tanker ready to scramble—we can send it."

"Even better. And Bob, don't tell anybody about it, nobody, not the FBI, no one! Lyra's life depends on it. Nobody is to know I'm on board, not even after takeoff!"

The deputy wing commander turned to leave, and Riley caught his arm. "One second. Get a hold of Frank Bandfield—he's somewhere in the South, I think, his wife will know. Get us linked up by phone if you can get him before I go, or by radio to the KC-135. If you can't get us in touch, tell him to go to Little Rock Air Force Base as soon as possible; phone ahead and get him permission to land there."

Pine Bluff, Arkansas/May 22, 1957

Helmut sat on the edge of the bed, weeping. Lyra lay at his side, pretending to be asleep. His eyes swept over her lovely body, still young and firm despite all she had been through. To think that that swine Riley had possessed her, that she responded to him, that they had conceived a child! It was an abomination. If she and Riley were reunited . . . the thought drove a spike through his heart. It must never happen.

Josten had known all along how improbable it was that she would respond to him, yet he had to take the chance. Now it was over; she had pretended to warm to him yesterday, but he knew her too well.

He'd thought by being gentle with her, playing some records of old German songs, he might create the mood. He even had some Henkell champagne that he'd gotten in New York.

Yet she could not conceal her shudder, her involuntary movement away from him even as he pressed against her. It hurt him deeply. When he kissed her, he felt the withdrawal, the intake of her breath. It ruined things—he could not get an erection, no matter what he did, not even when she pretended, pathetically enough, to respond to him.

So it was over. Tomorrow there would be the showdown in town. He would come back, and they could all have dinner together, Lyra and the children. Then he would end it.

Memphis, Tennessee/September 22, 1957

The Beeler Aviation office had the usual fixed-base operator's collection of Salvation Army desks, tattered calendars, and glass cases liberally studded with dead flies. In the part designated as the pilot's lounge, Bandfield sat on the edge of the battered sleep-sofa, an old-fashioned two-piece phone in his hands. He waved for silence. "Go ahead, Patty."

"I got a message from Bear Riley. He's going to Little Rock, thinks that Josten has Lyra and the children somewhere near there. He wants you to meet him there, at the Air Force base. He's got clearance for you to land."

"I'll be there, but what for? Isn't the FBI on the job?"

"I guess he can't tell them for some reason. Anyway, he wants you to be there, and not to tell anyone. But you be careful!"

"It sounds screwy, but of course we'll go. We might as well, we're sure not selling any airplanes."

"Call me as often as you can, keep me posted."

He relayed the news to Roget and Marshall, who said, "Sounds strange, Bandy, what can you do that the cops can't?"

"I don't know, but we'll find out."

Roget slipped his arm around Marshall's shoulders. "Bandy here knows Josten from the war; he may be able to figure out what he's thinking."

Marshall rubbed his fist in his palm. "Maybe I'll go into town and see Saundra."

Roget blew up. "See her? See her? You're a damn fool if you don't go into Little Rock, find her, and throw her over your shoulder. That's what the hell she wants; she's running around pretending to be looking for a cause, when all she wants is for you to make her do what she wants to do."

Marshall raised his hands as if to protect himself from the words.

"Listen, boy"—Roget had no idea that the word *boy* was insulting—"I've heard you moaning about not being recognized as an ace. I've heard you bitch about not breaking the sound barrier. Neither one of them two things means a damn! The only important thing for you is your wife, and you ought to get up off your Black ass and go get her."

Marshall spun around and walked out; Roget started to follow but Bandfield grabbed his arm.

"Damn it, Hadley, are you crazy? You got no business talking to him like that."

"I ain't? I ain't? Goddamn it, he's my friend, too, and he knows I'm right. You wait and see, I'll rag his ass till he does what he wants to do!"

Bandfield shook his head. "Hadley, you're incorrigible, and someday somebody's going to slug you for lipping off. Now let's let him take the TBM down, and you and I'll take the Catalina. Give you two hotheads a chance to cool down."

Little Rock Air Force Base, Arkansas/ September 22, 1957

The Airdrome Officer parked them in the VIP positions outside the Operations Section, where a crowd of airmen had gathered to watch the TBM and the Catalina being serviced. Navy planes were un-usual on the base—obsolete Navy planes, painted bright orange, were worth seeing. Colonel Dick May, the base commander and an old friend from Bandfield's Omaha days, was on hand to greet him.

"Dick, do you have a KC-135 inbound from Frederick?"

"Yeah, he should be touching down in about an hour; has a Code Six on board."

The Code 6 would be Riley. Bandfield called Marshall and Roget over. "Look, I don't know how long we're going to be here, or what we're going to have to do, but we might as well use this stop if we can. There's a lot of forests around here, they must burn like every place else. Maybe we can arrange a demonstration flight tomorrow. Go ahead and get the tanks filled with water and dye. We don't need any fuel. Okay?"

Marshall put up his hand like a kid asking to leave the room. "Bandy, I'm glad to do that. But this old bastard has convinced me. In the morning, I'm going to go into town. I've got the address where she's staying, and I'm just going to walk right up to her and make her come back with me."

Roget punched him in the arm. "That's the way to talk, John."

Bandfield shrugged. "Fine. But let's see what Riley wants us to do first, then you go ahead with Saundra. Do you think she'd mind flying in the TBM or the Catalina?"

Marshall shook his head. "As Rhett would say, 'Frankly, I don't give a damn.' She's coming, and that's it."

Pine Bluff, Arkansas/September 23, 1957

Weissman was very unhappy that Riley had brought Bandfield along.

"They'll have a lot of guards tonight—too many people will make too much noise."

Riley had been able to get some sleep on the tanker flight in, and he was feeling hopeful. "Look, Bandfield's an old woodsman, a regular Indian. He won't make any noise, and we might need help."

Weissman had parked in the barn, and he made them wait until three A.M. before starting in. "We'll walk in and wait. When he comes out, we'll all shoot, then rush the bus and get the woman."

"Are the children inside?"

"I don't know. I haven't seen them. There's a trailer about a mile away, they might be there."

Riley shook his head. "Christ Almighty, this is no good. Even if we kill Josten and rescue Lyra, we still have to get the kids."

Weissman felt resentful—he'd brought this man here to rescue his wife, and he was being critical.

Bandfield spoke up for the first time. "Let's don't shoot Josten, then, just jump him when he comes out. He's crippled, he can't resist us. We'll make him take us to the kids."

Weissman was emphatic. "Absolutely not. I can't take a chance that he'll survive."

Riley turned to him with an expression that commanded belief. "Erich, I guarantee he won't survive. When we get my wife and kids, I'll kill him myself, I promise you."

The Israeli reluctantly agreed. At three they roused themselves to walk as quietly as they could in the cool September morning, their eyes accustomed to the dark but still stumbling over branches and logs. Bandfield thought of the old James Fenimore Cooper novels, where the Indians and the good guys could walk through the forest without making a twig crackle. As hard as they tried, as slow as they went, they sounded like a herd of spastic moose.

As they neared the encampment, Riley pressed his mouth against Weissman's ear. "Something's wrong. Everything is too quiet."

Suddenly Weissman stopped. They crouched down as he looked around, making sure he was in the right place.

"They're gone. The bus is gone."

Riley screamed, "You stupid shit! You've let them get away. Now what do we do?"

Weissman looked shattered.

Bandfield said, "Back to the car. They must have gone into Little Rock. It'll be light in a few hours; let's get airborne in the Catalina and spot the bus. When we do, we'll call the cops in on them."

Weissman, still hurt, moaned, "The cops? The cops are cooperating. This is a state-wide, city-wide effort. The cops are on Josten's side."

Little Rock, Arkansas/September 23, 1957

Lyra sat with her arms around her children, their tears a mixture of joy at being reunited and terror at their strange situation.

Helmut shuffled awkwardly through the door to introduce the two women formally, though they'd met briefly before. "Lyra, may I present Elsie McNaughton? She was kind enough to have taken care of the children for us."

It was bizarre; the woman was obviously as nervous as she was. "They're lovely children, Lyra—we enjoyed having them."

Lyra looked into her eyes and saw only confusion. Elsie, dressed in a pretty silk robe, wearing huge furry slippers, stretched her arms out as if to embrace her. Glancing at Josten, who shrugged and looked away, she put out her arms to Elsie.

They hugged and Elsie whispered "Don't open this now." Backing away she said, "I fixed some sandwiches for you—I know what Ulrich likes. Be careful."

Helmut walked Elsie to the door. Just before she left, Elsie took Helmut by the arm and spoke earnestly to him. When the door opened, Lyra could hear the rough sounds of someone disconnecting the bus's electrical and service fittings.

They drove them for almost an hour in what sounded like a convoy of trucks. Helmut stayed with them in the living quarters, very contrite, telling her that when the operation was over, she and the children would be free to leave.

She did not believe him for an instant; she couldn't take a chance on believing him. He would never let them go willingly.

The bus jolted to a stop in a rough field. The children slept but she could not; three hours passed slowly. At six o'clock the bus reverberated with the scurrying sounds of men getting ready to march. Someone knocked on the door and Helmut left without a word. She immediately looked inside the package Elsie had given her. There were four peanut butter and jelly sandwiches—and a small-caliber pearl-handled pistol. She checked it carefully, making sure that it was loaded and the safety was off. She told herself, You better let him come close to you before firing. No, just wait by the door, shoot as soon as you can, just keep pulling the trigger until he falls.

Lyra hated that the children would have to see it happen, but there was no alternative. Suddenly it seemed as if it were a dozen years ago, in that miserable train in Germany.

Her tears stopped, and she was ready.

At Adams Field, Fitzpatrick was busy strapping Dixon Price into the luxurious gray leather chair installed for the governor's use in the right rear of the C-45. Price was excited, his face flushed, and he already had a headset clamped to his ears, but he looked up sharply as Josten eased himself into the aisleway. The man was obviously at the breaking point, his eyes darting from side to side, the corners of his mouth dotted white with dried saliva. God, was this the mastermind behind their arrangements?

Josten painfully edged up the aisle to sit directly behind the pilots. He had not been in an aircraft in a dozen years, not since the crash in his precious jet fighter. As luxurious as it was, this crackerbox with wings was nothing compared to a jet, but it had all the radios he needed to communicate with Ruddick on the ground, and, if necessary, for Dixon to talk to the governor.

There would probably be precious little talking to do. The whole operation, scheduled to begin in thirty minutes, would either be over with according to plan, or it would have gotten completely out of control. In either case, nothing Ruddick or the governor could do or say would matter, and his own role in it would be ended, just as his life would be in a few hours.

Yet within twenty minutes after takeoff, the airman within him had to appreciate that Fitzpatrick was a master pilot. In the early morning light, the man had the C-45 steeply banked flying perfect pylon eights on the bus below where Lyra and the children waited, never varying a foot in altitude, the wingtip aligned with the bus as with a transit. Price sat quietly in the back, monitoring the radios, watching intently, and Coleman seemed to be enjoying himself like a child at a circus, talking to Ruddick periodically as the Klan formed up below them.

The Storm Klan, smart in their trooper uniforms, swinging their billy clubs, ceremonial daggers at their sides, were in one column; the regular Klan, dressed in white robes—white on white and embroidered for the more affluent ones and sheets for the poor— were in a second column. They all struggled to keep their pointed hats straight as they brandished their clubs and sticks.

Josten took out his Walther automatic and checked it carefully. He had suffered so long, and the last week had turned the bus into a Dr. Caligari's cabinet for him, with Lyra's inability to mask her revulsion. Lyra had almost fooled him for part of the previous day, when she had said that she would be willing to stay with him. But she had never really relaxed, never given herself to him so that he was able to make love to her. That would have made all the difference, brought her back to him as they used to be. He felt strangely indifferent to the children; Ulrich was a stranger, totally Americanized, not at all as he would have been if Lyra had not run off. He would dispose of them, too; it didn't matter anymore. It would be nice to take Riley with them, but that was impossible. When this mess below was over, no matter how it turned out, he would end their suffering.

Coleman leaned back and motioned to him through the oval entrance to the cockpit. He leaned forward and Stan pointed to an orange flying boat that had entered into a circle over the encampment.

"Colonel, there's a strange airplane flying out there, a Catalina. I'm going to call Little Rock tower and see who they are."

Inside the flying boat, Marshall listened to Coleman's voice, so familiar from Korea, asking the Little Rock tower about the "big orange Catalina." The last time he'd heard him had been on the day he was shot down, the day Coleman had stolen his two victories from him. The bastard.

The Black pilot mashed down on his transmitter button. "Coleman, it's me, Bones Marshall. You remember me, you stole two of my MiGs, you white bastard."

Marshall turned to Bandfield and mouthed the word, "Sorry." Roget, seated in the back in the right blister, said, "Watch your tongue there, young man. We ain't supposed to get in no fight, we're supposed to find that blue bus."

In the Beechcraft, Fitzpatrick turned and put his finger to his lips, even as Coleman indignantly called into his hand-held microphone, "Stop your foul language on the air, Marshall, and clear the area. I'm speaking as the on-site commander."

Price screamed through the intercom, "For Christ's sake, Stan, shut up. It's bad enough they know we're here, don't admit to being the commander."

Josten shook his head in disgust; at least Dixon had some brains even if Coleman did not. Not that it made any difference anymore; it was almost seven, and the troops would soon be moving out.

Pointing to the Catalina, Coleman leaned over to Fitzpatrick. "Look at that, they're leaving. Can you imagine Marshall turning up here?"

"Why not? You heard Ruddick saying Marshall's wife was in town with the protestors; he's probably come in to protect her."

Below Ruddick winced at the transmission as the two columns moved out, joining into a single unit. If Marshall was here, Bandfield was, too; they were thicker than thieves. Probably here to get Marshall's wife. They might be too late. He hoped so.

Six miles away, the PBY, groaning under its eight-hundred-gallon load of water and dye, dove at 140 mph, the controls taut and heavy, the wind drumming against the big canopy.

Marshall turned to his copilot. "Looks like the Klan is getting ready to march through the Black part of town, where Saundra's staying. Let's make a run in on these guys."

"Sure you want to do it, John? We could hurt somebody with this stuff."

Marshall's eyes flashed as he glanced over. "I sure as hell hope so, Bandfield—do you want them lynching the poor Blacks down there?"

Bandfield hesitated until he saw the first line of Klansmen leaving the park where they had assembled to march off toward the first homes. Then he yelled, "Okay, I've got the equipment set up—just tell me when and I'll pickle it off!"

"Just dump half the load—we might want to make two passes. I'll come in at a hundred and fifty feet, try to get as many of these white-sheeted motherfuckers as I can."

Bandfield looked at Marshall, surprised at the obscenity from a man who rarely cursed, thinking how strange it was to be at war again, here in the United States, flying this old clunker.

The orange wings of the PBY were cocked at forty-five degrees as Bones reefed it around, leveled off, and headed straight toward the marchers, now only half a block away from the shabby street where the Black section of the city began. Marshall thought quickly how much it was like Italy again, or Korea—the keening dive to deliver bombs against an enemy. And these were truly his enemy, his people's enemy. This time he didn't have to use two rivets to aim with; Roget had installed a little open sight on the nose of the big flying boat.

Waiting until the sight coincided with the head of the column, he counted "One, two," and called "Water away!" He reefed the suddenly lighter Catalina around in a climbing turn, toward the circling C-45 as the yellow blob of water hurtled onward, blossoming out to hit the street immediately in front of the marching Storm Klanners, cascading up in a spreading spray, then rolling like a chrome-yellow blimp across them, covering them like a sticky clinging sheet. The first few hundred Klansmen were blinded and gasping for breath, their uniforms drenched with yellow; as a man they turned to run through the troops behind them, most of them smeared with the yellow dye, but not soaked like the front rows. One Storm Klanner screamed, "The niggers are using mustard gas!" and in that moment the march through "darkytown" was over.

Roget crowed, "Direct hit, Bones, you nailed their asses with that one."

Josten had watched, unbelieving, as the huge globular mass had detached itself from the flying boat to saturate his troops. He felt the blood pounding in his head as he saw the work of months turn into a rout, his troops fleeing in a tide of yellow that surged through the white-clad forces behind them. Berserk, he jabbed his finger at the Catalina.

"Ram them, damn you, ram them!"

Fitz shook his head. "Are you crazy? I ain't ramming nobody."

Josten looked at him momentarily, aimed his pistol at Dixon, and said, "Ram them, or I'll shoot your friend here."

Coleman said, "Wait a minute, Helmut, don't be—"

Josten raised his pistol and fired, the bullet shattering Price's forehead and blowing the back of his skull away. Josten jammed the hot barrel of the smoking revolver in Coleman's neck, saying, "Now ram them, or I'll do the same to your friend."

Fitz, suddenly believing, nodded shocked agreement as Coleman stared back in horror at Price slumped in the seat, blood from the massive wound pouring across the gray leather. His body quivered once, his arms and legs drawing up in a defensive spasm. Then he was still.

Fitz began talking to Josten. "Look, we don't have to ram them. We're faster and more maneuverable than they are. I'll come in on top of them, and slice their rudder off with my prop. That will send them in, and we can land on one engine if we have to."

Josten, suddenly aware that Lyra would now live on without him, yelled, "All right, try it. If it doesn't work, then by God we'll ram them." He wondered if Riley could be on board the Catalina—he was a friend of the Negro, that would be perfect.

Marshall had the flying boat in a turn, surveying the yellow chaos below, when Bandfield called, "Bones, isn't that a blue bus in the middle of the park with the Klan guys?"

Below them, in a panel truck near the bus, Ruddick saw the tide of white and yellow surging toward him. He stepped out, waving his arms. "Stop, you're not hurt. Stop . . ." He grabbed the first man to reach him, pulled him to the truck. As the crowd cascaded around them, the truck an island in the sea of fleeing men, the Storm Klanner looked at him in panic, pulled the ceremonial dagger from its sheath, thrust it in Ruddick's side, and ran on. Pain rippling through him like sheet lightning, unable to understand the panic or the stabbing, Ruddick staggered from the truck and fell. The next wave of stampeding Klanners trampled him into the asphalt, their cleated boots crushing his aquiline nose, grinding his glasses into those forever cold blue eyes, stilling his melodious voice.

A thousand feet above Ruddick's broken body, the Catalina circled, as Roget called, "Hey, that little bug-smasher's making a run on us. We better get out of here."

Marshall yelled, "Bandy, you call Little Rock and tell them where the bus is. Hadley, keep your eye on the C-45. Think he's got any guns on that thing?"

Bandfield twisted in his seat. "Doubt it, but we'll find out in a minute, he's easing in above us. Shit, I can't see him any-more!"

Roget called out, "I got him, he's high on our starboard side, closing in. Looks like he's trying to ram us . . . gimme a steep left turn, John!"

Marshall rolled the heavy PBY to the left and the Beech fell away.

Roget snorted. "Hell, he's trying to chop off our rudder with his prop."

"Where are they?"

"He's edging back in, about four hundred feet out, maybe fifty feet low. Why don't you get down on the deck, keep him from getting underneath us where we can't see him."

Marshall's voice was strained. "Okay, I'll let down. Just keep telling me where he is, distance and direction."

Marshall dove below the trees, cutting along the river's surface, hauling back to clear the boats below as the C-45 edged closer.

"Big mistake, Bandy; I've boxed us in down here, should have stayed high."

The stench in the Beechcraft had become intolerable; in death Price had lost control of his bowels and bladder. Fitz turned to Josten. "I'm getting sick. Can't we just go in and land?"

Josten cocked the pistol and pressed it to Coleman's head. "Ram him or chop his rudder off, one or the other, or I'll kill Coleman, and then you."

Coleman's lips barely moved as he whispered, "Do what he says, Fitz."

The pilot had already pushed the props and mixture forward; now he came in with the throttles, easing in closer, level with the Catalina.

Roget watched him, caught up in the excitement, able to see clearly inside the cockpit.

"There's a guy in there with a pistol big as a house."

Exasperated, Marshall yelled into the intercom, "Quit the fucking play by play and tell me where they are."

"Now they've moved back about ten feet, fifty feet high and two hundred feet back."

Bandfield, neck sore from swiveling around trying to see the Beechcraft, said, "There's a bridge coming up, Bones, just chop the power and land this thing, put it down on the river. If they haven't got any guns, they won't be able to hurt us."

Marshall's face was contorted in a snarl. "Bullshit, I'm going to nail this guy. Bandy, on the count of three, hit the JATO bottles. Hadley, when we get above them, yell, and we'll dump the water."

The PBY was at maximum power, jets of black smoke streaming from its exhaust as the C-45 moved in closer, its prop edging toward the Catalina's rudder.

Marshall's voice was brittle as he called, "One, two, three!"

"JATO on!"

As soon as he felt the surge of the JATO rockets, Marshall hauled back on the control column, pulling the Catalina's nose up. In the C-45, Fitz instinctively chopped the power to avoid a collision as the flying boat sailed above them, climbing at a thirty-degree angle.

Roget yelled, "Water away!" and Bandfield toggled the switch.

The second four hundred gallons rolled out of the Catalina's belly in a billowing cloud, inundating the Beechcraft with a gleaming yellow smear that covered the windscreen in a glaucous haze.

Fitzpatrick keyed his mike. "Little Rock tower, this is Beech Five Five; we got an emergency here, I'm going to need a ground-controlled approach. I can't see a damn thing."

As he spoke he saw the manifold pressure flicker and the rpms surge on first the left, then the right, engine as their induction systems choked on the aluminized water. Power dropped away and he lowered the nose to keep his airspeed.

Josten pounded on the back of Fitz's seat. "Faster. Get them."

Fitzpatrick shook his head. "Shut the fuck up, you Kraut bastard."

Josten looked at Fitzpatrick with hatred and raised his pistol to fire just as the Beechcraft hit the center pylon of the bridge in a massive explosion.

In the circling Catalina, Roget called, "My God, he hit the bridge."

Marshall, exultant, pounded the cockpit coaming, yelling, "How did you like that, Coleman? That one was for Dave Menard."

Bandfield called Little Rock tower and told them about Lyra in the van. It took a half-dozen transmissions before the tower operator could believe what Bandy was saying and agree to get someone out of the blue bus.

At the moment of the Beechcraft impact, Weissman and Riley had worked their way to the field where Josten's bus was parked. The remnants of the Klan ignored them as they streamed toward their waiting trucks, anxious only to get out of there, to get rid of their yellowed uniforms and robes.

Weissman was carrying a massive five-foot-long crowbar. He handed it to Riley. "You pop the door open, and I'll go in first; if Josten's there I'll kill him."

They crept to the bus and waited. There was no sound from inside. Riley jammed the crowbar in the door by the lock and heaved; the door popped open and Weissman flung himself inside. Lyra's first bullet caught him in the shoulder, the second went into the walnut paneling above his head, just as Riley yelled, "Lyra, don't shoot, it's me."

Weissman slumped to the floor in pain, wondering where Josten was. He realized they all were safe when Riley and Lyra embraced, the two children clinging to Riley's legs. As his shoulder throbbed with pain, he thought, Weissman the Wounded—that's too much.

Bandfield had called ahead, and when the Catalina pulled into the line at Little Rock Air Force Base, the base commander and a raft of staff officers and Air Police were waiting.

Colonel May shook his hand and said, "Bandy, we just got a call from Colonel Riley; he said to tell you that he has his wife and children and is on the way to the base."

"Thank Christ—did he say they were okay?"

"He didn't say—but he was gibbering with happiness, so I guess they are. Now tell me about this crazy business with the Air Guard C-45."

Marshall grabbed Bandfield's arm. "Can we do it on the way in? I want to get Saundra."

"You go ahead—I'll wait here for Riley. Okay, Dick?"

May nodded and Marshall edged the driver out of the seat. He waved, then burned rubber as he left the flight line, wondering if Saundra would come with him.

The streets were deserted. Two hours before, they had been streaming with the Ku Klux Klan—now they were empty. Marshall felt strangely comforted that he was in an Air Force car; it might help if he encountered any yellow-stained Little Rock policemen.

As he turned into Maynard Street he saw that his bombing had been right on the money; the dye had spread across the street and the park, but none of the houses on the block had been hit.

Most of the homes were small and unpainted, and few had their house numbers visible, but Saundra had described Lucy Tate's place to him when they talked the week before. He recognized it at once—neatly painted green and white, a picket fence surrounding a flower-laden yard. As he eased in to park, the front door opened and Saundra flew down the steps to the street, throwing herself, trembling, into his arms.

He kissed her, then asked, "Are you all right?"

"Everybody is all right. It was you in that airplane, wasn't it? You water-bombed the Klan! I was never so proud of anybody in my life. They were going to kill us."

"I'm taking you back with me. You're not going to put yourself in danger like this again."

He didn't let her reply, enveloping her with his arms, closing her mouth with a kiss.

Behind her screen door, Lucy Tate looked out with approval, saying softly, "That's it, that's what she wants, man. You got her now, you take her with you!"

Author's Note

It is sad that the Korean War has truly been the forgotten war, for it signaled so many social, military, and political changes for the United States. Even though the most powerful enemy in the Korean War was China, the war's most important effect was the final polarization of the two great powers, the United States and the Soviet Union. In the process, the war forced a major rethinking on the role of the American military. Where in the past the country had depended upon a well-prepared Navy to defend its shores until a tiny Army and Air Force could be expanded to meet a threat, it was now evident that full-time professional military forces would have to be maintained permanently.

This book tries to tell the story of how the military coped with that changing situation, complicated as it was by both the growth in air and space technology and by social changes caused by the growing civil rights movement. Although there were still many individual instances of discrimination, the military services in general, and the Air Force in particular, led the way in implementing the changes in the law and in our social consciousness that the civil rights move-ment achieved.

Researching material for this book took several years and would have taken more had it not been for the remarkable contributions of a number of individuals who gave freely of their time to provide me with material or to review what I'd written for accuracy. I was particularly concerned that my portrayal of black characters be accurate, and my special gratitude goes to a friend and colleague, Colonel Tommy Daniels, USAF, who was untiring in finding knowledgeable people to help me. Tommy put me in touch with a number of Tuskegee airmen as well as other black officers who had served during the period and experienced the problems of the times. I am grateful to Major General James Whitehead, Colonel John Whitehead, Colonel Charles McGee, Lt. General Frank Peterson, and Lt. General William E. Brown, Jr., all of whom were helpful in the extreme. And among the Tuskegee airmen, I was, like anyone who knows him, inspired by their stalwart commander, Lt. General Benjamin O. Davis, Jr.

Because I was even more concerned about my depiction of a black woman character, I sought and received help from Captain Julia Barnes, NC USN (Ret), a wonderful lady who has been successful in both military and nonmilitary careers. Carlos Camp-bell was also helpful in reviewing material.

The issue of the treatment of prisoners has always been a haunt-ing problem, and never more so than during the Korean War, when for the first time our soldiers and airmen were captured by hostile Communist forces. Colonel Walker "Bud" Mahurin, who scored twenty victories in World War II, scored four more in Korea before being shot down. I am indebted to him both for accounts of action in MiG Alley and for his hard-earned information on life in a Korean prisoner of war camp. Major General Frederick C. "Boots" Blesse, who scored ten victories in Korea, was also extremely helpful with insight into air combat. And former astronaut and Skylab commander, and now novelist, Dr. William R. Pogue filled me in on life in an F-84 outfit.

For the forest-fire fighting material, I am indebted to the dean of forest-fire fighting, Jack Wilson, of the Boise Interagency Fire Center, as well as to Fred Fuchs, of the U.S. Forest Service; George Patterson, of the Forest History Association; and Jonathan Jones, a forest-fire fighter.

Pearly Draughn, librarian of the Air Force Association, was always helpful, as was Paul Schlus of the Arkansas Air National Guard. And I want to thank Leo Opdycke for his insightful, if sometimes painful, commentary. I'm grateful, too, to Roy and Sandy Bradley for the information on Little Rock and its environs.

At Crown, I'm indebted to my editor James O'Shea Wade, his able assistant, Victoria Heacock, and to all the wonderful people who did so much to pull the book together. And, as always, I'm glad to have as my agent the gracious Jacques de Spoelberch.

WALTER J. BOYNE
Ashburn, Virginia